MOVING ON

Trisha Grace

ISBN: 1470049627
ISBN-13: 978-1470049621

To Jesus, the one who made it all possible.
To my dear fiancé, who is always so supportive of me.
To my mom, who is always encouraging of whatever
choice I make.

Chapter One

"After what you've been through with your parents and grandmother, you shouldn't have to be here," William Hayes said through his oxygen mask, his voice weak, soft, and wispy.

Along with a private doctor and two nurses, Kate sat in Mr. Hayes's bedroom, watching over him.

The king-size bed that used to be in the room had been replaced by a hospital bed. Different types of medical equipment, measuring every aspect of his status, stood all around them.

Holding his hand, she said softly, "Are you sure you don't want me to call Tyler?"

William Hayes's lids slowly drooped over his eyes. A teardrop slipped down from the corner of his eye and onto the white pillow case. "It was my fault. I abandoned him."

Kate pulled a piece of Kleenex and dabbed at his tear. "It isn't important now. Don't worry about it. Someday, someday he'll understand."

A series of coughs reverberated through William Hayes's fragile frame, and his wrinkled hand flew to his chest, clutching it. Kate quickly moved aside as the doctor and nurses rushed forward to attend to him. When his coughing fit ceased, his trembling hand reached between them.

Everyone immediately stepped aside for Kate.

She cupped her hands over his. "I'm here."

He pulled down his oxygen mask as she leaned in. "Help me to … to help him." His weak voice was barely audible, but Kate knew who he was referring to.

The one regret that he couldn't mend in time.

She didn't know how she could help him, but she nodded anyway.

Mr. Hayes was a good man; he deserved to go in peace.

She smiled at the frail old man lying in bed and moved forward, intending to put the oxygen mask back in place.

"Kate, promise that you'll help him," Mr. Hayes said, clasping her hand.

Her brows furrowed slightly, but she retained her smile.

Having known Mr. Hayes for nearly five years, she'd heard all the stories about Tyler Hayes as a boy. Now and then, Mr. Hayes would take out a photo album and tell her the stories behind the pictures.

But that was all she knew of Tyler—the boy behind all the stories.

She had never met Tyler Hayes in person.

Mr. Hayes and Tyler had long been estranged, and neither had tried contacting the other in the past twenty years. Throughout all the health episodes that Mr. Hayes had suffered in the past few years, Tyler never showed his face or graced Mr. Hayes with a phone call. He was basically non-existent.

She couldn't blame Tyler, though.

"Kate."

His frail voice brought her back to the moment.

"I promise."

"Thanks. Thanks, Kate. Thanks for letting me play the role of grandfather that I never stepped up to. You're the best granddaughter anyone could ask for." Then he closed his eyes, his hand slipping from within hers.

The muscles around his face relaxed, and it looked as if he'd simply fallen asleep. Only the long monotonous beep from the heartbeat monitor indicated otherwise.

Kate stepped out of the room while the doctor and nurses flew into a flurry of activities.

She didn't know how long she stood outside. Eventually, the doctor stepped out and gave her a grim pat on her arm while the nurses brought Mr. Hayes's body out of the room.

She turned away from the doctor as her tears fell.

Shortly after, calls started coming through her cell phone asking her about funeral arrangements.

She knew Mr. Hayes had listed her as his emergency contact, but she was in no way qualified to make such decisions. She needed to find Tyler Hayes immediately.

She went into the study and searched for the black leather Bible that Mr. Hayes had once showed her. She pulled out the Bible and ran her fingers along the cursive golden letters imprinted on the bottom left corner. *Tyler Hayes*.

Mr. Hayes had bought it with the intention of giving it to Tyler for his eighteenth birthday, but he never did. For nearly ten years, the Bible had sat in the bottom drawer of Mr. Hayes's desk.

Flipping all the way to the last page of the Bible, she pulled out the piece of paper stuck within.

Though there hadn't been any contact between them, the late Mr. Hayes had been keeping track of Tyler, making sure that he didn't lack for anything.

With a heavy sigh, she dialed the number written neatly on the piece of paper. She broke into a small smile when the line connected, surprised that it actually worked.

"Hayes."

For a moment, Kate lost her voice. She didn't know what she was supposed to say. "Tyler Hayes?"

"Who's this?"

There was no good way to go about delivering the news, so she took in a deep breath and gathered her courage. "I'm Kate, Kate Mitchell. I'm calling about your grandfather, Mr. Hayes." There was no response on the other end of the phone, and she had an inkling that Tyler would hang up the phone at any moment so she hurried to continue. "He … he passed away."

Again, Tyler Hayes was silent.

She waited, thinking he was probably dealing with shock or whatever feeling was coursing through his system, but the silence dragged out and she felt compelled to say something.

"The funeral home is asking about the arrangements. Should I get them to call you?"

"Who are you?" Tyler's voice was soft.

"Kate Mitchell. I'm … a friend."

A grunt came from the other side of the line. "Do what you deem fit."

"Wait, Tyler. I can't possibly make the decisions."

"Then don't do anything; leave him wherever he is."

Kate pursed her lips. That wasn't an answer she'd expected. She drew in a long, deep breath and continued. "All right, I'll settle the funeral arrangements. I know he wanted to be buried with your grandmother and your parents."

Even in the continued silence, Kate could feel Tyler's increased tension on the other end of the phone. Softening her voice, she said, "Come home. Come back home for the funeral."

There was a click and the line went dead.

Kate sighed and shook her head, hoping Tyler would at least consider attending the funeral.

She returned to the guest room that Mr. Hayes had set aside for her. She sat by the desk and glance at the queen-size bed in her room. She wanted nothing more than to hide under the covers and cry, but there were things waiting for her to do.

Shoving all her feelings aside, Kate switched on her laptop and began making all the necessary arrangements.

Tyler clutched the phone in his hand and waited for the grief to come, but it never came. Perhaps he'd already done his grieving twenty years ago. Perhaps his childish hopes that his grandfather would someday turn up at his door finally died.

Whatever it was, he couldn't find a single ounce of sadness or any feeling of loss.

"What is it, Ty?" Joanne asked. "Is it work?"

Tyler couldn't deal with Joanne right now.

He stood and strode away, hoping to put some distance between them before Joanne started her motions of coaxing, then whining, and eventually throwing a fit to get her way.

"Ty." Joanne sighed and hurried after him. "What's wrong?"

Tyler rubbed the bridge of his nose.

"You know you can tell me anything. I'm your fiancée," Joanne cajoled while Tyler cringed.

He didn't know how Joanne had got into her mind that they were engaged; they weren't even a couple. She was simply his friend's spoilt younger sister.

But he wasn't interested in dealing with that right now.

Going into his room, he slammed the door behind him—right in Joanne's face.

"Ty!"

He closed his eyes while Joanne continued shouting for him from behind the door. He wasn't in the mood to entertain her; he never was.

He sat on the ledge by his window and gazed out of his house. He'd wanted to go back to the mansion for the longest time. Not to visit his grandfather, but to look at the house he'd grown up in.

He hadn't been back there since his parents' funeral.

He remembered everything about that day. He remembered crying his eyes out when they lowered the coffins. He remembered Marianne embracing him while his grandfather turned his back to him and walked away. He remembered how he'd called after his grandfather, only to see him getting into a black sedan.

His grandfather didn't bother to turn back and offer him a hug or even some kind words.

Instead, almost as soon as the funeral was over, his grandfather got someone to pack up his things and ship him and Marianne off to another house.

Every day, he waited for his grandfather to come for him or at least to visit him, but he never came.

Each time the phone rang, he would race to it, only to hear another unfamiliar voice.

Not once did his grandfather call to check on how he was doing.

Once he was out of sight, he was out of his grandfather's mind.

Why should he go to his grandfather's funeral when his grandfather had never bothered to look him up for the past twenty years?

He never understood why his grandfather was so cruel to him. He was just an eight-year-old who didn't know any better.

Marianne had told him that his parents' death was an accident and it wasn't his fault.

Then why did his grandfather punish him by abandoning him when he needed his grandfather the most?

Tyler clenched his jaw and tightened the grip on his phone. Just when he'd made up his mind not to attend the funeral, his phone rang with another call from another unknown number.

He sighed and picked up the call. "Hayes."

"Tyler Hayes?"

"Yes."

"Good evening, Mr. Hayes. I'm your grandfather's lawyer, Joel Sawyer. Your grandfather insisted that I read his will in front of you, Miss Marianne West, and Miss Kate Mitchell after the funeral. You will need to be present before I can reveal the contents of the will."

Tyler rolled his eyes.

He didn't need any more money. The company that his parents ran became his when he turned twenty-one. There was only one thing he wanted—the mansion.

The mansion that he grew up in and was ripped from after having his parents taken away from him.

"Let me know what the contents are over the phone. You can call me after the funeral."

"There's a clause stating that if you do not turn up, no one else in the will gets anything."

Tyler drew in a long, frustrated breath.

"I'm sorry, Mr. Hayes. I'm merely following your grandfather's instructions."

Though he wasn't willing to attend the funeral, he couldn't allow the bad blood between him and his grandfather rob Marianne of what she rightfully deserved.

For the past twenty years, she was all he had. She was his only family; she was there for him when no one else was. He couldn't allow his anger to blind him to that fact.

He sighed and said, "I'll be there."

Chapter Two

A solemn atmosphere enveloped and percolated through the Hayes mansion as Kate listened to all the condolences. Though she'd been at the mansion so many more times than the other guests, she couldn't help feeling out of place.

Tyler should be the one speaking to the late Mr. Hayes's friends, the one listening to their condolences, not her.

She scanned the room of unfamiliar faces for the umpteenth time and finally spotted Tyler.

Recognizing him was much easier than she'd expected.

He hadn't changed much from the younger version she'd seen in the photo albums.

His dark brown hair was shorter than it was in the photographs, and his bangs that nearly reached his eyes were pushed to the side.

She leaned against the wall and watched him move around the living room in a black suit.

It wasn't the time to notice how well the suit fitted him or to admire the broad shoulders that made him the perfect rack for any style of clothes.

Her foot inched forward, but she paused when she saw him brushing his fingers across the surfaces of the furniture in the living room.

She took her eyes off him and glanced around the room.

The late Mr. Hayes had kept the design of the house almost exactly as it was before the tragedy occurred.

The coffee-brown leather couch that took up the largest space in the room, the chocolate-brown coffee table that sat above the furry beige rug, and the bookshelf against the white wall had all been around even before Tyler was born.

Even the renaissance wall finishes were exactly the same.

The late Mr. Hayes had only added some new pieces of furniture to fill the space where the grand piano used to be. Besides that, nothing much had changed.

The whole place was like a time capsule.

It must be difficult for Tyler to see the house after so many years.

She walked over and asked as she neared him, "Tyler Hayes?"

His head snapped up, and he frowned the moment he laid eyes on her. "Kate Mitchell?"

"Yeah, that'll be me."

His head bobbed up and down while his eyes scrutinized her.

"Is something wrong?"

"I was expecting someone … older."

She looked around and laughed softly. "I guess I'm pretty young among this crowd."

"You said you were his friend, so I thought …" Then he shrugged, not bothering to complete his sentence.

Kate smiled. "He wasn't exactly my friend. He was sort of my grandmother's friend."

"Sort of?"

"It's complicated."

Tyler gave her a look over and turned his back to her.

She'd thought Tyler would prefer some company, but she supposed she was wrong.

She pursed her lips and tucked her hair back behind her ear. "I'll leave you alone."

"Wait," he said and turned back to face her.

She stood where she was, her brows raised, waiting for him to say something.

"Never mind," he continued after a moment.

Kate could sense his hesitation. She watched his eyes sweep the room, observing the different faces.

She understood his silent struggle; neither of them seemed to belong where they were.

Moving next to him, she said, "I don't know most of them either. I believe they used to work with your grandfather in the past. Some of them are from the senior home where he volunteered. He made some good friends there."

Tyler crossed his arms across his chest.

"I'm sure you have questions."

"How long have you or your grandmother known him?"

"Around five years."

He nodded, his eyes still on the strangers in the room.

In the few minutes that Kate had spent with Tyler, she realized he wasn't a man of many words. She glanced around and thought about slipping back into the crowd and away from him, but she didn't want to be rude. "Do you want me to introduce some of his friends to you?"

"No."

Kate noticed Tyler drawing in a long breath as if her mere presence was annoying him.

She was trying to be nice, but it seemed he preferred her gone.

So she smiled and, with a light touch on his arm, walked away from him.

Tyler looked at Kate while she strode away. Her chestnut hair was tied up in a bun with the shorter strands falling out. He hadn't noticed much about her except for the small, friendly smile she had on.

She was right; he did have questions. He had so many questions, but he didn't think anyone could provide him with an answer.

He stared at the room filled with strangers, uncertain about what to do with himself.

When he had rejected Kate's offer, he'd braced for some form of coaxing or whining. Instead, she merely smiled and gave him space.

For the first time that day, something other than the harrowing memories of his parents' death got his attention. He observed Kate while she conversed with a cluster of elderly men.

Even with the sweet smile she had in place, Tyler could see the grief in her eyes.

How did she grow so close to a man who was so cold toward him? Why would she mourn the passing of a man so heartless?

Taking his eyes off her smile, he gave her a head-to-toe scan.

A black sash was tied around her waist and into a knot on her back. The ends of the sash flowed down toward the edge of her dress.

The heels she had on accentuated her slim legs. In her heels, she stood half a head above his shoulders.

He took a step toward her. One step, and that was it. He didn't know what he was doing.

Her conversation with the elderly men was none of his business. He gave another look around the house before turning and walking out toward the back.

Kate saw Tyler bolt from the house and figured he probably needed some time and space. She wanted to follow after him, to make sure he was all right, but she couldn't walk out of the house while everyone was still there.

By the time the guests left, the sun was already beginning its descent. The orange tinge streamed in through the long windows and cast a warm glow into the house, bringing along with it a hint of sadness. She took a sip of the coffee in her hand and gazed out at the distant horizon.

The mansion was set far apart from the rest of the world, and the acres of land around the house belonged to the late Mr. Hayes. Surrounding it was a wide expanse of trees that acted like a moat, keeping the house from the outside world.

She never understood what the late Mr. Hayes loved about this house. Looking out from where she was felt so lonely. She couldn't imagine how forlorn he must have been living all alone in the huge mansion.

Among the trees, a lone figure sat with one of his legs stretched out and his back against a tree.

She set the coffee down on the table and strolled toward him, pausing when she was a few steps away. "Are you all right?"

11

"Is everyone gone?"

She nodded. "Except for Marianne and Mr. Sawyer. Marianne's clearing away the food."

Tyler let out a heavy sigh. "Well then, let's see what the old man has in his will." Tyler got to his feet, dusted off the dirt on his pants, and headed toward the house.

Kate walked alongside him, tempted to observe the real-life manifestation of the boy from all the stories she'd heard.

She wanted to tell him how sorry the late Mr. Hayes was for abandoning him after his parents' death. She wanted to let him know that he was always on the late Mr. Hayes's mind.

But she knew in her heart that he wasn't ready. Her words would only end up pushing him away.

"Did you come alone?" Kate asked.

"Yeah. Just here to sit in for the will," he said a moment later.

If Kate hadn't known his story or seen his taut jaw when he took in everything within the house, his words would've made her think he was a cold-hearted person.

They returned to the mansion and headed into the kitchen in absolute silence.

Tyler wasn't ready to listen to anything that she had to say, and it was too hard for her to listen to what Tyler thought of his grandfather.

She didn't blame Tyler for being angry, but she couldn't bear listening to anyone speak badly of the late Mr. Hayes, not today.

By the time they got to the kitchen, Mr. Sawyer was already seated at the head of the table. The sixty-one-year-old veteran lawyer sat rigidly, his arm placed stiffly over the black folder on the table.

Kate took a seat across from Tyler and turned to Mr. Sawyer.

"Since we're all here, I shall begin. Miss Marianne West." Joel Sawyer faced the elderly woman seated next to him. "Mr. Hayes left you ten percent of all the money he had in his possession; that will be equal to slightly over four million dollars." Turning his focus to Kate, he continued. "You, too, Miss Mitchell. You will receive ten percent of the money. The rest will go to Mr. Tyler Hayes."

Kate blinked when she heard Mr. Sawyer's words. The late Mr. Hayes had always treated her kindly, but four million dollars? There must have been a mistake.

She shook her head, but Mr. Sawyer interrupted her before she could speak.

"There's more." He glanced at Tyler and her, his lips pressed into a thin line. "All the estates that the late Mr. Hayes owned will go to Tyler Hayes; all except this mansion."

Her jaw dropped while the loud scraping of Tyler's chair against the floor pierced the air.

"There must be a mistake," Kate said, leaning forward on the table as Tyler stormed away.

"Wait!" Mr. Sawyer called out. "There's more. You need to listen to all of it, or, like I said, everyone here will have to forfeit their share of the inheritance."

Letting out an audible sigh, Tyler stopped and leaned back against the wall. He crossed his arms and stared into space, not looking at any of them.

"This house cannot be sold. Miss Mitchell can choose to give up this house, but there is a clause to it." He paused, seemingly waiting for Kate to make her decision.

"Go on," Kate urged.

Blowing out a heavy breath, Mr. Sawyer gave her a wry smile. "If Miss Mitchell chooses to forfeit the house, it will be transferred to Mr. Tyler Hayes as long as the following conditions are met."

"Conditions?" she said.

"Mr. Tyler Hayes and Miss Kate Mitchell will have to stay in this house together for a year."

"What?" *A year?* The confusion was quickly morphing into anger. What was the late Mr. Hayes thinking?

She had told him before that she grew up having to take care of everyone and everything. Now that she was on her own, she'd come to treasure her freedom. She finally had the time to indulge in the things she loved.

Why would he make her stay with a grandson whom he hadn't seen for twenty years?

13

"Let me finish. It's rather detailed. You might as well wait to lose your temper at the end of the whole thing. It will save us some time."

She sighed softly and gestured for Mr. Sawyer to continue.

"Beginning tomorrow, for the next year, both of you will need to stay here each and every night. Both of you have to be back at the mansion before midnight unless you are out together. If either one of you is traveling, you will have to take the other along." He took a moment and glanced at both of them, seemingly making sure they were still listening.

"All house guests have to leave the house by eight at night. House guests are only allowed to stay overnight once a month. Only Miss Marianne West is allowed to stay in this house for as long as she wishes. The late Mr. Hayes appointed me to make sure that the conditions are met. Hence, I will be staying here in this house with all of you." Pausing, Mr. Sawyer turned back to her. "That's if you choose to forfeit the house."

Kate tugged at her necklace. "Is there any other way around this?"

Joel Sawyer shook his head. "If you choose to forfeit the house and the conditions are not met, the house will be torn down and the land will be sold to anyone except those present here. The receipts will then go to a senior home."

"Are you done?" Tyler asked brusquely.

"Yes, that's all."

When Tyler went marching out, Mr. Sawyer reached out and held Marianne's arm, stopping her from going after Tyler. "The late Mr. Hayes has a letter for you."

Taking the letter from his hand, Marianne shoved it into her pocket and half ran after Tyler.

Kate sat where she was, wondering how she'd got herself into such a spot.

"Miss Mitchell," Mr. Sawyer said and waited for Kate to look at him. "When he was forming this will, I told him that he was being very selfish. I know this is incredibly unfair to you. He asked me to apologize on his behalf and wrote a letter for you, too."

Taking out another cream envelope, he slid it across the table. "He said you were his last chance to make right a wrong. I'm sorry that you are placed in such a predicament. Think it through and let me know. We'll all need to move in if you decide to forfeit the mansion."

Kate twirled the letter in her hand. "Of course I'm going to forfeit it. This is Tyler's home. I can't take it or allow it to be torn down, but I need to talk to him. He has to be willing to accept the conditions as well."

Joel Sawyer nodded. "He knew you would do this for him."

She didn't know if she should smile or frown.

"One more thing, Miss Mitchell. Mr. Hayes wanted me to tell you that if you were to reject or give away the money he left you, he'll come back and haunt you." He paused and grinned. "He said you were like a granddaughter to him. He wanted to make sure that you'll be well taken care of no matter what."

For the first time since she heard the will, her lips parted into a smile. Mr. Hayes knew her well. Reluctantly, she nodded before going after Tyler.

You promised, Kate reminded herself as she plodded toward Tyler and Marianne.

"Don't be stubborn. You want the house, I know you do. Just accept the conditions," Marianne said.

Kate wanted to hang back, thinking it was better for Marianne to handle the situation. But when Marianne saw her approaching, she shook her head and repeated, "Don't be stubborn." Then Marianne turned to her. "I'll leave you youngsters to talk."

Kate pursed her lips and dragged her feet forward. Tyler's jaws were shut tight, probably still seething at what he'd just heard.

It didn't require a genius to figure out that his anger would be directed at her. She didn't choose to be in this situation, but she was sure she'd be treated like the antagonist.

"Forfeit the house. You can't sell it anyway. Forfeit it. We'll follow the conditions, and I'll pay you for that."

And so it begins. "I wasn't going to steal the house from you. I

15

know how much this house means to you."

"So what do you want?"

"To help."

He closed his eyes and shook his head. Though he didn't say anything, the contempt was clear.

"Look, accept the conditions. It's just one year," she said.

"That's his condition. What's yours?"

"Mine?"

"What do you want?" he asked, enunciating each word.

You promised. She drew in a frustrated breath, asking God to give her patience. "Like I said, to help."

"If you didn't want the house, then why would you stay by an old man's side to take care of him?" Tyler continued. "Why act so high and mighty now?"

Kate grappled with her anger. "I may not be as rich as you are, but I don't need the money from the inheritance, and I definitely don't need your house. I don't even like this stupid place; it's like a scene out of a horror movie." She was tempted to reach over and strangle him.

Reining in her anger, she took another deep breath and stepped away. "You're not angry with me; you're pissed about your grandfather's will. It disrupts my life, too. So before you start venting your anger on me, maybe you should think about that."

Tyler remained silent, staring into the distance.

"I'm going to tell Mr. Sawyer that I'm forfeiting the house. You decide if you want to go along with it."

Turning, Kate stalked away, wondering what she ever did to offend the late Mr. Hayes to deserve such punishment.

"So? What did he say?" Marianne asked when she entered the house.

She looked at the creases of worry etched in Marianne's forehead. Giving her a wry smile, Kate could only answer with a sigh.

Marianne handed her a glass of water. "Whatever he said, ignore him."

"Yeah." She nodded and took a sip of water. "I'm not going to steal the house from him."

"I never thought you would."

Marianne's immediate reply was comforting. At least someone didn't think she was a gold digger.

"Thanks." She took another sip from the glass, then handed it back to Marianne. "I'll inform Mr. Sawyer and head home. It's been a long day."

"Thank you for doing Ty this favor," Marianne said with a warm smile.

Kate returned Marianne's smile and headed into the kitchen.

No matter how awful Tyler was, she did make a promise to the late Mr. Hayes.

And it was just one year. It was the right thing to do.

Besides, the mansion was huge. It should be easy to avoid Tyler if she wanted.

After speaking with Mr. Sawyer, she left the house and slipped into her car. Inside, she pulled out the cream envelope from her back pocket. She played with it, twirling it around in her hand.

She didn't think it would be this tough to look at a letter, but it took her a couple of minutes before she could open the envelope.

Dear Kate,

I cannot begin to imagine your thoughts and feelings while you are reading this. Let me begin with a heartfelt apology. I am truly sorry for putting you in such a situation, but you are the only one I trust to handle this.

You know the one regret I had in my life was not mending the mistake I made with Tyler. He did not deserve the treatment he received. I should have been there for him, but I was so blinded by my own grief that I ended up letting down the most precious person left in my life.

As I leave to meet his parents, the shame is mine to bear. But Tyler does not deserve to be haunted by the ghosts from the past.

Kate, please help me give Tyler back his home.

Love,
William Hayes

Chapter Three

"You're really doing this?" Evelyn asked as Kate placed her sketchbook, stationery, and several folders into a box.

"No, I'm just packing up for fun."

"That line of sarcasm doesn't work for you; you do pack up for fun," Evelyn stated matter-of-factly. "Isn't it kind of rushed? Expecting you to move all your stuff in less than a day? And that Tyler, you said he was awful." Evelyn picked up the clothes that Kate had placed on the bed and dumped them into the suitcase.

Kate glowered at Evelyn. She pulled out the clothes, folded them, then arranged them neatly in the suitcase.

"Kate, I know you can't say no to helping people. But seriously, have you thought this through? You barely know the guy, and Mr. Hayes hadn't seen him in twenty years. He could be the Zodiac or some crazy guy."

They should stop watching such thrillers.

"One, I didn't say he was awful. I said he wasn't exactly a bundle of joy."

Evelyn rolled her eyes. "It's the same thing."

"Two, I don't have to pack everything. I just need some of my clothes and my work stuff. *And*, I'm not going to be there alone; Marianne will be there, too."

"Yeah, *his* loyal housekeeper. No one will be on your side."

"God will be on my side."

Evelyn rolled her eyes again as she shook her head.

Evelyn never condemned or made fun of Kate's faith, but she never believed in God. In fact, she didn't believe in ghosts, angels, or anything spiritual.

Kate stopped what she was doing and looked up at her best friend. She wished Evelyn would open her heart and trust that despite what she'd gone through, there was a God who loved her. But she never condemned Evelyn for her lack of faith either.

"Why would I need someone on my side? I'm not fighting a war," she said. "I know what I'm doing. I'll make sure to lock my door and windows at night. Happy?"

"Not at all. You're too trusting. You don't know the evils of the world."

If anyone else had spoken those words to her, Kate would've laughed. But Evelyn had been through the worst of the foster system and seen more than her share of evils, so Kate only nodded as though she were a child listening to a mother's lecture.

While she continued packing, Evelyn continued in her bid to get Kate to change her mind. Evelyn hovered around her, following her wherever she went, but not lifting a finger to help.

Kate didn't mind the lack of help. Evelyn's style of packing was to sweep everything into a suitcase, then hope that it would close—a complete opposite of Kate's style. But she hated having someone shadowing and getting in her way while she moved around the room.

No matter what Evelyn said, Kate was adamant about going through with her decision.

Leaving aside her promise, she couldn't allow Tyler to lose his house because of her, not when she knew what had happened to him.

Even as she got into her car, Evelyn was still going on and on about how dangerous it could be and how it wasn't her style to do something so ridiculous.

"Kate, I know you grew up taking care of people around you, but this isn't your battle. Please, just think it through again."

"I have. I need to do this," Kate stated before pulling the door close. She smiled brightly at Evelyn through the windshield and waved, ignoring the scowl on her face.

When she got to the mansion, three other cars were parked

outside.

She'd hoped Tyler wouldn't be around. Though she'd told Evelyn that she wasn't fighting a battle, she did have a strategy in mind. She'd head in, put her stuff down in the guest room, and return to the office—all before Tyler got there.

She glanced at the cross pendant hanging from her rear-view mirror. "I declare that today will be a good day, Lord. I know You're always with me and You'll help me in whatever situation I face."

Squaring her shoulders, she stepped out of her car and looked at the mansion, her home for the next year.

The beige exterior of the three-story mansion and the clear glass of the long windows stared back at her. Though the late Mr. Hayes had kept up with the maintenance, the walls were tinted with a hint of gray and dullness; probably due to the dust collected over the past few years.

The layer of dust cast a gloom over the mansion, making it seemed as if it, too, were in mourning.

She shook her head and headed toward the door.

Even before she was near the door, she could hear the lively racket within. With her luggage in hand, she cautiously pushed it open.

The moment she stepped in, all the clamor ceased. Everyone seemed to freeze in place, seemingly waiting for someone to react. That was until a shrill whistle woke everyone from their trance.

"You're Kate Mitchell?"

She moved toward the crowd and cast a quick glance at the four men and the woman present.

"Yup," she answered the man wearing a plain gray T-shirt that showed off his bulging muscles.

The same man let out a loud, boisterous laugh. "Well, Anne, you should start worrying now." He got to his feet and reached over with a boyish grin. "I'm Ryan Faris." Tilting his head to the left, he said, "That's Joseph Hansen and Dan Riley." Each smiled and waved when his name was mentioned. "The one sitting next to Ty is Joanne Riley."

"I'm Ty's fiancée," Joanne said while scrutinizing Kate from head to toe.

Kate shook Ryan's hand and nodded politely as she looked at the polished blonde sitting next to Tyler. Thick mascara lined her eyes and her nails glimmered with neon pink nail polish.

She couldn't help conjuring up the image of a Barbie doll when looking at Joanne.

"You're all here to help him move?" Kate took the chance to give everyone another look. All the guys appeared tall, their lanky legs stretched out casually in front of them, and all of them seemed to be at ease.

All except Tyler.

His legs were stretched out like the rest, but his arms were folded, and he was staring into space as though he was afraid to look anywhere else.

A moment of silence descended as everyone turned to look at the single piece of luggage standing by the couch.

"I want to say yes, but it'll be pretty obvious that we're lying. So, here's the truth: We're here to see who Ty is going to be living with for the next year." Ryan beamed another of his boy-next-door grins and winked.

Despite his hulking figure, his gregarious nature removed the threat of how his arm could easily crush her if he wanted.

"Is that all you have? Looks like both of you travel light," Joseph Hansen commented.

Kate turned to look at Joseph. If she hadn't known that Tyler was an only child, she would've thought they were brothers. They shared the same dark brown hair, except his was cut much shorter, showing a clear, radiant face. He gave her a small pensive smile as though he, too, was contemplating her character.

"Actually, I still have a box of work stuff in my car. But other than that, this is all I brought." Looking at Tyler, she said, "Your grandfather had a guest room prepared for me those times I stayed over. Is it all right if I take the same room?"

"You can have the master bedroom," Tyler answered.

"I'm more comfortable in the guest room. If there's nothing

else, I'll put my stuff in the room and head out to work."

Tyler gave no reaction.

She sighed but managed to catch herself before she rolled her eyes.

Silence meant consent.

She reached for her luggage, but Joseph Hansen rose and strode over.

"Let me." Taking the handle, he waited for Kate to take the lead.

"I'll get your box. Is your car locked?" Ryan asked.

"I'll get it myself." Kate made her way toward the door, but Ryan easily caught up with her.

Once they were out of earshot, Ryan smiled warmly. "Don't get offended by Ty's attitude. He's always been like that, even with us."

Quietly, Kate considered Ryan while he pulled the box out of the back seat. "May I ask how you got to know Tyler?"

Ryan grinned mischievously. "Why?"

"You guys seem to be on the opposite ends of the spectrum—character wise, that is."

"So you noticed, huh? I have no idea how we actually became good friends. He's kind of a weirdo," Ryan teased. "We went to the same school. He was *really* good at basketball, and I think we just hung around him because he was so good. Then we sort of became friends."

Kate shook her head and chuckled at his story. As they re-entered the house and headed up the stairs with Joseph, she could feel Tyler's eyes on her. Still peeved with his words from the night before, she kept her eyes straight ahead, refusing to turn back to him.

"Nice room," Ryan said as he placed the box on the dark brown desk.

"Yeah, it's pretty decent," Kate said as she scanned the familiar room. The white walls were matched with dark chocolate furniture, just as all the rooms were.

The large wardrobe took up the entire length of a wall while the queen-size bed and study desk stood against another.

Kate loved the simplicity of the room. She never liked seeing clutter, so this simple bedroom was perfect for her. There was also the one thing she did love about the house, the high ceiling that made the room feel so much more spacious.

Joseph twirled the luggage in his hand and asked, "Need any help unpacking?"

"No, I'm good." Reaching into the box, she pulled out her laptop. "I'll unpack tonight. I have to get to work."

Joseph peered into the box filled with folders. "What do you do?"

"I own an interior design firm." She strode out of the room with Joseph and Ryan following.

"Why are you still going to work? I heard you inherited quite a sum; I'm sure you can live off that," Joseph said casually.

Kate paused and narrowed her eyes, studying Joseph, considering if his question was of curiosity or accusation. "I'm not here for the money if that's what you're asking."

Joseph raised both his hands in a gesture of peace. "I was merely stating a fact. It isn't my money, so I don't care who gets it."

She turned and continued toward the stairs. "I've been very blessed to be able to do what I love," Kate answered simply. "I get to turn houses into homes for my clients to live and create great memories in."

"I think all of you should leave so we can settle down and rest," Tyler said as he emerged at the top of the stairs.

"I thought we only need to leave by eight? You haven't even given us a tour," Ryan complained.

Tyler only glared at him.

"If you don't want to, then Kate can give us a tour," Joseph added.

"Get out of here."

Kate pursed her lips to stop them from curling. Ryan wasn't joking when he told her about Tyler's attitude.

"It's okay. They can stay if they want. I'm heading out to work anyway." Kate took a step toward the stairs, but Tyler reached out, his hand firm on her arm.

"Stay," he said softly, almost like a plea.

Both Joseph's and Ryan's eyes widened.

"Is there something you need?" Kate stared warily at Tyler.

Last night, he'd made it pretty clear he wanted nothing to do with her. What could he want with her now?

"We should go," Joseph said.

Giving Tyler a pat on the back, both Ryan and Joseph made their way down the stairs.

"Stay for a while," Tyler continued. "The house—"

"Ty!"

Kate jumped at the sudden scream. Tyler's fiancée didn't seem pleased with his decision to kick them out.

"One minute." He plodded down the stairs.

She couldn't hear what was going on, but there was some commotion until a door slammed shut.

Ryan, Joseph, and Dan made their way back to their cars while Joanne continued screaming at the door.

"Forget it. You know what he's like. He isn't going to open the door," Ryan said.

Joanne's shoulders slumped.

Dan glanced over at his sister while he made his way toward his car. Ryan was right; it was a losing battle. Joanne could stand there and shout until her voice turned hoarse and Tyler still wouldn't bother about her.

Whenever Tyler chose to shut the world out, nobody ever got in.

Dan couldn't help rolling his eyes. He'd never understood his sister's obsession with Tyler. Since she was young, she had been the apple of his parents' eyes and had grown up pampered. Though everyone who saw how Tyler treated Joanne thought he was mean to her, Dan couldn't blame him.

Joanne was one clingy person who thought the world revolved around her.

"And you should stop telling everyone that he's your fiancé." Dan shook his head at the ludicrous statement she'd been making.

"He never denied it," Joanne whined. "Silence means consent."

Joseph and Ryan burst into laughter while Dan sighed heavily.

When Joseph finally managed to stop laughing, he said, "If you're referring to anyone else, I can't comment. But, Anne, we're talking about Ty. He barely answers half our questions, much less your insanity."

Ryan nodded. "Yeah. I don't even want to ask how you decided that he wanted to upgrade your one-sided relationship to fiancé-fiancée level. Everyone here knows that the two of you aren't even a couple."

"Yes, we are. He's been my boyfriend since we were young, and he's never—not once—denied it," she screeched.

Dan took a deep breath. "He just can't be bothered with you."

Dan had told her this countless times, but her skull was so thick that nothing ever got in.

All she had in her head were her stupid fantasies and make-believe world.

"Shut up. I won't let any of you sow discord between Ty and me."

"That's the problem; there is no Ty and you," Ryan mumbled under his breath, but everyone heard him.

Dan felt Joanne staring at him, probably expecting him to put up some sort of defense for her. But it was difficult when he was on Ryan's side. Voicing his opinion would only end up in an ugly shouting spectacle that he wasn't interested in having.

Joanne didn't have the ability to think logically, so any effort at reasoning would only be wasting his breath.

"Hey, Joe, you're working the night shift, right? Since you're dropping Ryan off, can you take Anne along? I have some work I need to rush." Dan didn't want to dump his idiotic sister on Joseph and Ryan, but he didn't want to have Joanne in his car. Once they were on their own, she would probably start throwing her tantrums, accusing him of never being on her side.

After all these years, he was tired of having to entertain her whims.

At least Joseph would have Ryan in his car, and that would be enough to keep Joanne's mouth shut.

Ryan was the one person in the group who had never allowed her to get away with anything. He loved teasing people, especially Joanne. He didn't have a problem putting Joanne down and laughing at her stupidity. She used to try fighting Ryan with outbursts of tantrums, but it never worked on him, and she finally learned to shut her mouth around him.

Joseph scowled at Dan. "Yeah, I'm sure you do."

Ryan turned to Joseph. "Guess we're in for one hell of a miserable ride home."

Joanne plodded toward Joseph's car and got into the back seat without another word. Joseph directed another glare at Dan and mouthed the words 'you owe me' before getting into his car.

Chapter Four

Once Kate heard the door shut, she moved toward the railing and saw Tyler coming up the stairs with his luggage.

"Is everything all right?"

He nodded without looking up at her.

What is wrong with this guy? She was leaving when he told her to stay. Now, he was refusing to look at her. "Okay, I guess I should go, too." She figured it was better to stay away from him until his resentment of her faded.

"Where are you rushing to?" he asked as he continued up the stairs.

Away from you. She wasn't interested in getting insulted by him again.

"Work. I—"

"Why did you choose to forfeit the house?" he asked as he walked past her, still not looking at her.

She drew in a slow, deep breath. This was why he'd asked her to stay—to pick a fight with her.

Help me to … to … help him. She wanted to roll her eyes when she heard those words play in her head. Why? Why did she make that promise?

Keeping her anger under control wouldn't help Tyler get his house back, but it would keep him alive—for now.

"I'm sorry, Mr. Hayes. I have no wish to start my day fighting with you." She turned and took a step away from him.

"I didn't mean …"

She paused and turned back to him.

"I wasn't trying to insinuate anything. I just want to know."

She stared right at him, seeing dark-gray ripples amid the dull amber in his eyes. In that split second, she realized he had been concealing his turmoil as aloofness.

This was only his second time in the mansion after twenty long years. The memories, even if he could remember any happy ones, were probably giving him nothing but misery.

The knowledge that he would never see those in his memories again and never be able to enjoy another smile with them must be painful.

The nostalgia could bring about such an ache that, sometimes, it would seem better to forget about everything.

It was a feeling she could empathize with.

Tyler waited, his eyes unblinking, seemingly giving her time to consider how she wanted to react.

She sighed softly and gave him a small smile. There wasn't any need for her to add to his agony.

He nodded and turned away from her, heading toward the master bedroom.

"Tyler," she said when she saw him reaching for the knob. Her fingers moved to the silver locket on the chain she wore around her neck.

Tyler didn't respond; he didn't even look over at her. His hand hovered over the doorknob as if a force field was keeping him from touching it.

She waited and noticed the scars on his right arm. They looked like teeth marks, huge teeth marks.

Her head tilted to the side as she observed the scars, but abruptly, he dropped his hand and turned to face her.

She took her mind off the scars and continued. "Your grandfather never made any changes to the room. The housekeepers have been keeping it clean, that's all."

He gave her a wry smile. "Just like the living room."

She pursed her lips and nodded. "The photos, the furniture, it's all the same."

Silence seemed to be his favorite style of response. He stared back at her, seemingly studying her, or maybe he was just glaring at her.

Again, she couldn't help feeling that she was annoying him with her presence.

She twirled the locket around her finger and looked away, trying to come up with an excuse to leave when he suddenly asked, "What was he like?"

"What?"

"What was he like to you?"

The late Mr. Hayes was like a grandfather to her. Whenever she got stuck with problems from work, she could always ask him for some insights. Whenever she wanted to complain about meeting an unreasonable client, he would be there to listen.

But she couldn't possibly say that to the grandson he had abandoned.

"He was a nice person," she said and glanced toward the study.

The door was closed, but she imagined herself walking in and seeing the grin that the late Mr. Hayes always had for her.

She closed her eyes and drew in a deep breath when she felt the burning in her eyes. "He loved telling me stories about you." She smiled, thinking of those times when the late Mr. Hayes pulled out the photo albums. "I think I can tell you the story behind every photo in this house."

Opening her eyes, she waited for Tyler's response.

Tyler remained frozen like a statue, staring out of the long window at the end of the hallway.

The late Mr. Hayes used to do that all the time.

Sometimes, she would come up the stairs and find him sipping his coffee and staring out at the woods.

At those times, she'd join him by his side and watch the trees along with him. She never asked what he was staring at. All she knew was that his heart was aching, and she hoped being beside him could bring him some comfort.

She sighed when Tyler turned his gaze to her.

When she'd agreed to stay in the mansion for a year, she didn't think it would be this difficult.

She didn't like where the house was situated. She didn't like the feeling of being separated from the world, but she'd just realized how difficult it was to be trapped in the house with all those memories.

Everything in the house reminded her of the late Mr. Hayes.

The memories of their conversations were still imprinted so vividly in her mind that she could almost see him right there in front of her.

She couldn't imagine the pain he'd been in for the past twenty years. As much as everything reminded her of the late Mr. Hayes, everything in the house must have reminded him of Tyler's parents.

Now she could understand why he thought it was better to move Tyler somewhere else than for him to remain in this house.

"The two of you were close," Tyler said.

She didn't know why, but she felt awful. She felt as if she'd stolen the one family that Tyler had. "I'm so sorry."

"Don't be. To me, he's been dead for twenty years."

Although his face remained straight and revealed none of his feelings, the anger rang clear in his words as his eyes darkened. Kate finally realized how much the late Mr. Hayes had hurt and was still hurting him.

Maybe she was jumping to conclusions. Maybe she wasn't irritating him. Maybe he just hadn't figured out how to deal with everything.

She was suddenly remorseful of all the indignation she'd felt.

She should've been more understanding.

He was abandoned right after his parents were taken from him, and he never got to listen to his grandfather's explanation. He never got the answers he needed.

"Would you say you were rather awful to me last night?" Kate asked.

"Excuse me?"

"Last night, you weren't the nicest person."

Tyler considered her words for a moment. "You haven't answered my question."

"What question?"

"Why did you choose to forfeit the house?"

"It's a pretty long story," she answered. "I'll tell you later when we're not standing around like idiots. And you haven't answered *my* question."

"Yes, I was. I'm—"

Kate lifted her hand, palm out, to stop him from talking. "I'm not looking for an apology. I'm hoping you can do me a favor."

He frowned, his eyes narrowing slightly. "What do you need?"

"Is Marianne staying on this floor with us?"

Tyler shook his head. "She used to have a room on the other side of the house and insisted on staying in the same room."

"Then will you stay in one of the guest rooms near mine instead of the master bedroom?"

The unspoken question was written clearly on his face.

"This is a big house. It's surrounded by trees, and it feels rather … scary." And lonely, she thought. But she didn't want to sound pathetic.

He smiled. "Like a scene out of a horror movie."

She grimaced as she remembered the awful comment she'd made about his house.

"I thought you stayed here before."

"Yeah, but I've never liked it. The house is big; the rooms are big, and it gets really quiet at night, except for all the strange noises coming from the woods." Kate smiled sheepishly.

Though she told herself that she was giving Tyler an out from having to stay in the master bedroom, she still meant what she'd said.

She never liked staying over.

It was a huge house, too huge. Everything creaked at night, and the noise was always magnified in the empty hallways.

In the light of day, she could appreciate the spaciousness. She enjoyed looking up at the renaissance finishings on the ceiling and imagining the stories that unfolded in the house.

At night, her wild imagination, coupled with watching way too many crime shows, won over any fondness she had for the place.

Without giving her a verbal answer, Tyler made his way toward where the three guest rooms were situated.

She saw him glance into her room before stopping by the

guest room next to hers. "So you're an interior designer?"

"You're the owner of Hayes Security and you didn't check up on me before moving in?"

"Did you check up on me?"

"My best friend would've made me do it if I knew how to. But I don't, so I'll have to settle for locking my door and windows."

Tyler grinned, his eyes creasing. "The windows? Do you think I'm Spiderman or something?"

It wasn't until now that she noticed how similar the late Mr. Hayes and Tyler were. Their smiles always seemed more polite than actually being happy.

That was the first hint of genuine joy she'd seen from him.

She returned his grin and gave an aloof shrug. "If we're done here, I'd like to get to work. See you later."

"Why are you in such a hurry to leave? And you didn't answer my question again."

"I don't think you're Spiderman."

He laughed. It was a short laugh, but it caught her attention.

"That wasn't the question I was talking about."

Kate arched her brow.

"You're an interior designer?"

"Oh, that." She chuckled and continued. "Yeah. I own an interior design firm with my best friend, Evelyn Jordan, and I'm not in a hurry to leave. I thought you might want to explore the house on your own for a while."

Tyler turned the doorknob and opened the door to his new room. "I haven't been ..." He said the words slowly, and she could hear the melancholy in his voice. "Maybe you can give me a tour." He pushed his luggage in and looked back at her.

Kate shook her head and made disapproving noises.

"What?"

"When your friends asked me for a tour, you told them to get out. Now you want me to give *you* a tour." Kate smiled, letting him know that she was teasing.

"You seem ready to head to work, so I guess you're not that tired."

"True." Then sighing softly, she looked at him apologetically.

"I didn't stay here much. And when I was here, I was mostly in your grandfather's room, the guest room, or the study. I don't think I can help much with the tour."

The late Mr. Hayes didn't mind her looking around, but she never ventured around on her own. Everything in the house seemed too personal and heartbreaking for her to touch.

Tyler nodded slowly.

She didn't want him to think she was refusing to help, so she continued. "But since I'm staying here for a year, we can explore it together."

"This isn't a castle. Exploring seems exaggerated."

Kate scowled at him. "There's nothing much on this floor. Besides the two of our rooms, there are another guest room, a study, the master bedroom, your grandfather's room and ..." She tipped her chin to direct his attention. "The gathering area."

"You just said an awful lot," Tyler said as he glanced around.

"Yeah, but they're mostly rooms with beds." Then breaking into a smile, she added, "I can give you a tour of the study. There's a beautiful table; I believe it's antique."

Already used to his lack of replies, she went into her room, put down her laptop, and strode toward the study.

She opened the door and leaned against it, ushering him in. "Before your grandfather got too ill, he spent a lot of time in here."

She sighed softly as she saw the room.

She was tempted to walk away and leave Tyler alone in it. She didn't want to be going through the late Mr. Hayes's things without him around. She didn't want to be in the room. She didn't want to be reminded that she wouldn't see him sitting behind the mahogany desk again or that she wouldn't hear another story from him.

But this wasn't about her.

She tugged at her necklace and forced herself to step in after Tyler. She kept her back to him as she moved around the room, pretending to be occupied with sweeping off invisible dust on the surfaces.

* * *

Tyler stood by the door for a moment, his eyes scanning the room.

The room appeared less cluttered than he remembered. There used to be files and paper stacked on the table, then more files on top of the cabinets lining the wall.

He entered the room and moved toward the antique table Kate spoke of.

Everything in the house was so familiar, yet so strange.

His hand skimmed the surface of the table, and he wondered how many times he had been in the room. He was fairly certain that he'd loved barging into the room even when he wasn't allowed to, but the memories seemed so distant that he wasn't sure if he'd imagined it.

He moved around the table and immediately saw the photo in a silver frame. A photo of a boy sitting on his grandfather's lap.

It took him a moment to realize that the boy in the photo was him. He couldn't recognize himself with the wide, carefree grin.

For the first time since being in the house, a happy memory surfaced; the camping trip he'd begged his parents and grandfather into bringing him on.

He was thrilled to be able to stay in a tent while his grandfather told him silly folklore.

Even as his lips curled into a smile, his chest tightened and he couldn't breathe.

He swallowed and looked away. That was when he noticed the black Bible sitting in the middle of the table.

"Your grandfather wanted to give that to you on your eighteenth birthday. He gave something similar to your dad on his eighteenth birthday."

Tyler turned away and shifted his attention to the cabinets.

"Your grandfather had one, too. The only verse highlighted within was 'Ask and it will be given to you,' " she said.

Tyler remained where he was, his back facing her.

"I once asked him what he was asking for. He said he'd asked for courage; courage to meet you, to talk to you."

"Then God failed miserably," he replied.

Kate shook her head. "Even when God parted the Red Sea,

I'm sure the Israelites didn't gain courage until they started walking and started seeing that God would keep the water from them. I'm sure that if he'd taken the first step, he would have realized that God had supplied the courage."

She didn't wait for a reply. Moving toward one of the cabinets behind the desk, she continued. "There's a safe in here. The password is your date of birth." Then she returned her gaze to Tyler. "The password to every safe in this house is your date of birth." Moving past him, she strode out of the study without another word.

Tyler trailed behind her, not knowing what to say.

He was thankful that he was with Kate. He didn't want, or perhaps didn't dare, to walk around the house on his own.

Before she arrived, he'd lounged on the couch downstairs, refusing to budge.

Since he was thrown out, he'd always wanted to come back home. Now that he was home, he couldn't understand the dread he was feeling.

He thought this house would help him remember all the good times he'd spent with his parents. He thought that by being back in this house, the lingering sadness that had shrouded him all these years would finally leave.

He was completely wrong.

Instead of the laughter, he only remembered the screams. Instead of the smiles, all he could remember was the agony on his parents' faces.

He hated feeling so out of place in what was supposed to be his home.

"Let's go to the other wing. Marianne can probably give us a tour," Kate said.

Tyler had so many questions for Kate. He wanted to know exactly how she met his grandfather. He wanted to know if his grandfather was who he remembered him to be.

He wanted to know how his grandfather was to her. He wanted to know if his grandfather was incapable of loving anyone or if it was just him.

"Did you hear what I said?"

"She's out buying groceries," he said as his eyes flitted to the flight of stairs leading to the attic.

His old room used to be in the attic. If his grandfather had kept his parents' room exactly as it was, there was a chance his was the same. Then again, his grandfather could have burned everything he'd ever touched.

He wasn't ready to find out the answer. So instead of heading up the stairs, he stopped and sat on the bottom step.

Kate moved to sit beside him, but she halted mid-stride. "Hold on, there's something you should have." She ran back down the hall and into the room they'd been in moments ago.

Tyler kept his eyes on the hallway, wondering what got her so excited.

Kate didn't have to do any of this, especially after how he'd treated her last night. He had no right to be angry with her or to accuse her of anything; she wasn't the one who came up with the will.

He had intended to keep the conversation between them to a minimum. He was never good with people, so staying away from her was the best solution.

But Kate was the only one who had been in the house in the last few years; at least, she was the only one he knew.

He'd offended her almost immediately, but she appeared to be quick to forgive; something he should learn.

When Kate returned, she had a bright smile on her face, and her eyes sparkled with such excitement that his own lips curled.

As she neared, she waved the small squarish box she held. She settled beside him and placed the box in his hand. "Open it," she urged.

He cradled the brown leather box in his hand as if it were a bubble. He didn't know what it was, but he knew it belonged to his parents. Somehow, he felt it would be ripped away from him at any moment.

"Go on, you'll love it," Kate said. "They were your grandparents', then your parents'. Now, they're yours to keep."

Tyler looked up and once again, her smile captured his attention. Her joy seemed infectious. She was like Ryan. They carried an air of blitheness with them; it was as if they were untouched by any sorrow.

Tyler surmised that Kate probably grew up in a world like Joanne's. She wasn't spoiled like Joanne was. Her only outburst had been his doing, but she must have grown up in a family who loved and protected her.

Surely that was the only reason why she was so quick to forgive and magnanimous enough to be smiling so radiantly at someone who had been so rude to her.

He wondered if things were different—if he hadn't lost his parents, if he grew up in the same world that Kate did—would he have the light-heartedness and generosity that she possessed?

"Open it," she said.

His attention returned to the box in his hand. He glanced over at Kate, then back to the box again. "Mine to keep," he muttered to himself.

"Yeah. Until you give them to your children, that is." Kate leaned closer and nudged him with her shoulder. "Open it."

He flipped the box open to see a pair of gleaming rings. One of the rings was set with three diamonds, the big diamond in the middle flanked by two smaller ones. On either side of the main diamond setting were another three miniature diamonds along the band. The rest of the band was carved with intricate flowers, which covered even the rim of the ring. The other ring didn't have any diamonds. Only a vein twirled around the simple band.

"It's white gold. You see the vein stretching across the ring?" Picking up the ring with the diamonds, she tilted it at an angle. There were more carvings of flowers underneath, except for the area right beneath the diamonds. "It's the same vein; it just blends into the carvings."

Placing it back carefully, Kate continued. "Your grandfather had it made for your grandmother. He said he couldn't afford expensive diamonds then, but your grandmother was excited to receive it anyway. When your grandmother gave the ring to your father, he replaced the diamonds and turned the original ones into a necklace for your grandmother. Then he used this ring to propose to your mom."

Tyler looked at Kate's blissful smile and couldn't help but beam back at her.

"Isn't that a sweet story? Oh, and the rings used to be yellow gold. Your father got them plated over with white gold."

Kate stared at him, seemingly observing his reaction, then she turned away for a moment before returning her gaze to him.

"Your grandfather said he was keeping them for you, for you to carry on the love story." Smiling apologetically, she continued. "I know it's kind of late. You've probably gotten a ring for your fiancée, but I'm sure she'll love this when she learns the history behind it."

Her fingers moved to tug at her necklace.

"She's not my fiancée." Tyler closed the box in his hand and set it down before him. Reaching over, he took the locket from her hand and examined it. It was a heart-shaped locket with the same vein design that curled into vintage-looking heart shapes. The veins formed a cage, encasing whatever was within. "What's inside?"

"But she said she's your fiancée, and you didn't deny it," Kate pointed out.

Without letting go of the locket, he looked up at Kate. She'd leaned in closer to prevent the necklace from straining on her neck. Flecks of honey amber, like petals of a flower, radiated out from her pupil. The flecks made it seem as if she had a sunflower in her eyes.

It suited her character; she was always smiling, and something about her just warmed him up.

"She goes around telling everyone that I'm her boyfriend, then recently she changed it to fiancé." Tyler had never bothered explaining to anyone about Joanne's strange habit, but he didn't want Kate to misunderstand. "When Dan and I became friends, she started announcing to everyone that I was her boyfriend. She was quite young, so I simply ignored her. She's just calling me that out of habit."

Kate chuckled at the bizarre anecdote. "Are you sure it's out of habit? She seemed rather serious."

Tyler shrugged. "What's inside?" he asked again, directing

Kate's attention back to the locket.

"The reason I'm here."

He turned to Kate and waited for her to continue.

Kate gave him a small smile. "My parents died in a car accident, and this is all I have left of them."

Car accident. His assumption about her background couldn't have been more wrong. Maybe she had great guardians. He was tempted to ask, but he wanted to know why she was here, why she was willing to do this for him.

He noticed her staring at the locket, so he continued. "This is all that's left? What about the house? I'm sure there were photos and—" He stopped abruptly when Kate sighed softly.

"I don't know. There's nothing left in the house."

"Nothing?"

She nodded. "My grandparents cleared the house. I don't know what they did with all the stuff."

"Why would they do that?"

"I don't know. I don't think their death was an accident. We never got the full story. My grandparents refused to talk about it. One day, they picked us up from school and took us home with nothing but the clothes on our backs and the school bags we'd brought to school. They told us that our parents had died in a car accident and that everything was gone. Even as we grew older and started asking questions, they stuck to their story."

"Us?"

"My sister and I. I have a younger sister, Lydia. She's studying to become a lawyer." Kate gave him a small smile, but he could tell she was extremely proud of her.

"What made you think otherwise?"

Kate shrugged. "I'd always assumed it was too painful for them to talk about it, so I never pushed. Lydia tried a few times, but each time my grandmother got so angry that she'd refuse to speak to us for a few days." She paused, pursing her lips. "Then when my grandmother got dementia, she started rambling on about some murder. At first, I thought she was confused, but I started piecing together the bits of information and I became suspicious. That was and is all I have—suspicions. It was difficult to get her to answer my questions properly."

"Until now?"

"It's impossible to ask now unless you know a good medium," Kate teased.

He blinked, stunned for a moment. "I'm sorry. I didn't know she'd passed away."

Kate nodded as she said, "Your grandfather volunteered at the home she was staying in. She thought that he was my grandfather, and he was kind enough to play along."

"So why is that the reason you're here?"

She took the locket that he was still holding and unfastened the small clasp before putting it back into his hand.

Inside lay a family photo; everyone was grinning as Kate and Lydia clung to their parents.

"A few years after their death, I realized I was beginning to forget what my mother looked like. My grandmother had photos of her, but they were all photos of her when she was younger."

Swallowing hard, Kate took a deep breath and looked away. "I began to have nightmares. I kept dreaming of my parents. We'd be in the park and I could hear them calling out for me, but when I ran to them, they would be faceless." She shook her head and continued. "I'd wake up screaming in the middle of the night. My grandmother would comfort me and get me to talk about whatever I could remember of them."

As she turned back to the locket in his hand, she gave him a wry smile. "And I remembered this. I remembered my mom wearing it all the time. I don't know how, but a few weeks later, my grandmother handed me the necklace with the locket.

"You know what the funny thing was? I thought I'd be over the moon to be able to hold the necklace in my hand. Instead, I cried; I cried so hard that it felt as if I'd lost them all over again. When I finally opened the locket and saw their smiling faces, saw myself smiling so happily in their arms, I couldn't stand to look at it."

Taking her eyes off the locket, she looked right at him. "So I understand. I understand what it feels like to have someone so precious taken from you so suddenly. I understand the heartache that even the good memories bring."

"Why do you still wear it?" Tyler asked, his voice in a deep whisper.

"The same reason you're still here." Kate closed the locket and placed her hand over it. "This house has great memories waiting for you to remember. It's scary and heart-wrenching. Right now, it probably seems easier to forget. But someday, it'll be worth it. Someday, it'll make you smile. The ache of them being gone never really leaves, but at least you can remember them when they were happy. Those memories will be good enough to make you smile."

Tyler swallowed hard.

Kate reached over and picked up the box he'd placed on the floor. "They're gone, but their love is encapsulated in you. They loved you, and now you have something from them. This house, these rings; they live on in all of these. Your memories, their stories. As long as you choose to remember them and to tell them, they'll live on."

"Ty!" Marianne shouted when she entered the house, jolting both Tyler and Kate.

Kate chuckled at their reactions, and they got to their feet. She handed him the box and headed for the stairs. "I *really* should get to work, or Eve will go crazy on me. She's already pissed with me for staying here."

"What time do you get off work?"

"Hmm, I guess anytime after I'm done with work," Kate answered. "I doubt I'll be home late. It's too scary to drive up here at night."

"It's quiet and peaceful," he countered.

"Maybe I've watched too many crime shows. This house sort of reminds me of the movie *When a Stranger Calls*. Have you seen it?"

"No."

"Well, good for you. I wish I hadn't."

"Evelyn, she's your business partner?" Tyler asked.

"Mm-hmm." Kate nodded in acknowledgment.

"Why is she angry that you're here?"

Kate flashed a smile while shaking her head. "She's just worried." Then her brows furrowed. "Ugh! I forgot my laptop. You go ahead."

Tyler leaned against the wall as Kate went back up the stairs.

"She told you to go ahead. You don't have to wait for her," Marianne stated.

He continued down the stairs, ignoring Marianne.

"You sure have plenty of questions for her," Marianne continued.

"I should know who I'm living with."

The corners of Marianne's lips turned up. "Really? I don't hear you asking about me."

"That's because you never stop talking," he said as he looked over his shoulder to see if Kate was coming down the stairs.

Marianne raised her knuckle and knocked Tyler on the head. "Watch your manners. And she'll be back tonight—you don't have to keep watch."

Something was wrong with him. He never bothered much about others. The things he knew about his friends were from what they told him. He rarely asked questions.

With Kate, there was so much he wanted to know. She understood what he was going through, something he hadn't quite figured out himself.

He tightened his grip on the box in his hand. Maybe someday he'd be able to let go of the horrors and hold on to the amazing memories his parents had once created for him.

"Bye, Tyler, Marianne. See you guys tonight!" Kate shouted as she went running out the door.

"Kate," he called out as he ran after her.

She was right; moving into the mansion disrupted her life, too. He didn't want her getting into trouble with her friend.

Kate paused and looked up, one of her feet already in the car. "Yeah?"

"Will you be all right?"

Her brows drew closer. "I'm lost."

"Evelyn, you said—"

"Oh." She chuckled. "I'll be fine. Don't worry."

He continued standing right where he was, and she probably noticed his uncertainty.

"I'll drop you a text once I get to the office to let you know that I'm alive and well. See you tonight." Kate slipped into her car, and he watched as the car disappeared from his view.

"Are you worried that she isn't coming back?" Marianne asked from behind him.

He was. There was so much more he wanted to know, and there was something about her smile ...

Chapter Five

Kate stepped into her office, keeping her head low as she hastened past Evelyn's room.

"Miss Mitchell, a client—"

Her index finger flew to her lips, trying to shush her employee.

"Why didn't you pick up your phone?" Evelyn asked, her voice deadly serious.

Sighing softly at her failed attempt to sneak past Evelyn's office, Kate turned around and lengthened her steps toward her own office while her hand dug into the bag. "Sorry, I didn't hear it. I thought I'd be in and out of the house in a few minutes so I left my phone in the bag, and I left my bag in the car. As you can see, I'm still alive and well."

Evelyn closed her eyes and took in a deep breath through her nose.

Not good.

"I'm kidding, and I'm sorry." Kate took out her phone and sent a quick text to Tyler. "Let's get to work," she suggested before Evelyn could continue her lecture on the 101 reasons why she shouldn't be staying with Tyler at the mansion.

Before she could put her things down and settle into her chair, her phone buzzed. The notification flashed across the screen; a text message from Tyler.

"Did he just text you?" Evelyn asked, incredulous. "I thought you said he was awful."

Kate glowered at Evelyn. "I didn't say he was awful. I said he wasn't a bundle of joy." Kate repeated what she'd said that morning as she read the text.

Everything all right? Hope I didn't get you into trouble with your friend.

Evelyn snatched the phone from her hand and turned away.

"Eve!" Kate tried to grab her phone back, but Evelyn was too fast for her. Evelyn used her back as a shield and stretched her hands forward, making sure that the phone was out of Kate's reach.

With lightning speed, Evelyn's fingers worked across the QWERTY keyboard.

"Are we in elementary school?" Kate grumbled as she stretched over Evelyn's shoulder.

She was so focused on getting her phone back that she hadn't realized all their staff was staring at them through the glass.

When she finally noticed the stares, she pressed the switch on the remote to fog up the glass.

"Give me back my phone."

The moment Evelyn returned Kate's phone, Debussy's Clair de Lune broke the momentary truce. She quickly turned and picked up the phone before Evelyn could snatch it from her. "Hey."

"Kate?"

"Yeah." She shot a warning glare over to Evelyn.

"Are you all right?"

Uncertain about what Evelyn had sent out in the text, she decided to come clean rather than pretend to know what was going on. "Sorry, Eve sent out the last text. I have no idea what she sent, but you can just ignore her."

"Marianne's cooking. Why don't you ask Evelyn over for dinner?"

"Dinner?" Kate cast an uncertain glance in Evelyn's direction.

"Then she can take a look around at where you're staying."

"But the eight p.m. rule about guests …"

"We can have an early dinner. I'm sure Marianne can get it ready by … six?"

She doubted a dinner at the mansion would shut Evelyn up, but she did have to stay there for a year. If there was a chance that Evelyn would back off, she'd take it. "All right. We'll be back by six. I'll tell her to play nice, but please don't expect it."

"Not a problem. See you at six."

Kate could sense Evelyn's eyes on her throughout her phone conversation with Tyler.

Once she hung up the call, Evelyn asked, "Where are we going?"

"To the mansion, for dinner with Tyler and Marianne," Kate said as she tapped into the message application to read the text that Evelyn had sent.

Yes, she is. She shouldn't be staying with someone she doesn't know. If you harm her in any way, I swear I'll hunt you down and bury you somewhere in the creepy woods.

Kate's fingers splayed across her eyes and forehead. "Eve, thanks for being concerned about my well-being, but *really*? Do you have to add in the part about burying him?"

Evelyn rolled her eyes. "It's a threat; that's what a threat looks like."

Kate sat and leaned back against her chair. "Can we begin our work now?"

She rushed through the proposal she had been preparing for the new bed and breakfast she was working on, a bed and breakfast aimed at attracting city dwellers like her to the country.

In order to make sure that the city dwellers not get a rude shock, or feel as though they were still in the city, she'd worked to put in country elements without over-cluttering it.

Evelyn had already managed to find a few pieces of the furniture she wanted.

Kate simply had to make the final decision on which items would make it to the actual installment. Though she had hundreds of photos of that place, she needed to take a trip down before making the final decision.

She had to get a feel of the place for herself and look at the changes that the renovations had made.

It would save tons of trouble as compared to getting the pieces of furniture and planning a room, only to realize that the new floorings or the colors of the walls didn't match.

She scanned through her calendar, trying to find a date when she could make the trip down and perhaps stay over for the weekend. Just before she set the date down in her calendar, she remembered the conditions of the will.

She would have to ask Tyler along.

He had been much friendlier that morning, and they seemed to be on better terms. Hopefully, he wouldn't mind taking a weekend off.

She would ask him later after dinner, after Evelyn had gone home.

Tyler hung up the call and found Marianne staring at him. "What?"

"Did you just ask her to come home for dinner? And to bring a friend?"

Tyler frowned, not understanding Marianne's bewilderment. "Her friend's concerned about her stay here. I think it'll save her some trouble if she brings her friend here to have a look around."

"Save her some trouble," Marianne repeated while her eyes continued to study him.

"What?"

"Nothing. I'm just trying to think of a time when you took the initiative to solve someone's problem."

"I've helped you and the guys before."

"Yeah, when we asked. You never offered."

"If you didn't ask, I assumed you could solve it on your own."

Marianne rolled her eyes. Tyler didn't understand what that was for, so he ignored her. "I'm heading to the office to get some things. Do you need me to get anything for you?" Tyler asked.

"Some helpers."

He paused. "There are maids, right? Get them to help."

Marianne opened the fridge and said as she bent in, "They're part-time, and they only clean the house, not cook."

"Then hire someone, whoever you want. Let me know when you've made your choice."

"That's the Tyler I know," Marianne said from behind the fridge. "The Tyler who'll offer a solution, but leave you alone to deal with it."

Again, he didn't understand what Marianne was grumbling about. She was always so particular about who was allowed in the kitchen while she was cooking. It only made sense for Marianne to choose her own helper.

Marianne popped her head up from the fridge. "Why are you so nice to her?"

Grateful, maybe. After how he'd treated her, she still chose to help him.

The conditions of the will stipulated that she had to stay in the mansion for a year, which was all she had to do. There wasn't any need for her to tell him the stories behind the rings and to assure him that things would get better.

He wasn't highly skilled at being a pleasant person. But if there was one thing he was good at, it would be making someone feel safe in a place.

Without answering Marianne, he shrugged and headed out of the house.

"You weren't kidding about the woods. It's just like the *When a Stranger Calls* movie we saw," Evelyn said as she stepped out of the car.

"Exactly. I think it's scary to look out at the woods. I guess we're both city people," Kate said with a shrug. "Tyler says it's quiet and peaceful."

"Well, he's in the security system business, so the house should be the safest place in the world, right?"

She thought about that for a moment. "Actually, if you've got the keys or know how to break the doors down, you're pretty much in."

"Or just break the windows," Evelyn added, her eyes on the long windows the mansion had.

Now that Evelyn had brought it up, it was making her rather uncomfortable.

"Having second thoughts about staying here, huh?" Evelyn asked with a smirk. "Big house and all, in the middle of the woods with no security. Imagine waking up and—"

"Shut up." Kate turned her key and opened the door.

A series of low, soft beeps went off.

She turned to Evelyn, seeing the same confusion reflected on Evelyn's face.

"What's that?"

"I don't—" Before Kate could finish her sentence, a shrill alarm went off and both of them cringed at the loud alarm resonating throughout the house.

Tyler came jogging out of the kitchen and keyed in the security code, stopping the alarm immediately. "Sorry, I should've texted and warned you about that."

Kate rubbed her ears. "That wasn't working in the morning."

Tyler opened his mouth to speak, but a phone call came through the landline. He moved over to pick it up while Marianne walked out of the kitchen.

"Hi, Kate, and you must be Evelyn." Marianne smiled warmly and stretched her hand out for a handshake. "The alarm, such a troublesome thing, isn't it? But Tyler said you thought the woods were creepy, so he spent the day updating and fixing the system."

Kate's brows rose.

Tyler had been much friendlier that morning, but she certainly hadn't expected him to do anything for her.

"Thanks," she said as Tyler joined the group. "Hope it wasn't too troublesome."

"Evelyn, you can leave your bag on the couch." Marianne placed a hand on Evelyn's back and led her into the kitchen.

Grinning at Kate, Tyler pointed to the security pad right beside the door. "The code is your cell phone number. You have ten beeps to key in the code. If you don't key it in, don't complete it, or key in the wrong code, the alarm will go off."

Tyler continued to explain the system as they strolled toward the kitchen. "Complete the code anytime to cut off the alarm, but a call will come in within the next minute to ask for another code, which is my cell phone number. If you say it wrong or don't know the code, a patrol car will be dispatched to the house within five minutes. All the windows and doors of the house are wired as well. Once we enter the same security code into the pad, the alarm will ring if any of the windows open."

"Thanks for doing this, but won't it be troublesome if we want to open the window in the morning?"

"Marianne's always up before dawn. She'll switch off the alarm once she's up."

Tyler pulled out a chair and waited for her to sit before taking the seat next to her. "There's more. There should be a small red button with a plastic cover by your bed. You can simply lift the cover and press it. Same routine: someone will call within one minute, and you either give them the password or they'll send the police. There's a security pad by the stairs of each floor. So if any of them gets triggered accidentally, any one of us can turn it off easily."

"What if someone who knows the passwords to the alarm creeps into her room without her knowing?" Evelyn asked, staring right at Tyler.

Instead of answering Evelyn, Tyler got out of his seat and jogged out of the kitchen.

Kate kicked Evelyn under the table and scowled at her. Stop it, she mouthed.

"He personally fixed up the system and even got some additional security items for Kate," Marianne interjected as she placed the food on the table.

Kate looked up, waiting for Marianne to elaborate, but Tyler was already back in the kitchen with a paper bag. He returned to his seat and took out a box from the bag.

With his eyes on Kate, he said, "This is mainly used for travel, but your friend seemed concerned, so I thought you could use this."

She took the box from his hand and turned it around, searching for the instructions. There weren't any that she could see.

He took the box from her and slid it across the table to Evelyn.

"I got two of them for you. You can attach them to the door and window." Tyler paused as his lips curled. "When someone tries to open either, the alarm will ring. The alarm will be triggered as long as the door or window is opened from the outside. Once you've set them up, no one from the outside can switch them off. I'll teach you how to use them later."

Covering her mouth with her fingers, Kate tried to hide her smile. "Don't you think this is too much?"

"It isn't too much," Evelyn said. "Make sure you use them. Anything else?" Evelyn put the box down and leaned forward, staring at the bag that Tyler was holding.

Without taking his eyes off Kate, Tyler continued as he pulled more items out of the bag. "Pepper spray—you can put it by your bed in case someone slips into your room. And flashlights—put one by the headboard of the bed, one in the drawer of your desk, and one in the bathroom. If I remember correctly, black out tends to occur whenever a storm comes in."

"I feel as if I'm being prepared for war. But thanks, it's very thoughtful." Kate shot Evelyn a glare, warning her to back off.

"Let's eat, then," Evelyn announced. "And Marianne, thanks for preparing dinner."

"Yes. Thanks, Marianne," Kate echoed while Tyler returned all the things into the bag.

"Is there a piano here?" Evelyn asked as she took a mouthful of the mashed potatoes. "Mm, this is *so* good. Is there cheese in it?"

"You play?" Tyler looked at Kate.

Kate shot her leg out again, kicking Evelyn under the table. "Just a little."

Evelyn didn't even wince. "Gosh, this is really good," she said, taking another spoonful of it. "She practices every day for at least an hour. Are you going to stop playing for the whole year?"

"I can go home and play the piano whenever I want. It's no big deal."

"If you say so." Evelyn shrugged and pointed to the mashed potatoes. "Try it."

"I'm sure there's a place for a piano in the house," Marianne said.

"No, there's no need. She's just trying to be annoying." Kate took a spoonful of the mashed potatoes. "This *is* good."

"I cook every night. You're welcome to join us." Marianne

turned to Evelyn. "You, too."

Evelyn grinned and nodded.

"Do you have a flashlight? I'm sure you'll need one," Kate said to Marianne.

"I do, dear. Thanks. But I think he got one for me just to make sure that you don't give yours away," she jested.

"Ignore her," Tyler jumped in before Marianne or Evelyn could continue. "She's still irritated with me for getting her to cook for so many people without help."

"This," Evelyn's finger drew a circle in the air, "is so many people?"

"For Tyler, two is plenty," Marianne replied.

Kate chuckled. "I'm sorry for the trouble. I'll make Eve wash the dishes later."

Evelyn groaned. "I thought I was a guest."

"You can help me while Ty and Kate set up the alarms. Then you can test them out for yourself to see if they work."

Evelyn thought about it for a moment, then nodded.

For the rest of dinner, Evelyn was preoccupied with Marianne's food and that gave Kate a break from her incessant nagging about her safety.

After dinner, Kate and Tyler headed upstairs to fix the alarms.

"Thanks for doing this," she said as Tyler set up the alarm for the window.

"Not a problem. This way, if Peter Parker tries to get in …" Tyler flashed a wide grin as he slid the window up and an ear-piercing alarm rang. "You'll know."

She covered her ears and recoiled from the blaring alarm.

Tyler cut it off. "You can set this up before going to bed." He picked up the bag on the table and went around the room, putting the flashlights into different drawers around the room and the bottle of pepper spray into the drawer closest to her bed.

"You know, I can just lock the door." She smiled sheepishly. "There really wasn't a need to get all this."

"Your friend's giving you a hard time, right? Now that all these measures are in place, you should be able to get a breather," he replied nonchalantly.

Tyler disappeared into the bathroom, then reappeared moments later.

"By the way, we're only on the second floor. I bet I can climb my way up even without whatever help Peter Parker has," she said.

"Please don't try."

She shook her head and turned away.

"What?"

"You sound like Eve. And speaking of her, I'm sorry for the way she was behaving. She thinks I'm too trusting, so she behaves all crazy to make sure that I'll be safe."

"Let's go back before she thinks I've kidnapped you."

When they returned to the kitchen, Kate announced, "My room is ready for inspection."

"I heard the alarm from here. It's fine."

"Really? You're not going to inspect the room?" She was astonished. She'd thought Evelyn would fight her all the way, but she seemed to be wrong about many things that day. "If you say so."

Once Evelyn had cleared her dish-washing duties, she thanked Marianne for dinner and left.

"I'm going to head back to my room. You kids need anything else?" Marianne asked.

"No," she answered while Tyler shook his head. "Oh, would you give us a tour of the other wing?"

Marianne arched a brow. "A tour? It's mainly more guest rooms, a store room for some necessary cleaning items, and a laundry room."

"Great." Kate hopped to her feet. "Can you show me where the laundry room is?"

"Whatever for?"

"So that I can do my laundry," she answered matter-of-factly.

"Don't be silly. We have maid service here. They come every day; they'll help with your laundry," Marianne said.

"But—"

"It's no trouble. Trust me. If you go down and do your own laundry, you'll end up affecting their workflow and cause more problems for them. There should be a basket in your bathroom; throw everything that you need to wash inside."

Kate pursed her lips; she was so used to doing her own chores.

Since her parents' accident, she had ended up taking over her mother's role. Her grandmother still cooked for her, but her grandparents were old so she had to do many of the chores on her own.

"If you don't want to cause them any trouble, then let them do their jobs," Marianne continued as if she'd sensed her hesitation.

"You're right. I'll do as you say."

When Marianne disappeared through the connecting walkway to the other wing of the house, Kate said, "So she's the only one staying on the other side of the house?"

"Don't worry about her. No one's dumb enough to mess with her."

"But criminals aren't usually the ones with the highest intelligence. Otherwise, they wouldn't be committing crimes in the first place."

Tyler looked up at her and narrowed his eyes. "Let me guess, your favorite TV show is *Criminal Minds*?"

"And *CSI,* and *Bones,* and all the other crime shows you can find."

"You should stop watching them, at least while you're here. I won't be entertaining you if you can't sleep due to some TV show."

"You know, your personality goes downhill with the sun."

Tyler grimaced. "I'm sorry about last night. I was—"

"Angry. I would've been, too. It's fine." Just as Kate finished her sentence, the doorbell rang. Kate met Tyler's gaze. "No one is allowed in after eight, right? I haven't had time to read the fine print."

Tyler stood, went toward the window nearest to the door, and pushed the blinds aside. "Mr. Sawyer."

"Right. He's supposed to be here, too."

Tyler strolled over and punched in Kate's number on the security pad before opening the door.

"Good evening, Mr. Hayes. Sorry for being so late; I was

swamped with work. Is Miss West here?"

Tyler stepped aside for Mr. Sawyer to enter, but he didn't bother to reply.

Seeing that Tyler had no intention of answering the question, Kate said, "Marianne is in the other wing of the house. We're staying upstairs. There's another guest room upstairs and some in the other wing where Marianne is."

Mr. Sawyer looked over his shoulder at Tyler, then turned back to Kate. "I think I'll join Miss West. Will you take me there?"

Kate got to her feet. "I can take you to the other wing, but I don't know which room Marianne is in or where the guest rooms are."

Without a word, Tyler moved forward and trotted through the walkway to the other side of the house. Kate and Mr. Sawyer followed.

"You only brought a piece of luggage, too?" Kate asked as she noticed the piece of luggage he was dragging along.

Mr. Sawyer laughed. "No, this just contains the files I need to go through for work. I haven't had time to pack, so I just grabbed two sets of clothes and the essential items."

"Essential items being the files?"

Mr. Sawyer sighed and nodded. "Yes. Sadly, they are my essential items."

Kate empathized; she knew how it was to be overwhelmed with work. "Why did you ring the doorbell? Don't you have the keys?"

"I only had two sets in my possession. I gave one to Mr. Hayes and one to Miss West."

Tyler kept his back to them even as he spoke. "You can ask Marianne where the spare keys are."

Mr. Sawyer gave Kate an apologetic look; a look that Kate immediately understood.

The late Mr. Hayes had an eccentric character. He didn't trust many people and was often quiet and deep in his own thoughts. It had taken him years before he confided in Kate over what had happened with Tyler's parents.

Mr. Sawyer must think that the young Mr. Hayes had inherited those traits.

But Tyler wasn't a horrible person.

He'd spent an entire day fixing up the security system for her and even got her all the gadgets to help her with her Evelyn issue. "Based on my observations, Mr. Hayes becomes grumpier as the day ends. He'll be better in the morning."

Tyler continued walking, completely ignoring them. Once he knocked on Marianne's door, he left Mr. Sawyer by the door and headed back to the other side of the house.

She said her goodnights and, seeing that Tyler had already turned the corner, hastened her steps to catch up. It was completely dark outside except for the dim, silvery moon rays, and she wasn't interested in moving around the house on her own.

"Oh!" Kate stumbled a few steps back as she turned and knocked right into Tyler.

He immediately reached out, holding her shoulders to steady her.

"Were you so frightened that you had to run back to your room?" Tyler laughed when he saw the grimace on her face.

"I had to run because you didn't bother to wait, Mr. Hayes."

Tyler frowned. "Ty, you call me Ty."

"Mr. Sawyer calls you Mr. Hayes."

"You're not Mr. Sawyer, and I was waiting for you."

Kate didn't understand the reason for his sudden seriousness, but she stopped her teasing anyway. "Why do you hate Mr. Sawyer so much, *Ty*?"

He started walking again, this time slower, probably so she didn't have to hurry just to catch up with him.

"I don't hate him."

"Then why didn't you reply when he asked you about Marianne?"

Tyler shrugged indifferently. "I didn't feel like answering."

"That's a horrible answer. Even if you didn't feel like it, you should have. It was rude and would've been awkward if I weren't there."

"Life will be tiring if you have to do everything you should."

Kate scowled at him. "Next time when someone asks you a question, I'm not going to reply. I'll sit back and watch how you deal with it."

"I won't care, but you won't be able to stand it."

"Challenge accepted," she said and laughed as he grinned.

Chapter Six

"What's with the alarm?" Ryan asked the moment Tyler entered the kitchen, where the boisterous crowd was already seated around the table.

He shrugged and settled into an empty seat. He was already used to seeing all the guys in his house. All of them had their own places, but everyone always gathered at his. They weren't there for him, though; they were all there for Marianne's food.

Ryan didn't bother to wait for his reply. Using his fingers, he picked up a strip of bacon and stuffed it into his mouth.

"We have forks here," Marianne said with a swat to Ryan's head.

Joseph was seated across from him, chatting with Dan, while Joanne moved over to sit next to him.

"Did you sleep well?"

He didn't bother to reply. He stood and reached over for the pot of coffee placed in the middle of the table.

"What's that?" Joanne asked as he poured his coffee. She reached over, pulled out the chain, and held the rings in her hand.

Tyler wanted to stop her, but he was holding a pot of hot coffee in one hand and his cup in another. He didn't want to make a mess.

He exhaled heavily through his nose as Joanne leaned in to take a closer look.

He could never stand her overwhelming perfume. It was so artificially sweet that it hurt his nose to breathe while seated beside her. He turned away from her and took a breath of fresh air.

"Are those for me?" Joanne shrieked the moment she saw the rings. "Oh, they're beautiful."

Putting everything down, he yanked the chain from her hands. "Don't touch them. They aren't for you."

He hated people touching his things without his permission. Actually, he hated people touching his things, period.

He let the rings hang free outside his shirt. The long chain that held his parents' rings swung freely right below his chest. "And you need to stop introducing yourself as my fiancée."

Joanne's brows furrowed and she pouted. "Why? We've been dating forever; it's time we move on."

A sudden stillness took over the kitchen.

Subtlety wasn't prevalent in the group.

Everyone was clearly surprised that he'd brought that up, and all of them didn't bother to hide their stares.

The guys had told him, more than once, to stop Joanne before she started believing her own imaginary story, but he hadn't bothered. He was certain that Joanne wasn't insane.

He never led her on.

His indifference toward her was obvious to everyone, so how could she think otherwise?

He pushed his chair away from Joanne, putting some space between them. Her overpowering perfume was giving him a headache.

Staring right at her, he continued. "We were never dating. I never corrected you because I thought it was only a habit that meant nothing."

Joanne leaned forward and tried to circle her arms around his, but Tyler rose from his chair and turned from the table, bumping right into Kate.

Ryan and Joseph shared a brow raise while Dan stretched across the table to grab his sister's arm. "Enough, Anne."

"Are you running to your room?" Kate teased and smiled at him.

The urge to leave the kitchen melted away. "How was your

sleep?"

"I'm pleased to announce that Peter Parker didn't visit me," she said as she leaned to the side to look at the crowd. "I thought last night was so-many-people."

"They don't count," Marianne said. "They're always around, sort of like furniture or clutter in the house."

Kate chuckled and waved to the rest of the guys. "Good morning, people. Breakfast smells great. Am I allowed to join?"

Tyler beamed at Kate and led her to an empty seat beside Ryan. The moment she sat, she gasped and reached for the rings hanging right in front of her.

She cradled the rings in her hand. "I can't believe you're wearing them. They're beautiful."

Thank you, he mouthed the words.

"You're welcome," she said and let go of the rings, turning to the table of food. "Mm ..." Kate took a deep breath. "I completely understand why they're here all the time."

No one commented on her words. No one said anything.

Kate glanced around the table and blinked when she saw everyone staring at her. "Did I say something wrong?"

Tyler took an empty chair and placed it next to Kate, forcing Ryan to move his chair and make room for him.

"You just touched his things," Ryan said as he got pushed aside.

Kate looked at Ryan, pursed her lips, then turned to Tyler, speaking as slowly as Ryan did. "Am I not supposed to?"

"Ignore them."

"When Ty says not to touch something, it means *nobody* is allowed to touch it," Ryan continued.

"Generally, just don't touch any of his things without first asking," Joseph added.

"Oh, I'm sorry. I—"

"Ignore them," Tyler repeated, then glared at Ryan. "Knock it off."

"Where did you get that?" Ryan asked.

Instantly, last night's conversation surfaced in his mind. Kate was already staring at him, probably waiting for him to reply

Ryan's question.

He gave Kate a smirk and shrugged.

She bit down on her lips and looked away from him.

He didn't know if she was trying to stop herself from answering the question or if she was trying to prevent herself from bursting into laughter. Regardless, he couldn't help grinning as he saw her struggling.

After drawing a long, deep breath, she tried imitating the shrug he gave. She failed miserably.

"It's killing you."

Kate closed her eyes, took another deep breath, wiped the smile off her face, and gave another shot at the shrug. This time, she succeeded.

"I'm impressed," Tyler commented.

She was still chewing on her lips, but the corners were slowly inching up. She gave Tyler a brief glance and the same aloof shrug she'd just mastered.

"You guys have an inside joke already?" Ryan leaned forward and directed the question to Kate.

Kate leaned forward and closer against Tyler. "Long story short, he was being irritating," she said to Ryan.

Tyler took in the vanilla scent from her hair as Kate returned to her position. She smelled like ice cream. There was something else, something flowery, but he couldn't quite make out what it was.

"I'm done eating and I'm going home to sleep. Coming?" Joseph asked Ryan.

Ryan groaned. "I haven't had my fill."

"Suit yourself. Nice to see you again, Kate."

"What? We're all becoming Ty now? How am I supposed to get home?" Ryan's bellow got louder with each question, but Joseph continued walking out of the house without even flinching.

"Ty, can we talk for a minute?" Joanne whined in her sweetened voice.

He hated that voice. It never failed to give him goosebumps.

"Where are you going?" Kate asked Ryan.

Kate had leaned in closer again, and he forgot all about Joanne when he felt Kate's hair brush against his arm.

"I can give you a ride home," Kate continued.

"I'll drive," Tyler interjected. The thought of Ryan getting to know Kate better didn't sit too well with him.

"Really?" Ryan eyed him warily. "The world's upside down today. But since my ride's gone, can I just crash in one of the rooms here?"

"Ty, just one minute. Pleeeease ..."

Kate turned to him, and her eyes flitted to the side.

He shook his head. "She's always like this," he whispered when her eyes returned to him.

Kate tugged on her necklace and returned her focus to the food before her.

"There are spare rooms on the other side of the house. Marianne will arrange a room for you," Tyler continued as though Joanne hadn't spoken a word.

"Ty," Joanne whined again.

He saw Kate pursing her lips before she gave him a pleading look. "Ty," she whispered even as he glared at her.

Undeterred, she cocked her head slightly toward Joanne.

"Ty?" Joanne sneered. "You've known him for like what? Two days? And you're calling him Ty?"

"That's enough," he said.

"But—"

"But nothing."

Everyone, even Ryan, froze.

Joanne's head snapped toward her brother.

"Don't need to look at him. You can leave if you're unhappy. No one will stop you."

Joanne got up, but instead of walking out, she picked up a random glass of orange juice from the table and splashed its contents into Kate's face. "Bitch."

Tyler was on his feet in an instant, but Dan had already pulled Joanne out of his way.

"Ugh."

Kate's soft cries immediately got his attention. Pushing the chair aside, he knelt down beside her.

Her hands hovered before her eyes, and she wouldn't stop blinking. "My contacts, something's wrong with them."

A tear slipped down her cheek, then more followed as she blinked.

"I'll find some eye drops," Marianne said, rushing out of the kitchen.

"Get Joe," Tyler said as he cupped his hands over Kate's. Ryan nodded and sprinted out.

Gently, Tyler pulled her hands down and placed them on her lap. "Stop blinking if it hurts, just close your eyes." He clenched his jaws, frustrated with himself.

He should've seen that coming.

She was only here because of him, and he couldn't even keep her safe in his own house.

"I can't help it. It stings too much to keep my eyes closed, and I can't keep my eyes open either."

Tyler wiped the tears away, wishing there were more he could do for her.

"Ty—"

"Enough." Dan grabbed Joanne by her arm and dragged her out of the house.

Tyler clenched his jaw and took a deep breath, turning his attention back to Kate.

He tucked her hair behind her ear just as she reached toward her eyes again. He grabbed her hands midway, stopping her.

"Let me try taking the contacts out. It really stings."

"I know, but just wait for a while. Joe will be here anytime. He's a doctor; he'll know what to do." He covered her hands with his and gave them a gentle squeeze.

"Yeah, he's already on the way back. Your fingers are dirty. Don't make it worse," Ryan added as he came running back into the kitchen.

"I'm so sorry," Tyler mumbled.

He sighed when Joseph finally came running in with Marianne's eye drops in hand.

"Here, let me take a look." Joseph tipped her head up. "I can see the lens in your left eye. The right lens is missing."

"I only know it hurts like crazy."

Her hands shifted, moving toward her eyes, but Tyler held them down. Instead of fighting him, she turned her hands over and held on to his.

"All right. I'm going to drip in some eye drops before taking out the one in your left. Keep staring up at the ceiling and try not to move your eyes around. It's going to sting, but try to focus on the ceiling," Joseph said in his soothing professional voice.

Her grip on his hands tightened as Joseph removed her lens. Her blinking worsened and tears rushed down her cheeks.

Shifting both her hands into one of his, Tyler reached up and wiped the tears away.

"It's the eyes' reflex to wash away the foreign liquid," Joseph explained to him.

"Focus on her."

"I'm going to take out the contact lens in your right eye now. I know it hurts, but close your eyes for me. Remember to keep your eyes focused and don't move them around." Joseph pushed softly along the edges of her eye. "Open your eyes now."

She forced her eyes open, her hands clutching tightly onto his.

"Got it. It's going to hurt. Bear with me, okay?"

She nodded. She clenched her jaws and held her tongue as Joseph pinched and tugged on the tinted blue edge of her lens.

Even Tyler had to cringe when he saw Joseph pulling out the lens from the corner of her eye. More tears gushed down Kate's face, and her grip tightened around his hands, but not a whimper escaped her lips.

"It's out." Washing her eyes with eye drops, Joseph announced, "Done."

Ryan gave Joseph a pat on the back. "Well done, Doc. I think your life depended on it." Ryan laughed as he cocked his head toward Tyler.

Tyler stood and lifted Kate's chin. She blinked, her eyes bloodshot, and she still didn't seem to be able to keep her eyes open.

"Her eyes are still—"

"It's normal. I'll write down the name of the eye drops and eye gel you can get at the pharmacy. And Kate, you'll need to stay off your contacts for at least a week."

"A week? I hate wearing my glasses; they give me such headaches."

She blinked a couple more times, and he could see the focus returning to her eyes.

"Don't look so worried. It doesn't sting so much anymore," she said, half laughing.

"Your eyes are bloodshot," he whispered, his thumb gently brushing along her jawline.

He sighed, frustrated that she got hurt because of him. He would have to talk to Marianne about keeping Joanne from the house.

"Are you all right, dear?" Marianne asked.

"Yeah." Kate nodded. "Sorry for being such a baby."

"Kate, when your contacts disappear behind your eyes, it can cut your optic nerves and you may go blind," Joseph said in all seriousness.

"Then maybe you should stay away from contacts permanently," Tyler said.

Kate sighed, and her hands moved unconsciously toward her eyes.

Tyler pulled her hands away from her face and frowned at her. "Don't do that."

She dropped her hands onto her lap. "I tried getting lower powered lenses and lighter frames for my glasses, but nothing worked. I can't wear my glasses for long periods."

"Lasik?" Joseph suggested.

"I've considered that, but I never had the time to check it out."

"Any recommendations?" Tyler asked Joseph.

"I'll text you the contact later." Scrawling across a notepad, he handed Tyler the list. "Here's the eye drops and eye gel. For today, apply the eye gel once every four hours and the eye drops whenever her eyes feel dry. Her vision will blur for about a minute or two after applying the gel."

Tyler nodded as he glanced at Joseph's note.

"Great. All's well that ends well. Now, Marianne, where can I get some sleep?"

"You're sleeping here? Can I crash here, too?" Joseph asked.

Tyler heard Joseph's question, but he didn't bother answering; Marianne would settle them.

He turned back to Kate. "Do you have to go to the office today?"

"I have some stuff I need to do, but I think I'll work from my room." Kate forced her eyes shut. "I don't want Eve to know what happened, not now anyway."

"I need to get the eye drops and gel for you. Will you be all right here?"

Kate scowled at him. "I'm not a baby, Ty. I can pick those up on my own."

He returned her scowl. "You can forget about that. You're not driving today." Taking a step closer, he stretched out his hand. "I'll take you to your room."

"I'm not blind," she said even as she took his hand.

Halfway up the steps, Kate threw her head back and gave an exasperated sigh. "I'm supposed to meet my sister for dinner tonight. I haven't told her that I've moved."

"Don't worry, I'll get you there."

"Don't *you* need to work?"

"The work will still be there when I get back. Anyway, I can work from home, too."

"I'm sorry."

"You're not used to people taking care of you," Tyler said. "Just an observation."

"Like my observation about your character going downhill along with the sun?"

His lips curled, but he didn't bother to reply.

When in her room, Tyler asked Kate where her phone was. "In case you need anything," he said and placed the phone by her bed. "Just call me."

"I *really* am fine." She lay back on the bed, staring up at the ceiling. She kept blinking her eyes, but it didn't seem to help.

"I didn't say you're not. I'll be back soon, and don't rub your eyes," he said, brushing her hair from her face.

He should stop touching her.

He hadn't been able to keep his hands from her. He'd told himself that he was simply wiping her tears away—like anyone would. She wasn't crying now, though. He had no business or reason to keep touching her.

Kate closed her eyes. "Yes, sir."

Tyler flexed his fingers, walked out of the room, and headed over to the other wing.

"Your friends are settled and probably snoring away right now. But you're not here for them, are you?" Marianne said.

Tyler ignored Marianne's jibe. "Will you stay with her until I'm back?"

"Why are you so worried? I've never seen you so concerned about anyone."

"She got hurt because of me."

"No, she got hurt because of Joanne." Marianne scrutinized his face. "You don't have to be so worried, Ty. She isn't going to disappear. Not everything good will," she said softly, almost in a whisper.

"Just stay with her until I get back."

"All right. Go get her eye drops. I'll keep her company."

He followed behind Marianne, turning to the door when she headed up the stairs.

So much for making the house safe for her.

When he opened the main door and saw Joanne sitting on the step, he sighed impatiently and thrust his hands into his pockets.

"I tried, but she won't leave without seeing you," Dan said after winding down his car's window.

Dan stepped out of his car as Tyler moved right past Joanne without giving her another glance.

"Wait, Ty."

He strode toward his own car while Joanne's heels clicked behind him.

"Let it go, Anne," Dan called out.

"What were you thinking?" Tyler stopped and asked Joanne.

Joanne skidded to a stop. She took a few steps back and looked up at him.

She rolled her eyes and pouted. "Who does she think she is? She comes in here, calls you Ty—"

"I told her to call me that. If you have a problem with that, you bring it up to me."

"She was trying to seduce you."

"Even if she was, it's none of your business," Dan said, exasperated.

"Ty," Joanne switched to her sweetened voice again.

Tyler sighed and continued toward his car.

Dan exhaled slowly through his nose. "Anne, I said enough. This isn't your house. You don't get to throw tantrums and expect everyone to give in to you. If you're so in love with Ty, then you should know this. He rarely ever cares about anything or anyone, but the few things and people he cares about, he's extremely protective of them. What you did, he'll never forgive you."

Protective? Yes, he was protective of Kate, he supposed. He should be. After all that she'd done for him, keeping her safe was the least he could do.

"He doesn't care about her! I'm his fiancée!" Joanne screamed in Dan's face. "What's wrong with all of you?"

Tyler saw Dan push his hands into his pockets as he took a step away from Joanne.

He'd heard Dan complain about Joanne, but he hadn't seen Dan this frustrated before.

Tyler pulled his car door open as he looked over his shoulder at Dan and Joanne.

"Ty owns the biggest security software and systems firm in Washington. His grandfather had the best security system installed in his house, but have you ever seen him use it?"

Joanne stared pointedly at Dan, not getting his point.

"He never used it because he didn't see the need. Yesterday, the alarm wasn't working. Today, it's up and running. Who do you think he set it up for?"

"Himself! Marianne! It's isolated here," Joanne screeched.

"Stop shouting," Dan said calmly, even as he took another step away from Joanne.

"I set it up for Kate," Tyler said before Dan had to grab Joanne by her shoulders and shake some sense into her.

"Why?" Dan asked.

He shrugged. "Because I could and I wanted to." He got into his car and drove off, hoping that for Joanne's own sake, she wouldn't be here when he returned.

When Tyler got back to the mansion, he found Kate chatting with Marianne. He couldn't make out what they were talking about, but he could hear them laughing away.

"Feeling better?" Tyler asked as he entered, interrupting their conversation.

"Yeah."

"I'll leave you two alone and go finish up my book," Marianne said. "Let me know if you need anything." She gave Kate a pat on the leg and left.

"Have you met Marianne before this?" he asked when Marianne stepped out of the room.

Kate blinked, and her hand reached for her necklace. "Why do you ask?"

"The two of you seem to be on friendly terms."

"Marianne is nice to everyone."

"Did she visit him?"

"I don't know what you're talking about," she said and quickly changed the subject. "Would you pass me the eye drops?"

He took out the box of eye drops from the bag, opened it, and handed her a vial. "You're a horrible liar."

"I'm not lying."

"You're just avoiding my question."

Kate dripped a drop into each of her eyes and turned to him. "Why don't you ask her instead?"

He shrugged, not saying anything else.

She sighed softly. "She didn't tell you because she didn't want to upset you."

He pulled out another box from the bag and opened the eye

gel. "We should've used this first."

"It's all right. I'll use it now." She took the tube of gel from him and tilted her head back. She squeezed the tube, but it simply refused to cooperate.

Sitting by the side of her bed, Tyler took the gel from her and lifted her chin. He squeezed a dab of the gel into each of her eyes. She blinked a few times, her brows moving to form a frown.

"This feels weird."

"It'll be fine after a while. Get some rest. I'll leave your door open. Shout if you need anything."

"Ty, are you all right?"

"Just close your eyes and rest."

Kate nodded, but when he was about to leave, she reached out and grabbed his arm. "He really missed you, and he wanted to see you. He just didn't know how to. He knew it was his fault."

Tyler clenched his jaws, and though Kate probably couldn't see him clearly, he turned his face away from her.

Didn't know how? He should've just shown up.

He had waited so many years for a visit, a phone call. He had waited until his heart grew cold from disappointments, and he learned not to hope.

"I'm not asking you to forgive him. I just want you to know that he knew the fault was all his." She ran her finger down along the taut line of his cheek.

Her soft touch startled him.

His hands kept finding their way to her, and she hadn't shrunk from his touch, but he was really aware that this was the first time Kate had touched him.

The resentment, disappointment, and hurt all melted away.

Unconsciously, he took her hand as it fell from his face and held on tight. He wanted to pull her into his arms, to hold her, to allow her warmth to dissolve the misery he'd carried for so long.

"I'm sorry," she suddenly said, pulling her hand from him.

She must've thought he was angry with her. "Don't be." He smiled. "I was just caught up in my thoughts."

Kate chewed on her lips, and her finger twirled around her locket.

"I'm fine." He tapped his finger against her nose. "Vision back to normal?"

"Yeah."

"Did it help?"

She blinked a few more times. "It did; my eyes feel much better."

"All right, then. I'll leave you to your work."

Once he was out of the room, Kate's words replayed in his head.

He never allowed himself to think much of his parents or grandfather.

Whenever he thought of them, he felt as if he were sucked into an undercurrent that dragged him deep into the abyss of darkness. He would end up drowning in the overwhelming memories of the night his parents died, the funeral, and the events after.

So he chose to shut those memories out.

Kate's gentle touch was like a breath of fresh air he'd so desperately needed, allowing him to break the surface of the water and simply breathe.

The perspective changed so drastically with the fresh air.

Everything he'd gotten himself to believe didn't make sense. If his grandfather had hated him, why would his photo be upfront on his desk? Why would he tell Kate all the stories about him? Why would he use his date of birth as the password to everything that held value for him?

Maybe things weren't like what he'd thought.

Maybe his grandfather's will wasn't another betrayal or punishment.

His perspective had changed, but he still couldn't wrap his head around the whole matter.

In some ways, Kate had given him the answers to some of his questions, but she had also confused him about things he thought he understood.

Since he couldn't get any answers, he dove into his own work, keeping himself occupied.

He stayed in his room until he heard Kate's door close and

figured she was getting ready for dinner. He changed and waited for her in the living room, reading another Patricia Cornwell novel on his iPad.

"You look studious," he said when Kate came down the stairs.

"Everyone looks studious with glasses."

"Feeling better?" he asked as they got into his car.

"Yeah."

"Are you sure?"

"Why ask if you don't believe me?" She narrowed her eyes at him before breaking into a smile. "I am."

He grinned, getting her point. "So what did you tell Evelyn?"

"I told her I'll be having dinner with my sister and had to head home to clean up the house."

"Do you often have dinner with your sister?"

"Not really. She's currently working on a project. She seemed rather excited about it. She told me that she *had* to meet me today."

"What time will you be done? I'll pick you up."

"Why don't you join us for dinner? Then you won't have to travel here and there. I'm sure Lydia won't mind."

He almost asked if she was sure, but caught himself at the last moment. "Sure."

When Tyler entered her two-story house, his eyes made a sweep of the living room and he smiled.

All the walls in her house were painted white, except for the largest section of wall that had a light blue wallpaper with columns of white flowers.

Three cushions, the same shade of blue as the wall, were positioned across her couch.

A long tablecloth lay across the middle of the dark brown dining table while a neat stack of home decor magazines sat on the coffee table.

"Why would Evelyn believe that you need to clean up your house?"

"She thinks I have some sort of compulsive disorder. Her house is …" She chuckled. "Is beyond messy. It's as if a tornado sweeps through her house every day."

Tyler scanned the area. "Your house's like a showroom."

"I work hard to keep it that way. Cleaning is one excuse she'll always believe." She gestured toward the couch. "Sit. I'll get you a drink."

Eyeing the polished black piano, he reached out and held her arm. "I don't need anything. Why don't you play for me?"

Kate bit down her lips as her fingers twirled around her locket. "I'm not really good."

"I don't play, so I can't judge." He moved toward the piano and sat on the edge of the bench.

Kate sighed softly as she sat beside him. Pushing up the wooden cover, she said, "Don't expect too much."

"Just play."

She removed her glasses and placed them on top of the piano. After a moment's thought, she positioned her fingers on the keys and played.

He watched as her fingers grazed across the keys.

Kate closed her eyes and filled her house with Debussy's Clair de Lune. Her initial self-consciousness faded, and she seemed absorbed by the music.

For him, the music fell to the back of his mind while his attention turned to her smile.

He'd thought Evelyn was exaggerating when she said Kate played the piano every night, but Kate clearly loved it.

It would be nice to fill the mansion with music, too. He remembered exactly where his mother's grand piano used to be. He remembered clambering onto her lap and watching her play. His mother had even taught him a duet so they could play it together.

When the piece ended, Kate smiled shyly. "Did I pass?"

"Flying colors."

"That's nice." At the same moment, the jingling of keys turned their heads toward the door. "It must be my sister."

"Kate! You need to see this." Lydia came bursting in with a thin brown folder in her hand.

Lydia looked a lot like Kate. They had the same hair color, high cheekbones, and green eyes, but Kate was at least a head taller than Lydia. And instead of the amiable character that Kate exuded, Lydia seemed to exhibit a more passionate and determined, maybe stubborn, personality.

"Hello to you, too," Kate said.

"Kate, I'm serious. You need to look at this."

The smile on Kate's face disappeared, and she swallowed hard.

Initially, he didn't know what caused her reaction. Then Lydia waved the brown folder as she moved over to the couch.

Kate had told him how her sister had pestered their grandparents for details on their parents' death. Judging from how excited Lydia was, she'd probably found the answer she'd been looking for.

"What is it?" Kate asked, her voice thick with dread.

Tyler strode over and stood beside Kate. "Is everything all right?"

Lydia's eyes widened for a moment when she noticed his presence. She quickly composed herself, gave him a look over, then turned back to Kate with her brows raised.

"Ty, this is my sister, Lydia. Lydia, this is my friend, Tyler."

Lydia gave him a quick nod. She wasn't the least bit interested in him. She patted the seat next to her and continued. "I'm working on some cold case files for my project, and guess what I found." She slammed the thin brown folder onto the coffee table and flipped it open. "They didn't die from an accident, Kate. That was why grandma and grandpa were always so evasive. Look at these photos."

Tyler stood across the table from the couch and saw Kate blanch as she peered at the pictures of her mother with her throat slit.

Kate flipped the photos over and closed her eyes.

Lydia opened her mouth to speak, but Tyler cut in, "That's enough."

Lydia frowned and opened her mouth, only to close it again. She cast her glance between Kate and Tyler before she gasped. "You knew. You already knew, didn't you? Why didn't you tell me? All these years I kept asking, but you never said anything."

"I didn't know for sure. I only began suspecting after grandma started saying stuff when she was confused."

"Why didn't you tell me?"

"Because I know how obsessed you are. Besides, does it matter? Are you happier knowing that our parents were murdered?"

Lydia stared back at Kate, her eyes wide with disbelief. "Don't you want to know what happened to them? To get real answers and justice? How could you go on with your life and pretend that it was *nothing*?" Lydia spat out the last word with disgust.

"What was I supposed to do? I only suspected, and digging would only reveal more questions. What's the point of chasing after ghosts of the past?"

"Just because you didn't want more questions, you chose to pretend?"

"No, she chose to let go," Tyler said. "I can assure you that no answer will satisfy you, no answer will be good enough."

Lydia rolled her eyes and glared at him with contempt. "What do you know? You have no idea what we went through, so keep your mouth shut."

"Lydia, you're angry with me. If you want to vent, vent at me," Kate said.

Tyler was tempted to move between them, to put himself in front of Kate, but he was blocked by the coffee table.

Lydia looked away. After a few moments, she sighed heavily and closed the file. "If you're not interested in giving them justice, I will." Lifting the folder, Lydia stormed out of the house.

Kate lay back against the back of the couch as the door slammed close. "Perfect."

"Are you all right?"

"What a day," Kate muttered.

"Sorry."

"For what? None of this is your fault. I'm sorry about what Lydia said. I know what happened; I can't imagine what you went through."

"The old man told you."

Her hands reached for her necklace as she nodded.

"It happened a long time ago. I'm all right now."

"Do you actually believe what you just said?"

No, he didn't. He'd thought he was all right. He thought he had let go of the past and moved on. But if he had, being in the mansion wouldn't have brought up all the pain and fear.

"Are you going to help your sister?"

"Am I being selfish if I don't?"

"Selfish?"

"I kept it from her on purpose. I took extra care to make sure that I didn't let slip anything my grandma had said. Lydia was always asking questions. Even when she got grounded and got her allowance cut, she continued trying to catch the inconsistencies in my grandparents' stories."

"Why is that selfish?"

"I was afraid; I was afraid nothing good could come of pursuing the past. And because of that, I'm not giving my parents the justice they deserved."

Tyler moved around the coffee table and sat on it. Leaning forward, he rested his elbows on his legs. "In this case, I think justice is over-rated. They're dead; I don't think they would care much about justice."

Her lips formed a small, uncertain smile.

"Marianne used to tell me that parents just want their children to be happy." He took the locket from her hand, pulling her closer toward him. "I'm sure all they care about is that you are happy."

"But Lydia has a point."

"I think both of you have your points, but you don't have to decide today." Giving her a warm smile, he released the locket and suggested, "Let's order takeout and get some food."

"Food would be a nice distraction."

While Kate was ordering takeout, Tyler took out his phone and wallet, laying them side by side on the coffee table.

"Getting comfortable?"

Tyler looked over his shoulder. "Play another song for me," he said and strode over to the piano.

"You need to stop ordering me around."

"Play another song for me, please."

Kate laughed softly, but she stopped abruptly and turned her attention to his phone. "Your phone is ringing." She moved over and took a glimpse of it. "It's Dan."

"Ignore it. I said please, but you're still standing there."

Kate shrugged her shoulders in imitation of him. Instead of moving to sit by him, she sat on the couch and picked up his phone. "Hi, Dan."

He shook his head and pressed random keys on the piano.

"Dan? It's Kate. Ty is ... busy at the moment." Kate beamed brightly when he shot her a glare over his shoulder. "His temper is that bad, huh? Does it erupt mostly at night?" Kate gave him a quick brow raise as he swiveled around to face her.

He watched as she grimaced, then laughed and said, "It's the irritating shrug. Mm-hmm. It's nothing, forget about it."

Tyler rolled his eyes. He got off the chair, went over, and pulled the phone from her hand.

"Oh—" Kate gasped.

"Have you apologized?" he asked brusquely.

"Yes."

Once he heard Dan's reply, he hung up the phone and threw it back onto the table.

"You didn't even say goodbye."

"I never do."

Kate tilted her head to the side. "Right." Turning her head back to him, she continued. "You hung up my call, too. That was so rude."

He drew in a long, patient breath and sat beside her. "How about this? You play for me, and I'll say goodbye when I hang up your calls."

"You should say goodbye to everyone."

He grinned and shook his head. "You don't play *that* well."

Her jaw dropped in a dramatic response, then she lifted her hand to check her watch. "Oh, right. It's nighttime. I forgot."

Tyler couldn't remember the last time he had this much fun talking with someone. He liked to keep his sentences short and to the point. He didn't see the point of small talk or joking around.

Ryan loved it. He and Joseph could go on for hours on some asinine argument. Whenever that happened, he either tuned them out or endured it.

Yet, he enjoyed all the banter he had with Kate.

Kate adjusted herself on the couch and leaned against her hand that was propped on the couch. "Are you seriously angry with Dan?"

As though the phone was trying to remind Tyler of what had happened in the morning, it buzzed with a reminder for Kate to apply her eye gel. Reaching into his front pocket, he took out the eye gel. "Not at him. Still, he should apologize to you. I know Joanne won't bother."

He twisted the cover off and tipped her chin to drip the gel into her eyes, then he handed her a piece of tissue to wipe off the residual gel.

"So what exactly happened this morning? She was angry with me for calling you Ty?"

"Before you came in, I told her to stop calling me her fiancé. I guess she was looking for a chance to throw her tantrums, and she chose to vent on the weakest link."

"*I* am the weakest link?" Kate asked, seemingly offended. "I can take care of myself."

He laughed when he saw the indignant expression. "Weakest link in the room, yes. She can't possibly take on any of the guys. All four of us learned judo, so unless she's looking to be slammed onto the ground, we're out. Then there's Marianne; not even Joanne will dare take her on."

Kate considered what he'd said. "I could've been a martial arts expert, too."

She seemed genuinely unhappy about being called the weakest link, so he masked his laughter in a cough. "So are you?" he asked in as serious a tone as he could muster.

"You'll never know."

He laughed and decided to drop the subject.

When the doorbell rang, Kate opened the door without checking who it was. He was behind her in a minute and paid for the food before she could get her wallet.

"You didn't even check who it was before opening the door," he said as Kate closed the door.

Kate frowned. "We ordered takeout; of course it was the delivery man. Who else could it be? Not many people come to my house, just Lydia, Evelyn, and delivery people."

As she gave him a run down of her list, Tyler realized that he didn't know a piece of vital information about her. "Boyfriend?"

"Probably, if I had one," Kate answered nonchalantly.

He grinned. The little piece of information was delightful enough that he almost forgot the lecture he'd prepared about her door opening habit—almost. "You should always check who's at the door before opening it."

"Like the way you did when Mr. Sawyer was at the door," Kate stated. "Just another observation."

"You should do that, especially when you're alone at home."

"You forget that I could be a martial arts expert." Kate smiled, then saw his seriousness. "All right, all right. Next time, I'll make sure to check before opening the door."

The answer wasn't good enough for Tyler.

He glanced around the house again, observing while he chewed his food. "You live alone, and you don't have motion sensors for your porch or a security alarm. You're not used to people taking care of you, but you don't take very good care of yourself either."

Kate followed his glance and looked around her house. "I always make sure that all my windows and doors are locked before going to bed or leaving the house. And unlike your house, I have neighbors who can probably hear me scream if anything happens."

"Probably," Tyler repeated. Probably wasn't good enough.

Chapter Seven

The next morning, Kate woke up and checked her email like she did every morning. She drummed her fingers on the table, her stomach growling while the laptop loaded.

She had only been living in the mansion for three days and her stomach was already spoilt by Marianne's cooking.

She smiled and shook her head, clicking into her email account. She was about to click on one of the daily devotionals she subscribed to when she saw an email from Lydia.

She blinked and took a second look.

One characteristic that Lydia had inherited from their grandmother was the cold-shoulder treatment. Whenever they had a disagreement, Lydia would disappear for days, ignoring all of Kate's texts, calls, or emails.

Kate skimmed through the email and sighed.

Lydia had decided to go back to their parents' house to take a look around, and she would be searching for the detective in charge of their parents' case.

She wished Lydia had discussed it with her beforehand. She had done both of those, and both were dead ends.

The detective had retired, and the police department refused to give her the address or even a phone number to contact the retired detective. As for the house, it had been stripped of everything except for the basic infrastructure of walls, doors, and windows.

She grabbed her phone, but after what had gone down last night, she was certain Lydia wouldn't pick up her call. Even if

Lydia did, she wouldn't believe anything that Kate had to say.

Putting her phone down, she slumped back against the chair.

She ran through her grandmother's ramblings and tried to sift them for some clues that she might've missed. She sat there, picking at her own brain, until Tyler's voice jerked her back to earth.

"Pass me your house keys."

"What?" She thought she'd heard him wrong. "*My* house keys or the keys to the mansion?"

"Your house keys," Tyler repeated, slower this time around.

"Why?"

"I'm getting someone down to fix up a security system and some motion sensor lights for your porch and the back of your house."

The pounding headache that she'd gotten from perusing her memories was getting worse. That, combined with the lack of answers, was already sending her mood in a downward spiral.

"Ty, I'm grateful that you fixed up the security here, but my house's fine. I'm the responsible one. I take care of myself just fine, so please don't come in here and command me about this and that," she said as she moved and stood by the door. Once she completed her sentence, she slammed the door in his face.

Tyler wasn't sure what happened. He was merely trying to make sure that she would be safe in her own house. Annoyed by her senseless reaction and frustrated with being snubbed, he was going to march off when he saw Marianne standing nearby.

He tried to stalk past her, but he should've known better.

Marianne reached out and grabbed his arm. "Ty, as much as you need your space, Kate will need hers. I know you're protective of the things you care about, but she's not a thing. She has her own way of thinking, and you'll need to learn to respect that and be patient."

"I'm trying to keep her safe."

"Not everything you care about will disappear in an instant, Ty. She is safe. You have the security up and running, and I'm always around the house."

"What about *her* house? There's no security there, and she lives alone."

Marianne shrugged. "She's here now. If you feel so strongly about that, then you should discuss with her, not decide for her."

He wasn't sure which was more frustrating; Marianne eavesdropping or the fact that she was probably right. Still, Kate didn't have to slam the door in his face.

Disgruntled, he went into the kitchen and was glad that there wasn't anyone else around the table.

Since Mr. Sawyer arrived, he hadn't joined them for any meals. Though he was probably staying over every night, Tyler hadn't seen him around.

Ryan and Joseph had gone to work. They had either extended their shifts or were crashing at their respective houses.

Dan was wise enough to stay away from him. Joanne, however, wasn't.

She had sent him quite a few texts and kept calling him all morning. Just as that thought came up, his phone buzzed and vibrated away on the table. Rolling his eyes, he picked it up. "Joanne, stop calling."

"Ty," Joanne's sweetened voice coaxed. "I just—"

"Stop calling," he repeated and hung up the phone.

Kate pulled off her glasses and put them down on the table. Pinching the bridge of her nose, she ignored the knock on the door.

She understood Tyler's intentions, but she wasn't in the mood to get pushed around.

Lord, what should I do?

"Kate, it's me."

Her brows furrowed when she heard Marianne's voice. Opening the door, she asked, "Is something wrong?"

Not waiting for an invitation, Marianne stepped in. "Nothing. I just wanted to tell you that breakfast's ready."

"Oh, I think I'll skip breakfast today."

She was sure that Tyler was already in the kitchen, and it was better to stay away from him after what had happened.

Marianne frowned. "You should never skip breakfast. Come, chat with the old lady for a while." Marianne sat on the edge of Kate's bed, gesturing for Kate to join her.

"Am I in trouble? If it's about Ty, I'm—"

"It is about Ty, but not about what happened," Marianne said, cutting her off. "I thought I'll give you a little insight or understanding about that eccentric boy."

She gave Marianne a small smile. "He's not eccentric; he just isn't incredibly sociable."

Marianne grinned. "You're being kind. Anyway, I suppose you know what happened to him when he was young?"

"Yes, Mr. Hayes told me."

"I'm not using that as an excuse, but since then, he's developed this intense protectiveness over things he cares about. It is as though he feels that anything he treasures will be stolen from him at any moment."

She could understand that.

She understood what it was like to have her world completely changed in one instant.

Shaking her head slowly, Marianne continued. "He had this storybook; it was the last book his mother read to him before ... before they passed away. *The Little Prince*. He treasured the book so much. Once, Joanne was browsing through the books he had on the shelf, and of all the books, she had to pull out that particular one. When Ty saw her flipping through the book, he snapped and barked at her. He warned her never to touch his things without permission, then chased everyone out of the house."

"He can be rather mean at times," Kate said.

"Yes," Marianne agreed. "He is older now and won't throw a fit when people intrude on his privacy, but he can still be harsh. The same thing happened when Joanne touched his rings. The boys learned long ago to keep their hands off his things, but Joanne always thought she was special; that girl never learned." Marianne sighed. "He yanked the chain away from her and told her not to touch them, but he didn't have a problem when it was you."

"That's because I was the one who passed them to him. Joanne had introduced herself as his fiancée so I thought he could give the ring to her."

Marianne pursed her lips and nodded. "Maybe. The point is, he cares about you enough to let you into his comfort zone."

"So his sense of protectiveness now stretches to include me."

"Smart girl," Marianne said with a pat on her leg. "I know he can be pushy, but tell him, let him know. He's not used to protecting people."

Kate wasn't trying to be a feminist; she simply didn't like to be ordered around. She had always been the one in charge, been the one taking care of others. She didn't appreciate being spoken to like a child.

Then again, Tyler wasn't trying to push her around; he was simply trying to help her.

Marianne didn't wait for her reply. She stood and walked out of the room.

Kate switched off her laptop and followed Marianne into the kitchen. Her stomach growled again as the mouth-watering aroma of Marianne's breakfast hit her. She couldn't believe she almost skipped breakfast.

For a moment, she seriously considered how Tyler would react if she tried poaching Marianne after the one-year stay in the mansion.

She settled on a seat across the table from Tyler and smiled at him, but he was staring at his iPad.

"I'm sorry. I didn't mean to blow up at you."

Tyler remained silent.

If enduring a grumpy housemate was the price to pay for Marianne's breakfast, she would gladly pay it.

After a few moments, Tyler said, "I shouldn't have made the decision for you. I thought …"

"You thought it was for my own good." She paused and gave him a small smile. "I understand your concerns, and you know what? You're right. I should have a security system installed. Since that's your area of expertise, I suppose you can advise me on what to install."

Tyler smiled and set his iPad aside.

She was glad they were back on good terms; she never liked getting into fights.

Tyler started explaining all the security installations she should get, giving her a rundown of what the system would do.

She agreed to everything Tyler suggested, everything except the motion-sensor that would trigger video recording. "That feels a little extreme."

"The recording is only activated if the password isn't keyed in. That way, you'll be informed of a break-in and be able to log in to your account from any computer to see who's in your house. It'll be more convenient for you, especially since you won't be home for a year."

She doubted anyone would break into her house. Her neighborhood had always been safe, but Tyler had a point. "Okay. But can we do it tomorrow instead? I've got some work to complete today. Should I pay you now or tomorrow?"

Tyler scowled at her. "I'm not charging you," he said, seemingly exasperated that she'd even asked him about it.

"Why not? It's my house."

She saw him drawing in a deep breath, but he didn't reply.

She thought he was going to leave it at that; he wasn't letting her pay, period.

"You're doing me a favor by staying here; I'm the reason your house will be empty. Let me return the favor."

She thought about arguing, but from the mere number of words he'd spoken, she knew he was trying hard to be patient. "Okay."

Tim Russell was sitting in his office when he heard the quick raps on the door. He glanced toward the door just as his a member of his staff, Marc, pushed the door ajar and popped his head in.

"Tim, Mr. Hayes is here."

"Here?"

"Yeah, he's in our department."

"What?" Tim got up from his seat and went over to the door. Marc stepped aside for him to take a look. Tim's eyes widened and he turned to Marc. "What's he doing here?"

"I don't know," his staff mumbled and hastily returned to his desk as Mr. Hayes neared.

Tim took a glance around and saw the question on everyone's face, the same question he had just asked Marc.

Though Mr. Hayes was the one who improved upon his parents' equipment and knew how to install each and every one on his own, he'd never ventured into the installation department. Not even when there was a major project in progress.

Barely anyone in the office ever spoke much to him. There was plenty of gossip about him, but no one ever had a real conversation with Mr. Hayes.

The company had many events for the staff, but he never attended any of them except for the annual company dinner. And even for that, he never stayed long. He would sit, not talking to anyone, for an hour or so before disappearing.

All the staff knew him as a man of less than a few words.

"Mr. Hayes, is something wrong? What can I do for you?" He couldn't help wondering what he'd done to bring their elusive boss down to his department.

"Do you have a spare team for an installation tomorrow?" Mr. Hayes asked, strolling into his office. He settled casually onto the available chair and waited for Tim to return to his.

Tim sighed quietly, glad that Mr. Hayes hadn't come down to fire him. "How many men do you need? What scale of installation would it be?" He figured it must be an extremely big and important project for Mr. Hayes to see to it himself.

In all the years he'd worked here, Tim had never seen Mr. Hayes personally handling a project. The sales department would liaise with his installation department. Mr. Hayes was never involved.

"A two-story house."

Tim's face blanked. "You bought a new house?"

He regretted his question the moment it was out of his mouth.

"Do you have a team to spare?" Mr. Hayes asked, ignoring his question.

"Yes, of course. I just need to know the system to install, the address, and the time for the installation."

After giving Tim the details he needed, Mr. Hayes told Tim to get all the equipment ready by the end of the day so that he could inspect it personally.

Inspect it personally?

It wasn't a huge project, but it was undoubtedly an important one.

"Not a problem. I'll have it ready and personally see to the installation."

He'd already made up his mind about going down to the installation site the moment Mr. Hayes had asked. It obviously mattered enough for the boss to take care of it himself, so he had to make sure that his men would be on their best performance.

Besides, he wanted to prove himself right. He was betting that this had something to do with a woman.

Mr. Hayes nodded and left.

Tim leaned back in his chair and thought about the gossip that his wife had told him. He'd heard quite a few rumors about how some of the female staff had shamelessly tried to throw themselves at Mr. Hayes, but he never gave any of them a second look.

The more Tim thought about it, the more interested he was in seeing with his own eyes the woman who had moved the ice mountain.

Chapter Eight

Tyler and Kate were already waiting in her house when the team arrived to install the system. Kate welcomed his team and asked them if they wanted tea or coffee.

He didn't like how she was troubling herself to serve his staff, but she'd always seemed concerned about doing what was right. He guessed being a good host was important to her.

While she prepared tea and coffee, the men got to work. He strolled around the house, watching them.

"Ty," Kate called to him, gesturing for him to join her on the couch while she set the cups of freshly brewed coffee and tea on the coffee table.

"Stop staring at them; you're making them nervous," she said softly, handing him a cup of coffee.

He took another glance at the men. "I'm making sure they're installing it right," he said and sat beside her.

"They've done this more than once, right? I'm sure they'll install it right. Besides, there's something I need to discuss with you."

"What is it?"

She switched on the laptop on the coffee table. "I need to head down to the bed and breakfast I'm working on. It's located in a small town in North Dakota. One of the conditions of the will states that you'll have to come along." She double-clicked on the calendar application. "I know it's troublesome, but I really have to make the trip."

"Okay."

Turning the laptop toward him, she asked, "When are you free?"

"Anytime."

A corner of Kate's lips turned up. She leaned back against the couch and looked at him. "What exactly do you do at work? You seem pretty free."

"I design and improve the system, and I make sure that everything is running smoothly in the company."

"You designed the system? I thought your parents came up with it."

Nodding, he continued. "They did, but I improved and changed some of the things. Technology changes; our security system can do much more now."

"So, you're kind of a computer geek?"

He smiled. "I'm good at developing software and equipment that keeps people safe."

"So you're a geek." Kate flashed him a wide grin. "Kidding. Then, Mr. Hayes, do you actually know how to fix the equipment? Or were you just poking your nose around, pretending to know what's going on."

"I fixed up the system at the mansion, didn't I?"

"True." Her head bobbed up and down. "How do you make sure that everything is running smoothly when you're not in the office?"

"I have an assistant. Don't you?"

Kate shook her head. "Never found the need for one. Maybe because I'm actually working in the office most of the time."

"You shouldn't be rude to someone who's trying to make your house safe."

"Someone once told me that life will be tiring if you have to do everything you should."

He laughed.

Kate grinned and turned back to her computer. "All right, then. Give me your details. I'll book the flights and all."

"Why don't you give me yours? I'll settle it."

"No, I've got it."

He opened his mouth to argue, but changed his mind. *Respect.*

Kate smiled when she saw his reaction. "It's *my* business trip. I don't want to trouble you."

"Okay." He nodded. "But do it later. Since we're here, you can play the piano while we wait for the system to be up," he said.

"I don't like playing when there are others around."

"You played for me." He saw her scowling, but he knew exactly how to get her to play. "If you don't want to play, then I'll just go back to watching them work."

"Are you blackmailing me?" Kate narrowed her eyes with feigned anger. "What makes you think I'll care?"

He shrugged and stood, turning toward the men who were installing the security system. Kate sighed and stood also.

"All right," she said, trotting to the piano. She sat on the right side of the bench, lifted the cover, and waited for him to join her.

Tim watched in amazement as he saw his boss conversing with Miss Mitchell. He'd never heard so many words coming out of Mr. Hayes's mouth. To top it off, he was laughing.

Laughing!

Tim couldn't even remember a time when he'd seen Mr. Hayes smile.

A joke had once gone around the office that Mr. Hayes probably had some muscle dysfunction, making it impossible for him to smile.

Tim thought back on those times during staff meetings. No matter how good the sales figures were, Mr. Hayes would only give a nod of approval. Sometimes, he wouldn't even have any reaction. He always appeared bored or angry.

Now, the same aloof boss was chatting and laughing with Miss Mitchell.

Maybe Mr. Hayes was only stern in the office. Maybe he was a different person when he was with his friends.

Tim doubted it. He was certain there was something special about Miss Mitchell.

Not only did Mr. Hayes personally arrange her installation, but he'd also taken time off to be here with her. That was on top of the specific instructions he'd given about not charging Miss Mitchell.

He stood behind one of the men and took another look at Mr. Hayes and Miss Mitchell. His wife would definitely be all ears for this story.

"Let's play a duet," Kate suggested the moment Tyler sat.

He placed his hands on the piano and pressed down on random keys again. He hadn't played the piano since his parents died, hadn't even touched one until the last time he was here with Kate.

Playing the piano was something he did with his mother. Since the night of her death, he had refused to play. Though there was a piano in the house that his grandfather had dumped him in, he never once touched it.

Somehow, everything that reminded him of his parents made him angry. Every one of those things only reminded him that he would never be able to see or spend another moment with his parents.

If Marianne hadn't stood in his way, he would've thrown the piano out without a second thought.

The mansion used to have a piano, too.

He guessed his grandfather had the same reaction toward the piano as he had. The only difference was that no one could stop him from throwing anything out of the house.

"You know how to play," Kate said, almost in accusation.

He looked up at her, wondering how she came to that conclusion.

"Your thumb; you placed it right at the beginning of a new chord, and you bent your fingers the way you should instead of placing them flat on the keys."

His focus dropped back to the keys. "I haven't played for a while," he said softly.

Kate didn't reply.

He turned and saw her pursing her lips, clearly worried that she'd hurt him. He reached over and pushed her hair behind her ear, getting her attention. "I'm fine."

"I can teach you if you want. It's okay if—"

"Why not?" He wasn't exceptionally keen, but she'd seemed so happy when she was playing the piano, and he wanted to be part of that.

She beamed and placed his hand on the correct keys. "*Heart and Soul.* Have you played it before?"

He gave a wry smile at the pure coincidence of Kate picking the one song his mother had taught him. He tried out the keys, playing the first few notes. "This is all I remember."

Smiling, she showed him a few notes at a time, then let him repeat after her demonstration.

"I love this song. My grandmother used to play it with me even when she was at the senior home, except she thought I was my mother," Kate said, shaking her head indulgently.

Tyler had spent his whole life avoiding anything that held any link to his parents. Any memories of them only made his heart ache, so he refused to allow himself to remember. That was the only way he could cope.

Seeing how fondly Kate could speak of the memories that her parents and grandparents had created for her, it felt safe for him to remember as well.

Though he would never see his parents again, perhaps he could still smile at the joy they'd once given him.

"And your sister?"

"She wasn't interested and never learned. Now I have someone to play the song with."

He smiled, pleased to be the someone she was talking about.

"Mr. Hayes, we're done," Tim said.

"Go ahead and play. I'll check it through first," he said to Kate before getting up and moving over to Tim.

Instead of playing, Kate swiveled around and watched him scrutinize the system.

Her attention on him lingered for a minute. Then she got up and attended to his staff, bringing out more glasses and a flask of water.

He rolled his eyes when he heard her apologizing for the lack of snacks. "Kate," he said, cocking his head to the side, gesturing for her to come over.

"Yeah?" she asked as she walked over toward him.

Nothing. He simply didn't want her to fuss over the men. He was worried that if he hadn't called her over, she might head out to buy snacks for them.

He didn't answer her question. He walked around the house with Kate by his side, explaining how the system worked while checking it.

Pointing to the corners where the small, thumb-sized cameras were, he continued his orientation on the security system. "There's one camera in every room, except bathrooms, of course." Pointing toward the window, he continued. "There's another one right outside all your rooms. The cameras will activate if you don't key in the correct password on the pad, but will be deactivated once you key in the correct code. When you leave the house and lock the door using the security pad outside, the cameras will be activated if the motion sensors detect movement."

With his hand on her elbow, he led her down the stairs. "As with the mansion, all the windows and doors are wired. If someone tries to open them or breaks the windows' glass when you lock down the house, it'll set off the alarm. Do you want to give it a try?"

"You want me to break the window?"

He blinked, then cracked a smile when he saw the mischievous glint in her eyes.

"I'm sure it's working fine. Is that all?" Kate asked.

Tyler nodded as he glanced around the house, satisfied with the security in place. When they returned to the living room, he nodded to Tim and the team started packing up.

Kate thanked his staff for their hard work as they trotted out.

"Have the codes been set?" she asked, closing the door behind his staff.

"Yeah. The password for the door is your phone number. The security code for the phone call will be your sister's number."

"Thanks. I wanted to use your number, so I'll only have to remember one set of passwords. But that would mean Evelyn and Lydia will know the password to the mansion as well. I didn't think you'd appreciate that."

He hadn't given Dan, Joseph, and Ryan the password to the mansion either. He was fine with them having the keys to his own house, but with Kate living in the mansion, he didn't want them entering and leaving as they would at his house.

"Do you want to choose the hotel?"

He frowned, and for a moment couldn't figure out what Kate was talking about. "Oh, the bed and breakfast trip ..." his words trailed off at the end. "Have you read the fine print of the will?"

Kate shook her head, her eyes still on the laptop. "No, why?"

"We have to stay in the same room. Separate beds are fine."

He laughed when he saw the shock on her face as she took in the news.

"Does Mr. Sawyer have to come along?"

"No—guess he figured the lawyer will be busy."

Kate sat in front of her laptop and started searching for plane tickets and a place to stay.

He sat beside her and watched her multitask through the various tabs on her web browser. "Don't you think it's kind of weird to be staying in a hotel so close to where the new bed and breakfast is?"

"Then what do you suggest?"

"Why don't you deal with the tickets while I settle the accommodations?"

She took out her glasses and placed them on the table. "Sure."

They were done in less than an hour. It would've been much faster if they hadn't debated on who should foot the bill.

In the end, it was a compromise. Kate paid for the flight while he paid for their accommodations.

When they were done with that, they began chatting about their work.

He realized Kate knew plenty about him, but he didn't know much about her. He asked her question after question, finding out how she and Evelyn started their company in her grandmother's garage and how they had grown their company from scratch to having five teams of designers working for them.

Though she still worked on her own projects, she would also advise and improve the designs of other teams, making the final decisions.

"That sounds like a lot of work," Tyler commented.

"Yeah, but I love my job."

He was about to ask another question when Kate interjected, "Enough about me. My turn to ask the questions."

"You already know plenty about me."

"No. I know plenty about the young Tyler, not the one sitting with me."

He smiled. "What do you want to know?"

"How did you get that scar on your arm?"

Flipping his hand over, Tyler stared at the bite marks on his arm. "Got bitten by a dog."

"Ouch. What happened?"

He shrugged and said, "It came out of nowhere."

"Did it hurt?"

"It was so long ago. I can't remember."

"Am I boring you?"

"No, why?"

She laughed softly. "Your answers are really short."

He wasn't bored; it was his habit to keep his sentences short. He paused for a moment, thinking of something else to add to the story. "I do remember it was a complete pain to start learning how to play basketball with my left hand."

"Ryan said you were really good at basketball."

"And when did he say that?"

"First day at the mansion."

"So you were checking up on me?" he asked.

"No, I merely asked him how you guys became friends."

He nodded, saying nothing else.

"Tell me about your work."

"You already know what I do. As I said, I inherited the company from my parents and improved the system. Now I just make sure nothing goes wrong."

"And when things do go wrong?"

"My assistant tells me about it. I'll come up with a solution, and she hands out my instructions."

"So you don't work with anyone else but your assistant."

"That's why I have an assistant."

"So you don't have to talk to anyone else at work?"

He shrugged. Things were simpler that way. He didn't have to entertain stupid questions and unwanted attention. It was more efficient, too. He didn't have to explain his actions. Instructions would be passed down to the different departments, and everyone got to work to solve the problem quickly.

"Your grandfather used to go on and on about how smart you are. He said the company was growing fast with good, quality products that you've worked on."

"He was good to you."

She smiled, seemingly embarrassed. "Yes, he was."

"What did the two of you do together?"

"Nothing much. He told me lots of stories about you. I think I know the young Tyler better than you do."

She was probably right.

After so many years of pushing his memories aside, they had started to fade. He couldn't remember much about his younger days except the night his parents died.

His brain seemed determined to torture him with those memories.

No matter how he tried, he could never forget the horror on his parents' faces.

Sighing, he pushed those thoughts from his mind and returned to their previous topic. As they chatted, he mentioned that Hayes Security regularly hired ex-policemen for their security team or as trainers for their new recruits.

"So you have contacts in the police force?"

"More goodwill than contacts," Tyler corrected.

Kate fiddled with her locket.

"What is it?"

"Do you think your goodwill can help me find a retired detective?"

He looked at her, studying her expression. "I'll help as long as you're sure that's what *you* want."

She chewed on her lips while she began winding and unwinding the chain around her index finger. "I don't know. I can't help but feel that if I were to do nothing, I'd be betraying my parents."

"Those are strong words."

Kate sighed. "I just feel guilty."

"Have you been happy?"

She thought about his question.

"It isn't a difficult question," Tyler stated when he saw her struggling to come up with an answer.

"I'm not sure. I'm proud of my achievements and grateful for what I have, but I'm not sure if I'm ... happy."

"Then I'm sure your parents would rather you work on that."

She nodded slowly.

"But I'll try to get the information anyway."

She gave him a small smile. "Thanks."

"Out of curiosity, what makes you happy? You—not about other people—just you. Like playing the piano; I can see that makes you happy."

"Yeah, I love playing the piano. I play whenever I get the time. I think that's the one indulgence I allow myself to have. And I love designing, especially old houses. I love being able to keep the memories alive while giving the house a newer and more contemporary look."

"Are you happy at the mansion?"

"Yeah, I am," she said without hesitation. "It's the first time I don't have to be the one in charge." Chuckling at her own thoughts, she continued. "And who wouldn't be happy to have Marianne cooking their meals?"

Tyler grinned and shook his head. "She's the only reason the guys are always gathering wherever I stay."

"I can't blame them. I'm thinking of poaching her from you after the one-year stay at the mansion. You'd better start treating her better or she might leave with me."

Or you can stay. Tyler didn't voice his thoughts. He didn't even know what he was thinking. "If she makes you happy, I'll let her go. Then the guys and I will just be here a lot."

Kate laughed. "I don't think my table can fit her groupies," she said. "And I don't think she's good for me. I might get really fat. That's the only reason I haven't asked."

After Kate had cleaned up the house, he drove both of them back to the mansion. As usual, the road wound uphill with both sides flanked by trees as far as the eye could see. Kate stared at the trees.

The orange tint that filled the sky filtered through the trees, beaming into the car as they drove.

"This is the first time I've actually paid attention to the woods," Kate said.

"Still find it creepy?" he asked.

She stared out at the trees and smiled. "Not so much, not when there's someone beside me."

"It's peaceful."

"Hmm …" Kate continued gazing out of the window. "It's somewhat nostalgic."

"Nostalgic?"

"It feels as if the trees have many love stories and secrets that are waiting to be discovered."

His lips curled as he looked at the elongated shadows of the trees caused by the setting of the sun. No matter how many crime shows she watched, Kate was still a romantic at heart.

He loved the woods.

It was a huge playground that he could spend hours in. His favorite thing to do was to run around in the woods and watch how his shadow changed as the sun retired.

With all his love for the woods, he'd never thought of it as a place that held love stories.

Her words did remind him of a place he wanted her to see.

He was just about to tell Kate one of the secrets that the woods held when he saw the bright-pink mini-Volkswagen parked in front of the house.

He sighed, turning Kate's attention toward him.

He felt her eyes follow his gaze and heard the breath she sucked in.

The last thing he wanted was for Joanne to be anywhere near

Kate, so instead of stopping the car right in front of the house, Tyler turned and steered the car toward the left side of the mansion.

Joanne hopped out of the car and waved her hands about, but Tyler had no intention of stopping.

"Where are we going?" Kate asked. "You're not going to drive us through the wall to avoid speaking to her, are you?"

"Call Marianne. Tell her to open the garage door."

"There's a garage?" Kate pulled out the phone from her bag, scanning through her contact list.

"Hi, Marianne. It's Kate. Yeah, he wants you to open the garage door. Okay." Kate turned back to him. "I think she knows Joanne is by the front door," Kate mused while she hung up the call.

He wasn't quite as amused as she was. "Then she should've told Joanne to leave."

"Maybe she did, but Joanne refused. What do you expect her to do?"

It was probably true. Marianne had never taken a liking to Joanne and would have no qualms about chasing her away.

The car came to a stop in front of the garage door that was still closed. He drummed his fingers impatiently on the steering wheel while eyeing the rear-view mirror.

"I think she's still angry," Kate said as she looked in the rear-view mirror. "You're going out to speak to her, right? You can't just leave her waiting out front for you."

He turned to Kate. "The person you're talking about almost made you blind."

Kate chuckled. "Don't you think that's a bit of an exaggeration? Painful, yes. But I seriously doubt I was at risk of going blind."

He shook his head, but otherwise remained silent.

Sighing, Kate took off her glasses and wore them like a headband over her hair. She closed her eyes for a moment and rubbed her temples.

"It's giving you a lot of trouble."

"I'm just not used to it. And if there's a garage, why are we parking our cars up front?"

"I don't have the clicker installed on my car, so it has to be opened from inside the garage. Marianne hates it when people disturb her while she's cooking." He took a glance at the rear-view mirror and continued. "But if you want, I can fix it up for you."

"It's okay. I was just curious."

When the garage door rolled up, he drove in with his eyes focused on the rear-view mirror.

"She isn't going to materialize out of thin air, and don't crash into the wall."

Tyler grinned and took his eyes off the mirror, parking the car.

"Go talk to her, and please don't be angry about the juice incident. It's over and I'm fine."

He shook his head as they stepped out of his car. "Kate, stay away from her. I'll keep her away when I'm around. But if, for whatever reason, you find yourself alone with her, call me, then turn and leave."

Kate ignored him and went up to Marianne. "What's for dinner?" she asked and hooked her arm around Marianne's. Marianne beamed and outlined the menu for the day, but their conversation was interrupted by the doorbell.

Joanne was pressing the doorbell so many times and so quickly that the tune from the bell wasn't able to complete itself. The bell played its tune like a broken radio trying its best to function but failing pathetically.

Without another word, Tyler took a deep breath and marched toward the door. Kate caught up with him and gently grabbed him by his arm. "Ty, please don't be mean."

He stared back at her, observing her for a few moments.

Don't be mean, Kate mouthed.

He exhaled slowly through his nose and nodded. He continued his stride toward the door and waited for Kate and Marianne to go into the kitchen before stepping out.

Joanne immediately stopped pressing the bell and flashed her sweetest smile. "Ty!"

He could see her hesitate before taking a big step toward him and wrapping her hands around his arm.

He pulled his arm away from her and took a step back while he stared into the distance, bracing himself for the whining that Joanne would definitely rain down on him.

He thought about what Kate had said. He still couldn't believe she was actually concerned about someone who went crazy on her.

This was why he had to be protective of her; she was too nice for her own good.

He wasn't intending to be mean to Joanne, but he *was* going to tell her to leave and slam the door in her face.

He supposed he couldn't go with his original plan now.

"Where did you go with that woman?"

He kept quiet, finding no need or reason to explain anything to Joanne.

"Ty, why is she making you drive her around? Is she pestering you? I can tell her to leave you alone."

Tyler turned and finally looked Joanne in her eyes. "Stay. Away. From. Her."

"Ty!"

"Joanne," Tyler said, his voice low and stern, just as Dan had spoken that morning. "If you're not here to apologize to Kate, then leave."

"Ty! Wait, don't just leave. Do you know how long I've waited here for you? Marianne wouldn't even let me in. She was completely unreasonable; don't be unreasonable, too. That Kate is a nobody. Why do you care what I splash in her face?"

He couldn't believe what he was hearing. He'd known Joanne was spoiled, but he never knew she was out of her mind.

"I was the one who told Marianne not to allow you into the house." He wanted to end his reply there, but Tyler finally felt the need to make things clear with her.

"Joanne, I don't know what's wrong with you, but this is crazy. There's nothing between us; there never was and never will be. We've never gone out on dates or anything, so I don't know where or how you got the idea that we're a couple. To me, you're just Dan's sister. The end. And if you were to ever do anything to hurt Kate again, I'll call the cops on you."

That was the longest conversation he ever had with Joanne, and he could see the shock in her eyes. He wasn't sure if the shock stemmed from his long speech or the contents of it, but he couldn't care less.

She stared at him, pouting.

He rolled his eyes and turned away.

He wasn't interested in pacifying Joanne; he wasn't interested in anything she had to say.

He'd already fulfilled his not-being-mean part. He went back into the house, making sure to close and lock the door behind him.

Both Marianne and Kate smiled warmly when he entered the kitchen.

"Has she left?" Marianne asked. "I told her to leave, but she wouldn't listen."

Kate was silent, but she looked at Tyler expectantly, waiting for an answer to her silent question.

"I tried to be as nice as possible," he stated.

Marianne's head swayed between them. "Your parents used to do this, this mental communication thing. She'd give your dad a look and only he would understand what was going on."

Neither of them said anything in response to Marianne's statement.

Marianne had lived with and taken care of him for over twenty years. He was grateful that she'd always been there for him, but he couldn't help shooting her a glare.

"We'll be heading to North Dakota this weekend. Kate has to work," Tyler said, hoping to stop Marianne from rambling on.

"All right. Give me a call when you're coming back, and let me know if you kids want to eat."

After dinner, Kate thanked Marianne for preparing the food and returned to her room. She wanted to get her ideas for the bed and breakfast ready before heading over.

Over the next few days, Kate was busy with her work. Dinner became the only time when Tyler could talk to her.

While Kate was busy getting her portfolio ready, Tyler was

busy searching for a grand piano. There was also the task of rearranging the furniture in the living room to make space. His grandfather had shifted things around, taking up the empty spot where the grand piano used to stand.

Kate was probably the best person to consult, but since it was meant to be a surprise, he had to figure it out himself.

If he could design a whole system backed with technology to keep buildings and homes safe, surely he wouldn't have a problem with rearranging furniture.

Or so he thought.

Each time he gave Marianne the instructions for the movers, there was always a problem. It would be too cluttered in that corner, the dimensions weren't right, or there wouldn't be enough walking space. The problems went on and on.

In the end, he decided that he didn't need all the furniture in the living room. There wasn't a need for the extra couch, the additional chairs, or the desk that no one used. All those could be taken apart and sent up to the attic, instantly solving his problem.

Leaving Marianne with the finalized instructions, Kate and Tyler left for North Dakota.

Chapter Nine

Tyler rented a car at the airport, and they headed out toward the hotel. He wound down the car windows, taking in the fresh country air.

He looked over at Kate. Her hair flowed back with the wind; her eyes closed as she took a deep breath.

"This is nice," she said as she looked out of the window.

Throughout the drive, Kate couldn't take her eyes off the view outside.

"Never been to the country?"

"Not many country houses to design." She cast a glance over her shoulder to look at him. "It's beautiful out here. There's so much space. It feels so free, so relaxed."

"This is free and relaxed, but the mansion is creepy?"

"It's different. We're not surrounded by acres of trees. Here, you can see as far as the horizon."

He contemplated the work it would take to remove all the trees around the mansion for Kate to see as far as the horizon. The land belonged to them, so it wouldn't be an issue for him to cut down the trees. Thinking aloud, he said, "But I don't think it's possible to remove all the trees."

Kate took her eyes off the scenery, laughing as she turned to him. "I don't think it's possible either. And there's no need—it can be rather beautiful at times."

She took a look at the map and frowned. "Am I reading the map wrong or is the hotel pretty far from the bed and breakfast?"

"It's the nearest hotel I could find outside town. I didn't think we'd be welcome if they found out you're with the new competition."

She nodded. "Did you bring any work along?"

"No, why?"

"If you're busy, I'll drive there on my own."

There wasn't any way he was letting her drive around in a place she'd never been to, especially after the way she twirled the map around in her hands and still got the direction wrong. "I'll go with you."

"Great, then I'll have a free chauffeur for the next two days."

When they arrived at the hotel, he parked the car and took their bags from the trunk.

"This is the first time I don't have to worry about the bags or take care of the check-in," Kate said as they got to the room.

Taking a quick glance at her watch, she took out her phone and sent a text.

"Do you need to be somewhere now?" Tyler asked.

"No, it's fine. I just texted Ben to let him know I'll be late. It was a long drive; you should get some rest."

Tyler walked over to the space between the beds and set her luggage down.

Kate pointed her chin toward the beds. "Which side do you want to take?"

"The one nearer to the door."

Kate plopped onto her designated bed. "Do you want to go look at the bed and breakfast with me? Or would you prefer to go scout around on your own?"

"I don't mind going along if I won't get in your way."

"Looks like I'll have a bodyguard as well as a chauffeur." She grinned at him. Walking over to the window, she pushed up the window pane and leaned out to take a deep breath of the summer air.

Her smile was always so mesmerizing.

He leaned against the wall by the window and watched her smile.

"What?" she asked. "Is there something on my face?" She brushed her hand against her cheek, trying to wipe off whatever she thought he was staring at.

He pulled his gaze from her and turned to the scenery outside. "Nothing," he said, his eyes on the dry, knee-length grass that was bending to the will of the wind.

"Look, someone's riding a horse."

He grinned at her amusement. "It's just a horse. I'm sure you've seen one before."

"Yeah, but not like this. I've seen them in pictures, movies, and zoos, but never like this."

"You never rode before?"

"No," Kate answered while still staring at the horse.

Kate glanced over at Tyler as he stopped the car opposite the under-construction bed and breakfast. He had only studied the map for a minute before he returned it to her and got them to their destination without a second look.

"Thanks for accompanying and driving me around," she said.

He shrugged. "It's nice to get away from the city once in a while."

The moment she got out of the car, Benjamin came jogging out of the bed and breakfast, clutching a bouquet of flowers.

She sighed softly. That wasn't a good sign.

"Is there something I'm missing?" Tyler asked as he strode over to join Kate by her side.

Strictly business, I promise. She rolled her eyes as Benjamin's words replayed in her head.

"We used to date."

They continued toward Benjamin, who had halted midway when he laid eyes on Tyler.

"Hi, Ben," Kate said awkwardly.

Squaring his shoulders, Benjamin handed Kate the flowers. "Hi there." He leaned in to kiss her on the cheek before turning to Tyler. "I didn't know you were bringing someone."

"You seem to have forgotten that I no longer need to let you know who I'm going out with," Kate said, hoping it would remind him of their professional standing. "Ty, this is Benjamin Anderson, owner of the bed and breakfast. And Benjamin,

Tyler."

Benjamin nodded at Tyler before he placed his hand on Kate's back and led her toward the bed and breakfast. "You never asked me along for any of your projects."

"I don't think I owe you any explanation." She stepped out from Benjamin's arm.

"I tried calling your house the other day, but it kept going to the voicemail. I was in town and thought I could drop by," Benjamin continued as she moved toward Tyler.

"Oh, I've moved in with Ty. I guess you can try to get me on my cell phone next time." Casually, she wrapped her hands around Tyler's arm.

Benjamin's jaw slackened. "Moved in?"

She nodded, praying Tyler would play along with her little charade.

Tyler had appeared stunned for a moment, probably surprised by her sudden touch. Once that moment passed, he folded his arm to support her weight as she leaned in.

Disbelief flooded Benjamin's face. "When?"

"Last week," Kate chimed. Since Tyler hadn't pulled away from her, she took that as his consent to participate. In gratitude, she beamed up at Tyler and leaned closer as he returned her smile.

"How long have you known him? You moved in with him after knowing him for what, three months?" Benjamin asked with complete confusion. "I asked you to move in with me— twice—but you refused. You said—"

"I know what I said," she cut in before he could finish his sentence.

"Were you seeing him before we broke up?"

"I'm not you."

Benjamin swallowed hard and cleared his throat.

"Things are different with him. I've moved in with him, and I'm happy. All of which shouldn't matter to you. You promised this was strictly business."

Benjamin grunted and stared at Tyler. "What's so special about him?"

She glowered at how rude Benjamin was. "Completely different and absolutely none of your business. I think you've made your stand pretty clear. Find someone else for your project; I can't help you." She turned to leave, pulling Tyler along.

A sudden and forceful grip on her arm made her gasp and jolted her to a stop. "Let go!" She tried to shrug off Benjamin's stronghold.

Before Benjamin could respond, he was down on the ground.

She wasn't exactly sure what had happened.

She saw Tyler stepping between her and Benjamin. The next thing she knew, Benjamin's hand was no longer on her arm, and she was staring at Tyler's back while Benjamin was moaning on the ground. She took a step to the side, trying to get a clearer view of what had happened.

Tyler stretched out his arm, preventing her from moving forward. "Touch her again and I'll break your hands." Taking her hand, he strode with her back toward the car.

She went along with Tyler, placing the flowers on top of Benjamin's car as they walked past it.

"You were serious about the judo thing. I didn't even see what you did. You have to teach me."

"No," he said without thinking as he pulled out of the parking lot.

"Why not?" she asked, disappointed with his blatant rejection.

Tyler's lips turned up as he saw her reaction. "You'll get hurt if you don't know what you're doing. If you need someone to fight for you, give me a call."

"That's sweet of you. It's kind of condescending, but sweet." Taking a glance out of the window, she continued. "Is he going to be all right? I mean you didn't break his bones or anything, right?"

"I can take you back if you feel bad," he answered coldly.

"I just don't want to get you into trouble."

He ignored her comment and said, "So I guess you don't have to work this weekend."

She gazed out of the window and sighed softly. "Evelyn warned me. She was certain that it wouldn't work, not with

Benjamin in it. But instead of listening to her, I chose to trust Benjamin. Now, I've wasted all of our time and effort." Turning back to face Tyler, she smiled apologetically. "I'm sorry to make you come all the way out here only to go all the way back home."

"Then we don't have to go all the way back home, not immediately anyway."

She frowned.

"We can stay, take a look around, and enjoy ourselves. We can see a real-life horse up close."

A grin spread across her face. "We are already here anyway, and I like the horse idea."

"Good." He returned her grin. "Shall we get something to eat before we start scouting for one?"

"Yes, please. I'm starving."

As they stood in front of the restaurant, Kate ran her fingers along the logs that made up the walls. "Lovely—the classic country style."

Tyler opened the door to the small restaurant, and the few people looked up at them before returning their focus to what they were doing.

"Welcome. Table for two?" A young lady wearing jeans and a striped T-shirt smiled brightly at them. Tyler and Kate nodded and followed the waitress to their table.

"Is there something you want to ask?" she asked Tyler after the waitress had taken their order.

He was quieter than usual.

"What happened between you and Benjamin?"

She pressed her lips into a thin line. "I caught him in bed with someone else."

"Do you still have feelings for him? Is that why you're still angry with him?"

"Who says I'm angry?"

"He's the only person I've seen you being rude to."

She shook her head. "I have no feelings for him and have absolutely no intention of getting back with him." She laughed once without humor. "He basically told me it was my fault that he slept with someone else."

She paused and took a sip of water. "Apparently, by refusing to sleep with him, I caused him to make that mistake," she said. "I guess I'm frustrated that he thinks I'll get back with him once I've cooled down. I mean, seriously? Do I seem so pathetic that I'll go back to someone like him?"

"I guess he's just hoping for the best."

"Well, it isn't going to happen," she said. "I'm sorry for letting him think we're in a relationship."

Tyler shrugged. "Technically, you told the truth. We did sort of move in together."

Her head bobbed up and down. "I know, but still, I'm sorry for pulling you into the pretense. I owe you one."

"Were you … upset? He asked you to move in twice; I suppose the two of you were serious."

She pulled out her locket, and her fingers twirled around it. "The truth?" She gave him a small smile. "I guess, somehow, I knew we weren't meant to be. In the first place, I don't believe in moving in. But when he asked, I couldn't even bring myself to imagine living with him. Frankly, for me, our relationship ended before I found out he was sleeping with someone else."

Before Tyler could ask another question, her phone rang.

She broke into a grin when she saw the name on the screen. "Evelyn," she informed Tyler before picking it up.

"He called you?" Kate asked when she picked up the phone.

"He asked if you really did move in with a guy named Tyler."

"Did you corroborate my story?"

"I told him that it was none of his business and hung up."

She laughed.

She didn't think Benjamin would be stupid enough to call Evelyn; he should know better.

"Are you coming back now?"

"No, we're going to do some touring and find a real-life horse that I can view up close."

"The two of you are getting close," Evelyn said.

"I'll call you when I'm coming back."

"All right."

She hung up the call and turned to Tyler. "Sorry, she goes crazy when I don't pick up her calls."

Tyler laughed. "She seems to be crazy a lot."

"That's her normal reaction whenever she gets worried, but I'm sure you already know that side of her."

"The two of you are close."

"She's like a sister to me, even more of a sister than Lydia is."

Tyler didn't reply, but his smile grew wider. "So did she corroborate your story?"

"She scolded him and hung up."

"She isn't just crazy to me, then."

She chuckled softly. "That's my friend." Then shaking off the laughter, she continued. "You may think she's crazy, but I trust her with my life. And it isn't her fault that she doesn't trust people easily. She grew up in the foster system and went through a lot, more than enough to instill in her that she can't trust anyone but herself."

"You're as protective of her as she is of you."

"I told you, she's like a sister. But don't worry. I'll keep you safe from her."

Tyler laughed again, a carefree laughter that she'd gotten used to.

It had merely been a week ago that he was the walking definition of gloom.

Being back home was good for him.

"Thanks, but I think I'll do the protecting."

She rolled her eyes.

"Shall we go look for a real-life horse now?" Tyler asked as they finished their lunch.

She nodded and reached into her bag for her wallet.

"I'll get it."

"You keep paying for our meals. I'm already not paying anything for the food back at the house."

She drew in a deep breath as Tyler shrugged.

He must have sensed her frustration. "It isn't right to let a lady pay."

"I thought you didn't care about what people think."

He shrugged again, but this time, she laughed. He slotted a fifty-dollar bill into the folder and stood.

"You're so bossy."

"So are you," he said.

"No, I'm not." When was she ever bossy?

He opened the car door for her and continued when he got into the car. "You told me off for not hanging up the phone the right way, and you basically ordered me to speak to Joanne and not be rude to her."

"Ordered you? Who dares?"

Tyler took the map from her, studied it for a moment, then handed it back to her. "You, apparently."

She narrowed her eyes at him, but that only made him grin.

She wanted to be angry with him, or at least pretend to be, but she loved his brilliant smile.

She'd always found him good-looking, even Evelyn thought so as well. Without the shroud of despondency, without the resentment, his smile was alluring.

"Let's go," Tyler said.

"Where are we heading?"

"You'll see."

She sighed. "Your short replies can be rather irritating."

"You'll love it. I promise," he said simply.

Turning the map in her hand, she looked at him. "That's it? One look at the map and you know the way?"

"Even without the map, I'm sure I'll find the place before you do."

"What do you mean?"

"Do you know how to read a map?" he asked, casting a quick glance over at her.

"What makes you think I don't know how to read a map?"

"You keep turning it this way and that. It's clear you have no idea which direction we're heading."

He was right.

She had to look out for landmarks and check them against the map before she could get the orientation right. "You can't blame me; my car has a GPS that tells me to turn right or left," she retorted.

He shook his head. "Well, I used to be in charge of map reading whenever my parents and I went on holiday. So don't worry, we won't get lost."

Pursing her lips, she wondered when was the last time he'd spoken of his parents. She observed him for a moment. Since he didn't appear upset, she continued. "Did your family travel often?"

"Every holiday. We have a beautiful cabin in North Carolina. I'll take you there when you're free."

"Was that where you went fishing with your dad and grandfather?"

"Yes. Do you fish?"

"No, but I've seen a real-life fish up close."

Tyler laughed.

"Tell me about the cabin."

"It's surrounded by trees." He turned, seemingly to check her reaction.

She bit down on her lips, but the corners turned up anyway. "Your family loves trees."

Ignoring her jibe, he continued. "There's a lake right in front of it, and we have a small boat. When we're there, I'll row you out. And if you want, you can try rowing it, too. It's fun."

"I haven't said yes. You know how I feel about houses surrounded by trees."

"It's beautiful. I promise you'll love it. If you don't, we can leave immediately," he said as they pulled into a ranch.

She opened the door and stepped out with her bag without commenting on what Tyler had said. He joined her outside the car, just as a tanned young man wearing faded jeans and T-shirt came jogging out from the ranch. "Hi, are you looking for something?"

"Do you have horseback riding lessons here?" Tyler asked.

"Horseback riding?" Her head snapped toward Tyler. "Aren't we a little too old to learn horseback riding?"

"No, ma'am." The young man smiled warmly as he addressed her.

"Not we, just you. I already know how to ride."

She shook her head vehemently. "I don't think I can do this. I've never been good at sports. I don't think horseback riding will be any different."

The young man stood uncertainly between them, waiting for them to come to a decision.

"Get the horses ready," Tyler instructed.

The young man immediately nodded and scooted off before Kate could voice any objection.

"Ty …"

He sat on the hood of the car and smiled. "We're already here, so why not give it a try?"

She didn't want to embarrass herself. She wasn't an animal fan and had never been athletic.

"How about riding with me?" Tyler asked when he saw her hesitating.

"We can do that?"

Tyler gave a dramatic sigh and stood. "I'll go make the arrangements. Wait here."

She sat on the hood, waving him away. Taking her phone from her bag, she took a few pictures of the surroundings.

When she saw Tyler jogging back with a clipboard, she switched her camera to video mode and started recording. "This is the man who's trying to get me to ride a horse at the age of twenty-five. Eve, if I fall and hurt myself, he's the one you need to hunt down." She made sure she spoke loud enough for Tyler to hear.

Tyler broke into a huge grin. "You need to sign this."

She took the clipboard from him and perused the document.

"It's a declaration that if you fall and hurt yourself, it isn't their fault."

She signed and returned the form to him with a sly smile. "Doesn't matter. Eve knows who to go after."

He stretched his hand out and pulled her back onto her feet. "I won't let you fall," he said in all seriousness.

"I know," she said and placed her bag in the car.

The same young man whom they had met earlier led them to

a gray stallion. "As you requested, Warrior is strong but disciplined. He should be easy to handle."

"I'll take a ride on him first," Tyler said and took over the reins.

She cringed when Tyler slotted his foot into the stirrup and swung himself up.

The young man saw her reaction and grinned. "It doesn't hurt the horse."

She nodded, but that wasn't the only reason she'd cringed. She was mainly wondering how she was going to get onto the horse.

"Your boyfriend's good with the horse. I'm Mike, by the way." He stretched his hand toward her.

She took his hand. "Kate. And he isn't my boyfriend, we're just friends."

"Oh." Mike nodded. "He seemed awfully concerned about your safety."

"I've got a crazy friend who'll kill him if I get hurt."

"Ah …"

Tyler rode around in circles before bringing the horse to a complete stop right in front of her.

Still holding the reins, he hopped off and gestured for her to go over.

Gingerly, she took a step forward.

With his hand on her back, Tyler brought her closer to the horse. He instructed her on how to get onto it and waited patiently as she hesitated.

"I'll hold on to the reins; it won't go anywhere."

"Okay," she said, but remained right where she was.

She thought Tyler would urge her to give it a try, but he didn't say a word. He waited behind her, allowing her to take all the time she needed to gather her courage.

Lord, please don't let me fall flat on my face.

Taking a deep breath, she slipped her foot into the stirrup and pushed herself off the ground. Almost immediately, she dropped back down, laughing.

"What are you doing?" Tyler asked, his eyes creased in

amusement.

"Sorry, I kind of freaked out."

Tyler laughed softly. "Give it another shot. Remember to swing your leg over."

He made it sound so easy.

"I can't help it if my leg refuses to cooperate."

"I'll catch you if you fall."

She would rather not fall at all.

Nodding, she took in another deep breath. This time, she pushed herself off and swung her leg over.

"It's easy, right?" he said and got up behind her.

It was reassuring with Tyler behind her, but she still didn't dare to move. Then she felt him pull her phone from her back pocket.

"It may drop. I'll keep it for you," he said before she had to turn around.

"Have fun," Mike said with a wide grin.

Tyler adjusted himself on the horse; his arms safely flanked her sides, forming a cage. Though she wasn't leaning against him, she could feel the heat radiating from his chest as he tilted forward.

"Ready?" he asked.

"I guess so."

"Have more confidence in me. You can hold on to its mane, just don't grab it too tightly or it'll affect the maneuver." Tyler made a sound with his tongue and the horse started trotting forward.

Even though he had already told her not to grab the mane too tightly, her reflexes defied his orders. Her eyes slammed shut, and she pursed her lips as the horse moved.

She didn't think Tyler could see her, but he suddenly whispered into her ear, "I won't let you fall."

His voice, so deep and low, reassured her. Her tensed body relaxed, and she opened her eyes as she leaned back against him.

"Better?"

She smiled and looked over her shoulder at him. "You're good at this."

"Do you want to head out? There are a few trails we can take."

"Okay."

Moving back toward Mike, Tyler informed him that they were ready to head out.

"The trails are obvious; just follow the paths that don't have any grass," Mike said as he led them out of the corral.

They nodded and started down the trail. Once they began on the trail, Kate trusted Tyler enough to let go of the mane before asking for her phone. Shifting the reins into one hand, he took it out of his pocket and handed it to her.

She snapped random photos of the scenery. Having grown up in the city, she was fascinated with the spaciousness the countryside offered.

When she was done with the scenery, she turned to one side and tried to take a picture of Tyler. She forgot about her balance and almost slipped off the horse.

She gasped, but Tyler's arm was already around her waist, pulling her back in place.

"Be careful," he chided.

"Sorry." She smiled sheepishly. Angling her phone, she leaned back and took a picture of them. She was admiring it when Tyler took the phone away from her.

"Stop taking pictures. Give it a try," he said and tried to push the reins into her hands.

She clenched her fists and pulled her hands away from the reins. "No. You're doing a mighty fine job. I'm satisfied with simply being on a horse."

"It's pointless if you're just going to sit and enjoy the view; you can do that in a car." Taking her hand in one of his, he pressed the reins into it.

The sudden change in tension caused the horse to jerk forward, throwing her off balance again. She slipped to the side, pulling the reins along with her and causing the horse to turn sharply toward the right.

Tyler held her steady and immediately tugged on the reins to pull the horse back on course.

"That was a good start."

"You have very little faith in yourself."

"I don't trust myself with sports or animals of any kind."

Again, Tyler placed the reins into her hands. Except this time, he covered her hands with his own and guided her. "Make sure you're not holding on to it too tightly; otherwise, you won't be able to control him." Then he pulled her left hand slightly back; the horse shifted along with her control. "See, just a little tug and the horse knows what you want."

For someone who didn't speak much, even with his closest friends, he was being extremely patient with her. Not once did he roll his eyes at her frantic nerves or show any sign of impatience.

His warm hand on her outer thigh brought her attention back to earth. "Keep a firm grip using your thigh, but keep your waist soft or the horse won't be able to move properly and your back will ache."

"When did you learn to ride?" she asked, not realizing that Tyler had let go of the reins.

"Since I was able to, I guess. I can't remember exactly when."

"Do you still ride?"

"Whenever I'm free. I own a horse at a ranch near the cabin; I'll let you ride him when we're there."

Laughing softly, she twisted her waist and turned back to face him. "You keep talking as if I'm definitely going. I haven't even agreed."

"Good. You know how to turn without needing me to save you."

Though it was true, she still scowled at him. "Why do you like riding?"

"I never said I did."

She shrugged. "You won't get this good at something if you don't like it."

"This is the first time you're riding. I seriously doubt you're a good judge of that."

"I was trying to praise you because you've been so nice to me, but I'm beginning to change my mind. Is it getting late? Is that why you're getting grumpy?"

Instead of a rebuttal, he took over the reins and made a series of "click-click" sounds. Then he shifted his body forward and sent the horse sprinting ahead.

She screamed and grabbed onto the horse's mane while Tyler slowed the horse back to its original pace.

"Sorry," he said, flashing an apologetic smile. "Bad idea of trying to be funny."

"Do. Not. Do. That. Again."

"You have my word," he said as he bowed his head in apology. Taking out her phone, he returned it to her. "Here, take your photos and enjoy the view."

Once the phone was in her hand, she tapped on the application for her camera. Leaning back against him, she lifted her hand and took another photo of them.

Changing it to video mode, she twisted around and interviewed Tyler. "So, you haven't told me why you like riding."

He turned his face away from the lens, but grinned and answered after seeing that she wasn't going to back down. "I just like it." Without notice, he took the phone from her and placed the reins into her hands.

She fumbled for a moment before gaining control.

"How's your first ride coming along?" Tyler asked, this time with the phone's camera on her.

"It was fun until someone tried to kill me." She glowered at Tyler.

They continued riding for over an hour.

When they got back to the stables, Mike was already waiting for them. Tyler hopped off the horse and raised his folded arm for her as she got off.

It wasn't until she tried to stand that she realized she could barely feel her legs.

She grabbed onto Tyler's arm as she felt her legs quivering.

"Sorry, I should've turned back earlier," Tyler said.

"No, it's fine. I'm sure I'll be all right after a while. I was having lots of fun anyway." Despite saying that, her legs didn't seem to be recovering.

Tyler took her hand and hooked it over his elbow, letting her lean against him as they slowly strolled back to the car.

She heaved a sigh of relief as she settled back against the seat. "I feel like an old lady."

"We'll order room service. That way, you can rest."

"That's a fantastic idea."

"Did you have fun?"

"Yeah, but I think there's a real chance that I'll be bedridden tomorrow."

Chapter Ten

Tyler hung the towel over his shoulders as he walked out of the shower in his T-shirt and long sweatpants.

Kate sat in front of the desk, her hair still wet from the bath, transferring the photos and videos she'd taken onto her laptop.

He bent forward, leaning over Kate, to look at the photos. It was strange to see himself in some of them.

He never enjoyed taking photos, but she was having so much fun that he didn't want to be a wet blanket. "May I?" he asked, his hand hovering over her phone.

"Go ahead." Kate switched off her laptop and went to sit on the bed.

He scanned through the photos and sent several of them to his own phone.

Yawning softly, she stretched her neck, and her hand kneaded along the side of her shoulder.

He should've known it'd be tough on her. He shouldn't have taken them out on such a long ride. "Is your back aching?"

She flashed a sheepish smile. "A little."

"I'm sorry."

"It's my fault for not exercising enough. Don't worry, it's worth it anyway." She grinned and stretched her back.

"You're wearing your glasses again."

Once the week that she was supposed to stay off her contact lenses was up, Kate had immediately returned to them.

He preferred Kate in her contact lenses. Without the additional layer of glass, the radiating flecks in her eyes were clearer.

"I was afraid that I might fall asleep with my lenses in, so I took them out in the shower."

"Speaking of which, Joseph gave me the contact for the Lasik surgeon." He sent Kate a text before handing the phone back to her. "You should make an appointment. That way, you won't have to wear your glasses anymore. Especially since they're giving you headaches all the time."

"You sure are making a lot of plans for me."

He grimaced, realizing he was overstepping his boundaries again. "Sorry, I was just—"

"I was kidding. Maybe I'll go for it next year. Then I won't have to fumble around the mansion after the surgery and disturb the rest of you."

He sighed and said, "You should have it done this year, so you'll have someone to watch out for you after your surgery."

Kate yawned again and nodded at his statement, but he doubted she heard a single word.

Almost immediately after dinner, Kate fell asleep.

He switched off all the lights and lay in bed, browsing through the photos on his phone. A grin spread across his face as he thought about the day.

Choosing a photo that Kate had taken of them, he set it as his wallpaper and returned the phone to the table. He got back into bed and smiled, planning their itinerary for the next day.

Kate turned to her side, jostled by another groan. She opened her eyes and rolled herself over as she heard yet another groan. Sitting up on her bed, it took her a moment to remember where she was.

She slipped out of bed and pressed the button on her phone to get some light into the room.

She took a few unsteady steps toward Tyler's bed. Despite the air conditioning in the room, he was perspiring and appeared to be in pain.

Just as she wanted to ask if he was all right, his head snapped to the side and he groaned again.

"Tyler," she said softly as she knelt down beside his bed, uncertain if he was awake. "Ty." Gently, she laid her hand over his, thinking of waking him. But he immediately grabbed her hand and pulled it toward his chest.

Tyler squeezed her hand and pinned it tight against his chest as though he was afraid that she might slip away or take her hand back.

She froze, stunned by his sudden action.

She tried to pull her hand back without startling him, but he was holding on so tightly that it was impossible.

She realized Tyler was probably having a nightmare. Her free hand pushed his hair aside, and she saw the fear on his face.

She knew exactly what he was dreaming of.

"Tyler." She gave him a light shake, but he only tightened his grip on her hand.

She didn't know what to do. She didn't want to jostle him from his sleep, but he seemed better off awake.

She tried waking him a few more times, calling out his name softly, but he seemed trapped in the nightmare.

Not knowing what else to do, she wrapped her hand around his and prayed, "Lord, take away his nightmare. Give him rest." Still holding on to his hand, she told him that everything was all right.

Though her words appeared to have calmed him, Tyler never eased the grip on her hand. Curling up on the floor beside his bed, she leaned against it and continued to tell him that everything was all right until she dozed off.

Tyler gasped and felt his lungs constricting. The ache in his chest was getting worse as his lungs screamed for air.

He was curled up under the table and could feel the heat as the fire drew closer. He couldn't open his eyes; it hurt too much.

It didn't matter anyway. The smoke was too thick for him to see anything.

Then he heard it—his parents screaming his name.

No! Don't come over! He tried to warn them.

Forget about me! Leave! He tried to scream, but he couldn't.

123

He tried again; he had to let them know what would happen if they came over for him, but he couldn't get his voice working.

He cupped his hands over his ears as he saw a piece of the ceiling fall. Despite that, he heard it. He heard the bone-chilling scream from his mother as she got pinned by a concrete slab. He heard his father's cry of agony as he tried to pull his mother out from under the slab.

"Stay under the table," his father instructed.

He didn't know what to do. He pulled his legs tighter against his chest and squeezed his eyes shut as the fire crept up on his mother.

His father wasn't going to leave his mother behind.

Then another slab fell, knocking his father out.

He had once thought he'd be next.

He couldn't stand the pain throbbing in his chest. He couldn't fight the dark rims invading his eyes.

But it wasn't his time.

He felt himself getting hauled out of the house. Then standing outside the house, he stared blankly as the house crumbled.

Soon, everything started to fade.

The noise was always the first to go. The roaring of the fire fizzled out, and the shouting of the firemen ceased. All that was left was a deafening silence.

Next, the colors disappeared.

He watched the scene as if it were one of those black-and-white silent films. Adults he didn't know walked about; each wore a grim and solemn expression.

Some of them came over to talk to him, but he couldn't hear what they were saying.

After that, their faces began to blur, and the same darkness that had invaded his sight returned.

He tried to grab on to something, to someone. But everything he touched always crumbled away.

Eventually, he was the only one left standing in the Stygian darkness.

He began walking, searching. But no matter which direction he took, there was nothing but darkness.

Twenty years, that was how long he'd had this nightmare. And for twenty years, it was always the same.

He would keep moving and searching until the darkness depleted his strength. He would then give up and wait, wait to wake up with an aching loneliness.

But this time as he waited to be consumed by nothingness, he heard a voice.

He heard someone calling his name, then felt a warm and gentle touch on his hand.

He held on, holding the hand close to him, worried that it'd slip away like everything else and leave him alone in the dark again. As he held on to the hand, a glimmer of light shone through the darkness. Soon the light invaded the emptiness and the darkness left.

The colors returned, and the voice got clearer.

He could finally see the face of the person he was holding on to—Kate.

She was beaming radiantly at him. "It's all right. Everything is all right," she said, her hand skimming down along his jaw.

The next morning, Tyler opened his eyes and became conscious of the hand he was still holding on to. He jerked upright, pulling Kate's hand along and jolting her awake.

He released her hand as she gasped and ran her hand through her hair, seemingly disoriented.

When she turned and saw him, she immediately sighed.

"Sorry," she mumbled. "I fell asleep." Leaning her elbow against the bed, Kate tried to push herself up from the floor.

She couldn't get herself up. She dropped back onto the floor and buried her face in the bed. "I can't feel my legs."

He got off the bed and scooped her up in his arms, gently placing her onto his bed. "You slept on the floor for the whole night?" he said as he started kneading her calves.

He couldn't believe he'd stupidly held on to her hand, causing her to sleep on the floor.

"Not technically. I'm not sure what time I woke up," she said before closing her eyes.

At first, she didn't have any reaction as Tyler kneaded up and down her calves. Then she suddenly flung her hands out, grabbed his arm, and screamed for him to stop.

The pins and needles must have started.

He immediately let go, but her fingers dug into his arm.

Her eyes squeezed shut, and she bit down on her lower lip, seemingly trying to stop herself from screaming any more. "Gosh," she said through clenched teeth and leaned back on the bed, using the pillow to cover her face.

He ran his hand through his hair while he kicked himself for being the cause of her pain.

Kate continued to writhe in agony for a few minutes as she wriggled her toes.

Once the pins and needles subsided, she sat up and smiled sheepishly at him. "Sorry for that … um … sorry. I tried waking you up. But you didn't, and I fell asleep."

"Kate, please. Please stop saying you're sorry. I should be the one apologizing. I'm such an idiot. I—"

Kate scowled at him. "What idiot? You were sleeping; you didn't know." Then lowering her voice, she asked, "Do you get nightmares often?"

"Every now and then," he said. "I'm sorry I woke you."

She lay back on the bed. "It isn't your fault, but you can make it up to me by letting me sleep now." She flashed a toothy grin.

He laughed; it was always easy to laugh around her. "Go ahead. I'll get breakfast."

Kate nodded, her eyes already closed. "Goodnight."

He closed the curtains before leaving the room.

Once he was out of the room, Tyler called Marianne to inform her that they would be extending the trip for another day. She hated it whenever he disappeared without first informing her.

"Kate's work not going well?" Marianne asked.

"We'll head back tomorrow," he said.

"All right."

When he got back to the hotel room, he was surprised to find Kate awake. Her bag lay neatly by the door, and she was replying to emails on her laptop.

"I thought you wanted to sleep."

"I tried, but I couldn't get back to sleep. Don't worry, I'm wide awake. I can drive us back to the airport if you want."

"We're leaving today? I thought we could do more exploring. We can go hiking at the national park."

"Hmm, I don't have any other projects on hand. So if it doesn't affect your work, then I'm fine with it."

"Great. I've already extended our stay for another night."

When he saw her blank expression, he grinned. "Sorry, I thought that even if you didn't want to stay, you could rest and we wouldn't have to rush."

She shook her head but was already smiling. "I'll call the airline and change the timing, then."

"I've done that as well."

"Huh." She glanced around after switching off her laptop. Then she scanned the room again, seemingly uncertain about something. "So, what should I do now?"

"Eat." Tyler laid out the food on the desk.

Kate moved her laptop and asked, "Are we really going to the national park?"

"If you want."

She narrowed her eyes and looked up at him. "Really? I thought you liked to make all the decisions."

He pulled up a chair next to hers. "I'm sorry. I know I overstep my boundaries at times."

"I was kidding," she said. "But there will be times when I'll disagree with your decision. You know that, right?"

He leaned forward in his chair, looking right into her eyes. "I know I must seem pushy; making decisions for you, altering plans without first discussing with you. But if you'd said no, I would get us back to the mansion today, even if it meant buying a private jet."

He waited for Kate to say something, but she reached for her locket and tugged at it.

"I didn't mean to make you uncomfortable. I just wanted you to know that if you do disagree with me, I'll listen."

Kate turned back to him with a puzzled look.

"You always play with your necklace when you're uncomfortable or nervous. Unless I'm making you nervous instead of uncomfortable." He grinned and winked, hoping it'd make her feel better.

"I'm not uncomfortable or nervous," she said, looking away from him. "The last time someone went out of their way for me was when my grandmother got this locket back."

"Maybe because you never let anyone do anything for you. You had to do your own laundry, carry your own luggage, open your own doors. And when your sister wants to pursue something that you've chosen to leave behind, you see the need to step in and help. Maybe it's time you let someone do something for you."

She gave him a small smile. "Then don't complain when I don't do anything."

"I look forward to that."

After breakfast, they spent the day hiking in the park. Kate continued taking photos and videos of them and their surroundings.

After two hours of hiking, the dense trees came to a stop. They stood by the riverbank, beside a series of fold mountains.

"This is beautiful." Kate bent down and skimmed her fingers across the surface of the water.

He took the phone from her hand and snapped a picture of her, and another when she turned to look at him. She raised her hand to block her face, but he'd already taken the photo.

"You've been taking photos of me and of us the entire day, but I can't take one of you?"

She shrugged. "This is amazing." She sat by the riverbank and took in the scene around her.

Settling down beside her, he said with a grin, "The cabin has a fantastic view, too."

Kate nudged him with her elbow as she laughed softly. "Stop. Stop selling me the cabin idea. I don't know why you want me to go there so badly, but ..." She raised her finger to stop him from interjecting. "I'll go."

He grinned brightly.

"I can't promise when. Since I've been rather busy with the bed and breakfast, I haven't had time to catch up with my teams. And there may be hiccups here and there, but I'll let you know once I can free up a couple of days."

"That's fine with me."

They continued chatting by the riverbank until it got too warm, and they decided to head back and have their lunch.

He made sure he matched Kate's pace.

Every now and then, whenever the path was uneven, he'd hold out his hand for Kate to use as support.

He really had to stop finding excuses to touch her.

The trek down took slightly longer, and he figured that Kate must be exhausted.

He didn't mind the slower pace; it was his fault that she was tired. The horseback riding, the uncomfortable sleeping situation, and the two-hour hike were probably taking a toll on her. "Are you all right? We can rest for a while if you want."

"No, I'm fine. Sorry, I know I'm slowing you down."

"I get to see more." Taking her hand, he folded his arm and hooked her hand over his. "Lean on me if you're getting tired."

He didn't think that she would. From previous conversations, he'd surmised that she didn't like others to think she was weak.

But the combination of events was clearly too much for her. She leaned against him as her pace slowed further. Though she was clearly tired, she didn't complain or whine about needing rest. She kept her feet moving. Only when they got back to the car did she sigh and stretch her limbs.

Tyler laughed at her, but she merely scowled at him. Probably too exhausted to banter with him.

They had dinner nearby, and she seemed invigorated after that. She shopped at the gift shop, examining the items and picking out T-shirts for both of them.

"I don't want it." He pushed her hands away when she tried to see if the T-shirt would fit.

"Why not? It'll be a fun reminder of our trip."

"I don't need a T-shirt to remind me of our trip. I have a good memory, and you have enough photos."

She sighed softly and placed the T-shirts back onto the shelf. "All right," she said with discontent as she moved on to the rest of the store.

Tipping his head back, Tyler shook his head, exasperated with himself. He grabbed the T-shirts she'd put down, brought them over to the counter, and paid for them. When he turned, Kate was standing beside him with the biggest smile.

Thank you, she mouthed.

When he saw the smile that two T-shirts brought, the thought of owning a cheesy T-shirt didn't seem that bad after all.

That night, the same nightmare plagued him again. But he was no longer drowning in the fear and loneliness that the dream always brought him. This time, he knew that at the end of it, Kate would be there in the sunlight, bringing light into the darkness that enveloped him.

Chapter Eleven

Kate opened the door and got out of the car while Tyler took their luggage from the trunk. She was getting used to this whole letting-others-take-care-of-her thing.

She strolled up to the mansion and opened the door. As expected, the door wasn't locked. It never was during meal times.

She tilted her head to the side and blinked as the living room greeted her.

The whole living room looked different.

The writing desk was missing, and in its place stood a black grand piano. "Ty, you didn't have to do this," she said when she felt him coming up behind her. "Was it because of what Eve said?"

"I thought it'd be more convenient for you. Then you don't have to travel between places to play your piano."

She broke into a wide grin and went forward to try out the piano. Lifting the cover, she tried out a few keys.

"Huge present, isn't it?" Evelyn's voice drew Kate's attention.

"What are you doing here?" Kate stepped away from the piano and hugged her friend.

"Checking if you're hurt and if I need to hunt him down."

"I had so much fun." She handed Evelyn the laptop. "Go ahead. I'll join you in a bit."

Evelyn took the laptop and went back into the kitchen while Kate returned to the piano. Her fingers skimmed across the surface of the keys, but she didn't play them.

"Do you like it?" Tyler asked.

"Yes, very much. Thanks, Ty. This is really nice of you."

"As long as you're happy."

Standing, she threw her arms over his shoulders. "I am. Thanks," she said and stepped back, the grin still plastered on her face. "Let's eat something."

She stepped into the kitchen and took a quick glance. She was glad that only the guys, Evelyn, and Marianne were present and secretly relieved that Joanne wasn't present. Joanne and Evelyn being in the same room would result in a mega explosion.

"Hello all," she said.

All of them uttered some form of acknowledgment, but their attention was mainly on the laptop. They had all crowded around Evelyn's chair, trying to look at the photos.

"Ty, you're in a lot of the photos," Joseph said.

Ryan looked up at Tyler and gave him a sly smile before adding, "And you're smiling—a lot."

"People smile when they're taking photos," Kate stated plainly. "Ty's an amazing rider; he was really good with the horse."

"You rode with her? Seriously? The last time we wanted to try riding, he got us instructors and dumped us on them," Dan complained.

Kate laughed at the funny image of two grown men on the same horse. "So you wanted to ride with him?"

Dan rolled his eyes. "No, I'm merely stating the huge contrast. He left Anne there, too."

Joseph cleared his throat while Tyler shot Dan a glare. "Sorry, I was—"

"It's okay," she said. "I told you it's nothing to worry about. Is there enough food for us? I'm starving."

Marianne's eyes were glued to the screen. She nodded and waved, gesturing for Kate to go ahead without even looking over at her.

When Kate heard her own voice on her laptop, she knew Evelyn was playing one of the videos. It was the one she took while they were seated on the riverbank. "So, tell me more about the cabin in North Carolina."

Tyler went on to describe what he could remember of the place. When the video ended, Ryan asked, "Wait. You have a cabin in North Carolina? Why haven't we stayed there before?"

Evelyn closed the laptop and shifted it to a countertop nearby.

Shrugging, Tyler answered, "I didn't like going there."

Everyone around the table fell silent and dug in.

Seemed like everyone knew how Tyler avoided everything that had to do with his parents.

"And you feel like going there all of a sudden?" Evelyn asked, apparently unaware of how quiet everyone had become.

Kate kicked Evelyn under the table and scowled at her.

What? Evelyn mouthed to Kate.

"I think Kate will love the place, and I want to show her my horse," Tyler answered.

Kate turned to Tyler, surprised that he'd answered Evelyn's question instead of shrugging it off.

She picked up her fork and pointed its tines at Evelyn's plate.

"Kate," Dan said as he stood and stretched his hand toward her. "I'm sorry about what Joanne did."

She grimaced and sighed. "Dan, I told you it's all right." Still, she shook his hand so he could return to his seat.

"I know, but you deserve an apology, and I want to make it up to you."

She opened her mouth to speak, but Dan continued before she could say anything.

"I've paid for a Lasik consultation with the doctor Joseph recommended. Whenever you're free, you can head down, get your eyes checked, and decide if you want to have the operation. Then you can stay off contact lenses altogether." Dan cast a quick glance at Tyler as he finished his sentence.

Seemed like everything within the group was public information.

"Did you ask him to do that?" she asked Tyler.

"No, he didn't," Dan said. "I asked Joseph how you were doing, and he told me about your glasses giving you trouble and the Lasik thing. I thought it'd be a good idea."

"Thanks."

"So when is Joanne coming to apologize for herself?" Evelyn asked, staring right at Dan.

Dan blinked, then smiled awkwardly.

"When pigs can fly, when hell freezes over, when the sun stops shining, when—"

"I think she got it, Ryan," Joseph said, stopping Ryan's mindless ramble.

"Eve, let it go. I'm fine," Kate said softly, but a tone of warning lingered in her words.

Evelyn raised both her hands and shrugged, then returned to her food.

"So, you guys stayed and had a mini-holiday?" Ryan asked.

He had asked it casually enough, but Kate couldn't help feeling that she was being tested. "Yeah, you saw the photos."

"You asked and he agreed?" Ryan pressed.

Kate frowned and turned to Tyler.

"Ignore him."

She turned back to Ryan and smiled. "We were already there anyway."

"Do you know Tyler hates taking photos?"

"Ryan." Tyler stared at him. "Enough."

Ryan was clearly trying to push a point across, and Kate could feel the blood rushing to her cheeks.

Clearing her throat, she turned to Evelyn. "So, Eve, what are you doing here?"

Evelyn swallowed, then using the fork, she pushed the food around on her plate. "One of our teams screwed up *majorly*. I just got a call from an extremely pissed-off client. I thought you'd want to know about it."

Kate sighed and braced herself for the news. "Which one?" Then burying her face in her hands, she continued. "Please don't tell me it's the one I handed over to Laura so I could work on the bed and breakfast."

Evelyn's silence answered her question.

"Perfect. What happened?"

"They messed up with the ordering and got the wrong pieces of furniture. But instead of telling us, they thought that somehow, miraculously, the owners wouldn't notice the difference."

Kate stared at Evelyn, completely dumbfounded. She opened her mouth to speak, but Evelyn raised her finger and pursed her lips. "And," she said after a moment, "they damaged one of the owner's desk. Instead of apologizing, they just threw it out. They even argued that the owners agreed to remove it in the first place."

"Have you spoken to them? Maybe there was a miscommunication."

"I knew you'd say that." Evelyn shook her head. "Trust me. They knew they screwed up, but they chose to be complete idiots instead of owning up to it."

Kate sighed heavily.

Why didn't she just listen to Evelyn? Why did she have to trust Benjamin?

She could go on listing all the whys, but it wasn't time to wallow in what she should and shouldn't have done. She sat back against the chair and asked, "Is there a possibility of retrieving the desk to restore it?"

"Nope. It's long gone."

She nodded. "What did the Harpers demand?"

"Mrs. Harper was just screaming into my ear." Then smiling coyly, Evelyn said, "I held the phone away from my ear and agreed with everything she said. You know I'm not good at handling people, so I figured I'll let you do the talking."

"Okay. Once you get back to the office, check if we still can get the original pieces we wanted. If it's out, find alternatives. Find out from them exactly which desk was thrown out and check if we can replace that as well."

"I can tell you right now that it can't be replaced. It's a handcrafted desk."

"Then you'll need to work your magic," Kate said.

Evelyn was great at handcrafted furniture. She was attentive to details and always made sure that it was flawless before presenting the final product to the clients.

"It was made from a particular wood. It won't be easy to find, and I'll need time and pictures of the original desk. Based on how she was screaming on the phone, I don't think the Harpers will be willing to provide either of those."

"I can help with that," Dan interrupted. "I know someone who provides special wood, I'm sure I can get him to give you some for the desk."

Kate turned and smiled at Dan. "Thank you. That will be very helpful." Looking back at Evelyn, she explained, "Dan owns a construction firm."

Dan returned her smile and shrugged. "Not a problem."

"What about Laura?" Evelyn finally asked.

"She's going to prepare an apology for the Harpers. I want it in writing. After I approve it, she'll read from it—word for word. We'll discuss how to deal with her after we settle the debacle."

"Oh, I got that covered. Dismiss her and the rest of the team."

Kate pursed her lips while her fingers tugged at her locket.

Though someone in the team should've spoken out about what was happening before it got out of hand, sacking the entire team seemed too drastic.

It was the team leader who made the decision.

"I know you won't want to do that," Evelyn said. "I'll let you decide what to do with the rest of them, but Laura's got to go."

Kate nodded.

"I guess I'll get back to work and leave you to deal with the incensed client." Evelyn stood and said her goodbyes.

Dan stood and followed Evelyn as she left.

"Sorry for talking about work at the table. Must've bored you guys."

"Don't worry. I'm too tired to talk anyway," Joseph said while Ryan nodded.

"Good luck." Ryan gave Kate a pat on the shoulder before heading out.

"I'm going to crash, too." Joseph stood.

"Joe." Tyler's voice stopped Joseph in his tracks. "Can you check Kate's eyes again to make sure they're all right?"

Though she insisted that nothing was wrong with her eyes, Joseph turned to her. "Don't bother. He won't let me get any rest until I've checked your eyes."

She shook her head, but didn't want to give Joseph any more trouble. So she sat and allowed him to check her eyes, moving them according to his instructions.

"Her eyes are fine."

"I know. Thanks," she said.

When Joseph stepped out of the kitchen, she yawned softly and stretched.

"Are you leaving now? I'll drive you there."

She smiled and shook her head. "You've already been driving me around for the past two days. I can manage."

"Evelyn said the Harpers were really angry. Are you sure it's all right for you to go down on your own?"

"I'll be fine. They'll probably yell at me, but I'll be fine."

"Why don't you ask those who screwed up to solve the problem instead?"

"And let them make things worse?"

"Let me drive you. I'll wait in the car."

"No. I know it sounds serious, but screw-ups will continue to happen, and clients will continue to get upset. You can't protect me from all future yelling. So, no. Just go rest."

Tyler didn't reply. He stacked some of the dishes on the table and turned back to Kate. "Then when you're done at the Harpers, will you drop me a text to let me know how it went?"

"I can do that."

"Will you be back for dinner?" Marianne asked.

"I guess so; there isn't much I can do when offices close anyway."

"Good. I was thinking of making dessert. What do you like?"

Kate thought about it for a moment. She wasn't in the mood for any dessert. Besides, she didn't want to trouble Marianne. "I'm fine with anything."

"No, I want to make something you like. Tell me, or I'll have to spend the whole day thinking about which dessert to choose and if you'll like it. It's so much more troublesome."

"Apple strudel. I don't know if it's possible to make it at home; I always buy it. If you want, I can buy some on the way back."

Marianne scoffed. "You'll have apple strudel tonight. Oh,

right, I almost forgot. Mr. Sawyer asked for your plane tickets and hotel receipts to verify that the conditions were met."

"I was starting to think Mr. Sawyer wasn't living here at all. I haven't seen him since the first night we moved in. I'll pass them on to him tonight." Then turning to Tyler, she continued. "I'll text you."

But Tyler stood, took her laptop, and walked out beside her. "If you need anything, call me."

"You don't have to be so worried. You can't protect me from everything, but God can. If hordes of angels are with me to keep my feet from dashing against a rock, they can keep me safe from a screaming client."

He looked blankly at her.

Her lips parted into a smile. "Psalm 91," she explained.

"You have a lot of faith."

"You have to believe in something, right? I choose to believe that the words in the Bible are true." She paused by her car. "Seeing Jesus as a very real presence in my life helped me a lot when I lost my parents. Whatever I do, I always imagine that they are there with me, that they are among the angels who surround me." She shook her head, smiling wryly. "I will call you if I need anything."

Taking the laptop from Tyler, she slipped into her car. "Thanks for getting the piano." She beamed at him, closed the door, and drove off.

When Kate reached the Harpers', she closed her eyes and muttered under her breath, "Give me favor, Lord. Help me."

Taking a deep breath, she pressed the doorbell.

The moment Mrs. Harper saw her, she folded her arms across her chest before drawing a long, frustrated breath. "What do you want?" she asked, ending her question with a sigh.

Kate gave her a small smile.

She'd already expected such a reaction from Mrs. Harper. At least Mrs. Harper hadn't slammed the door in her face.

"I'm here to apologize and fix the mistakes."

Mrs. Harper rolled her eyes. "I loved that desk. That Laura girl just threw it out, then had the audacity to say that I was the one who told her to do so. I still have the drawings of the design we'd agreed on, and it didn't include throwing away that desk."

"I understand, and I know it was entirely our fault. I know I can't give you back the original desk, but my business partner, Miss Jordan, is searching for a replacement. If we can't find it, we'll make a replica for you. I know it can't replace the memories you had before, but at least we can return you one that's as similar as we can achieve."

With her fingers rubbing her temple, Mrs. Harper continued. "And the rest of the furniture? So many of the pieces are wrong; they don't fit the house."

Kate nodded. "I'll fix all of that. Let me take a look so I know exactly what needs to be done. Miss Jordan is already checking on the availability of the furniture that we agreed on. If they aren't available, she'll search for alternatives, and I'll get back to you." She paused, waiting for a reaction. But Mrs. Harper merely closed her eyes and looked away.

"I know our mistakes inconvenienced you. I don't want to end things like that. I want to end this right. I promise we'll make it up to you. There will be no further charges, and I'll completely waive our original designing fees. Also, I'll give you a further thirty percent discount off the original furniture we agreed upon."

Mrs. Harper drummed her fingers against her elbow. "When can you get it settled?"

"Give me a week to get the design right and change the furniture for you. As for your desk, if we can't get it, Miss Jordan is going to make another one for you. So regarding that, I'll need to check with her before I can confirm it with you."

Sighing, Mrs. Harper nodded. "All right."

"Thank you. I promise you won't regret it."

Mrs. Harper stepped aside, allowing Kate to enter.

As Kate walked around the room, she pointed out the wrong pieces and described how the original ones were supposed to be.

"Did I miss anything?" she asked politely.

"No, you got it all."

Kate nodded. "Again, I'm so sorry for all the headaches we've caused."

Mrs. Harper pinched her lips together, giving her a nod.

"Thank you for giving us another chance."

Before leaving, Kate apologized again and promised she'd correct the mistakes as quickly as possible.

She sat in her car and emailed Evelyn the list of furniture that had to be replaced, then sent Tyler a text, letting him know that she was done with the Harpers and was leaving for the office.

She headed to the office and spent the rest of the day on the phone, trying to rectify the mistakes made. After much negotiation, pleading, and some groveling, they got all the furniture they needed. All except the desk. That would have to be recreated by Evelyn.

Kate called Mrs. Harper to inform her of the latest updates, then headed back to the mansion with Evelyn's car behind hers.

As she drove toward the mansion, she found herself looking forward to seeing Tyler, to tell him how her day went and find out how his day was.

Maybe they could spend some time playing the piano after dinner.

But as she turned around the bend and saw the pink mini-Volkswagen, she sighed. *This isn't good.*

She took out her phone and called Tyler, letting him know that she was outside the mansion and so was Joanne.

As expected, he told her to stay in the car and hung up.

She was intending to hide out in her car anyway. She tightened her grip on the steering wheel as the car came to a stop and prayed that Joanne would just leave her alone—a prayer that wasn't answered.

Joanne stormed over and started pounding on her car's window, yelling and gesturing for her to wind it down.

Kate closed her eyes and focused on her breathing. She wasn't interested in getting yelled at today.

Then, the pounding stopped.

She opened her eyes, thinking that Tyler had come out from the mansion. But she was wrong. "Oh, no." She'd clean forgotten that Evelyn's car was right behind hers.

"What do you think you're doing?" Evelyn shoved Joanne back.

As Joanne staggered back on her heels, Evelyn took another step forward and gave Joanne another shove.

Kate, got out of the car, hurried forward, and grabbed Evelyn's arm. "Eve, please." She turned and tried dragging Evelyn away from Joanne.

Those two didn't make a good combination. They needed distance.

"You went on a trip with my Tyler?" Joanne screeched.

Kate shook her head, suspecting that Joanne had some suicidal inclination.

Evelyn easily shrugged off her hold and stepped closer to Joanne.

"Eve, please," Kate repeated, hoping that Joanne would finally register the deadly vibes radiating from Evelyn. *Jesus, please. You know I can't stop her when she's bent on fighting.*

Before Evelyn or Joanne could do anything, Tyler came sprinting out the door. He stopped in front of Kate, stretching his arm out protectively in front of her.

"I called Dan. He's on the way," Tyler said before asking, "Did she hurt you?"

"No, she was just pounding on my car's window." She let go of her grip on Evelyn and placed her hand on Tyler's outstretched arm. "It's okay. I'm all right."

"Go inside," Tyler said softly, but she knew he'd meant it as a command. She sighed, looking between Evelyn and Tyler.

"No," Evelyn said. "Kate will be here for a year. If this girl has something to say to Kate, then thrash it out now."

"Just stay away from my Tyler!"

Kate's hand tightened on Tyler's arm, but she immediately released her hand when he pushed her half a step further behind him.

She wasn't frightened. Joanne's scream simply caught her by surprise, but her reaction definitely made it worse for Joanne.

"I'm not *your* Tyler. I never was, and I never will be. I told you that the last time. Who I go out with is none of your business."

"She's just pretending to be all sweet and nice. She's trying to get your money."

Evelyn took a big stride forward, staring Joanne down. "Say that again and I'll rip out your tongue."

"I'll say—"

Evelyn grabbed Joanne by her wrist and jerked her forward. "I dare you."

Joanne's eyes widened.

"Stop behaving like a spoiled brat. Nobody will ever see you as anything more than a spoiled brat unless you grow up. If you think the rest of the world will condone your actions as your family does, then you're wrong. I dare you to try me."

Joanne drew a sharp breath and finally learned how valuable silence was.

"Let me make it clear. If you ever dare to go crazy on Kate or do anything to hurt her again, I'll make sure you receive double of everything you do to her. Do you understand?"

Joanne stared back at Evelyn, her chin jutting out stubbornly.

With another rough jerk, Evelyn repeated, "Do you understand?"

"Eve …"

Evelyn shot her a glare and turned back to Joanne. "Do you understand?" Evelyn asked again, raising her voice.

"Yes," Joanne finally said, almost in a whisper.

Evelyn let go of Joanne's hand, the red imprints of her fingers clear against Joanne's porcelain skin.

Joanne spun around and headed toward her car, but Evelyn cut her off. "No, you don't. You don't get to come here, yell at Kate, then go home. You owe her an apology for splashing juice in her eyes. And now, you owe her an apology for coming here to terrify her."

Joanne's eyes turned red and tears brimmed over in an instant.

Kate sighed and closed her eyes.

Tears wouldn't make Evelyn back down. Once Evelyn began on a warpath, no one could stop her—not even Kate.

Evelyn didn't believe in begging or crying. She hated people who used tears as weapons. She grew up learning to fight hard to win her battles.

And right now, it was clear that Evelyn wasn't letting Joanne leave without any consequences.

Evelyn fastened her hand around Joanne's arm and turned her back to face Kate. Tightening her grip, Evelyn demanded, "Apologize now."

Joanne swallowed hard. She turned to Tyler, but he didn't say a word to defend her.

"Sorry."

Scoffing, Evelyn tightened her grasp. "Who is sorry and for what?"

Kate stepped out from behind Tyler and said, "Eve, that's enough." Joanne's behavior was ridiculous, but so was theirs. "Stop it."

"No."

"Eve, come on. That's enough."

"Tyler, are you convinced that Miss Joanne here won't ever come back to harass Kate? Am I going too far?"

Tyler pulled Kate back behind him. "I think you do owe Kate a proper apology."

"Ty."

Evelyn shot Kate another glare. "You can get angry with me, but I'm not letting this girl go until she learns her lesson."

"I don't need your help!" Joanne screamed and brushed away the angry tears with the back of her hand.

Kate's fingers splayed across her eyes. She couldn't figure out what was wrong with Joanne. Was she so proud and stubborn that she would turn down help from the one person who was willing to do so?

Kate couldn't stand watching them, and Joanne clearly didn't want her help. She turned away from them, intending to head into the house, but Tyler's hand held her in place.

"I'm sorry for splashing juice in your face, and I'm sorry for making a scene here today."

Evelyn released her death grip and took a step away from Joanne. "See, that was easy. Now get out of here. Don't let me find out you're harassing Kate again."

Seething, Joanne got into her car and sped away.

Kate pulled her hand from Tyler's and stormed into the house, heading straight for the kitchen.

"What's wrong?" Marianne asked.

She exhaled heavily through her nose and leaned against the counter. She was too agitated to sit.

Evelyn entered the kitchen and pulled out a seat. "Go ahead, start your lecture."

She glowered at Evelyn. "That was so wrong."

"Wrong? That girl's insane, insanely spoiled."

"So? That doesn't mean we can bully her."

"She went crazy on you twice. I went crazy on her once. She got off easy."

"Eve!"

"All right, all right. I'm sorry."

Kate rolled her eyes at Evelyn's patronizing apology.

She went on and on about how awful they were to Joanne, how Evelyn shouldn't have been so rough with her, and how she couldn't believe Tyler took Evelyn's side.

Both Tyler and Evelyn kept their mouths shut and allowed her to rattle on until the doorbell rang.

She wasn't sure how long she'd vented, but she pulled out a chair and sat, as usual, by Tyler.

She had stopped her lecture, but she was still feeling uneasy about the whole thing. "Maybe I should give Dan a call and apologize."

"What do you have to apologize for?" Dan's voice got their immediate attention.

"If you apologize, I swear I'll hit you," Evelyn said before Kate could open her mouth.

Evelyn gave Dan a rundown of what had happened before she continued. "I'm not sorry about it. But if you want to blame someone, you can blame me."

Instead of getting angry, Dan gave Evelyn a pat on the back. "Thank you," he said. "I hope she learns something." He sat on one of the chairs, sneaked a peek to make sure Marianne wasn't looking, then picked up a potato wedge and popped it into his mouth.

Kate and Evelyn shared a confused look.

"She's really spoiled, and no one ever sets her right. So, thanks," Dan continued. Curtailing his jubilance, he said to Tyler, "Sorry about her coming here again. My mom is encouraging her to fight for what she wants." Looking over at Evelyn, he asked, "Are we still on for tomorrow?"

Kate arched a brow at Evelyn, but she simply smiled at her.

"Yes—that's if you're still willing to introduce your wood guy to me."

As they chatted, Joanne was quickly forgotten, and Kate was smiling again by the time Dan and Evelyn left.

Marianne then shooed Kate and Tyler out of the kitchen so she could clean up.

Since she had some free time on her hands, Kate decided to try out the piano.

Tyler sat on the couch behind her, watching her play.

"Thanks, Ty. This is a great piano," she said without turning to look at him. She played another piece before looking over her shoulder and cocking her head to the side. "Still remember what we played the other day?"

He sat beside her and suddenly said, "I didn't mean to push Joanne too far, but if I'd helped her, she might come here again. I want to make sure you're safe. I'm usually back before you, but what if I'm not? I don't want to risk that."

She laughed softly. "I was still feeling slightly guilty over what happened to Joanne. But you know what, maybe God allowed this to happen so that you can finally see."

"Finally see what?"

"See that you don't always have to worry about me. I was so tired today that I didn't want to ask Evelyn over for dinner. But she asked, and I agreed. God won't leave me unattended, okay?"

He sighed, clearly unconvinced.

"Okay. Even if God isn't real and there are no angels in this world, Marianne will be here. And if I can't get you, I can always call Eve. You saw how she was," Kate said.

He grinned. "She's a good person to call. I'll give you Dan's number, too."

She nodded, took his hand, and placed it on the piano keys. She didn't want to think about Joanne anymore.

She'd had a long day, and she'd be busy solving the issue with the Harpers for the rest of the week. That was enough problem for her.

She waited for Tyler to begin the melody before joining in.

Just a few notes into the melody, Marianne came dashing out. The two of them stopped and looked up at her.

"What's wrong?" Kate asked when she saw Marianne's bewildered expression.

Her question brought no reply. Marianne merely moved closer to the piano, staring at their hands.

"Were you playing?" Marianne asked Tyler.

Tyler didn't bother to reply.

"Is he not allowed to play?" She turned to Tyler, wondering if she did something wrong.

"She's just surprised," he assured her. "Don't worry."

Before Kate could return her gaze to Marianne, she felt Marianne's arms around her. She coughed, trying to replenish air in her severely constricted lungs.

"Marianne, you're hurting her." Tyler pried Marianne's arms from Kate. "What's wrong with you?"

"Is everything all right?" Kate asked as she rubbed her palm against her chest.

"Yes, dear. Play, ignore me," Marianne said and returned to the kitchen with the widest grin.

Kate blinked and turned to Tyler, who simply gave her a slight head shake. It seemed she wasn't going to get any answer, so she placed her hands back on the piano.

They played for another hour before returning to their rooms. She wanted to spend more time with him, but she was exhausted.

After a quick shower, she stepped out from the bathroom and was walking over to her desk when she heard someone playing *Heart and Soul* on the piano.

She frowned, wondering who was playing it.

Joseph and Ryan weren't around. Maybe it was Mr. Sawyer.

But it was a duet.

She got out of the room and headed down the stairs, smiling as the cheerful piece continued.

Just before she got off the final step, the melody suddenly stopped.

She stepped off the stairs and turned to the piano. No one was seated in front of it. The cover was down, and the seat pushed in; exactly how she'd left it.

Her head tipped to the side, and her brows drew closer.

"Mr. Sawyer?" She went into the kitchen, but nobody was around either. "This is …"

It had been a long day.

She was exhausted, and the tune was probably stuck in her head from before.

She shook her head and returned to her room, going up the stairs two steps at a time.

Chapter Twelve

Evelyn stepped into Dan's office and found two desks on opposite sides of the wall.

Joanne sat behind one of the desks, filing her nails. She wore a peach-colored lace headband that pushed her wavy blond curls back.

Evelyn could never pull off that kind of headband. It was simply too sweet for her personality.

It didn't suit Joanne either. She wasn't sweet; she tried to be, but it always came out so forced, so feigned.

Across from her, another blonde sat behind the second desk. Unlike Joanne, she wore a white, buttoned-down shirt. Her hair was tied up in a neat ponytail, and she appeared to be actually working.

"Hi, can I help you?" the working blonde asked as she glanced up from her computer.

"I'm Evelyn. I'm looking for—"

"What are you doing here?" Joanne barked, putting down her nail file.

Rolling her eyes, Evelyn continued without acknowledging Joanne. "Dan."

The working blonde nodded politely and picked up the phone, but Joanne marched over and snatched the phone from her, slamming the phone down.

The assistant sighed softly and gave Evelyn an apologetic smile.

"What business do you have with my brother?"

Evelyn shook her head. *This girl never learns.* "If you think I won't dare to beat the brat out of you simply because this is your brother's company, then you're wrong." Taking a step closer to Joanne, Evelyn glared at her. "Get your brother out before I put actions behind my words."

"Are you threatening my daughter?"

Evelyn turned around as a heavily made-up woman sauntered in with a series of click-clops announcing her entrance. Despite the layers of freshly applied powder on her face, the age lines that were deeply carved into her face were crystal clear.

Evelyn pursed her lips as she took in the skin-tight dress and the chunky necklace around the creased skin of the woman's neck.

She tried to stop herself from giggling at the absurdity of the old woman's outfit. People in their sixties shouldn't be dressing as if they were still in their early twenties.

"Were you the one who threatened my daughter?" the woman asked as her eyes scrutinized Evelyn from head to toe.

Joanne crossed her arms and smirked.

"Yes," Evelyn replied without hesitation.

Joanne's mother raised her hand and swung her open palm at Evelyn. Without even flinching, Evelyn easily caught her attacker by the wrist and shoved her back.

Evelyn even had time to grace Joanne with a smirk of her own.

"I grew up with people much worse than you. If you think I'm a lamb that you can intimidate, think again. I don't care how old you are. If you dare try that stupid stunt again, I'll peel your flaky skin off you."

"What's going on?"

Evelyn heard Dan's voice, but she didn't turn around. She kept her eyes on the outrageous woman in front of her.

"Evelyn, are you all right?" Dan asked as he strode up to her.

"Yeah," she said. Her eyes flitted over to Dan, trying to judge if she would have to fight him, too.

She relaxed a little when he smiled at her. "I just came to realize that your sister is a monster because she was brought up

149

by one. How did you turn out so well?"

Mrs. Riley's jaw dropped, and she stared at Evelyn with disgust. "Are you going to let her speak about us that way?"

Dan merely shrugged.

That's a smart choice. There was no right answer in this situation. No matter what answer he gave, he wouldn't be able to appease both sides.

Taking her hand, Dan pulled her out of the office.

"Sorry about that, but you seem to have handled yourself pretty well," Dan said when they were out of earshot.

"Are we still going to meet your wood guy or are you throwing me out of your office?" Evelyn asked as she was dragged to the parking lot.

"Of course we're still meeting my wood guy. But if you are too distraught by what happened, I can take you home."

She pulled her hand from Dan, laughing at the thought that a pair of spoiled mother and daughter could scare her. She pointed to her own car. "I drove. I'll follow your car."

"That's just wasting gas. I'll drive you there. After that, we can have lunch, and I'll send you back here."

"Are you trying to spend more time with me?"

He blinked and laughed. "Is that all right?"

Evelyn shrugged half-heartedly. "Is it all right if I ask Kate to join us for lunch?"

"Sure."

She took out her phone and sent a text to Kate as she got into Dan's car. "Why are your parents so protective of Joanne? Did she almost die when she was a child?"

Her candor stunned Dan for a moment, but he recovered quickly and answered, "No. It took my parents a long time to have the both of us, and they'd always wanted a daughter."

Her head bobbed up and down as she came to an epiphany. "That's why they spoiled her. And since their attentions were focused on her, you grew up to be independent and successful while your sister lives off you like a parasite."

"I didn't know you were an expert on families."

"I'm not. I've just seen more than my fair share of

dysfunctional families."

Dan didn't say anything, but she knew the question he had in mind.

"I grew up in foster homes. It's all right to ask. If you haven't realized it, I'm pretty straightforward. I say things as they are; no drama, no secrets."

"What happened to your parents?"

"I don't know. I've never met my dad. And all I remember of my mother was her dropping me off at the hospital and never coming back."

"I'm sorry."

"Don't be," Evelyn said with a wry smile. "And don't look at me that way."

"What way?"

"The oh-poor-thing way. I survived it. I'm still in one piece, mentally and physically. And I must say I'm at a pretty good place in my life."

"How do you know Kate?"

"We met in college, but that's a long story. Speaking of Kate, I want you to know that even though I'm grateful you're introducing your wood guy to me, I'm still going to say this. If your sister does anything stupid to Kate, I'll kill her."

"It's difficult to believe you and Kate are friends."

"I know, she's like the complete opposite of me," she said with an indulgent smile.

When they finally got to the warehouse, Dan's wood guy had everything she needed. And thanks to Dan's good relationship with him, she would be able to get the wood before the day was over.

At lunch, Kate couldn't stop thanking Dan for his help and insisted on picking up the tab. When Dan went to get his car, Kate hung back and pulled Evelyn aside. She had to warn her friend.

"Eve, I know you like to have fun, but please don't get involved with Dan."

"I have no intention of doing so. But out of curiosity, why

not?"

"Because he's the nice, serious sort of guy. The type who's interested in relationships, something you avoid at all costs. I can tell he's fond of you, but unless you change your mind about relationships, please don't mess with him."

"I haven't changed my mind. Relationships are a hassle and are doomed to fail."

"Then don't—"

"Don't worry, I won't get involved with Dan. Things between you and Tyler are weird enough. There's no need to add Dan and me to the equation. And speaking of fondness, it was really sweet of Tyler to buy you that piano, huh." Evelyn hooked her arm around Kate's and pulled her closer.

"It isn't for me; it's for the mansion."

Evelyn rolled her eyes. "*Please.* It's for you. You do know you have to stay there for a year."

"I know." She knew what was at risk; there was no way she'd jeopardize Tyler's claim on the mansion. "We're just friends."

"Do you like him?" Evelyn's eyes slitted as she scrutinized Kate.

"What?"

"I can hear the disappointment in your voice."

"I don't know what you're talking about."

"We're just friends," Evelyn mimicked, then displayed a dramatic pout.

"Don't be ridiculous. I'm going back to the office. See you later," Kate said and got into her car.

She shook her head as she steered the car from the curb.

What was she thinking? She barely knew Tyler.

There was no reason for her to be disappointed or upset. She chose to move in knowing full well of the one-year time limit.

She shook the thoughts from her head and returned to the office. She had plenty to do.

Over the next few days, while Evelyn worked on replicating the desk that Laura and the team had damaged and thrown out, Kate removed the wrong pieces of furniture and replaced them with the right ones.

A few of her staff from Laura's team were helping her, but instead of serving as part of the solution, they were giving her more problems.

Perhaps it was the angst of having to work under the close scrutiny of their boss right after screwing up. She found herself having to repeat her instructions several times to get things done properly.

She was already exhausted from having to do all the brainwork. Their lack of ability to understand simple instructions quickly pushed her beyond her boiling point.

In the end, she banished all her staff from the Harpers' house, kicked off her heels, and moved the furniture on her own.

By the end of the week, Evelyn managed to recreate the desk, and the two of them personally installed it in the Harpers' house.

When they were done, Kate sat on the couch and took in the new look of the house. She wanted to make sure that everything was perfect for the Harpers; she wanted to close the project on a good note. After going through the house, checking everything over and over until she was satisfied, she declared the house done and ready for the Harpers.

The Harpers viewed the house the next day. Kate trailed behind them and watched the Harpers closely, observing their reactions.

Their pinched lips slowly eased into a small smile as they moved from room to room. When they saw the replica that Evelyn made, Mr. Harper broke into a grin while Mrs. Harper gasped.

Mrs. Harper couldn't believe the wonderful job Evelyn had done with the desk.

In the end, despite Kate's insistence on giving them the discount she'd promised, the Harpers paid her in full.

Kate was delighted, not with the check, but that the Harpers were willing to give them a chance to make things right.

That night when she got back to the mansion, even Marianne's food couldn't keep her awake. Skipping dinner, she took a shower and collapsed onto her bed.

Sometime in the middle of the night, the sudden blare from

Kate's phone jarred her from her sleep. She sat up, half-dazed and with a minor headache. She pressed her hands against her face and took a deep breath before reaching over to grab her phone.

The bright contrast between the light from her phone and the dark room made her cringe, and she had to force her eyes open to look at the number displayed on the screen.

But it only showed that it was a blocked number.

"Hello?" Kate said, her voice thick with drowsiness.

"Kate Mitchell? This is Officer William Hurst. We have a situation at your house."

"My house? Officer? What's going on?"

"Your alarm was set off a while ago. When we arrived, we found a rather drunk lady trying to smash up the alarm. She claims she's your sister, but she doesn't have any ID on her."

The word 'sister' instantly snapped her out of her torpor. She threw her head back as she realized she'd forgotten to inform Lydia about the alarm. "Did you say she was drunk?"

"Yes. I'm sorry, but we'll need you to come over now so that we can clear this up."

"I can log in to the video stream to check if it's her," she said.

"I'm sorry, ma'am, but she's rather drunk. I don't think it's wise to leave her sitting alone in her condition."

"I'm on my way." She ended the call and got out of bed. Putting on her sweater, she grabbed her handbag and left her room.

She stood outside her door and hesitated for a moment. She wasn't sure if she was allowed to leave the house in the middle of the night without Tyler. She had been reminding herself to find the time to read up on the fine print, but between the failed project and the screw-up by her staff, she simply hadn't had the time.

Unwilling to take any risks, she decided it was better to wake Tyler and ask him along. She walked down the hall to the door next to hers and knocked on it. "Tyler?"

"What's wrong?" he asked as he opened the door and pulled her into his room, keeping her a step behind him. "I didn't hear the alarm."

The urgency of getting back to her house faded, and she laughed at his reaction. "Nothing's wrong, not in this house anyway. No one broke in. But my sister tried to get into my house, tripped the alarm, then tried to smash it. The police are at my house."

Tyler relaxed his stance. He went back into the room and pulled on a T-shirt before grabbing his keys.

Outside the house, Tyler strode over to his car, but she grabbed his hand. "I got mine, I'll drive. Sorry to wake you up at three in the morning."

"It's fine, I'll drive," he said, jiggling the key in his hand. "You can get some rest in the car." Without waiting for her reply, he continued toward his car.

She shook her head but followed him anyway.

"So why did your sister try to smash the alarm?" Tyler asked as the car started winding down the road. "I'd have thought a future lawyer would behave better."

"The officer said she's drunk," Kate said. "She must've been frustrated with the dead ends she met in my parents' case."

"How do you know she met with dead ends?"

She gave him a wry smile. "Because I met with the same dead ends."

"Did you tell her that?"

"Nope. She wouldn't have believed a single word I said. She has to go out there and face the dead ends for herself before she'll believe it. She's that kind of person; she won't give up without a good fight."

"Good trait for a lawyer, I suppose."

"Not too good a trait for a sister."

When they got to Kate's house, a patrol car was parked right by her mailbox. Lydia was seated in the back seat, her head hung low, appearing to be sound asleep.

Kate hurried over and handed her ID over to the police officer who had stepped out.

The porch light was on, and the officer immediately smiled. "I'm sorry you have to go through the trouble, but we have to make sure."

"I understand."

The officer opened the door and helped Lydia to her feet before removing the cuffs. "Here, young lady, you're free to go."

Lydia stumbled forward, but Kate managed to catch Lydia in her arms.

She thanked and apologized to the officer, then struggled with keeping Lydia from smashing into the floor.

Tyler stepped forward and effortlessly lifted Lydia into his arms.

"Thanks," Kate murmured, grateful that she didn't have to balance her sister's weight while trying to get through the door.

"Just leave her on the couch," Kate said as she hurried up the stairs and brought a blanket down with her. She laid it over Lydia and turned to Tyler. "Do you want to stay here tonight? I have a guest room."

"Why not? I'm sure you don't want to leave your sister alone."

"Thanks." She led him up the stairs and to the guest room. "Sorry, I haven't been home all week. I'm sure it's a little dusty. I'll change the sheets and—"

Tyler grabbed her wrist as she reached to pull out the sheets. "It's fine, Kate. Don't worry about it. You should get some rest."

She glanced nervously around the room, feeling awful that she wasn't a better housekeeper. "I'm really sorry about everything. Waking you up in the middle of the night, then making you sleep on dusty sheets. Maybe we should just go back to the mansion." She tugged at her necklace. "I'm sure Lydia will be fine."

He took a step closer to her. "Thanks for putting my comfort over your concern for your sister, but I'm sure you won't be able to get any sleep with Lydia here and you back at the mansion. Waking up in the middle of the night is fine. The room and the sheets are fine. Now, go rest." His arm went around her waist, and he brought her to the door. "I'll be all right. Goodnight," he whispered as he leaned closer.

Her heart fluttered. His face was so close to hers that she thought he was going to kiss her.

She gazed up at him, caught up in the moment. It felt almost natural to tip her chin back to kiss him.

Stop it. What do you think you're doing? Right, what was she doing?

Throughout the week, whenever she had thought about Tyler, she would remind herself of what was at stake. The house meant a lot to Tyler. She couldn't let whatever was wrong with her mess things up.

They had to stay in the mansion for a year. The last thing they needed was to kiss, then be all awkward about it.

She took a step away from him. "Goodnight," she said and hurried back to her room.

She had set her alarm earlier than usual, hoping she would be up before Tyler. She knew he was an early riser, but she had no idea exactly what time he woke up.

Whenever she was up for breakfast at the mansion, he was already in the kitchen.

She stepped out of the shower, got ready, and went downstairs to put two aspirins and a glass of water next to her snoring sister. She wanted to get out of the house before Lydia woke.

Tyler opened his door just as she was returning to her room.

"I'm ready to go," she said. "Did you sleep well?"

Tyler nodded. "Marianne said she didn't know we weren't at the mansion, so she made breakfast for us. Are you hungry? If you are, we can just have breakfast nearby."

"No, I'm fine. Let's head back and have our breakfast."

"And Lydia?"

"She'll be all right here."

"No, I'm not. My head's killing me," Lydia said as she staggered up the stairs. "Thanks for the aspirin, but why weren't you home last night? And what's with the alarm?" Lydia asked as her fingers rubbed her temple.

Kate was hoping to avoid having this conversation in front of Tyler. She played with her locket nervously. "I ... um ... was staying at Tyler's." Taking a deep breath, she rushed out the rest of the words. "And I'll be staying there for the time being."

Lydia's hand dropped from her temple, and she stared at Kate with widened eyes. "You moved in with him?" Her finger moved from Kate to Tyler as she tried to grasp the new information.

"But you don't believe in moving in, that's what you told Benjamin. You said—"

"I know what I said, but this is different. I'll tell you about it another time," Kate said as she tried to make a hasty retreat. She grabbed Tyler's arm, dragging him down the stairs.

But Lydia stretched out her arm, stopping Kate. "No, no, no. You're not leaving here without giving me a proper answer."

Kate rolled her eyes. That was Lydia, she had to have every minor detail before letting things go.

"What did she say about moving in?" Tyler asked.

"She said she'll only move in with someone when she gets married." Lydia sat on a step of the stairs. "So why did you move in with him?"

Kate sighed. "I know I said that, and I still mean it." She pointed her finger at Lydia.

"Then why did you move in?" Lydia repeated, sweeping her finger away from her face. "Did you get married without telling me?"

"I'm not in court, Lydia. Don't use that tone with me," Kate said. "It's a long story. I wanted to tell you about it the last time we met, but things didn't really go as planned. I'll fill you in another time. We need to go back to the mansion now."

"So are you married?"

"No!"

She had to grin when Lydia recoiled from her answer.

"Mansion? As in where you're staying now? I'm coming with. Give me a minute, and don't you go speeding out of the house without waiting for me." Lydia waited for Kate to give her a nod before she brushed past the two of them. "Lend me your clothes."

On the way back to the mansion, Kate filled Lydia in with what was going on. Lydia listened and didn't seem surprised by Kate's decision.

"So you put in the alarm system in gratitude?"

"No," Kate answered for Tyler. "He just thought it'd keep the house safe. Stop speaking to him like he's a suspect."

"It must be tiring to stay with miss-take-care-of-everything."

Kate's jaw dropped, and she looked over her shoulder at Lydia. "Don't forget who's paying your tuition fees."

"She makes me happy," he said without taking his eyes off the road.

She made him happy?

He was simply trying to be nice; she was reading too much into it, she thought.

"I'm sorry that you feel that way about her, but she's welcome to stay as long as she wants," Tyler continued.

"Even after the year?" Lydia asked.

"Even after the year." This time, he turned to grin at Kate.

She gave him a small smile. She supposed she could be like one of the guys, turning up at the mansion all the time to enjoy Marianne's cooking.

"Are you guys dating?"

Shaking her head, Kate looked at Tyler. "Ignore her."

"Do you have a girlfriend?"

"No."

"Do you always give such short answers?"

"Yes."

"And sometimes, he doesn't even reply. You should be glad that he bothered to answer your nosy questions," Kate added—loudly—reminding Lydia of her hangover and saving Tyler from further mundane questions.

When they arrived at the house, Marianne broke into a smile as they entered the kitchen. "Oh, you two look so alike."

Lydia was momentarily stunned to see the crowd in the house.

"Sit," Marianne said.

"I'm sorry about how I reacted to the case, and I'm sorry about last night," Lydia whispered as she leaned toward Kate.

Kate wrapped her arm over Lydia's shoulders and gave her a squeeze. "It's all right."

"Anyway, I couldn't find anything. I tried to search for the detective in charge of the case, but he'd retired and disappeared into thin air. There was nothing left in the house either. Even the few neighbors whom I tracked down couldn't tell me anything."

"Who are you trying to track?" Ryan asked as he overheard

their conversation. "Sorry, I didn't mean to listen in. You're searching for a retired cop? I'm sure Ty can help with that."

Lydia looked at Tyler. "Really?"

Instead of replying Lydia, he turned to Kate.

"I've already asked. He said he'll look into it for us," Kate replied.

"Oh, Kate, thanks. I'm sorry for being so rude the last time," Lydia said as she threw her arms around her. "And Tyler, I like you. You have my blessings for Kate to stay here."

Ryan's brows flickered up, and he flashed Joseph a wide grin. "Since everyone is so happy, I've got a suggestion." Ryan turned to Kate. "Joseph, Dan, and I have decided that tonight will be our once-a-month-stay-over-night!"

Tyler stared at the trio as if they'd gone crazy. "The house guests don't get to decide when they want to stay."

"Oh, come on. Ryan and I finally have a day off tomorrow, so we can have a movie marathon tonight," Joseph said.

"Sounds fun. Am I allowed to join?" Kate asked.

"Definitely. Everyone will pick a movie, and we'll watch them all," Dan answered.

"Great. I'll buy popcorn," she said. "I haven't done this since high school—can't wait."

Ryan flashed a boyish grin at Tyler. "You in?"

Tyler took a deep breath and shook his head.

"You're joining us, right?" Kate asked as his eyes met hers.

He sighed. "You won't enjoy it, trust me."

"Oh, come on. I'm sure it'll be fun," Kate pleaded.

Tyler gave his aloof shrug while the trio exchanged an accomplished nod at each other before Ryan said, "No one is to reveal the movie they've chosen until tonight."

"Lydia, you're welcomed to join us if you want. You can pick a movie, too," Joseph added.

"I would love to, but I've got research to do and reports to write. You guys go ahead and enjoy yourselves."

"And Evelyn," Dan said. "She can join us if she wants."

"We had a busy week. I told her to have an early weekend and go enjoy herself. I'll ask, but I doubt she'll want to join us."

Chapter Thirteen

Kate sat, looking at the team of fidgety staff who were either casting glances at the door or staring intently at the floor.

Evelyn sat beside her, her irate glare doing nothing to calm the nervous staff.

Only Laura was missing from the team; Evelyn had fired Laura after informing Kate of the situation.

"If it were up to me, all of you would've packed up your stuff along with Laura," Evelyn said. "But your other boss wants to give you guys another chance. The rest of you will be demoted to probationary basis."

Nodding, Kate added, "You'll be on probation for the next six months. One more mistake and you're done here. All of you will be split into the remaining teams. You'll need to report every decision you make to your new team leaders. If any of you don't agree with how we're handling the situation, you're free to resign. Otherwise, let's put this behind us and get on with our work."

All of them mumbled some form of agreement and apology before heading out of her office and to their respective desks.

Once they were out, Kate leaned back against her chair. "Thanks, Eve, for coming in to do this with me. We're having a movie night back at the mansion. Do you want to join us?"

"Can't, sorry. I've got a date."

She shrugged it off. "I figured, but I told Dan that I'd ask."

"All right, then. I'm going off for my early weekend. Call me if you need anything," Evelyn said as she took her bag and

161

sauntered out of the office. "See you on Monday."

There was plenty of paperwork for Kate to settle, but she decided that she deserved an early day off, too. So, she got off work earlier and went out to buy a DVD before returning to the mansion.

That night after dinner, everyone gathered around the coffee table in front of the television.

"I brought *Resident Evil*, part one. Figured there's no point watching the later episodes if Kate hasn't watched the first one," Ryan said with a wide grin.

Dan laughed. "Great minds think alike. I brought *Dawn of the Dead*." The two gave each other high-fives while Joseph threw in his DVD with the other two. "*The Others*."

She hadn't watched any of those movies, but she knew what they were; movies she avoided at all costs—zombie and horror films.

Perfect.

She'd spent the whole afternoon thinking of a movie that everyone could enjoy. She was certain that none of the guys would want to watch a chick-flick, so she struck those out.

But the guys clearly didn't spare any thought for her.

She turned to Tyler while the guys were giving each other the approval of great movie choices. "He brought episode one of the zombie movie for me."

Tyler's lips curled.

"What movie did you bring? *Twilight*?" Ryan asked.

She cleared her throat. "I thought this was supposed to be a night of entertainment."

"Oh, come on. I bet you chose some romantic chick-flick," Dan replied.

"No, I didn't. I chose a comedy that I thought everyone could enjoy," she said and returned her gaze to Tyler. "What movie did *you* bring?" *It'd better not be part two of the zombie film.*

Tyler threw his DVD onto the table. *Pirates of the Caribbean.*

"See! That's a neutral film." She smiled at Tyler. "Thank you."

"So, what movie did you bring?" Joseph repeated Ryan's

earlier question.

"*Fun with Dick and Jane*," she said softly. What she'd thought would be a night of entertainment was going to become a night of horror. She probably wouldn't be able to get a good night's sleep for months, not with her mind filled with images of zombies and ghosts, and especially not when she was staying in a mansion surrounded by nothing but trees.

"You don't have to watch these. I can kick them out," Tyler said. "It's not eight yet."

The rest of the guys burst into a series of grunts and groans.

She wasn't the least bit interested in watching any of the movies that the three guys had chosen, but she couldn't ruin movie night for them. "You know what? I asked to be a part of this, so I'll watch whatever they chose. But just so you guys know, next month I'm bringing *The Notebook*."

Ryan hooked his arm over Kate's shoulders in a brotherly manner and gave her a tight squeeze. "That's the way. Let's begin."

"Go set it up." Tyler picked up a random DVD on the table and flung it toward Ryan, hitting him in the chest.

Ryan barely caught the DVD, but his smile only grew wider at Tyler's sudden interruption. Then, ignoring Tyler, Ryan lifted up the DVD. "The movie marathon shall begin with … *Dawn of the Dead*!"

She rolled her eyes.

Pulling her legs up on the couch, she sat cross-legged with a cushion on her lap.

She tried to enjoy the movie, but fifteen minutes into the show, she found herself struggling to keep her eyes open.

She crushed the cushion against her chest as the camera panned toward the door that was left ajar and zoomed in to reveal the silhouette of a young girl in a nightgown.

She had to turn away.

Her fingers covered her mouth, and she channeled all of her concentration onto a spot on the wall.

"Ooh," Ryan, Dan, and Joseph groaned in unison, and she knew someone must have died or someone's blood was spilled.

She drew a deep breath and forced herself to turn back to the television.

Her fingers moved to her necklace, and she pulled the locket to her lips, watching as the main character made a mad dash away from the zombie infestation.

A sudden warm touch on her arm made her jump at the same moment the guys erupted into another round of 'ooh' and 'aah.'

The touch became a gentle squeeze on her arm, keeping her from falling out of the couch.

"Are you all right?" Tyler asked. His brows furrowed, but the corners of his eyes were creased.

"Yeah," she said, smiling sheepishly.

"Stop watching it. You clearly hate it."

"It's all right; I'm just kind of gutless when it comes to this stuff. It's good training, I guess." She forced a smile and turned her face back to the screen.

She tried, she really did try to maintain her position and dignity, but the constant fear that something would jump in front of the camera was too strong for her to handle.

The anticipation, the wait, and the uncertainty were causing her more distress than the zombies themselves.

Their gruesome looks and choice of diet didn't sit particularly well with her stomach, but the anticipation was worse.

She endured for as long as she could until goose bumps covered both her arms. She closed her eyes and leaned on Tyler's shoulder while her fingers dug into the sleeve of his shirt. "Let me know when the zombies are no longer around."

"Kate," Tyler whispered.

"No, I want to watch. I want to know what happens to them in the end."

She continued watching the movie behind the filter of Tyler's sleeve. Despite the few thousand times her eyes squeezed shut out of fear, she managed to pry them open.

When the black screen came on and the credits started rolling, she gasped with disbelief. "Seriously? What kind of stupid ending is this?"

"Kate, it's just a movie," Joseph said, slightly amused at her reaction.

Leaning back onto Tyler's shoulder, she continued. "Yeah, but those poor people in the movie. It's so unfair. This is a stupid movie."

She knew it was just a movie. She knew no one actually got hurt. Still, it was a horrible ending. She hated stories with horrible endings.

"This is it. Movie night is over. Get out." Tyler stated, rubbing his hand down her back.

"Oh, come on!" Ryan protested and nudged her.

She scowled at him, but he nudged her again.

"I'm fine. Let them watch the rest of the movies," she said after narrowing her eyes at Ryan.

"Fine. But you're not watching another movie." With his arm still over her back, Tyler pulled her from the couch and led her up the stairs.

She sighed as she followed him. "You knew this would happen."

He laughed and pulled her closer, holding her tight. "I've known them for a long time."

"I should've listened to you," she said. "Do they always bring such movies?"

"Yeah."

"And you always join them?"

He nodded.

"Why?"

"I have nothing to do anyway."

"You watch all those horror movies and you still find the trees around your house peaceful?"

He shook his head and laughed. "Unlike you, I can differentiate between reality and fiction."

"Really? After watching that movie, you don't look outside." Her gaze followed her finger as she pointed to the long window. "And—"

"I think we should change the topic before you decide to move out tonight."

She sighed again. He was right, she needed to occupy her

mind with something else. "Can we watch the movies we chose? I don't think I can sleep now."

Grinning, he agreed. "Come downstairs with me. Let them know you're all right."

She was sure the guys couldn't be bothered about her. They were just glad they could continue watching the movies they'd brought.

Tyler probably knew that as well. He simply didn't want to leave her alone, and she must admit she was immensely grateful.

As they plodded down the stairs, Tyler paused for a moment. "Keep your eyes from the TV."

Only after she nodded did he take her hand and walk over to pick up the DVDs they had brought.

"Are you all right, Kate?" Dan asked. "We have a doctor in the house."

Tyler shot all of them a glare. "I'll bring these back down when we're done."

"Keep them; I brought the entire set of *Resident Evil*. I thought if we had time, we could watch it all. We'll definitely have time now." Ryan grinned brightly. "The two of you can enjoy your movies."

An entire set? Something was severely wrong with them.

As they went upstairs, Tyler noticed that Kate still had a faraway look in her eyes. "You're not still thinking about the movie, are you?"

Kate ran her fingers through her hair while her face displayed a mixture of chagrin and embarrassment. "I know it's absurd. But when I watch something, whatever the show is, I need to know the ending. I need to know that everything worked out fine in the end."

"And you love crime shows?"

"Those that I watch or read always catch the bad guys."

"So if the group of people had survived and lived happily ever after, you'd be completely fine."

She pursed her lips. "Not completely, but I'd definitely feel better." Chuckling, she continued. "I remember watching this horror movie when I was young. I don't even remember what the title or the story was. My parents were afraid that I'd get nightmares and told me not to watch it. But I'd already started, and I wanted to know the ending. So I watched, then I didn't dare to go to bed. In the end, I had to sleep with my parents for an entire week before getting over it."

"And you didn't learn your lesson."

"Nope. But *The Ring* really got to me, and that was when I swore off horror films."

"Then why did you insist on watching the movie just now? You knew the bad reaction you'd get."

"I know," Kate said, exasperated with herself. "I thought I would've outgrown the fear. I'm not a kid anymore. I'm twenty-five, Ty. It's kind of pathetic that I react this way to a movie."

He tried to conceal his grin, but Kate saw right through him.

"I know, it's stupid."

"*Pirates of the Caribbean* doesn't have too good an ending either —that's if I remembered it correctly."

She nodded. "I do like happy endings, but this is way better than the movies they brought."

"You need to know that everyone is well and fine."

"Not everyone. It's just that through a book or a movie, you grow to like certain characters. And when the ending sucks, it's just wrong."

"We'll watch your movie, then. It's a good ending, right?"

She smiled.

Of course it was. She wouldn't choose something that didn't have a good ending. He grabbed the DVD and set up the player, smiling to himself as he thought about what she'd said.

She wasn't just used to taking care of herself; she was used to taking care of everyone, making sure that things went well for everyone around her.

It was the same thing with Ryan and Joanne.

When Ryan didn't have a ride home, Kate had offered to drive. When Joanne was trying to get his attention but got ignored, Kate couldn't bear to let it continue, so she stepped in to help.

She was the complete opposite of him.

"Do you think we can steal some popcorn from them?" she suddenly asked.

"I'll get it." He stood, then stopped and asked, "Do you want to come along?"

She went down the stairs with him, but didn't follow him over to the couch. He figured she probably didn't want to risk putting more gory images into her mind.

He strolled over, pulled the bucket of popcorn out of Ryan's hand, and headed back toward Kate.

"Hey!" Ryan hollered after Tyler, but he didn't bother to glance back over at him. "Can you guys eat that much? Share some with us."

Kate laughed at the dismay on Ryan's face. "Food is everything to him, isn't it?"

Tyler grinned at her observation.

"It's all right, we can share. He was kind enough to rent episode one of the zombie films just to make sure that I didn't miss out on anything," she said, then rolled her eyes.

"That's right," Ryan shouted. "I love you, Kate."

Joseph elbowed Ryan, shutting him up immediately.

"In a friend or brotherly kind of way," he quickly added, then flashed Tyler an apologetic smile.

That brought more laughs from Kate. "The things he'd say for food." Taking the bucket from Tyler's hand, she pulled him into the kitchen. "Since he loves me, I guess we have no choice but to share."

He knew Ryan was just being Ryan, but he'd never felt more inadequate as he did then. He found himself loathing his aloof personality and suddenly found himself jealous of Ryan's cheerful disposition.

"What's wrong?" Kate asked, breaking his thoughts.

He gave her a small smile and shook his head.

"I thought I was the one in the bad mood," she said.

"Ryan made you happier."

A corner of her lips turned up. "It's always nice to be loved, I guess." She paused, tilting her head to the side, scrutinizing him.

"You protected me. If you hadn't dragged me away, I probably would've watched the next zombie movie, and I probably would've lost my mind before the night was over."

He said nothing as she moved away to take a bowl, pouring some of the popcorn into it.

With her back to him, she continued. "I like you the way you are. Ryan is ... Ryan," she said with an indifferent shrug as she turned around and leaned against the counter. "You guys are very different, but I like you just the way you are." She smiled and strolled out of the kitchen. "I'll bring our portion upstairs. You can return the bucket to Ryan."

He grabbed the bucket and walked out alongside Kate. He'd never thought himself capricious, but by the time he got back to Ryan, he was all smiles. "Your popcorn."

His smile, so genuine, seemed to worry Ryan.

"Did he add something to my popcorn?" Ryan shouted over to Kate.

Kate looked at Tyler, then shrugged.

"You won't do that," Ryan said and watched their reactions, but they simply ignored him and went up the stairs.

"Do you think he'll still eat the popcorn?"

"He will," Tyler said and pressed the play button on the remote.

He and Kate watched the two movies they brought. Halfway through the second movie, he felt her head against his shoulder.

He turned and smiled as he saw her sleeping soundly.

He continued watching the movie, keeping as still as he could so he didn't wake her. He only lifted her from his shoulder when the credits began rolling. He laid her down on the couch and pulled off her glasses as gently as he could.

Pushing aside the hair that had fallen over her face, he couldn't resist running his finger down the side of her face.

He smiled, then headed into her room to get her a pillow and blanket.

When he got back, he slipped his hand under her neck and slotted the pillow in, smiling as he accomplished his task without rousing Kate from her sleep. After draping the blanket over her, he sat on the floor and leaned back on the couch with his iPad in hand.

He was midway through the new crime novel he was reading when Kate moaned.

"No …"

He turned back to her just as she flinched.

The peaceful expression on her face had been replaced by a frown, and her head pressed against the pillow as if she were bracing for something painful to happen.

Whatever she was dreaming of definitely wasn't pleasant.

"Kate." The moment he touched her, she screamed and shot upright, flinging her hands about.

He leaned back, avoiding her swinging arms, then held her hands firmly in his. "It's me," he said.

Her hands relaxed within his.

He let go of her hands, got up beside her, and wrapped his arm around her, running his hand up and down her arm. "It's all right; it was just a nightmare."

Kate pressed her face into her hands.

"Is everything all right?" Joseph said as the three guys sprinted up the stairs. They all skidded to a stop when they saw his arm around Kate.

He shot them a glare, irate with them for bringing the horror films. In his arms, Kate had stopped screaming, but he could still feel her shaking.

"Sorry," Ryan mumbled, and they quickly retreated down the stairs.

"Are you all right?" Tyler asked softly while Kate appeared to be in a daze. He wasn't sure if she was fully awake.

"Yeah," she said after a moment. "Oh my God, was I screaming? Did I wake you?"

"Yes, you were, but you didn't wake me." He had thought it was better for him to stay near her, just in case she had a nightmare, but he didn't think she would have such a bad reaction. "Feeling better?"

He waited, but there wasn't any reaction from Kate.

"It's all right. It was just a nightmare."

"I know, but I couldn't get out of it. I couldn't find a way out."

"It's over now," he said as he let go of her. If he could, he would keep holding her, but he didn't want her to feel uncomfortable. "Go back to sleep. I'll be right here."

She glanced around, then down at the pillow and blanket. "Thanks," she said as she tugged at the blanket.

"If it isn't too uncomfortable, then sleep here tonight. I'll be here if you have a nightmare."

She lay back onto the pillow. "You're going to stay here with me for the whole night?"

Brushing aside her bangs that had partially hidden her face, he assured her, "Yes, go back to sleep."

But she didn't. Instead, she pushed the blanket aside and sat up. "I can't let you stay up the whole night just to accompany me."

"I'm not tired anyway."

She shook her head. "Then let's do something together."

"Like?"

She hesitated for a moment. "I want to show you something, but I'm afraid that you'll get upset."

"What is it?"

She got up and went into his grandfather's study, returning with a thick photo album. Tyler narrowed his eyes at the thick album. He wasn't sure what was in it.

Gingerly, Kate sat and opened the album, showing him pages that had yellowed along the edges. "This is the cabin you were telling me about, right?" she asked, pointing to a picture of young Tyler, who was smiling so brightly that all his teeth were showing. "And that'd be you."

He eyed the picture and smiled at the younger him who was beaming so elatedly.

"You were so cute then." She looked up at him and pretended to scrutinize him. "You're not too bad now either," she said and laughed softly.

"Good enough for you?"

"Oh, Ty, no one is ever good enough for me." Then she laughed. "I'm kidding."

"It's all right. I agree."

Shaking her head, she turned back to the album. "Tell me more about the cabin." Flipping the pages, she stopped at one with Tyler on a pony. "Look at you on the pony."

Pointing to another picture, he laughed. "That's the boat I built with my dad."

"Will it fit both of us?"

"If it doesn't, I'll build another."

"Build another? You had your dad the other time. You probably just knocked in a couple of nails or sanded off the surfaces. I don't think I'll dare step into a boat you build on your own," she said.

"You'll step in even if you see it filling with water, just to make sure that you don't hurt anyone's feelings."

"No, I won't. I'll stand there and criticize how awful the workmanship is and put the person down until there isn't a shred of dignity left," she countered.

"Why are we talking about Evelyn?"

She burst into laughter, but playfully smacked him on the arm. "Don't make fun of my friend."

That night, they talked about the photos, about all the things he used to do at the cabin. He made plans for their time there, and they joked and teased each other along the way.

They hadn't even realized that the sun was up and that the guys below had fallen silent until Marianne came walking up the stairs. "I was wondering where the two of you went. There are three huge guys snoring downstairs, but the two of you were missing. I thought you guys went out in the middle of the night again."

Their heads snapped up, but neither moved away from each other.

"We were just talking about the cabin," Kate said and stretched her back. She took the glasses that Tyler had removed from her and got up. "I think it's time for bed."

"Eat something first. You've been up the entire night; I'm sure you must be starving."

Kate stood where she was, seemingly trying to weigh which

was more important. "I am, and I doubt I can sleep with my stomach screaming for food."

"Good." Looking at Tyler, Marianne continued. "I suppose you'll be coming with us?"

He stood without answering Marianne's question. Putting the photo album down, he headed down the stairs with Kate and Marianne.

"How was the movie marathon?" Marianne asked, looking over her shoulder at Kate.

He smirked while Kate shook her head. "It was a disaster. I think I'll be having nightmares for the next month."

"They brought horror movies," he explained.

"They brought horror movies?" Marianne gasped in disgust. "I thought the boys would know better. I'll give them a piece of my mind later."

Kate chuckled. "Don't, it's fine. I ended up having a good time anyway."

"Really?" Marianne turned to Tyler, giving him a coy smile. "Did you enjoy yourself, Ty?"

A corner of his lips sneaked up.

"Good, good," Marianne mumbled and gestured for them to go on into the kitchen while she woke the guys.

During breakfast, Marianne chided all the guys for being insensitive to Kate. The guys smiled and apologized, appearing genuinely sorry.

"We didn't mean for you to get nightmares from the movie."

That was when Kate finally realized what happened. "You guys heard me scream."

"And saw Ty hugging you," Ryan added as he swallowed his bacon.

Kate froze for a moment, her hands unconsciously moving toward her necklace as she struggled to find a response.

"You can just ignore them. I do," Tyler suggested when he saw her twirling her locket. "If you haven't noticed, Ryan tends to say whatever is on his mind without thinking."

Kate smiled gratefully for Tyler's rescue and did what he suggested.

"So, are you going to keep running into Tyler's arms each time you get scared?" Ryan continued after a moment.

"I didn't run into his arms," Kate said, narrowing her eyes at Ryan.

Ryan nodded. "So, Ty, are you going to keep hugging Kate each time she gets frightened?"

He had no intention of entertaining Ryan.

"Of course not," Kate answered.

"Really?" Without any warning, Ryan shouted in her face and pretended to lunge toward her.

She screamed and leaned into Tyler while he instinctively wrapped his arm around her.

"I guess you're wrong," Ryan said jokingly, and the rest of the guys burst out laughing at them.

Tyler was used to Ryan's antics, but he didn't appreciate Ryan treating Kate that way. He shook his head and was about to tell Ryan off when Kate lifted herself slightly off Tyler's chest and gave him a mischievous smile.

He frowned, not understanding Kate's reaction.

She leaned back into his arms and started making sniffing noises while her hands curled against his shirt.

Everyone froze and stared at Ryan.

"Crap. Kate ... I'm sorry, I was just joking ..." Ryan stammered.

She continued hiding in his chest for a couple more seconds while Ryan panicked.

Tyler finally understood what she was doing and laughed as Kate straightened herself and smiled at Ryan.

"Whoa, good one, Kate!" Dan said.

"That isn't fair," Ryan contested.

"Too bad. You started it." Kate turned back to Tyler and smoothed down the creases in his shirt. "Sorry about that."

"I was still right anyway," Ryan said.

Marianne knocked Ryan on the head. "If you intend to continue eating here, I suggest you shut up."

Everyone laughed while Ryan raised both his arms by his chest.

Having filled their empty stomachs, they went off to their respective rooms to get some sleep.

Tyler stopped outside Kate's room, leaned against the door, and asked, "Will you be all right?"

"It's broad daylight. I doubt I'll be haunted by nightmares. But if I do, I won't hesitate to wake you."

His smile grew into a wide grin. "Make sure you do that."

Chapter Fourteen

Conversations crisscrossed the table as Kate took a mouthful of mozzarella cheese salad and nodded at something Ryan had said.

She tried to pay attention to the conversations, but she was exhausted.

With one less team to work with, the projects that were handled by the original team ended up on her desk.

She hadn't worked this hard since she and Evelyn started out their company.

But no matter how busy she was at work, she always made it back home for dinner. That was the only part of the day she looked forward to.

Marianne's cooking was fantastic, but food wasn't the lure that made her pack up her work and leave her office on time.

Dinner was the only time she could talk to Tyler. And if she got home in time, she could sometimes spend an hour playing the piano with him.

Otherwise, they would drink their coffee and chat about work, or she would take out another photo album and make Tyler tell her the stories behind the photos.

She'd heard many of the stories before, but she loved seeing Tyler's smile whenever he spoke of them.

At times when he couldn't recall what happened, she would tell him what the late Mr. Hayes had told her instead.

The only downside to the conversations they had was Tyler's habit of making plans for them to head down to wherever the picture was taken.

She'd love to go to all those places with him. She'd love to see and do everything he said they could, but all they had was a year.

It started out exciting when he began planning their trip to the cabin. But as more places sprang up, the plans became reminders of how short a time she had with him.

There was no way they could do all the activities he'd planned in one year.

They would probably still be friends. They might still see each other once in a while, holidays perhaps. But things wouldn't be the same.

"Tired?"

She woke from her daze and turned to Tyler. "Yeah, I had to run around quite a bit today."

"Things will get better once the probation is over," he said with an encouraging smile.

She nodded.

"Tell you what. If you want, we'll make the trip to the cabin after the probation is over. I'll arrange everything."

There really wasn't a need for six whole months of probation, was there? She was sure the team had learned their lessons.

"If you want to go, that is."

"I'd love that."

"Great," he said with a grin. "And are you free this Friday night? It's the company's annual dinner, and I'm afraid that it may drag beyond midnight."

"I didn't think you'd bother to show up for these events."

"I have to show my face."

Chuckling, she nodded. "Yeah, I can go with you. Is it formal?"

"Is that all right?"

"Are you going to change the dress code for me if I say no?" she asked with a teasing grin.

"If that's what you want."

"And I bet you know that I won't. Anyway, Eve's been pestering me to go shopping with her; I can get a dress then."

She finished up her dinner, and for the first time since she'd been back from North Dakota with Tyler, she went straight to her room.

She wanted to spend some time with Tyler, but she couldn't keep her eyes open. Besides, shopping trips with Evelyn were always arduous events; she needed to recharge and prepare herself for it.

The next day, as she'd suspected, Evelyn was ecstatic that she wanted to go shopping.

They went from shop to shop, but even after Evelyn was carrying bags of new haul in both hands, Kate couldn't find any dress she truly liked.

Those that Evelyn chose were too revealing for her taste, and she couldn't find one that would make her look presentable enough for the dinner.

Stepping out of what was probably the fifteenth changing room, Kate brushed down the midnight-blue dress she had on and tilted to an angle to see how she looked in the mirror.

"You look great in the dress, and I'm not saying it because I'm getting tired. I'll tell you if they sucked, but you look great in so many of them," Evelyn said.

"I don't know …"

"Why are you so nervous about the dinner?"

"I'm not nervous. I just want to be presentable."

"You look more than presentable. You're slim and tall; you look nice wearing anything."

Awkwardly, Kate pulled on the satin material around her chest. "It's sort of revealing."

"No, it's not. The back isn't cut that low, and it's not showing enough cleavage."

"We can make some alterations for you and pull the material closer around your chest," a sales assistant said from behind her.

"That would be great," she said before Evelyn could send the sales assistant away.

Evelyn watched her through the mirror as the sales assistant pulled the satin closer around her chest and pinned it up. "Are you guys getting serious? You've been spending a lot of time together."

Kate kept her eyes on the mirror, pretending to concentrate on what the sales assistant was doing, and avoided Evelyn's watchful eyes.

"I've been bugging you to come shopping with me, but you kept insisting on going back for dinner. Now you're getting yourself all flustered over a dinner."

"It's a company dinner. I don't want to disgrace him."

"He likes you. He treats you differently," Evelyn said as if she had known Tyler for years. "Dan says he's never seen him so happy. He says that Tyler speaks to you more in a week than to all of them combined throughout the years."

"You met Dan again?" she asked, surprised that Evelyn hadn't mentioned it to her.

"He asked me out for dinner, and I said yes." Evelyn shrugged and waved it off. "It's nothing."

When she changed out of the dress, the sales assistant took it to make the alterations that Kate wanted.

She moved to sit beside Evelyn. "He keeps making plans for us. I can't help but feel that once the year is up, once we go back to our individual lives, all the plans will fall to nothing."

"And you're afraid that they will?"

"No. I don't know."

"Oh, Kate. If you were in any other situation, I'd tell you to go ahead and have fun. But you guys are stuck together for a year. If things don't go well—"

"There's nothing between us, and there will be nothing between us. The house is way too important to him. I'm not going to mess it up." She wasn't interested in continuing the conversation, so she stood and went over to the counter to pay for her dress.

On Friday, Kate stood in the altered dress and sighed.

She hadn't brought any of her accessories over to the mansion. Even if she did, nothing would match this dress. She hadn't been to many formal events and never had the need or desire for clunky jewelry.

She couldn't believe she had been so muddleheaded.

She'd taken half a day off work to get her nails and hair done. Her nails glimmered with classy French manicure while her hair was tied up in a loose bun.

Without her hair over her shoulders, even with her mother's locket, her neck seemed bare.

It was too late for her to go out in search of something that would match her dress. This was the best she could do.

Taking a deep breath, she stepped out of the room to find Tyler leaning against the wall by her door.

He was wearing a black suit with a white shirt under the jacket. He had left the top two buttons of his shirt unbuttoned, and the edge of the sleeve peeked out from his jacket at his wrists.

His suits were clearly tailor-made, but his structure, the broad shoulders, the lean, muscular chest, and the lanky legs combined to make that simple ensemble perfect.

"Sorry to keep you waiting," she said. Her fingers reached over and fiddled with her locket.

"It's fine …" His words trailed off as he took in the sight of her in a long satin dress.

"Do I look all right?" she asked as she saw Tyler giving her a scan.

"More than all right."

She sighed, relieved. "Good. I don't want to embarrass you." Then she noticed the black, squarish box he was holding. "What's that?"

He followed her gaze to the box in his hand. "Oh, right. I wanted you to have this," he said as he handed her the box.

"What is it?"

"Open it."

She did as she was told and gasped when she saw the diamond necklace, earrings, and bracelet. "You didn't buy this, did you? I can't accept this. It's too expensive."

"I didn't spend a cent. It was my mother's. I remembered she had it, and Marianne said most of her stuff was in the attic, so I just dug it out."

"Your mother's? Then all the more I can't accept this," she

said and remembered what was in the attic. "You went up to the attic?"

She never thought he would venture into the attic. Since they moved into the house, not once had he peeked into his parents' room or taken a step up the stairs to his old bedroom.

"I went up there for this." He pointed at the box, redirecting her attention back to it.

"It's beautiful, and I appreciate the thought, but I can't take your mother's jewelry."

Tyler took the box from her. With his hand on her arm, he guided her back into her room. Setting the box on the table, he took the necklace and leaned in, hooking it in place behind her neck before removing her locket. "Then just wear it tonight. It isn't doing any good collecting dust in the attic anyway."

She didn't hear a single word he'd said.

As he spoke, she angled her face toward him, closed her eyes, and took in his fresh, manly aftershave.

It was times like these, when it was just the two of them, when he spoke in his serious but gentle voice, that she couldn't stop her heart from racing and herself from wishing that he would kiss her.

She opened her eyes as he straightened, his cheek nearly grazing hers. His gaze paused on hers for a moment—just a moment—and she forgot how to breathe.

He turned from her, seemingly unaware of the reaction he had caused, seemingly unaffected. He laid the locket gently by the box and reached for the bracelet.

Lifting her hand, Tyler clasped the bracelet around her wrist.

She stared at the hand holding hers. His hand was so warm.

"I'm sure my mother would love for you to wear it. They look great on you."

She finally took her eyes off Tyler and turned to the mirror.

The necklace, though diamond-studded, wasn't clunky in any way. It draped beautifully around her neck and down to the opening of her dress.

As Tyler reached for the earrings, she took them before he did and put them on.

The close proximity and his warm touch were making her heart flutter, putting the attic completely out of her mind.

"Just tonight, then."

He grinned, took her hand, and walked down the stairs with her.

"You found them!" Marianne exclaimed when she saw the jewelry on Kate. "They look wonderful on you, dear."

She blushed. "Thank you. Do I look okay?"

"Of course you do. You'll make Tyler the envy of everyone at the dinner."

Laughing, she shook her head. "I wasn't aiming for that. I just hope I look decent."

"I told you, you look better than that," Tyler said.

Throughout the whole drive toward Tyler's office, she couldn't stop fidgeting. She kept reaching for her locket, only to realize she wasn't wearing it.

"Stop worrying."

"I'm not worried. Maybe a little nervous."

"Why?"

"I don't go to events like this. I don't know if I'm dressed right; I don't know how to behave right."

"You look beautiful," he said, looking into her eyes. "I'll be right beside you the whole night."

She smiled and nodded.

He always made sure she was well taken care of. Fixing up the security system, riding with her at the ranch in North Dakota, taking her away from movies that she shouldn't have been watching in the first place. There was nothing for her to be nervous about.

Her nerves eased, only to return in double the potency when they stepped into the ballroom.

The moment she and Tyler entered, all eyes turned to them.

She froze, clutched Tyler's arm, and inched closer to him.

"They're just surprised that I came with someone," he said.

"You've never brought anyone to your company dinner?"

Tyler shook his head.

She scanned the room and all the unfamiliar faces who were

blatantly staring at her. Tyler led her into the room, ignoring all the eyes focused on them.

She didn't know how he did that. Was he so used to people staring at him that he no longer cared?

All the attention was making her regret her decision. She didn't belong at events like this.

When her eyes finally registered a familiar face, her eyes lit up and she smiled warmly. "Mr. Russell."

Tyler stopped as Tim Russell hurried over with a woman by his side.

"Miss Mitchell, nice to see you again. You look amazing." Tim smiled politely.

"Thank you, and you can call me Kate."

Tim nodded and introduced the lady next to him. "This is my wife, Adrianna. She works for the company, too."

"Hi, Adrianna. You look beautiful." She turned to look at Tyler, but he continued his silence and merely nodded in acknowledgment of Adrianna. "And this is Mr. Hayes. He works here, too. I've no idea why he brought me here only to keep quiet," she said, a less than subtle hint to Tyler that he wasn't being sociable.

Adrianna and Tim laughed nervously.

"I brought you here so that you can answer questions for me, which you so commonly do," Tyler replied with a grin.

She narrowed her eyes while Tim and Adrianna laughed, less nervous this time.

"Will we be sitting together? It'll be nice to know someone at the table," she said.

"Yes, I made arrangements for them to be seated at the same table," Tyler answered as he stepped away from Tim and Adrianna, continuing toward their table.

She said her temporary goodbyes hastily as she got dragged along.

"That was mighty rude of you," she said to Tyler once they were out of earshot.

"What was?" Tyler asked, appearing to be completely clueless.

"We should've chatted with them, asked them how they were

and so forth."

"We're already seeing them at the table later," he replied matter-of-factly, as though that explained his actions.

She shook her head but let the matter drop. Settling onto the chair that Tyler had pulled out for her, she continued. "Aren't you going to walk around the room and talk to some of your staff?"

"I never do that."

"Really? So what do you normally do at such dinners?" she asked as she leaned her chin against her hand.

"I show up."

She couldn't help chuckling at his answer. "That's it? So you brought me here to *show up* with you?"

The smile on Tyler's face faded. "I'm sorry if you're bored. I'm not used to … I don't usually—"

She laid her hand on his arm, stopping him. "I didn't mean to make you feel bad. I was joking. I don't mind being here with you. It's all right with me if you're the only one I speak to for the rest of the night."

His grin returned. "Thank you."

"For what?"

"For being you." Tyler leaned in, closing the distance between them.

Again, her heart pounded. She couldn't move.

She probably could if she wanted to, but she didn't want to.

She closed her eyes as he neared, feeling the warmth of his breath on her lips. But before his lips touched hers, a loud clearing of throat rang through the speakers.

They woke from their trance and moved apart as all the staff members took their seats.

She turned her head away from Tyler and took a deep breath before looking back at him and smiling as though nothing had happened.

She needed to stop wishing he would kiss her.

All around, everyone continued to look at her with what seemed to be part curiosity and part surprise.

Ignoring all the stares, she smiled warmly at Adrianna, who

was seated right next to her. But Adrianna seemed fixated on getting the cutlery at the right angle, tweaking the utensils to the left and right, then up and down.

"Are you all right?" Kate asked softly so she wouldn't bring any more attention to herself.

Adrianna gave a nervous grin and sighed softly. "Yeah, it's just that everyone seated at this table belongs to the higher management. I feel a little out of place here."

"You mean you don't usually sit at this table?"

Adrianna's hesitation answered her question.

"I'm so sorry ..." Kate let her words trail off as she turned to Tyler. "Ty, you made Adrianna and Mr. Russell sit at this table just to make me feel comfortable?"

"I thought you'd prefer a familiar face," he said slowly, seemingly aware that she wasn't pleased with his decision.

"You made them sit with people they don't know; it isn't fair to them. They won't be able to enjoy their dinner."

"I'm sorry to interrupt, but it's all right. We're fine. Please don't get upset because of me," Adrianna said.

"I'm not upset. I just feel awful that you're made to sit here because of me," she replied and shot Tyler a glare.

"If you want to change your seats, go ahead."

Pursing her lips, Kate turned back to Adrianna. "He meant: he's sorry, too, and thank you for keeping Kate company."

Adrianna laughed. "You're welcome."

Tyler shrugged as he usually did.

"And thank you, Ty. I know you're trying to make sure that I don't feel out of place, but please don't do that again. As I said, I can just talk to you."

As the night progressed, she divided her attention between Tyler and the Russells. Adrianna had lots of questions for her, and she answered every single one of them.

When another wave of cold air washed across them, she rubbed her palm against her arm as a chill ran through her.

A shawl. She knew she'd forgotten to bring something.

She was sighing at her own absent-mindedness when she felt a warm coat placed over her shoulders. She smiled at Tyler and pulled his coat closer. Thanks, she mouthed.

"So where did the two of you meet?" Adrianna asked.

She saw Mr. Russell glare at his wife, but she smiled and told him that it was all right. "We met at a funeral."

"Oh ..." was Adrianna's reply, then she quickly proceeded to the next question. "How long have you been together?"

"We ... I ..." Kate stammered as she tried to structure a proper sentence.

"A while," Tyler interjected. His lips curled as she turned to him. "It's the easiest reply," he whispered into her ears.

She had to agree. It would be too long and too strange a story to tell Adrianna about the will and all, so she smiled politely and nodded.

Tyler listened in while Kate chatted with Adrianna and Tim and answered all the questions that Adrianna had about her.

He wasn't paying full attention to the conversation. His mind was still thinking about the almost-kiss he'd had with Kate.

She hadn't moved away when he'd leaned in, but her reaction after that was baffling. She appeared embarrassed, then pretended as though the moment never occurred.

Maybe he was being impetuous.

He sighed softly, putting the thought out of his mind.

Once dinner was over, everyone moved around, taking part in the various lucky draws and competitions.

He and Kate were the only ones who remained seated at the table.

No one was around them, but he could feel the stares and almost hear the gossip going around.

He knew the ongoing conversations in the room revolved around them.

Kate must have felt it, too. She reached for her necklace again, only to release it immediately.

"Are the stares making you uncomfortable? We can leave." He shouldn't have lied to her and asked her to come along.

He'd never stayed longer than an hour at the dinner. There was no way it would've dragged over the midnight rule. But since the trip to North Dakota, he'd missed spending time with her away from their usual gang, and the dinner was a perfect excuse and chance to do so.

"It feels a little awkward." She gave him a small smile. "But I'm good."

Just as she finished her sentence, he noticed the familiar face moving toward their table. He bent close to Kate and said, "Give me a minute. I'll be right back." But as he stood, he hesitated. "Will you be all right alone? Should I get Adrianna to accompany you?"

"I don't need a babysitter," she assured him. "Go."

He headed over and took the piece of paper that his employee was holding. "This is the current address?"

His employee nodded.

"Thanks," he said and returned to Kate. He'd barely left her for a minute and already she was surrounded by a group of women. But the moment he neared their table, the women dispersed.

"How do you work with them when they're all so frightened of you?" Kate asked.

"I work better alone."

She nodded and changed the topic as the man he'd spoken to walked by. "Is everything all right?"

He pulled his hand out from the pocket, leaving the piece of paper inside, while he considered his reply.

"You don't have to tell me if you don't want to. I shouldn't be so nosy."

He ran his finger along her jaw as he gazed into her eyes. "I don't mind you asking. I'm just worried that my answer may upset you."

Her brows furrowed. "What is it?"

"The favor you asked. Do you still want your answer?"

Understanding flooded her face. "You found the retired detective?"

"Do you still want to find him?"

She thought about it for a moment before nodding. "Yes."

Tyler sat, looking into her eyes. "Then I want a promise in

return. Unless you make me this promise, I won't give you the address."

"I promise, whatever it is," she replied without any hesitation.

"You haven't even heard what I want."

Pulling the coat closer around her, she shrugged. "It'll be something that will keep me safe."

He grinned; pleased with the confidence she had in him. "When you go look for him, you have to take me along."

"I probably would've asked you anyway."

"Good."

Reaching into his pocket, he took out the piece of paper with a name and address written on it. He slid it across the table to Kate. Instead of picking it up, she slipped it into her purse without even looking at it.

"I'll look at it tomorrow. Tonight, there seem to be some activities going on. Let's check them out." She stood and waited for Tyler to get to her side. "Do you know what they've organized?"

"Not a clue," he answered, slightly guilty that he couldn't play a better host for her.

"It's all right. Let's find out together." She shrugged off the coat and returned it to him.

He slipped on his coat and the same flowery scent that Kate carried got on him. "What's this scent?"

"What scent?" She took a whiff of the air. "I don't smell anything."

"This flower scent from you."

"Oh, my moisturizer. Sorry, is it that strong?"

"No, it isn't. I was just wondering."

"It's my rose moisturizer."

"Rose," he mumbled as they strolled around the various booths.

Kate stopped and looked at a poster on the wall. "You're rather generous with your lucky draw gifts—even if you don't know it."

"Excuse me, Mr. Hayes."

They turned.

A young lad with a clunky professional camera hung over his neck grinned nervously. "Sorry to disturb, but do you want to take a photo with your girlfriend?"

"Sure, she loves taking photos," he said while looking at Kate.

"Great!" the young lad exclaimed with a little too much exuberance.

Tyler took a step closer to Kate and wrapped his arm across her back. At his touch, she looked up at him and smiled as their gazes met.

A bright flash went off, turning both their heads toward the young lad. The young lad grinned proudly and nodded while he checked the photo.

"Send me the photo through email," Tyler said before leading Kate away.

"Not a problem, sir."

Moving along, Kate pointed to a crowd gathered at a particular section. "Look, they're playing *A Minute to Win It* games." When he didn't reply, she explained, "It's a game show where contestants have to complete tasks in a minute to win."

He allowed her to drag him along.

The moment the woman in charge of the game saw them moving toward the booth, she announced their arrival and pleaded for them to participate.

The woman pleaded, but her hand was already on Kate, pulling her toward the booth.

Tyler held on to Kate, refusing to let her get dragged away.

Though she was interested in watching, he was certain that she didn't want to participate.

But the woman was so determined, and their tug-of-war was getting somewhat ridiculous.

"There are six thimbles and six marbles. You need to bounce the marbles off the table and onto the thimble," the woman rattled on, pulling Kate further away from him.

When the woman finally let go of Kate, they were standing at one end of the table while he was still at the other.

"I'm horrible at games," Kate said.

"Oh, it's easy. Someone already won a hundred dollars from

this game," the same woman announced, her hand returning to hold on to Kate.

Kate glanced up at Tyler, her eyes pleading with him to get her out of the situation.

He stepped forward, but the woman was faster.

"One game, please."

Kate sighed in resignation. "All right. One game."

"Fantastic! You have one minute, starting ... now!"

A large digital clock projected on the wall behind Kate started counting down with loud ticks from the speakers.

Kate took a deep breath before picking up the first marble.

She cast a quick glance at Tyler and smiled sheepishly, then started bouncing the marbles.

She laughed at her own luck while the crowd cheered when two of the marbles landed and stayed in the thimble, but that was all she managed.

Tyler watched, laughing as she did.

Though they were surrounded by a crowd that was getting larger by the second, her eyes always found his whenever she looked up from the table.

Maybe it was because he was the only one she knew, but he loved how she looked to him amid the crowd and noise.

When the one-minute alarm rang, she shrugged. "I tried."

He strode over to her with a big smile. "You really are horrible at games," he said as she buried her face in his chest.

He instinctively wrapped his arm around her shoulders. He didn't want to release her even as she looked up and tried to take a step back.

"Well, Mr. Hayes, if you're so good, why don't you give it a try?" she said from within his arms.

Everyone cheered while her smile broadened.

Again, he looked only at Kate and continued. "Since I'm ultimately paying for the hundred dollars, let's bet on something else."

"What do you want?" she asked with a half shrug.

"If I win, you keep the set of jewelry you're wearing now."

By then, more people had gathered around the booth, but

everyone fell silent as he spoke his request.

Kate wiped off her smile and stared at him sternly. "Ty …"

"If I win, in one try, you'll keep them." He could see Kate considering the situation.

Her gaze remained fixed on him even as the silence around them grew deafening.

"I've never played it before," he added.

"One try."

He beamed. He took off his coat and put it into Kate's outstretched hands. Folding up his sleeves, he nodded at the same woman, and the same cycle repeated itself. He spent the first twenty seconds experimenting with the strength and the bounce of the marble, but once he got the first one in, the rest followed smoothly.

He even had time to give Kate a smirk while she stared in disbelief.

Another round of cheers and applause sounded when he completed his task. He looked at Kate and winked. "We had a deal."

"How did you do that?"

He steered Kate out of the cheering crowd and headed back to their table, thinking they'd enough excitement for the day.

"Ty."

He immediately continued. "We had a deal. Are you going back on your word?"

Kate waited until they were seated before saying, "I know we had a deal, but these belong to your mother. Are you sure you want to give them to me and not keep them for someone else? Someone more important."

"I'm sure." And he was.

In a matter of months, Kate had not only returned him the happy memories he'd lost, but created so many more for him.

She pursed her lips, but sighed and nodded after a moment. "All right. But if you ever change your mind, just tell me and I'll give them back to you."

He scoffed. "They are yours, yours to keep forever. I don't take back the things I give."

"Thank you," she said, looking at the bracelet on her hand. "They're exquisite."

That night was the first time since taking over the company that Tyler stayed throughout the dinner and the lucky draw winning announcements. It was the first time he sat through an entire dinner without once feeling bored or checking his watch.

When they got home, he got out of his car and jogged over to the passenger side door. Kate took his hand, and once he closed the door, she turned toward the mansion.

He tightened his hand and stood on the spot, stopping her from moving further. "Do your feet hurt?"

"No," she answered. "Why?"

He slipped his free hand into his pocket and took out his phone.

Kate watched curiously as his finger tapped away on the screen. She stepped forward to peer at what he was doing, but he shifted his arm away before she could see the screen.

When he was done, he placed the phone on his car and turned back to her. "You look gorgeous tonight." He pulled her close against his chest and placed his arm on her back. "Tonight was the only time in my life I actually wished there would be dancing at the dinner," he said as the music started playing.

She laughed softly in his arms. "This is rather nice, too," she said, leaning her head against his chest. "What song is this?"

"*Remember*. Dan was playing it in his car some time ago."

"So you kept it on your phone, waiting for a chance to whip it out for a dance?"

"No, I just thought it was a nice song."

"It is," Kate said as she swayed along with him.

"Did you have fun tonight?"

"I did. And you?"

"I did."

Kate nodded in his chest. "That's good."

He held her and moved slowly along with the song, hoping it would never end. He took a deep breath, and her rose and vanilla scent wafted into his nose. "You smell like ice cream, rose-flavored ice cream."

"Is that good or bad?"
Everything about her was good to Tyler, but he didn't reply.

Chapter Fifteen

Tyler sat at the dining table, staring at the empty seat next to his. Kate would usually be in the kitchen by this time, but there was still no sign of her.

He glanced over his shoulder, expecting Kate to walk in any second.

"You can start eating. I'm sure she'll come down soon," Marianne said as she set the plate of waffles down.

When Kate finally strolled into the kitchen, Tyler looked up at her and smiled, pulling out a chair for her.

"Did you kids have fun last night?" Marianne asked as Kate sat.

Instead of answering Marianne's question, Tyler and Kate smiled at each other.

"You're a bad influence, Ty. She's learning to ignore questions already," Ryan said.

Kate looked up and smiled at everyone. "Good morning, everyone. I had a lot of fun," Kate replied to Marianne. Then, glancing around the table, she noticed that the usual group wasn't complete. "Where's Dan?"

"I don't know. He's been rather secretive these past few days. Always disappearing," Ryan said with a shrug.

Joseph grinned. "Probably seeing someone. And he was asking if you'd gone for your Lasik review."

Kate grimaced. "No, I forgot all about it. But I promise I'll find time, soon."

"You had time to go to dinner with Ty, but no time to get

your eyes fixed?" Ryan questioned as he stared at Kate.

"Stop it," Tyler stated and shot a glare at Ryan.

Ryan's eyes widened when Marianne neared him with her knuckles raised. "Okay, okay," he said and stuffed a whole sandwich into his mouth.

"The dinner was at night. If the clinic's open at night, then I'll definitely have the time," Kate replied anyway. "Speaking of work, I've got to go—got to do some accounting and probably clear Evelyn's paperwork as well." She stood and turned to Tyler. "See you tonight."

"Bye," Ryan and Joseph echoed, then kept quiet until Kate was out of the door.

Once the door closed, Marianne shifted to where Kate had sat and smiled coyly. "How did last night go?" she asked.

Tyler continued sipping his coffee as though he didn't hear Marianne's question.

Marianne waited patiently, staring right at him to let him know she wasn't giving up. "I can wait. I'm an old lady; I have nothing else to do for the rest of the day. And if you ever intend for me to cook another meal for anyone here, you'd better start talking."

"Just tell her already," Ryan said.

Joseph laughed and shook his head. "I think your threat will work better if you say that you won't cook for Kate and will be horrible to her for the rest of her stay here."

Before Marianne could upgrade her threat, Tyler answered, "As she said, we had fun."

"Photos? I thought she loved taking photos," Marianne said.

"We didn't take any. She was busy answering questions."

He could feel Joseph watching him, so he looked up and waited for his question.

"Something's different, though. Something happened last night?"

He gave up the fight to control his smile as he thought about the night before.

Everything felt perfect. Somehow, his arms always found their way to her. And when they danced, she fitted him so perfectly. It felt as if she were made for him.

But it seemed too good to be true.

How could someone so kind be meant for a detached person like him?

"So? Did something happen?" Marianne nudged him, bringing his attention back to them.

"One year is too short."

"Then ask her to stay. I love her. She's so right for you."

She was with her ex-boyfriend for two years and couldn't bring herself to move in with him.

He'd only known her for a couple of months.

And right for him? Their personalities couldn't be more different.

"Don't let her slip away just because you're afraid," Marianne said softly and gave him a gentle pat on the shoulder before clearing the table of the empty plates.

Kate stared at the clock and smiled, glad that she'd cleared her paperwork in less than an hour. She leaned back in her chair and took a sip of coffee, smiling as she thought about the night before.

She sighed softly, wishing that the night hadn't ended and that she had more time to sit and indulge in the memories.

But she had to clear Evelyn's paperwork as well.

All of Kate's receipts were always neatly kept. They were all properly categorized and arranged from the earliest to the latest date. Anyone could look at them and settle the accounts without trouble.

Evelyn, however, always dumped everything into a wooden box.

Evelyn never had a clue about which receipts were for which projects, so Kate would have to go through the various projects and countercheck against the amount before she could assign the receipts to the proper projects. And only after all of that, could she begin to settle the accounts.

Putting her files away, she headed over to Evelyn's office. She knocked softly on Evelyn's door.

Evelyn looked up at her. "Good morning," she chirped. "Done with your paperwork?"

Kate nodded while she eyed Evelyn suspiciously. She was never this chirpy in the mornings.

"Sit. Chat. Tell me, how did last night go?"

"Great, sort of." She moved over to the couch and sat, then stacked up the magazines that were strewn across the coffee table.

"How was it sort of great?"

"I don't know. Everything just seemed to fit between us. Everything feels so right around him," she answered, smiling blissfully as she thought about their conversations and their dance.

"And the mansion?"

She sighed. "Thanks."

"I'm only saying it because I know you'll start rationalizing things when you're on your own."

Kate pushed the stack of magazines to the center of the table and obsessed with fanning them out evenly.

"Look, forget about the mansion. All your relationships last longer than a year. Besides, I don't remember ever seeing you talk about Benjamin or anyone like that."

"Like what?"

"Like a love-struck idiot?" Evelyn grinned as Kate glowered at her. "Everything just seemed to fit between us," Evelyn mimicked what Kate had said in an annoyingly sweet voice.

"Stop it."

"He's good for you. You don't know how to protect yourself. He can protect you."

"I grew up taking care of myself. I do fine."

"No, you grew up taking care of other people. You don't do too well on yourself."

Kate folded her arms and observed Evelyn for a while. "And the two of you are pretty alike." She strode over to Evelyn's desk and took the wooden box with all the receipts.

Just then, a commotion outside drew their attention.

"Ugh! Seriously? As if I don't have enough things to do

today," she complained when she saw Joanne trying to barge into her office.

"Really, that girl *never* learns," Evelyn said through clenched jaws.

"Eve, please."

But Evelyn was already out the door.

She hurried after Evelyn, hoping and praying that nothing disastrous would happen.

"Hey! She's here," Evelyn hollered across the office, capturing everyone's attention.

"Joanne, please. Please leave while you can," Kate pleaded, extremely conscious of all the stares on them.

Joanne squared her shoulders and stuck out her chin. "I'm here to tell you that I love Ty. I've loved him all my life, and I'm not letting this go without a fight. If you think I'm just a spoiled brat, then you're wrong."

"Oh, please. That's all you are. That's why Tyler never took you seriously. That's why he never took you to his company dinner—the same company dinner he took Kate to last night."

Kate glared at Evelyn, wondering if she'd gone out of her mind.

"I'm not a spoiled brat," Joanne repeated.

"Then tell us, since you stomped in here so gloriously, tell everyone here what you've achieved in your life."

"I'm not a spoiled brat."

Evelyn nodded condescendingly. "Right. You're just Dan's sister, then. That was what Tyler said to you; all you are to him is his pal's sister."

"Eve, please," Kate said in hushed tones. "I think she's gotten your point."

"I'm not just Dan's sister!"

Kate cringed at Joanne's outburst.

"Prove it," Evelyn said.

Kate's brows drew closer as she turned to Evelyn. Those two words sounded ominous.

"Fine."

Evelyn smirked and nodded. "Good. Starting tomorrow, you'll

have a real job. You'll be Kate's assistant for the next few months until some of our staff complete their probation. If you can stick through it and do a good job, I'll admit that you're not just a spoiled brat. I'll even put in a good word for you in front of Tyler."

Kate's jaw dropped, and she sighed a breath of disbelief.

Evelyn issued the challenge, Joanne accepted it, but she got stuck in the middle of it.

"Between the two of us, I think you need an assistant more than I do," she said.

"But if Barbie loses, she'll say that I was too harsh on her. There's no way she can say that about you." Evelyn glanced over at her. "Don't worry, she won't last."

"I'll be here tomorrow morning," Joanne said and straightened her dress before storming out the door.

Trying to contain the frustration that was threatening to erupt, Kate strode into her office without another word.

She could hear Evelyn's steps following her, but neither spoke until the door to her office was closed and the windows fogged.

"What were you thinking? I've already got enough things to handle. If you want to play her for a fool, then do it yourself."

"You can't have her harassing you all the time, right? Let her do this. And when she fails, she'll give up on Tyler, solving your problem once and for all."

Kate shook her head slowly as she listened to Evelyn. "And during? Eve, I don't mean to be rude, but it's a stupid idea."

Evelyn laughed.

Kate's brows rose, and her frustration inched up another notch. "Is this supposed to be funny?"

"Listen to yourself, Kate. You're completely pissed off with me, but you're still afraid of hurting my feelings. You need Tyler."

Running her hand through her hair, Kate finally asked, "And if she succeeds? What are you going to do?"

"I'll apologize; I'll tell Tyler that she was tougher than I thought. But he only has eyes for you. I don't know if you've noticed it, but his gaze is always on you. The first thing he did when he came sprinting out of the house that night was to put himself in front of you. It won't matter to him whether she succeeds or not."

"But it will matter to her," she said, enunciating each word. "Don't you see how naive she is? She's going to think that by succeeding, she'll have a chance with Ty. She'll be crushed."

"Someone's pretty confident of herself." Evelyn wriggled her brows.

Kate pinched her lips together, then breathed in slowly through her nose. "You know what? I think I'll finish up your paperwork at home."

"Oh, come on, Kate."

Gathering her things, she left Evelyn in her office and strode toward the parking lot. She got into the car with the intention of driving back to the mansion, but she had to tell Tyler what happened, and she didn't want to wait until dinner.

Taking out her phone, she called him.

He picked it up on the second ring. "Kate? Is everything all right?"

"Are you busy?"

"No."

"Do you want to meet for lunch? I'm already in my car. I can meet you at your office."

"Are you all right?"

"Yeah."

He was silent for a moment before he gave her the address to his office and waited for her to key it into her GPS before hanging up.

When she entered the office, she nodded as she saw the few familiar faces. She glanced around, uncertain of the way to Tyler's office.

"Miss Mitchell?"

Kate turned toward the voice, seeing a young lady in a peach-colored blouse and black pencil skirt walk toward her.

"Miss Mitchell?"

"That'll be me," she answered as she racked her brain for a name. She was certain she hadn't met the lady at the dinner, but the young lady greeted her with such familiarity.

"I'm Ella Price, Mr. Hayes's assistant."

Kate relaxed. "Just call me Kate. For a moment I thought I saw you last night and forgot your name," she said with a warm smile.

"Oh, I was in charge of the event last night. I was running all over the place and didn't get the chance to meet you, but Adrianna told me all about you," Ella said.

Kate wasn't sure how she felt about being discussed behind her back, so she just smiled politely. "I'm looking for Ty, I mean, Mr. Hayes."

"I know, he has informed me. I think he's expecting your call. But it's all right, I'll take you to him."

She followed Ella, and everyone at their desks looked up at her when they passed by.

"Is he busy?" she asked, trying to distract herself from the curious looks. "If he is, I can wait. There's no need to disturb him."

"He's free. He's just waiting for you," Ella replied.

"You ran the event last night, but he still made you work today?"

"No, no. Mr. Hayes usually lets me take the rest of the week off, but I wanted to go on a vacation with my fiancé, so he allowed me to have a longer holiday at a later time instead. A lot of people think he's aloof, but he's extremely understanding." Ella stopped by the desk in front of Tyler's office. "He's never brought anyone to the company dinner before, and he never stayed throughout the dinner either," she added.

"He never stayed throughout dinner?"

"Yeah. He usually stays for an hour or so, that's all."

She couldn't stop her widening grin. So much for the risk of the dinner dragging on past midnight. "Thanks," she said.

Ella smiled and left her outside Tyler's office.

She knocked on the door, but there wasn't an answer from within. "Busy?"

Tyler looked up from his desk, surprised to see her.

"I was waiting for your call," Tyler said as he stood.

"I know, but I was afraid you'd rush if you knew I was waiting in the car."

"What's wrong?"

She closed the door behind her. "Joanne came to the office."

Tyler's eyes widened. Placing his hands on her shoulders, he gave her a look over. "Are you all right? Did she hurt you? What did she do?"

She laughed, amused by his reaction. "It was more what Eve did."

Tyler looked at her, waiting for further explanation.

She told him everything. When she finished her story, his response was immediate.

"No. Give me your phone. I'll call Evelyn and tell her to forget it."

She smacked his hand away. "Even if you can get Eve to rescind her challenge, Joanne won't back out of it. She seems determined to prove herself to you."

"I'll call Joanne and tell her to stop her nonsense."

"No, don't. She's already upset enough. Eve was awful to her. I just …" She paused and sighed. "I just want to go to lunch."

She could see Tyler's hesitation. For a moment, she thought he wouldn't back down until the situation was resolved to his satisfaction. But instead, he smiled and headed out of the office without another word.

They had lunch at a restaurant nearby where Tyler chatted with her about everything under the sun. They discussed the novels he'd read, many of which she had read as well. Despite his constant teasing about her interest in crime novels, he was a fan as well.

They chatted about everything and anything, except about Joanne and Evelyn.

"What do you want to do next?" he asked as they stepped out of the restaurant and back into her car.

"Don't you have to go back to work?"

"I have nothing on. What do you want to do?"

She contemplated that question, but she couldn't find an activity that both of them could enjoy together.

"What do you like to do when you're free?"

"Play the piano and watch movies."

"We can rent *The Notebook*," Tyler suggested.

"Did you watch the movie before?" she asked.

"No, why?"

"Do you know what it's about?"

"A love story?"

"You won't want to watch it."

"I don't mind. It's just a movie anyway."

"That's really sweet of you, but I don't want to bore you. Besides, I always cry when I watch it."

"Then why do you still watch it?"

"Because it's a really romantic story."

"Good ending?"

"Yes and no ..." She knew her answer was confusing, so she told him the gist of the story. "He loved her so much. The heartache he put himself through just to get that few minutes with her."

"Kate," he said with an indulgent smile. "You really should stick to movies with absolute good endings."

She laughed at herself. "I know, I'm ridiculous. Still, it's one of my favorites."

"So which movie tops that list?"

She twirled her chain around her finger. She'd never told anyone what her favorite movie was. She loved watching it from time to time, but it was a secret that even Evelyn didn't know.

"What could be so embarrassing about a movie?"

"It's not exactly a movie ... more of a cartoon."

"You like cartoons?"

"No, it was a movie." She rolled her eyes. There wasn't any point in beating around the bush. "*Beauty and the Beast*."

"Disney's *Beauty and the Beast*?"

"That's the one."

He shrugged. "It does have a happy ending."

"Yup."

"Let's watch it, then."

"Really?" she asked. "You're going to watch a cartoon with

me?"

"Why not? It's better than one that makes you cry."

After buying the DVD, Tyler drove them back to the mansion and pulled out his keys to open the door. She smiled, realizing that she hadn't been using the keys much. She was always back around dinner time, and the door was always unlocked then.

They watched the movie on the second floor, munching on the popcorn they'd bought.

"You really like this movie," Tyler stated as he watched her.

She didn't reply. Instead, when Belle burst into a song, she sang along, getting every single word of the lyrics right. She even mouthed some of the dialog that the various characters spoke.

By the time she was done with her demonstration, Tyler was laughing so hard that his arms were cradling his abdomen.

"I'm glad you're enjoying yourself, but if you ever tell another soul about this, I'll kill you," she said.

"I think," Tyler struggled to form his sentence amid his laughter, "this has become my favorite movie as well."

"Well then, next time I'll have someone to watch it with."

"Anytime," he said, leaning closer against her, his arm resting across the back of the couch.

She pulled up her legs and sat cross-legged, her knee resting on Tyler's leg.

Throughout the movie, she would hum along with the music and that never failed to put a smile on Tyler's face.

After the movie, Tyler handed her the DVD. "You should keep this."

"Thanks," she said.

"Do you want to go for a walk with me?"

"In the woods?"

"I promise there's nothing scary in it."

She chuckled. "I'm only saying yes because you watched this with me." She waved the DVD in her hand.

She returned to her room, putting away the DVD before going out for the walk.

Again, Tyler placed her hand around the crook of his elbow as they strolled along, pointing out to her all the bumps and rocks on the ground.

"Where are we heading?" she asked.

"What makes you think we're heading somewhere?"

She shrugged. "You seem to be directing us toward a particular way rather than taking a leisurely stroll."

He grinned and nodded. "There's a shed, sort of like a play house for me when I was younger. I thought we could have a look."

"Do you still know where it is?"

"I used to come out here every other day. We'll do fine."

In less than fifteen minutes, they reached the shed that Tyler was talking about. She was expecting a dilapidated shed with broken windows and maybe a collapsed roof. After all, she thought no one had been there for twenty years.

But when she saw the shed, it was nowhere near dilapidated.

A small white shed with a wooden platform extending out in front of it stood in the midst of the trees. Around it were pots of colorful flowers that appeared to have been well taken care of. She turned to Tyler, thinking that he'd already been here before, but the same look of bewilderment was on his face.

"It's exactly how I remembered. I didn't think …"

Exactly how he remembered.

The late Mr. Hayes must have been maintaining the shed as he had the house. A time capsule that locked everything in its place before the accident happened.

"Your grandfather."

"He didn't mind getting rid of me, but he kept everything else exactly the way it was."

"It wasn't like that." She had to make him understand. "He thought removing you from all that you'd known would help you to forget what happened and allow you to move on." She waited for Tyler to say something, but he continued staring at the shed. "He'd always blamed himself. He said if he had been there, your parents wouldn't have died. He was heartbroken, and he made a mistake; a mistake he regretted his whole life."

Tyler said nothing. He sat on the ground, his gaze still locked on the shed. "I waited so long for him, but he never turned up."

She took a deep breath and fought back the tears brimming in her eyes. "Ty, he knew he was wrong, but he couldn't find the courage to make it up to you. He thought that after so long, it was better for him to remain out of your life." She sat next to him, pressing her shoulder against his. "As much as he wanted you to move on, he never did. Marianne said he'd sit in your parents' room and cry. If she hadn't packed up the rooms and moved your parents' things to the attic, they'd still be exactly where they were twenty years ago."

"I thought he dumped the things there because he didn't want to see them."

"He loved you very much. He used to tell me stories about you, and he'd show me all the photos he had of you. Not just you —he told me quite a few stories about your parents, too. Like this shed—I think your father built it originally for your mom so that she could sit and admire the plants she had. But you loved to hang around her, and it eventually became your playhouse."

Kate waited for Tyler's reply, but when his silence continued, she stood to leave, thinking he'd prefer some space and time alone.

Instead of allowing her to walk away, he stood with her and pulled her into his arms. One of his arms wrapped around her back while his other hand weaved its way into her hair. "Stay. Just for a while."

She wrapped her arms around his back, holding him. "As long as you want."

She sighed softly, holding him like he always did with her whenever she was afraid.

When they got back to the mansion, Kate could hear Evelyn and Dan talking in the kitchen.

At least she wouldn't have to do the explaining to Dan.

She stepped in, and Evelyn immediately turned around. "I bought apple strudel! And when someone said she was going home, I assumed it was to her own house, not here," Evelyn said. When Kate remained quiet, she continued. "I've drawn up the contract for Joanne, same pay as those on probation. And I promise I'll keep my eye on her. I won't let her cause you any problem. If she tries, dismiss her."

"Are you sure about this?" Dan asked.

Kate sighed. "What's done is done. Let's just see how it plays out."

She didn't want to talk or think about it. There was no way this would end up well, but there wasn't anything she could do. So she'd rather not think about it.

Besides, Tyler had enough on his mind, and she didn't want him worrying about her.

"Kate, my sister is——"

"I know. And truthfully, I didn't have much of a choice. I was kind of dragged into it. But Joanne seemed determined. I doubt anything can change her mind now," she said. "But if anything happens, please remember that this whole thing is Eve's idea."

Chapter Sixteen

Kate's eyes flew open to absolute darkness. She turned over and reached for her phone when she heard a thud.

Only when the light from her cell phone hit her face did she realize that whatever she heard wasn't just a sound in her dream or from her imagination.

She directed her glance up toward the ceiling when she heard another thud from above her.

Gingerly, she stepped out of bed with her heart pounding away.

She stood beside her bed, waiting and listening for another sound. But instead of a thud, she heard low, muffled voices humming along to a tune.

It was a song.

It sounded as if someone was playing it on the radio.

She moved toward her door, and the music grew louder, clearer.

Stars shining bright above you
Night breezes seem to whisper 'I love you'
Birds singing in the sycamore trees …

She smiled and followed the music, thinking Tyler was playing it.

She left her room and went over to Tyler's room. The door to his room was ajar, but he wasn't in it. The music wasn't coming from his room either.

She continued trotting forward, listening for the source of where the song was being played. She stopped in front of the long window and looked out.

The song continued playing, and right outside the house, on the empty space before the trees, a couple danced along to the music.

The lady wore a green sleeveless retro dress while the man wore a gray button-down shirt.

Something about the couple seemed familiar to her, but she couldn't figure out what it was.

She watched and smiled as the blissful couple danced to the song.

"Kate?"

She jumped and spun around, then sighed as she saw Tyler.

"What are you looking at?"

"There's a couple dancing," she said, turning back to the window.

"There's someone outside?" Tyler asked and strode forward, pulling her behind him.

That was when she realized how quiet it had become.

"There's no one out there."

"What? But I saw ..." She stepped forward and gazed out. "Okay. This is ..."

Tyler laughed softly. "Were you dreaming?"

"Maybe. But I was wide awake that day when I heard someone playing the piano."

"You heard someone playing the piano? When?"

"A while ago." The more she thought about it, the more she was scaring herself. "You know what? Forget it. Like you said, I was probably dreaming."

"It's okay," Tyler said softly. He must have realized the state she was working herself into. He ran his hands down her arms. "Next time you hear something, tell me."

"I heard some noise upstairs, too."

"And you decided to check it out alone?"

"I went to your room, but you weren't there."

Tyler grinned. "Because I was the one making the noise. I was packing up the attic. But if it ever happens again and I'm not in my room, wait for me before you check anything out."

She nodded. At least she wasn't completely crazy. "Why are you packing up at this time of night?"

"I don't want to be like my grandfather."

"I don't understand," she said. Her eyes flickered out the window again, looking at where the couple had been.

"I couldn't sleep." Tyler took her hand and headed up to the attic. "I don't want the accident to shape my life anymore. I don't want to remain trapped."

"I'm awake now. I can help."

"What was the piece you heard? The one from the piano."

"The same one we were playing, *Heart and Soul.*"

Tyler nodded, then changed the subject. "I was thinking. I know you're busy, but would you like to help me redecorate or redesign the house? You said you like to work with old houses."

"Why did you ask about the song?" She saw him hesitating, so she urged, "Tell me."

"It was the same song my mother taught me."

She drew a deep breath. She shouldn't have asked.

"So," Tyler said, seemingly as interested in changing the subject as she was. "Redecorating the house."

"Are you sure?"

"Yeah. Will you help?"

"Of course." Her eyes swept the attic.

The attic was huge. The ceiling was painted baby-blue and decorated with wispy white clouds. Against one of the walls, over a dozen large boxes were stacked up on each other and a few opened ones were on the floor.

"This was your room, right?"

He nodded as he sat on the floor, before one of the opened boxes. "I'm sorting through everything to see what I should keep or discard."

She looked into one of the opened boxes filled with brushes and paints. "Your grandfather said your mother loved painting. Did she paint these clouds?"

"Yeah. She painted the walls inside the shed, too. Flowers and hummingbirds. We'll go back when we have time."

She nodded while her eyes scanned the open boxes.

She was glad that he'd decided to move forward and not remain locked in the time capsule just as the late Mr. Hayes had. But looking at all the things in the boxes was depressing.

She pulled out one of the brushes that still had paint on it. She stared at it as a tear rolled down her cheek, falling onto the floor.

Tyler jumped to his feet. "What's wrong?" he asked, wiping away another tear hanging on the corner of her eye.

"I'm sorry. It's just heartbreaking that your parents left so suddenly. There's still paint on the brushes."

Tyler pulled her into his arms. "Don't be sad; she wouldn't want it. My grandfather and I spent twenty years mourning their deaths; that's enough."

"In the shed, is there a drawing of a train?"

"Yes, why?"

"Your grandfather and father said that all the flowerpots and paintings on the walls were too feminine for it to be a boy's playhouse, so your mother drew a train on the lower half of the walls to appease them. She drew you as the driver."

He ran his fingers down her hair. "I remember. I remember being really proud of it even though I wasn't the one who drew it. I mentioned it to everyone I saw."

She chuckled. "You were so cute when you were young."

"And I know nothing about the younger you. Doesn't seem fair."

She stepped out of his arms and peered into another box. "You need to stop hugging me each time I scream or get upset. I may get used to it."

Tyler grinned. "You're trying to change the topic. Tell me something about yourself."

"What do you want to know?"

Tyler asked her a series of questions about her family. One question led to another, and Tyler suddenly asked, "Have you told Lydia about Detective Cooper?"

She blinked, realizing that she'd forgotten about it. "No, I haven't even taken it out of my purse. Are you free this weekend?

Once I tell her, she'll insist on going immediately."

"Anytime."

Her head bobbed up and down as she considered her own schedule. "Okay, we'll go this weekend, then."

Time always flew whenever she was with him. They had barely gone through two of the boxes when she noticed sunlight streaming in through the window.

She sighed. It was time to get ready for work and face Joanne.

"Are you going to work? I'll drive," she said. She was the reason why his car was back at the office anyway.

"Yeah."

Back in her room, Kate took out the piece of paper and sent a text to Lydia, letting her know about Detective Cooper. Lydia called back almost immediately, trying to pry more information out of her.

Kate refused to give Lydia the address.

That was the only information keeping Lydia from going to Detective Cooper's house on her own.

Eventually, Lydia gave up trying to get any further information from her, but she did extract a promise that they would head over that weekend.

Kate showered and changed into a pair of denim jeans, then pulled on a black satin shirt. At the last minute, she changed into a black cotton shirt.

She loved that satin shirt and wasn't going to risk wearing it around Joanne.

Then she picked out a pair of comfortable heels; one that she wouldn't have a problem running around in—just in case there was a need to.

If she could put on armor without looking weird, she probably would. Since she couldn't, she headed down for breakfast dressed as she was.

Tyler didn't mention a word about Joanne during breakfast or on the drive to his office. Instead, he went on and on about the shed, telling her everything he could remember.

Only when he was getting out of the car did he casually tell her to call him if she needed anything.

She nodded, then headed over to her own office. She couldn't remember ever dreading the sight of her office so much.

As Kate plodded into the office, not a single one of her staff glanced up. All of them kept their heads low and their eyes on whatever was on their desks.

She stopped in her tracks when she saw Joanne sitting at Laura's desk.

Seeing her, Joanne stood and walked over with a cup of coffee in her hands. "Good morning, Miss Mitchell. Miss Jordan says I should get your coffee ready and ask you what I should do."

Kate took the coffee, but she didn't dare drink from it. She took out Evelyn's wooden box from her bag and handed it to Joanne. "These are some receipts from a few of our previous projects. Find out which projects the different receipts belong to. Do you know how to use Excel? Categorize them, then tabulate it and send me a copy. If you don't know what to do, ask any of them," she said. "Also, I need to meet a client later. I'll email you a list of all the forms I need. Get them ready for me before lunch."

She wasn't sure if Joanne could do any of that, but she figured she might as well flood her with work rather than let her be free to cause mischief.

Joanne nodded before adding, "Miss Jordan says I need to go meet the clients with you."

"All right." Kate turned and walked toward her office, reminding herself never to speak to Miss Jordan again.

"Good morning," Evelyn sang her words as she entered her office, clearly trying to cheer her up.

Kate didn't bother to greet her; she didn't even bother to look up at her.

Evelyn sat on the chair across from her desk. "Don't tell me she's already screwed something up."

Kate pushed her coffee over to Evelyn. "She made this. I don't intend to drink it, but you should definitely give it a try."

"This isn't like you. Do you distrust her that much?"

"No, I have absolute trust in her. I have no doubt of her determination to win Tyler's heart and of her hatred of me."

Evelyn leaned forward. "Are you jealous or worried?"

She continued as though she hadn't heard a thing from Evelyn. "Have you set up an email for her? I need it."

Evelyn scrawled the information on the notepad and pushed it across the table. Then she took the cup of coffee and took a sip as she stood. "Tastes pretty normal to me."

"I almost forgot. Ty asked me to help with redecorating the house and I agreed."

"Just let me know when you need me," Evelyn said and walked out.

Kate switched on her laptop and checked her emails before she began working on one of the four projects on hand. She went through the designs, noted down the details of the furniture she wanted, then emailed them over to Evelyn.

She tried clearing as much of her work as possible, but there was too much to do. She had the drawings, but there were still the quotations, the presentation, the forms to fill out, and the contracts to prepare.

With so many things to do, she doubted she could begin working on the design for the mansion for another month or so.

It was time to delegate some work.

So she emailed those on probation, telling them to get all of that done by the end of the week.

She was just reaching for her phone when the alarm rang, reminding her of the meeting; the meeting where she had to bring Joanne along.

Kate sighed and picked up the phone, informing Joanne that they would leave in five minutes. She sighed again as she packed up her things, dreading her time alone with Joanne.

As expected, an awkward silence hung in the car throughout the whole drive to the new client's home. Kate fiddled with the radio stations, playing some music to get rid of the silence, and was ever so grateful that the client's house was a short drive away from the office.

The moment she stepped out of the car, the same song that she and Tyler had danced to played on her phone.

She'd loved the song so much that she downloaded it and set it as her ringtone that morning.

She picked up the call and answered, "What can I do for you, Mr. Hayes?" The realization that Joanne was right next to her came almost immediately, and she cleared her throat while turning away from Joanne.

"Just wondering how's your day going so far."

"Everything's good," she assured.

"Are you outside?"

"Yeah, meeting a client."

"Has she given you any trouble?"

"Nope."

"Please don't tell me you're with Joanne right now."

"How do you know?"

"Your answers are extremely short."

She laughed at how predictable she was. "Like Ryan said, you're a bad influence."

"Call me if you need anything—anything."

"I will."

"Ty called?" Joanne asked once Kate hung up the call and returned the phone to the bag.

She nodded and continued moving forward, unwilling to enter into a conversation about Tyler. "Are you sure you brought everything?"

"Yes," Joanne answered in a conceited tone, as though the things she was told to do were beneath her.

Kate let the attitude slide and pressed the doorbell to the Campbells'.

Mrs. Campbell's maid opened the door and ushered them into the living room where Mrs. Campbell was seated, her back straight and her eyes on the book she was holding.

A pot of tea with matching cup and saucer sat on the table in front of her.

Mrs. Campbell put the book down and nodded at Kate, gesturing for them to sit.

Kate sat and went through the usual questions, finding out what Mrs. Campbell wanted to change about the house.

The conversations with clients were important to Kate.

She didn't just listen to what the clients wanted. Through the way they spoke of the house, she'd know more about their personalities and be able to design something that would suit their characters.

In Mrs. Campbell's case, it'd be easy to design her house. She was detached, and her imperious character was obvious from her words and demeanor. Grand and luxurious minimalism would suit her perfectly.

Beside Kate, Joanne sighed a couple of times. Kate stole a quick glance at Joanne and found her staring into space.

Having an attitude with her was one thing; behaving so unprofessionally in front of a client was another. A talk about manners was in order; a talk she wasn't going to have until Evelyn was around.

Maybe she should leave the talking to Evelyn altogether.

Shelving that thought, Kate asked if she could take a look around the house. Since Mrs. Campbell shoved the responsibility of showing the house onto the maid, Kate told Joanne to give Mrs. Campbell the forms that she needed to fill in.

Kate was away for less than five minutes when she heard Joanne and Mrs. Campbell erupting into a scream fest.

She turned to the maid, and after a moment of confusion, they hurried back to the living room to find out what was going on.

"How stupid can you be? You can't even get simple documents right," Mrs. Campbell said scornfully, rolling her eyes at Joanne. "I don't know why anyone would hire a bimbo like you. You are a complete disgrace to women in general."

"Everyone makes mistakes. Do you have to be such a bitch about it?"

Kate's eyes bulged as her lips formed an O. "Joanne, that's enough."

"Did you hear what the old hag said about me?"

Just as Kate took a deep breath, Mrs. Campbell picked up the few pieces of paper on the table and flung them in Joanne's face.

"You're too old to be behaving like a brat," Mrs. Campbell seethed.

"Mrs. Campbell!" Kate hollered as she stepped in front of

Joanne, putting herself between the incensed client and an enraged Joanne. "I know she was rude, but you weren't exactly kind either. You didn't have to do that," she said, looking down at the papers on the floor.

"I'm the client; I can do whatever I want."

Kate turned away from Mrs. Campbell and said to Joanne, "Are you okay? What happened?"

"Ask her! It's not as if you'll believe me anyway."

Speaking to Joanne was like speaking to a child. She really knew how to try Kate's patience.

"Stop shouting," Kate said calmly and softly. "I'm asking *you* what happened."

"I brought the wrong folder; it was the expenses you told me to tabulate for the previous projects."

She waited for Joanne to continue, but that was it. She couldn't believe Mrs. Campbell had blown a fuse over such a trivial matter. "Was that it? Mrs. Campbell?"

"Was that it? It was a complete waste of my time. Your assistant's completely useless."

Agitated, Joanne took a step forward, pushing herself against Kate, seemingly ready to continue the argument.

Kate took a step back, pushing Joanne along with her.

"Mrs. Campbell, I know Joanne was rude, but like I said, you weren't particularly kind either. And there really was no need to make such a fuss simply because both of you were throwing words at each other. Since I doubt you'll be willing to apologize to my assistant, I don't think we can work together." She bent down and picked up the pieces of paper on the floor. "Have a good day, Mrs. Campbell. We'll show ourselves out."

She dragged Joanne out of the house and asked again, "Are you all right? Do you want to go home? Or do you want me to call Dan?"

"No!"

Her sudden reaction startled Kate. Was someone in the Riley family deaf? Why did she have to shout all the time?

"All right. I won't call Dan."

"I'm fine."

217

"Okay," Kate said and got into her car.

The moment they got back to the office, Evelyn came out of her office and asked Kate how the meeting went.

"We're not taking the Campbell project. Mrs. Campbell's attitude is horrible."

"So horrible that even her big fat check can't help it?" Evelyn asked with a wide smile.

Kate shook her head. "No amount of money will make me want to work with her. And that reminds me, Joanne, you need to be on better behavior in front of our clients. Even if you're not interested, pretend to be."

Evelyn glowered at Joanne but didn't say anything else.

Quietly, Joanne followed Kate back into the office and closed the door behind her.

"Why didn't you tell Evelyn what happened?"

"It wasn't entirely your fault, and it was too long a story to tell," Kate answered right before Evelyn walked into her office with a bouquet of pink tulips.

"I was in such a hurry to find out how things went that I forgot to pass you this." Evelyn smiled and placed the flowers on her desk. "Aren't you going to ask who sent them?"

If the flowers were from Benjamin, Evelyn would've thrown them out.

And among all the questions that Tyler had asked while they were packing up the attic, one was about her favorite flower.

"It's from Tyler," Evelyn said when Kate didn't reply.

"Thank you, Eve. Thank you."

"Ty bought you flowers?" Joanne asked.

Evelyn made some disapproving noise and answered Joanne's question, "It's none of your business who sends flowers to your boss."

Sparing Kate the need to interject before another quarrel broke out, Tyler himself stepped into the office.

"Ty?"

"Oh, right. He called just now and asked where our office was, so I told him."

"Of course you did," Kate muttered.

"You said you like pink tulips," he said when he saw the bouquet of flowers on her desk. "Free for lunch?"

"Hi, Ty." Joanne bounced in front of him. "Can I come along?"

"I'm here to take Kate to lunch."

Kate shook her head, wondering if Evelyn and Tyler were in conspiracy to make Joanne go into another episode of her dramatic explosion.

She took her bag and headed out the door without speaking to any of them. Tyler followed while Evelyn hollered for them to enjoy their meal.

This time, as Tyler and Kate sauntered past the desks, everyone in the office stole glances at Tyler. They were clearly curious about the person whom Joanne was fighting her for.

When they got out of the office, Kate finally said, "You need to stop being so mean to Joanne."

"I thought you were afraid that she'd get hopeful and then get hurt. I'm trying to show her that there's no reason to get hopeful in the first place."

"So sending me flowers and meeting me for lunch are gestures to prove a point?"

"You sound disappointed."

Disappointment wasn't exactly the right word to describe how she felt. She was more annoyed than disappointed. Annoyed that she'd actually allowed herself to think otherwise. "I'm not."

Tyler reached out for her arm and stopped her. "They weren't gestures to prove a point. I sent the flowers and dropped by in hope of making you smile; it just so happens to serve another purpose."

She couldn't stop the corners of her lips from turning up.

When they returned from lunch, she refused to allow Tyler back into her office. She stood at the entrance of the elevator and turned around, preventing him from stepping out.

"See you later," she said.

"You're chasing me away?"

"I think you've proven your point to Joanne."

He took a step forward, moving closer toward her. "So as long as she's working here, I'm not allowed in your office."

She was beginning to wonder if he knew the reaction he caused her each time he did that. She raised her hand and placed it on his chest, stopping him from moving any closer. "I'll see you back at home."

"I hope she'll screw up soon," he said with a grin. Then he leaned in and whispered, "See you tonight."

She should say something, but her mind was still occupied with the thought that he was going to kiss her.

She stood right where she was until the elevator's door closed.

Next time, she was going to take a step away from Tyler instead of daydreaming about a kiss that was never going to happen.

Knowing that Tyler would be home earlier to pack up the attic, she cleared her work quickly and decided to head back earlier.

Taking the bouquet of tulips with her, she took a peek outside to make sure that Joanne wasn't looking before heading out.

"Miss Mitchell!"

Kate sighed and turned around to see Joanne hurrying after her. "Yes?"

"Can I have dinner at the mansion tonight?" Joanne asked earnestly.

Kate hesitated and Joanne immediately added, "After working hours, of course. I promise I'll behave."

She couldn't bring herself to say no, so she agreed. "Yeah, I'll tell Ty." The thought of Joanne joining them for dinner did erode some of her joy, but she had enough to spare.

Once she got back to the mansion, she hopped up the stairs to the attic and found Tyler sorting out another box.

"Need help?"

Tyler looked up from where he was seated. "You're back early." He stood and walked over to her. "Forget about the packing. Let's go to the shed. We didn't go in the last time. I want you to see the train; I'm inside it, you know."

"Really?" She beamed at him. "You know, the curse of your mood getting worse as the sun sets seems to have lifted."

They took the same trail to the shed; her hand hooked around his arm the whole way there.

The shed was well maintained on the outside. The pots of flowers were still blooming, and there wasn't a hint of yellowing on the wooden panels. Inside, however, wasn't doing as well. Many of the paintings had faded and the train tracks were barely visible.

She pursed her lips as she saw his disappointment. "Your grandfather couldn't paint. But," she said, leaning closer to the wall. "I can still see the miniature you inside."

He bent down beside her and took a closer look, his finger tracing the outline of the silhouette.

She stood and moved around the room. "Ty! Look at this. Is this your old toy?" She held a toy car in her hand, imagining the young Tyler pushing it around the shed while his mother painted.

As he neared, she took his hand and placed the toy car on his palm. "Your grandfather said your toy cars used to be a hazard around the house."

He brought the toy car up to his eye level and scrutinized it. "I used to place the car against the wall and run it along the tracks my mother drew."

"That must be why the tracks are curved all over the place, so you could have more fun."

They sat inside and talked about the pictures on the walls, about how Tyler's father was great at building things. They were so caught up in the conversation that they lost track of time.

Evelyn turned the doorknob and was surprised that it was locked. Whenever she'd come with Kate, the door was always unlocked.

She rang the doorbell and cast a glance at Joanne while she waited. "You promised to behave."

Joanne nodded.

Marianne opened the door, her lips set in a thin line. "Joanne, I told you that Ty doesn't want you in the house."

"It's all right, Marianne. She asked Kate. Where is Kate anyway? She isn't answering my calls."

"I don't know where they disappeared to. I'm sure they'll turn up soon," Marianne said as she stepped aside for them to enter.

All the guys were already in the kitchen, and Marianne told them to go ahead once the food was ready.

Fifteen minutes into the meal, Tyler and Kate finally turned up.

"Hello everyone," Kate said as she came into the kitchen. "Sorry we're late."

"Don't be. We didn't wait, so it's fine," Ryan said with his mouth full. "But I'm extremely curious about where you guys were."

"Somewhere," Tyler answered.

"Somewhere," Kate agreed with a smile. "And I forgot to inform you and Marianne that Joanne was joining us for dinner. Sorry about that."

Tyler scooped a spoonful of cheesy mashed potatoes and placed it onto her plate. "Stop apologizing and start eating."

Evelyn saw Joanne watching Tyler and Kate and noticed her swallowing hard before looking away.

They weren't doing anything intimate, but their attraction for each other was clear to everyone.

"What a crowd."

Everyone turned to the unfamiliar voice.

"Mr. Sawyer! They're here all the time. You're just too busy with work to notice," Marianne joked. "Join us. There's plenty of food."

"Are you sure? It definitely looks appealing."

"Join us, Mr. Sawyer. Marianne loves it when we lick up every single bit of food," Kate said. "You've been busy. We haven't seen you around since the first night here."

"Yes, I was busy. But that's over now. So if I'm welcome, I'd love to have dinner here more often."

"That'll be great," Marianne replied. "It's a great excuse for me to cook more. Everyone, this is Mr. Sawyer."

The three guys and Evelyn all nodded politely while Joanne kept her eyes on her plate.

"So, Anne, how was your first day of work? Did Kate bully

you?" Ryan asked while looking at Kate. "Is she a monster behind that friendly mask?"

Kate laughed softly, then put on an exaggerated pout. "I thought you loved me."

"Oh, I still do. I'd love you even if you were a monster."

The two of them laughed heartily.

Tyler's smile faded, obviously jealous of Ryan. But that changed when Kate turned back to him and smiled. "And you? Do you think I'm actually a monster?"

"No."

Kate's smile broadened.

"And would you still love her if she actually *was* a monster?" Evelyn asked.

Kate turned to her and narrowed her eyes. "Ignore her."

"I know she isn't," Tyler answered, looking right at Kate.

"I'm going home," Joanne suddenly said. Then she stood and left the kitchen without another word.

Everyone was silent for a moment, but Evelyn didn't allow Joanne's sudden departure to interrupt the conversation. "You should try messing up her house and see what happens."

"Really? You want to bring that up?"

Kate and Evelyn jumped into a lively debate over a house-watching situation. They hollered at each other, half laughing while accusing each other of going overboard.

When they could no longer contain their laughter, the debate finally stopped, and Ryan asked, "So was I the only one who got lost in that conversation?"

As Kate laughed, she unconsciously shifted closer to Tyler. And even though he probably didn't have a clue about what was going on during the war of words, Kate's giggles were enough to make him smile. His arm draped across her chair as Kate turned to him.

"Some time ago, I had to make a business trip. So, I asked Evelyn to watch the house for me. When I came home, her clothes, food, and wine bottles were strewn all over the floor."

"Oh, it wasn't *so* bad," Evelyn argued. "She has compulsive disorder. Everything has to be in the right place or it's a disaster."

"I do not. I just don't appreciate having spaghetti on my carpet, wine stains on my couch, and dirty clothes all over my floor and sink! Gosh, I can't even imagine what situation would cause your clothes to end up in the kitchen sink!"

Evelyn rolled her eyes. "Fine. But you guys know what she did? She made me clean up the house while she dictated from the couch."

"Which, thankfully, I checked or would've sat right on a wine glass," Kate retorted.

Ryan and Joseph laughed even as their jaws dropped.

"Her house must be an interesting sight," Joseph commented.

"I'll take a video next time I'm there." Kate paused, casting a quick glance over to Evelyn before looking back at Joseph and Ryan. "You'll be amazed."

"I would've thought you'd simply walk out. Who would dare to stop you?" Dan asked.

"Which is my point exactly; Kate is definitely capable of becoming a monster," Evelyn said and smiled at Dan.

Kate leaned back on Tyler's arm as she shook her head. "So will all of you when you see the destruction she brings whenever she stays over."

"Is that why she isn't watching your house while you're here?" Tyler asked with a grin.

"Yes, one year is a long time. I was only gone for a week that time. I can't imagine putting my house in her hands. My life, yeah, she'll protect me with her life, but the house ..." Kate shook her head. "Never!"

Evelyn pulled out a piece of tissue, crushed it, and threw it at Kate.

It wasn't anything dangerous, but Tyler instinctively hooked his arm over Kate's shoulders and pulled her toward his chest, protecting her from the crushed-tissue missile.

"Whoa, Evelyn. I suggest you don't do that. Tyler is a judo expert. You don't want to hurt Kate in front of him," Ryan said.

Smiling smugly, Evelyn replied in all confidence, "Even if I did hurt her, she would never let Tyler hurt me."

Kate sat up but didn't pull herself out of Tyler's arm. "Unfortunately, that's quite true."

Evelyn watched as Kate spoke, turning to Tyler whenever she smiled. Within the short stay at the mansion, Kate seemed to have grown so comfortable with being near Tyler; something which wasn't frequent with Kate.

Kate was kind to everyone, but she was only comfortable with a few, and nothing like how she was with Tyler.

Evelyn wasn't the only one observing them.

Marianne and the guys were all staring. But oblivious to the stares from around the table, Kate and Tyler started chatting between themselves, completely forgetting the rest of the room.

Chapter Seventeen

Kate sat quietly beside Tyler on the drive toward ex-detective Thomas Cooper's house.

She glanced at Lydia in the car's wing mirror and noticed how Lydia's brows were furrowed while her eyes stared into the distance.

Kate knew how important this was for Lydia.

Throughout Lydia's life, she'd always suspected that something wasn't right with the story their grandparents had told them. She'd tried to push their grandparents for information, but she had only ended up agitating them and a cold war always ensued.

As the car got nearer to their destination, Kate couldn't help wondering if she'd made the right decision in helping Lydia pursue the case.

She was worried about how Lydia would react to the information or the lack of it.

Either way, by going over to Thomas Cooper's house, she was igniting a spark that she might regret. She was giving Lydia permission to chase after ghosts that their grandparents had worked hard to keep from them.

It was a chase that might never lead to anything; a chase that might never end.

Taking her eyes off Lydia, Kate turned to Tyler.

The conversation they'd had at her house resurfaced, and again she wondered if her parents would agree with their choice of going after something that had happened so long ago.

When Tyler's car pulled to a stop, everyone looked out at the small, pastel-blue house with white picket fence, but nobody said anything. All their eyes were on the house, but no one moved.

For a moment, Kate thought that perhaps even Lydia might hesitate. But she sighed as Lydia flung the door open and stepped out.

Jesus … She didn't even know what to pray. *Jesus, just let everything be good.*

She reached out for the door's handle, but turned back to Tyler as she felt his hand on her arm.

"Are you sure about this?" he asked.

She shook her head and gave him a small smile. "No, I'm not. But I think Lydia needs to know, and it's too late to go back now."

"And you?"

"You've given me the answer I needed. Parents just want their children to be happy, right?"

Tyler smiled. "Let's go, then. Otherwise, I think your sister will head in without us."

By the time they got out of the car, Lydia was already standing right in front of Detective Cooper's door. She pressed the doorbell twice and tried peering into the house through the window by the door.

"Who is it?" a grumpy voice bellowed from within the house.

Once Tyler heard the voice, he widened his strides and placed himself in front of Kate.

"I'm … We're …"

They got up to the steps with Kate standing half a step behind Tyler.

Kate turned and stared at Lydia, confused. She thought Lydia would have an entire speech prepared.

"We're here to ask you some questions regarding a case you handled before your retirement," Tyler answered.

The door opened, and a pudgy old man eyed them suspiciously from his wheelchair. "Who are you?"

"Lydia Mitchell." Lydia stretched out her hand, but the old man merely glared at her and turned to stare at Kate. Lydia took a deep breath and dropped her hand. "That's my sister, Kate."

"I've seen you before, in a picture. Your grandmother came and pestered me for a locket from evidence."

Kate smiled apologetically as she fiddled with the locket. "I'm sorry if that caused you any problem."

The retired detective grunted.

"You have a fantastic memory, Mr. Cooper. Do you still remember our parents' case?" Lydia asked.

Even as Lydia spoke, Mr. Cooper turned to Tyler. "And you? I don't remember they had a son."

"He's my sister's boyfriend," Lydia answered impatiently before repeating her question. "Do you still remember our parents' case?"

"I remembered your grandmother; I remembered you and your sister. You think I've forgotten about the case? Whatever you're here for, I have nothing for you." Backing his wheelchair away from them, he reached for the door.

Lydia immediately took a step forward, pushing the door back against the wall. "No, I need to know. There's barely any forensic evidence or witness statements in the file. Why is the police file so thin? Did you take something with you or throw evidence out? Like how you returned my grandmother the locket even though it was evidence for an open case?"

Kate pushed her hair behind her ear and pursed her lips.

Common sense should tell Lydia not to accuse someone she needed help from. And Lydia was to be a lawyer. Shouldn't she be better with her words?

The old man clenched his jaws. "Insolent child. Get off my property now."

But Lydia hadn't come this far to be turned away. She stuck out her stubborn chin and continued. "No. Why isn't there anything in the file, then? There's barely any evidence or clues. You were obviously not doing your job."

"Forensic evidence wasn't like what you have now. We solved cases based on our manual footwork. And since no one saw or heard anything, I'd nothing to go on. As for your mother's locket, your grandmother came to me begging. She told me that your sister was having nightmares and the locket would help her. I told her no; I told her it was evidence. But she kept coming back; she kept pleading. The locket had been checked, and it didn't hold any clues. So I risked my job and returned it to her."

"Really? I did my own manual footwork, and I heard you had a reputation: A reputation for making things go away for the right amount."

"Leave my property, or—" Thomas Cooper coughed violently, his face turning red as he struggled to continue. "Or I'm calling the cops."

"We should go," Tyler said to Kate. He wrapped his arm over her shoulders and turned away from the door.

Kate followed, grabbing Lydia's wrist and pulling her along.

But Lydia wrenched her hand from Kate's grip and, again, stopped the door from slamming shut. "I know what you did. I'll prove it."

Kate ran back to Lydia and jerked her away from the door. "I'm sorry, Mr.—"

Before she could complete her sentence, Thomas Cooper rammed his wheelchair into Kate's shin. She screamed at the sudden impact and was thrown off balance.

She tumbled backward, but Tyler caught her before she hit the ground. She tried to stand up straight, but her right foot was twisted at a weird angle, caught underneath the footrest of the wheelchair.

Tyler must have realized it. He set her down on the porch and was about to move forward when Thomas Cooper reversed his wheelchair, grazing skin off Kate's foot.

Kate winced and turned into Tyler's chest, but she didn't give Thomas Cooper the satisfaction of hearing her scream again.

Tyler's arms held her tight. Rigidly, he scooped her into his arms and returned to the car without another word.

Behind them, the door to Thomas Cooper's house slammed shut.

Though Tyler hadn't said a word, she could feel the anger he was suppressing.

Lydia sprinted ahead and opened the passenger-side door for

Tyler.

Tyler placed Kate down on the seat and knelt down in front of her, lifting her feet up to rest on his thigh.

The place where the metal footrest had scraped across was already bleeding. He pulled off her shoe as gently as he could and checked her ankle.

"I'm sure it'll be fine after a while," she said as she saw the muscles along his already tensed jaws twitch.

He glanced up at her and slowly rotated her foot. She had braced for some form of pain, but she gasped at the unexpected jolt shooting up her leg.

"I think you sprained your ankle, but we had better get an X-ray just to make sure."

"Gosh, Kate, I'm so, so sorry. I'm sure he was trying to knock me down."

Tyler carefully shifted her leg into the car. "Get in," he commanded without looking up at Lydia. "We're taking her to the hospital," he said in a carefully controlled tone.

Lydia obeyed immediately.

Once in the car, Lydia took out a packet of tissue for her. "I'm sorry, Kate. I thought I could get something out of him."

"You tried that on grandma and it never did you any good or gave you any new information. As a soon-to-be lawyer, I thought you'd know better than this. I can't believe you jumped into accusing him without first trying to coax it out of him."

Lydia chewed on her lower lip. "I'm sorry. I really am."

"Forget it. Don't come back here again. I don't think any of us will be welcomed." Kate adjusted her position in her seat and bent forward to look at her foot. It was already beginning to swell, and an ominous violet patch was starting to appear. She sighed and lay back against the seat.

"Does it hurt?" Tyler asked.

"Nothing I can't handle."

When they got to the hospital, Lydia decided to wait in the car.

Kate didn't blame her.

Tyler hadn't said much, but his eyes were cold and dark, and his silence was causing even Kate to worry.

Lydia wasn't exceptionally skilled at keeping her cool or at getting information out of people. But even to her, it was clear that staying away from Tyler was a wise choice.

They sat in a waiting room so crowded that Tyler had to stand while Kate filled in the form, but they didn't have to wait long for her turn. Tyler made a call to Joseph and got them bumped up ahead of the queue.

They were out of the hospital in less than an hour.

Kate sat in a wheelchair and held a brown envelope while Tyler pushed her back to his car. He stopped the wheelchair beside the car and pulled the door open.

Kate pushed herself off the wheelchair, but before she could take a step, Tyler lifted her into his arms and set her down on the passenger-side seat.

"What's that?" Lydia asked as Tyler went to return the wheelchair.

"The X-ray film. He wants Joseph to take a look at it."

With the pain medication in her system, Kate fell asleep before Tyler returned. She only woke when she heard Lydia closing the car's door.

She stretched her back and turned to Tyler. "You look as if you want to murder someone."

"Feeling better?" he asked without a hint of a smile.

"Are you going to turn back and kill Mr. Cooper if I say no?"

He sighed softly. "I'm sorry. I should've paid more attention."

Her lips curled at his reply. "You're not God. You didn't know what was going to happen. How is it your fault for not being able to predict the future? Please don't blame yourself. I'm fine, really."

"Your angels are asleep today."

She shook her head with a smile. "It's so easy for us to blame God, isn't it?"

"Weren't your angels supposed to keep your feet from dashing against rocks?"

"I hate stepping out on the streets after it has rained. I hate the puddles of water on the ground, and I especially hate it when the water splashes onto my leg."

Tyler's brows drew closer, probably trying to judge if she'd somehow injured her head without him knowing.

"Three years ago, I parked my car across the street from my client's house. I'm usually very careful about where I step, making sure I avoid all puddles of water. But that day, I went around the car and my feet landed heavily in a dirty puddle of water," she said. "I froze on the spot, then groaned and complained to God, asking Him why didn't He open my eyes to that. I pulled out a piece of tissue and bent over to wipe off the water. And this whole thing lasted only for a few seconds."

She looked right at him, and her smile broadened. "As I bent over, a car veered right past me, missing me by an inch, and crashed into the tree behind me. The driver had fallen asleep while driving. If I hadn't stepped in the puddle of water, I would've been right in the path of the car; I would've gotten pinned between the car and tree.

"So, I don't claim to know how everything works, but I know God causes all things to work for the good of His children. I still hate the puddles of water after the rain, but I no longer complain when I step into one."

Tyler didn't say a word. He got out of the car and sprinted over as she pushed herself out of the seat, wobbling dangerously as she tried to balance on one leg. He lifted her into his arms and strode toward the opened door.

"I can walk."

"Oh, dear Lord, what happened?" Marianne said.

"It's only a sprained ankle. The doctor said I just need to rest and keep it elevated. And Ty, I'm serious. Put me down. This is embarrassing."

"The doctor said to rest."

"I'll lean on my other leg."

"Actually, you shouldn't do that. It'll be better if you keep your injured leg elevated and don't use it at all," Joseph interjected as he strode out of the kitchen. "I believe you have the X-ray for me?"

Tyler placed her on the couch and took the envelope from

her. He handed it over to Joseph and waited while Joseph lifted the X-ray to the light, getting a better look.

"She's fine. It's a very mild tear. Rest your feet, ice your wound, and keep it elevated."

She nodded dutifully. "I'll rest as much as I can. Where's Lydia?"

"Hiding in the kitchen. She's afraid Ty will kill her when he gets the chance," Joseph said.

Marianne laughed. "With that look, I can understand why. Wipe that frown off. Kate's fine, and I'm sure she won't be too happy if you frighten her sister."

Kate stood from the couch, getting better at balancing on one leg. She hopped back when Tyler moved toward her. "I can walk."

Tyler looked over at Joseph.

"You're not walking; you're hopping. And seeing how you're wobbling, there's an extremely high chance of you falling and hurting your other leg or aggravating your injury."

Rolling her eyes, Kate knew she was fighting a losing battle, so she cut Joseph off. "Fine. But can you give us a minute alone?"

Joseph and Marianne went back into the kitchen without another word. Marianne glanced over once, her brows furrowed, probably wondering what she was up to.

Kate waited until she was sure that they couldn't hear her before continuing. "You cheated. You used Joseph to force me into agreeing with you."

Tyler frowned and narrowed his eyes, observing her. "What do you want?"

She broke into a grin. "I'll let you carry me around if you stop blaming yourself and forget this whole thing," she said. "And forgive Lydia."

He drew a deep breath and shook his head.

Rearranging his features, he gave her an incredibly forced smile before stepping forward and lifting her into his arms. "You're injured, and you're still trying to make sure that everyone around you is fine."

"Mr. Sawyer!" Kate exclaimed when she saw him sitting in

the kitchen beside her sister.

"Are you all right, Miss Mitchell? I can help you press charges if you want. The late Mr. Hayes made me promise to watch over you. He said you'll get bullied if no one does."

She wasn't sure if she should be grateful that the late Mr. Hayes was so concerned about her or be insulted that he thought she couldn't take care of herself. "No, it's all right. We were at fault, too."

Tyler sighed softly.

"Actually," Lydia said and swallowed, "it was all my fault. Sorry, Kate. I'm so sorry. I never thought you'd get hurt. Sorry, Tyler."

Kate arched her brow at Tyler.

He pressed his lips into a thin line and forced a smile. "Forget it."

"As you wish," Mr. Sawyer said. "As for trying to force more information out of him using legal means and your sister's locket as evidence, it may not have much effect. He is right. Forensic evidence wasn't considered a priority, and the judge will probably slap him with a small punishment for returning the locket. Besides, your sister would have to return the locket to evidence and might never get it back."

Kate reached for her locket. There was no way she was giving it back.

"No," Tyler stated with deadly seriousness. "She's not going to return the locket." He looked Lydia right in the eyes. "Drop the idea."

"Idea dropped," Lydia said without hesitation.

Wow. She needed to learn to speak in that authoritative tone of his, Kate thought. She'd never managed to talk Lydia out of anything, and Tyler simply commanded Lydia out of it.

"You said you know what he did. What did he do?" Tyler asked, his voice low and tone controlled.

He was clearly still piqued with Lydia, but at least he was making an effort to conceal it.

Kate's eyes slitted as she thought back on what Lydia had said outside Thomas Cooper's house. "Yeah, what did he do?"

Lydia gave a nervous laugh. "I was only scaring him. I have nothing. I managed to dig up his reputation, but everything else was a dead end. I just can't believe that nobody saw anything; it was broad daylight."

"If he were a corrupt cop, he could've intimidated witnesses into keeping their mouths shut. I've seen cases like that: policemen being too forceful, witnesses recanting their statements, or people confessing to crimes they never committed," Mr. Sawyer said.

Lydia nodded along as Mr. Sawyer spoke.

"Drop it, Lydia. How long will you keep chasing after the case? I don't mind helping you when there's a clue, but I don't want you to keep pursuing it when there's nothing left to go after," Kate said, knowing that Lydia was probably thinking of some form of alternate plan.

Lydia's right shoulder inched up, giving her a half shrug.

This was exactly why she needed to learn Tyler's style of speaking.

Despite the excitement that morning brought, routine resumed after lunch. Joseph went back to work, and Lydia left along with him while Kate and Tyler continued to pack up the things in the attic.

There was nothing more she could do about her parents' case now. She had done her part and was ready to put the whole thing behind her.

She turned her attention to the box of paints sitting in one of the boxes. She took a peek over her shoulder to make sure that Tyler wasn't looking before she quickly memorized the brands and colors.

She had been racking her brain to come up with a present for Tyler's birthday, and she'd finally come up with the perfect gift for him.

"Feeling sad for the brushes again?" Tyler suddenly asked. "I think I'd better get rid of them soon. It isn't helping if you're crying up here all the time."

She scowled at him. "I was just looking."

* * *

After three days of being carried around, Kate finally managed to argue her way into getting back to work. She wasn't in a hurry to return to the office, but as long as she stayed at home, Tyler was there with her. She needed him away from the mansion so that she could work on his present.

"Eve, may I borrow your car?" Kate leaned against the entrance of Evelyn's office and asked as sweetly as she could.

"Why? I thought you're not supposed to drive yet."

"Ty's being overboard. Please?"

"Are you sure you can drive? Because if anything happens to you, I'm pretty sure he'll come after me."

"Then Dan will protect you."

Evelyn's face went still, removing all hint of emotions. "I don't know what you're talking about," she said and threw the key over. "Don't crash."

"I haven't seen Dan around the mansion recently, and I haven't heard you mentioning any guy for quite a while."

"That's because you have been too busy with Tyler to notice."

Kate smiled and gave Evelyn a half-hearted shrug, ignoring her jibe. "Really? Tell me, then. How many cute guys have you met recently?"

Evelyn turned back to her computer. "Don't you have someplace to go?"

"Don't let him fall in love with you unless you're ready for a relationship. Oh, and can you ask him what they normally do for Tyler's birthday? I'll appreciate it if you don't tell Dan or mention to anyone else that I'm leaving the office during office hours."

Evelyn waved her away. "I guess this has something to do with the paints, brushes, and other stuff you told me to buy?"

Kate's brows flickered up as a corner of her lips curled.

"My lips are sealed. Have fun and don't crash my car."

She had to admit it was rather difficult to drive with one ankle wrapped up in bandages. And since it still hurt whenever she applied force on her right foot, she had to drive with her left foot, shifting it between the gas and brake pedals.

She couldn't be certain if Marianne had super-hearing powers or if Evelyn's car was too noisy, but Marianne opened the door to the mansion even before she could get out of the car.

"Are you all right, dear? Is your leg hurting? Why are you driving? You should've stayed at home. I know you think Tyler's overreacting, but you're injured—"

"My leg's fine, Marianne. It isn't hurting much. I need to go down to the shed. Can you lead me there? I'm not sure if I still recognize the way," she said as she made her way into the house and toward the kitchen. "Let me grab a bottle of water first."

"I'll get it for you," Marianne said. She pulled Kate to a stop and helped her to the couch. "Sit. I'll get it."

As Marianne disappeared into the kitchen, Mr. Sawyer strode out. "Hi, Miss Mitchell."

"Mr. Sawyer, how's life without work?"

After working so hard for such a long time, Mr. Sawyer had decided to take a break. His doctor had told him that his heart wasn't as strong as it used to be, and he should consider slowing down.

"Good."

She smiled politely and turned her attention to Marianne as she came hurrying back.

"Why do you want to go down to the shed?"

There wasn't any way she could hide it from Marianne. She had to tell her; otherwise, Marianne might let it slip in front of Tyler.

"The paintings inside have faded quite a bit. I want to restore it. It'll be my birthday surprise for him."

The frown that Marianne was wearing disappeared. "That's a great idea. I'll be sure to keep my mouth shut, but are you sure you can make it down to the shed like that?"

"Oh, it doesn't hurt anymore."

"But there's no reception there. If anything happens …"

"I can accompany you. I'll bring my book along." Mr. Sawyer offered.

"No, I'll be fine. Tell you what, if I'm not back in two hours, then come look for me." She continued when Marianne pursed her lips. "Please? I don't have much time. His birthday is two weeks away, and I can only work on it during lunch."

"Oh, all right."

It wasn't easy getting to the shed on one leg, but she didn't complain. She didn't want Marianne to drag her back before she could do anything.

Once she was inside, she started work immediately. She set a countdown alarm for an hour and a half, making sure she had ample time to head back to the mansion before Marianne got a panic attack.

She shook her head when the alarm rang. She'd only completed a small portion of the train tracks, and she wondered if she could complete the whole shed in time.

She was tempted to stay longer. But since she couldn't call Marianne from the shed, she didn't want to risk having a rescue team haul her back.

Half hopping and limping back to the mansion was much easier without all the paints and brushes. She would still need them anyway, so she might as well leave them in the shed.

She got back to the mansion in twenty minutes. Once she greeted Marianne to show her that she was still alive and well, Kate washed up and headed back to the office.

"You have flowers." Evelyn walked in with a bouquet of tulips. "Your favorite flowers."

Smiling broadly, Kate told her to put them down by the couch.

"By the way, they were hand-delivered."

That statement immediately took the smile off. "Ty was here? What did you tell him?"

"I told him you were with a client and shooed him off."

She nodded gratefully. "Good, thanks."

"So, are you going to tell me what you're doing?"

"As long as you tell me what's going on with you and Dan."

Evelyn shook her head. "We're just friends. We hang out, have dinner, and sometimes lunch. That's it."

"That's it? Dinner and lunch?"

"Yeah."

She shrugged and proceeded to fulfill her end of the deal,

telling Evelyn what she was doing.

"Right, that reminds me. They usually just go over for dinner. He asked if I wanted to chip in for the present, and I said yes. We're getting him some high-tech watch. Do you know your boyfriend is a geek?"

"He's not my boyfriend. We're friends."

Evelyn rolled her eyes. "A friend who's causing you to rush to and from work in your condition and to brave the jungle in order to restore something his mother did for him," she said. "You're not just friends. When you laugh, you move closer to him without thinking. And when you're afraid, you lean toward him. I've never seen you do that with anyone."

"How did you know I lean toward him when I'm afraid?"

"Dan told me about the movie night and Ryan's prank. Don't worry, I gave him a hell of a lecture."

Laughing, Kate said, "Thanks. Did he tell you what Ryan said? Brought episode one just for me." She threw her hands in the air.

"So there's something?" Evelyn pushed.

"No, there's nothing. We're housemates; we can't be more."

"Can't?" Evelyn raised her brow. "Meaning you want more, but you're afraid that things won't work out and he'd end up losing the mansion? Kate." She paused. "I'm asking if you feel anything for him. Forget about the mansion and the situation you guys are in. Just think about what you want." She stood and walked out of the office, stopping right outside her door. "Oh, he's fetching you tonight. You know that, right?"

"You're not coming for dinner? Will Dan be missing from dinner, too?"

"Think about it," Evelyn said and closed the door behind her.

For the rest of the week, Kate rushed between work and the mansion. She tried to keep within the two-hour limit, but Tyler's birthday was getting closer, and there was still so much to be done.

In the end, she ended up leaving at lunchtime and returning to her office only to pack up and head back to the mansion.

And with that, her own work began piling up. She had no

choice but to bring her work home, retreating into her room once she was done with dinner.

Chapter Eighteen

Tyler watched while Kate returned to her room to complete her work. He knew she was short of a team at work, but she'd only missed three days. Surely there couldn't be so much backlog that she had to bring back work each night.

Over the last week, whenever he'd asked her out for lunch, she would tell him that she was busy with a client.

He never questioned further, but he couldn't help getting worried.

Something was wrong.

He couldn't help feeling that she was hiding something from him, and it was making him uneasy.

Then there were the lacerations on her arms.

She'd brushed it off when he asked, saying she was careless and had fallen at work.

The more he thought about it, the more his mind started gearing in one direction; she was helping Lydia to dig further into Detective Cooper.

It could be something else, but whatever it was, he was determined to speak to Kate about it.

The next day, without calling her, he went to look for Kate in the office. Like the past week, she wasn't in the office.

But Joanne was.

"Ty!"

He nodded before asking, "Where's Kate?"

Joanne smiled—an ominous sign. There was no reason for Joanne to smile when talking about Kate.

"She has been leaving work every afternoon and doesn't come back until we're supposed to end work. Maybe she got herself a new boyfriend."

That explained her smile.

"Evelyn said she was with a client," he said.

"I'm her assistant. I don't see her scheduling lunchtime with clients, and she's crazy organized. If she has a meeting with a client, I'll know."

"And she has an insanely good memory. The meetings happened to be at lunchtime, so she didn't see the point of recording them. She knows she'll remember anyway," Evelyn suddenly said. "And she's your boss. If you want to gossip about her, don't do it in the office or you're fired."

Joanne pouted. "I was simply saying that I don't see her working on any other projects except on the Winsors."

"You're new here. We don't tell you everything," Evelyn replied. "I'll tell her that you dropped by."

Tyler nodded and headed out of the office with Joanne's conjecture nagging at him.

That idea never crossed his mind. But now that she'd mentioned it, it seemed like a reasonable explanation for Kate's behavior.

Regardless, he was in no mood to return to work, so he drove back to the mansion.

When he turned into the mansion, he frowned when he saw Evelyn's car parked outside.

He had just seen her back in the office. He was sure she couldn't have beaten him back.

He walked into the house with the same confused look, expecting to find Evelyn in the house. Instead, he saw Marianne and her hasty retreat into the kitchen when she caught sight of him.

"What's going on?"

Marianne pretended that she didn't hear his question and hurried into the kitchen.

Raising his voice, Tyler asked, "Is Kate here?"

"I think so. Somewhere in the house, I'm sure. I need to

prepare dinner. I'm making her favorite dessert."

"Where is she exactly?"

"Ty, this is a big house; you can't expect me to know where she is at every moment."

He could tell Marianne was hiding something. Whatever it was, she wasn't going to tell him.

He decided to do a sweep of the house instead of wasting time bandying words with her. He went around the house, searching even the other wing, but Kate was nowhere to be found.

"She is not here. Where is she?" Tyler asked, enunciating each and every word when he got back to the living room. He stared at the phone in Marianne's hand and sighed impatiently. "Marianne—"

"Fine. She's at the shed, but Ty—"

He was out of the house before she could finish her sentence.

He hurried toward the shed, frustrated that she'd gone there on her own, without anyone with her and with an injured leg.

Marianne should have stopped her. How could she let Kate go into the woods alone?

Sprinting, he got to the shed in a couple of minutes.

The door to the shed was open, so he stepped in without knocking, ready to unleash his anger at her utter lack of concern for herself.

Kate's back was to him, and she was wearing her earphones, oblivious to his entrance. She held a brush in one hand and a palette in the other, her full concentration on the wall.

He took a deep breath through his nose.

She was all the way out here alone and was wearing earphones. What if it were someone else who had come by?

He sighed and shook his head. Then he finally noticed the walls. He glanced around and looked at the restored paintings on two of the walls. He moved toward one of the walls, his finger grazing the newly touched-up paintings. It was restored to how he remembered, exactly how his mother had drawn them.

"Ty! What are you doing here?"

He took his eyes off the wall and crossed the room toward Kate.

Standing in front of her, he tipped her head back and pulled her into a kiss. One of his arms wrapped tightly around her waist, pulling her close, while the other hand moved to the back of her head.

His fingers weaved into her hair as her lips parted. He had kept himself away from her for as long as he could.

Now, he couldn't let her go.

He held her in place while he tasted her, his hand gently kneading down her neck.

"Oh, no," Kate suddenly said and pulled back from him.

That wasn't the reaction he'd expected, not after the way she'd kissed him back.

"Oh, no. It got on the floor."

He glanced down at the drips of paint on the floor while she put the brush and palette aside. She reached for a wet towel and was about to stoop down and clean up the mess when he took her arm and gently pulled her back into his arms. "Leave it."

She held her arms out awkwardly behind his back. "My arm's dripping with paint."

He laughed and let go of her to reach behind his back. He pressed her arms against his shirt before returning to hold her. "I don't care about the shirt." His hand stroked down her long, silky hair. "Is this where you've been coming during lunch?"

She nodded. "It's supposed to be a surprise for your birthday."

"And the injuries on your arms?"

She buried her face in his chest. "I wasn't careful and tripped over a rock."

He wanted to launch into a lecture, telling her the list of things she shouldn't have done. She shouldn't have come down to the shed alone without anyone accompanying her. She shouldn't be walking through the woods with her injury. She shouldn't have her earphones on and not realize that someone had entered the shed.

But he held his tongue.

He didn't want her to step out of his arms, so he merely nodded. "It's beautiful. Thank you."

"I think I can get it done before your birthday. At least I hope

I can."

"Since it's my birthday, do I get a say?" He continued when he felt her nodding. "Leave it until your leg is completely healed. We'll come back together, and you can complete it then."

"But that will be too late for it to be your birthday present."

"I've already gotten the best present I could ask for," he said, wrapping his arms tighter around her.

She looked up at him, and he couldn't stop himself from kissing her.

"Since you're here, can you help me pack up? I need to return Evelyn's car," she said as she pulled back to catch her breath.

He added another item to the list of things she shouldn't have done; driving while she was injured. But he shoved that to the back of his mind. "I'll get Dan to pick her up and drive her here for dinner."

"You know they're seeing each other?"

Unwillingly, he let go of her and started packing up, placing the paints and brushes into the box lying in the corner. "He spoke to me about it to make sure it was all right. I assumed Evelyn told you."

"No, she didn't. I guessed it on my own. Does Dan know that Eve doesn't do relationships? She detests relationships, thinks it's pointless and doomed to fail."

"You'll have to ask him."

Smiling, she nodded. "Let's get back to the mansion, and I'll call Evelyn from there."

Since Kate refused to let him carry her back, he wrapped his arm around Kate's waist and lifted her across any branches that were larger than twigs.

"Told you she was fine," Marianne grumbled when she saw them walking in. "Now you've ruined her surprise for you. Do you know how much effort she's put in? Rushing here and there every day, then having to bring home her work just to give you a surprise. Inconsiderate boy."

"I know," he said softly, leaning in to give Kate a peck on her lips. "Thank you."

Marianne stared, seemingly wondering if she had just

imagined what she saw.

"That's a direct result of me heading to the shed to look for her. Still grumpy?"

"No, can't say that I am," Marianne answered with a wide grin.

"And now that I know, she doesn't have to rush between work and here to finish it up."

"Good, good." Marianne couldn't wipe off her grin. "Good. I'm making apple strudel today."

Kate laughed at Marianne's reaction.

"Thank you," Kate said. "I need to call Eve and inform her that Dan will be picking her up." Then waving her arm that was streaked with paint, she continued. "And to wash up."

He pulled her closer against him. "You go wash up. I'll get your phone."

Kate wiped the water off her arm and took the phone from Tyler before he went to change out of his shirt.

Fifteen missed calls.

Evelyn was going to kill her.

She sat and switched on her laptop, checking her emails while calling Evelyn.

"Where are you? Tyler was here. Joanne saw him and went on and on about you disappearing after lunch. I think he suspects something," Evelyn said the moment the call went through.

She sighed. She thought something had happened at work. "Well, the secret's out. He got home and, long story short, found me at the shed."

"Oh, I'm sorry. I know you wanted it to be a surprise."

"It was still a surprise, and I won't be too sorry about it."

"Huh. Why not?"

"We kissed."

"Finally."

She shook her head. "I'm not going back today. Tyler's calling Dan to pick you up. See you for dinner?"

"Yeah, okay."

"Sorry to ruin your date."

"It isn't a date. It's two friends having dinner."

"And the two friends can't have dinner together with everyone else at the mansion?"

"That's exactly what I'm doing tonight," Evelyn said. "As for you, don't think about dating. Complete your work."

She laughed, her head dropping back. "Being responsible doesn't suit you. See you later."

By the time she stepped out of her bath, the responsible self returned and she couldn't help but fret. The will, the mansion …

She could hear movements in the attic, so she trotted up, thinking of talking to Tyler.

There was so much at risk, and he needed to know, to think things through rationally before jumping into a relationship.

"Busy?"

"I thought you wanted to finish up your work. Miss me?"

His carefree manner made her smile, changing her mind about speaking with him. "Nothing, I just came to check on you. I'll go now."

"What's wrong?"

"Nothing." She turned to leave, but Tyler stopped her.

"You look as if you regret what happened."

"No," she quickly said. She didn't want him to misunderstand. "Worried, maybe."

"About?"

"We've only known each other for three months. There's still nine more months to go. What if things don't work out? I can't let you lose the house."

Tyler ran his finger down her cheek and smiled. "You don't have to take care of me, too. Don't worry about the house, and don't start thinking so responsibly when it comes to me."

"Don't start? When did I stop?"

"Moving in with a stranger. Giving up your work. Driving with an injured leg. Hopping through the woods on one leg for my birthday present. None of these seems responsible to me."

"I didn't give up my work; I brought it home. My leg's fine; you're making a big deal out of it."

"And driving?"

"I haven't crashed, have I?"

"And moving in, after having met me once when I wasn't at my best."

She scowled. "I like to help people."

"You *compromised*. You didn't believe in moving in, but you did. You know you shouldn't drive, but you did. You know you shouldn't go trotting into the woods in your condition, but you did. And you know you shouldn't have returned my kiss, but you couldn't help yourself." Then he stepped forward, closing the gap between them. Lifting her chin, he said, "You're the best thing that's happened to me in a long time. I don't care about the house. I just need you."

He bent down and kissed her, softly and tenderly.

"But—" she said as she broke from the kiss.

"No buts."

She opened her mouth to speak but decided against it. She nodded and was turning to leave when Tyler took her hand.

"Help me unpack."

She pursed her lips. She did have some work to complete.

"Please."

Narrowing her eyes at Tyler, she studied him for a moment. "Why?"

"I'm afraid you'll go back to your room and start getting worried again."

She gave him a lopsided smile. He was right; she probably would. So she stayed and helped him with the packing.

They went through his parents' belongings, looking at all the things they used to own.

Tyler flipped through the old records and pointed out those that his parents used to play. "They used to love this song."

She leaned over to have a look. "Dream a little dream of me," she muttered. The same song she'd heard that night when she saw the couple dancing away.

Then, it hit her.

She got up and headed to the study.

"What's wrong?" Tyler asked as he followed.

"I just want to check something." She went over to the

mahogany desk and pulled out the lowest drawer, taking out a photo frame.

Standing side by side, Tyler's parents grinned at the camera with their hands intertwined. His mother wore a green sleeveless dress while his father wore a gray button-down shirt.

"What?"

"They were the couple I saw," she said, feeling the goosebumps on her arms.

Tyler took the photo frame from her hand and pushed her fringe behind her ear. "You probably saw this picture before; you were probably half asleep."

That was true.

"Yeah." But it seemed too much of a coincidence. Shaking the thoughts from her mind, she continued. "You're right. I'm thinking too much. This is a nice picture; we should put in into an album or something."

He nodded, putting the frame down on the table. "Later. Let's pack up the attic first."

She glanced over at the picture again before leaving the study. "Yeah, let's pack up the attic."

By the end of the day, they had his parents' belongings sorted.

He was only keeping the valuables and the photos; the rest would be thrown out or donated.

She knew how difficult it was to part with some of the things.

The last book his mother was reading with the bookmark still in it. The blueprint of an unbuilt playground with his father's notes scrawled all over it.

Her heart ached to see those items, and she couldn't imagine how Tyler must have felt. But he didn't appear upset. He went through the items, smiling as he placed them into the respective piles.

"Are you all right?" Tyler asked as she skimmed her hand over the boxes.

"I should be the one asking you that question."

"I am." He pulled her into his arms, giving her a kiss on her forehead. "Stop worrying about me," he said and gave her a light tap on her nose. "I'll take the boxes out."

Evelyn arrived while Tyler was moving the boxes.

It was still too early for dinner; Evelyn probably just wanted to get more details out of her. While Dan sat watching television downstairs, Evelyn and Kate went to her room to chat.

"So, tell me everything," Evelyn asked as she closed the door behind her.

And Kate did. She told her everything, from what happened at the shed to the talk she had with Tyler.

"And now? What do you think now?" Evelyn asked.

"When he's around me, when he tells me that he's willing to risk it all …"

"But?"

"But when I'm here, sitting and thinking about things, I can't help worrying."

"Because that's who you are—you worry. You have to make sure that everything will be perfect for everyone before you can feel good."

"That isn't true."

Evelyn rolled her eyes. "I don't believe in love or relationships, but I must say this is different. Everyone here keeps saying he's like another person when he's with you. But it isn't just him. *You* are another person when you're with him. I've never seen you like that around another guy."

Kate stared blankly at Evelyn.

"You're always so independent. If the situation of your injured leg happened while you were with Benjamin, you would've thrown him out if he had tried to interfere with your work. This is the first time I've seen you let someone take care of you."

"But we've only known each other for three months. What if one month down the road he realizes that he jumped into things too quickly? What if reality sets in and he realizes this is a mistake?"

"Do you think it's a mistake?"

"No."

Evelyn's head bobbed up and down. "You know, the events leading up to you staying here at the mansion are uncanny. It seems like fate."

"Fate?"

"You don't believe in fate?"

"I don't believe that Evelyn Jordan is telling me about fate."

"Just say yes when he asks you to marry him."

"What?"

Evelyn sighed. "I guess the people involved never see things the way they truly are. What I've heard from this whole conversation is your fear that he'll wake up and realize he's made a mistake with you. I'm telling you now that your fear is stupid."

Kate narrowed her eyes.

"Kate, the way he looked at you on the first night I was here … that was the first time in my life, that for a moment, I wished someone would look at me like that. Nothing in this world can make him regret kissing you; nothing in this world can change his feelings for you. Stop worrying."

"That's a long speech from someone who doesn't believe in love."

"I believe it for you." Evelyn raised her index finger when Kate was about to speak. "Don't start trying to convince me that it's for me, too."

That night, the guys cheered when Tyler walked in with his hand intertwined with Kate's. The news had clearly been disseminated even before they got to the kitchen.

Evelyn, being her usual self, warned Tyler that if he ever hurt Kate, she'd still hunt him down.

Even Mr. Sawyer was all smiles, congratulating the both of them.

Only one person remained silent throughout it all—Joanne.

Evelyn had told her about the conversation Joanne had with Tyler. Joanne must've expected to see a disgruntled Tyler or even a fight between them.

"So what has she been doing all these afternoons?"

"She was here, preparing his birthday present," Ryan answered.

"Touching up of some drawings in a shed that Ty will never take us to," Joseph added, and Dan laughed in agreement.

"You all knew?" Joanne asked.

"Since you've already gotten your first present, we can reveal ours," Joseph said, ignoring Joanne.

"Yeah." Ryan made the drum rolls, and Joseph gave Dan the honor of announcing it.

"On your birthday weekend, we're all going to North Carolina! You can bring Kate to the cabin, and the rest of us can just stay at the ranch to give you two some privacy."

"I thought you guys were giving him a watch?"

"I lied," Evelyn said. "I'm going, too. Dan says he'll teach me how to ride."

Ryan gave a booming laugh. "Are you sure, Dan? You aren't Ty; you haven't been on a horse for a while."

"It's like riding a bicycle; you won't forget," Dan said.

"Everyone can stay at the cabin," Tyler stated.

The entire hullabaloo instantly ceased, and everyone turned to stare at Tyler. Kate beamed at him and leaned on his shoulder.

"Are you sure?" Joseph asked.

"Yeah," he said as he pulled Kate's chair closer and hung his arm over her chair.

"Marianne, you'll join us, right?" Kate asked.

"Of course. If I'm invited, that is."

"Of course you are. We won't go anywhere without you," Ryan said. "And you too, Mr. Sawyer."

Mr. Sawyer smiled back politely. "Well, thank you. I'd love to join all of you."

Kate couldn't help but notice that Joanne hadn't said anything, and she didn't dare ask if Joanne wanted to go. She seemed to be the last person Joanne wanted to see.

Thankfully, Evelyn seemed to have read her mind.

"Joanne, do you want to come along? It's over the weekend, so you won't have to work anyway."

"It's all right. I'd rather not."

Soon after, Joanne said she was tired and left without even finishing up her dinner. Moments after she left, Kate stood and went after her.

Tyler grabbed Kate's wrist, stopping her right by the chair. "Don't. Just let her be."

"I'll be right back." She gave him a peck on his hair and hurried after Joanne, catching up with her by the car. "Joanne."

"What?"

"I'm sorry."

"Really? If you're really sorry, then return Ty to me."

"He was never yours in the first place. And even if he were, I'm sorry, but I won't—I can't," she said.

Joanne rolled her eyes and opened the door.

"Look, the first time we were at my house, he asked me if I was happy. I couldn't give him an outright answer. I think I've done quite well in life, but I couldn't give him an answer. I have the answer now. I'm really happy, and for that, I'm selfish enough to hang on to it. And I think I make him happy, too."

"The two of you have only known each other for a few months. Do you actually think you'll last? What's his favorite food? What's his favorite color?"

"I don't know. But I know he loves the sunrise more than the sunset. I know we both love crime novels. I know he doesn't like animals, except horses, because he was once attacked by a bulldog while playing basketball with the rest of the guys. And when it attacked, Tyler pushed Ryan away and ended up getting bitten, which explains the scars on his right arm. I know he's humble because he merely told me that he was bitten. Marianne filled me in on the rest. I also know that he's determined. When his right arm got injured, he learned from scratch and trained his left arm without a word of complaint. I know he's extremely good at figuring out games though he may not be particularly fond of playing them. I know he's a good dancer."

As she rattled on, the concerns she had about them being together disappeared.

She had thought that the only thing holding them together was the mansion, that Tyler treated her differently because she knew the stories about the house and the photographs. She was afraid that once she'd told him everything, once he remembered everything about the house, then he wouldn't need her. She was worried that once the year was up, they'd move on with their lives, and there would be nothing to keep them together.

But having said some of the things she knew about him, she realized it wasn't the house keeping them together.

The house had brought them together, but it was the things they loved, the way they could talk to each other about everything, and the way they wanted to share their happiness with each other that was keeping them together. All that had nothing to do with the house.

"You're the shiny new toy," Joanne interjected to stop her from continuing with her list.

"I'm not. I'm the one person whom he wants to tell things to. I'm the one person whom he doesn't mind touching his things without permission. I'm the one person whom he wants to protect without being asked." She smiled, shaking her head at how the situation turned out.

She had intended to apologize and leave. But she'd stayed, and the more she spoke, the more certain she was of them.

She thought for a moment and continued. "And he's the one who makes me happy, the one I want to share my joy with, the one I can't take my eyes off, the one I can't stop thinking about, and the one I'm head over heels in love with." She laughed at her own words, realizing how needless her worries were.

Tyler walked out from the mansion and took her hand, lifting it to his lips. "I love you."

"And I love you, too."

"No buts?"

"No buts." She couldn't stop smiling. Looking into his eyes, she could see his sincerity and heartfelt joy. His amber eyes were radiant, and the gray lines of turmoil within his eyes appeared lighter, glowing like polished silver.

They looked up when Joanne's door slammed closed and watched her drive away.

"Gosh, we were so rude," she said, guilty for not considering Joanne's feelings before speaking.

"Personally, I thought your speech was well said."

"You were eavesdropping?"

"You left the door open. I just happened to hear it from where I was standing."

She laughed and gently elbowed him in the chest. "Excuses."

Chapter Nineteen

Kate looked out of the window on the lone, single drive up to the cabin. Treasuring their privacy appeared to be a Hayes family trait.

The cabin stood right at the end of a long driveway, and all around was nothing but acres of trees. The deciduous forest was magnificent in autumn. Trees in myriad colors of honey-yellow, peach-red, green, and gold stood on both sides of the road.

At the mansion, the sun helped bring out the sweet and wistful sentiment of the trees. Here at the cabin, the trees seemed to speak of romance.

"This is so beautiful," she said and stepped out of the car, then walked toward the cabin as she watched the video recording she'd made while Tyler drove them up to the cabin.

"I knew you'd love it."

She cast a quick glance over at Tyler and grinned. "I still don't understand why we have to come a day earlier."

"To make sure everything is in order. I haven't been inside for a while. I've asked someone to clean up the place, but I'm sure you want to take a look too, right?"

With her eyes still on her phone, she laughed. "This isn't my house, so I don't have to worry about clean sheets and all. You could've just admitted that you wanted to spend some time alone with me."

"I want to spend some time alone with you."

"Just so happens, I don't mind spending more time with you." She leaned over and gave him a peck on the cheek.

"And the house is mine, so it'll be yours, too."

"Oh, now that you've done packing up the attic, have you thought about what you want to turn it into?"

Tyler took her hand and asked, "What do you want it to be?"

"Me? I think it'll be a great study or a library, or both I guess. You can build a platform to segregate it into a mini-library and study area. It's rather spacious."

"It could be a room for our kid."

She shook her head and chuckled. "You did the same thing when you were trying to get me here."

"You're here now, so I guess it worked," he said.

"What are we going to have for lunch?"

"I believe the fridge should be stocked. I'll cook."

"You know how to cook? You lived with Marianne your whole life. When would you ever need to cook?"

"When I pissed her off enough for her to ignore me for days."

Laughing, she nodded. She understood what he was saying. When Lydia bugged their grandmother about their parents' case, the same thing had happened. Though she wasn't the one who made her grandparents angry, she was made to suffer along with Lydia.

That was how she learned to cook as well, through the lack of choice and the need to feed a growling stomach. "I can't imagine it'll be any good, then."

He pulled her close, draping his arm over her shoulders. "Then I hope you can sleep well with an empty stomach."

She glowered at him and pushed him away, but his arm held firm, keeping her in place.

"I'm kidding. I won't starve you. We'll cook together. So if it's bad, you can't blame me."

"You know, I could be as good a chef as Marianne is."

"Like how you could be a martial arts expert?"

She would have retorted, but she finally took her eyes off him and saw the lake in front of the house. "Wow." She continued moving toward the wooden platform leading out to the lake. At the end of it, a wooden rowboat was tied to the platform's beam. "It's still floating."

From behind, Tyler wrapped his arms around her shoulders. "Of course. Let's go put away our bags and cook lunch. If we have time, and if we haven't burned the kitchen down, we can row the boat out."

"Sounds great."

Turning around, they strolled toward the two-story log home that was twice as big as Kate's own house. Tyler took their bags from the car, and they went into the house together.

The interior of the house was made of wood as well. The light yellow wooden planks were matched with dark brown furniture.

Privacy and simplicity. That summed up the mansion and the cabin, and Kate guessed whatever other properties were under Tyler's name.

Tyler stood and took in the scene.

"Is everything just as you remembered?" Kate asked.

"Yeah," he said with a smile. Shifting the bags into one hand, Tyler took her hand and headed up the stairs. He walked straight toward one of the rooms and placed her bag inside. "Your room."

"I don't get to choose?"

"This is the biggest room, and the only room with a huge bathtub."

"Oh, but what about you? Don't you want this room?"

"Are you inviting me to share?"

She gave him a sweet smile and blinked, then closed the door in his face.

Once she'd freshened up, she bounced down the stairs. "Ty?"

"In here."

She followed his voice, finding him in the kitchen. He'd started preparing their lunch, chopping up mushrooms on the granite countertop. "We're really doing this?"

"Were you hoping that I hid Marianne in the trunk?"

She moved over. "I didn't know you were funny."

"I don't have a favorite food. My favorite color used to be blue, but now it's green, like your eyes."

"What can I do?" she asked, smiling at what he'd just said.

"Boil water? We're having spaghetti."

"Do you know how to make the sauce?"

"There's ready-made sauce in the fridge."

It didn't take long for her to find a pot and accomplish her task. She poured in some oil and a spoonful of salt before taking a seat on a chair across from Tyler. She leaned her head on her hand and watched him work.

"If there's ready-made sauce, why are you still chopping up mushrooms?"

"Because Ryan says women love men who can cook. I can't do any serious cooking, so I pretend that I can by chopping up mushrooms and dumping them into readymade sauces."

"Someone is in a good mood."

"I'm here with you."

"Aw ..." She got up from her seat and walked over to him, wrapping her arms around his waist. "That's sweet."

It didn't take long for them to cook up a meal with the ready-made sauce, but they took their own sweet time finishing their meals. After more than an hour of eating and chatting, Tyler cleared the plates and washed up while she wiped them dry.

"We work well together," Tyler said.

"And?"

"Nothing. I just like to state the obvious."

Once they were done, they went out to the lake. Tyler stepped into the boat, stretching out his hand for Kate. She took his hand, but didn't take a step forward.

"What's wrong?" Tyler asked. "Are you afraid of the lake or something?"

"I'm waiting to make sure that the boat doesn't sink; you had a part in building it, after all."

The corner of Tyler's lips sneaked up, and he gave her a strong tug, pulling her right into the boat and into his arms. The boat wobbled dangerously, and she curled her fists, grabbing tightly onto his shirt.

He held her firm and laughed. "I won't let you fall in."

"I could have."

"Then I would've gotten you out."

"And I would've waited until you dragged me back up here

before killing you," she said as she gave him a punch in the chest.

He allowed her to do it before grabbing her wrist and lifting up her hand to plant a kiss on the back of her fingers. He took in a deep breath and smiled. "You always smell so good."

"The spaghetti isn't filling enough?" she asked, drawing her hand back.

"You're really angry? I'm sorry. I didn't mean to scare you."

She scowled at him.

"I really am. Please forgive me."

"Shall we?" she asked with a smile and sat.

"We shall." Tyler sat across from her and picked up the oars.

"Is this the first time you've rowed the boat? I don't think you could've done it when you were young."

"This isn't the first time I've been back here." Smiling at her surprise, he continued. "Quite a few times, when I was at the ranch, I'd come over. At first, I only came to look at the boat. Then I got into the boat and started rowing. Since then, I've come by quite a few times."

"But you've never gone into the cabin."

"I couldn't."

"And today?"

"I've been thinking about bringing you here for a while. I wanted you to see this place, and going into the cabin didn't seem like such a big deal."

"I'm glad I came."

"That's good enough for me." He grinned. "I know this may not be the best timing, but I need to tell you something."

"What is it?"

"I want to tell you what happened to my parents," he said as he shipped the oars.

She blinked, uncertain about how she should react. She knew all about the accident. So whenever they spoke of the past, she always tried to protect him from that memory and skipped to another topic. "You don't have to. I know."

"I know my grandfather told you, but I need to tell you."

She pursed her lips and nodded.

Tyler drew in a slow, deep breath and said, "We were on a

holiday. We had a great time that day, and I was so exhausted that I don't even remember how I got to my bed. I also didn't have a clue that the cabin was on fire. I didn't smell the smoke or feel the heat. I only woke up when I felt my mother shaking me. By the time they got to me, the rest of the house was already on fire. We were trapped in the room while my father tried to pry the window open." He paused, swallowing hard as he remembered that fateful day he lost his parents. "Then all I remember was my mother screaming, and she was on the floor with what seemed like a piece of the ceiling on top of her. My father went hysterical, screaming for me to get under the table while he tried to pull my mother out."

She saw him tearing up and couldn't bear having him go through the harrowing experience all over again. She reached out, took his hand, and gave it a gentle squeeze. "You don't have to continue."

"No, I want to tell you. I want you to know because I told you, not from someone else. And because after today, I'm going to move on from this memory and make better ones with you."

She gave him a small smile and squeezed his hand again.

"So, I hid under the table, but my father never got my mother out. Another piece of ceiling collapsed onto him, and they were both crushed underneath it. I watched the fire devour them. My father shouted over the fire for me to close my eyes, and I did. I don't know how, but eventually, a fireman carried me out of the house. He probably came in through the window, but I'm not too sure.

"I don't remember much after that, except for the funeral. I remember a man telling me that I needed to pack up my things while my grandfather got into his car and drove away. I kept thinking that he'd come back to get me, but he never did. Disappointment became sadness, then bitterness and anger. Up until I saw the shed, I was still angry with him."

"And now?"

"Now I realized he never moved beyond my parents' accident, and I don't want to remain trapped as he was." His hand covered hers and he continued. "Now, I'm extremely grateful

261

that his seemingly ridiculous will brought you into my life."

Her lips curled into a wry smile. "The nightmares that you have, are they about the fire?"

His smile reflected hers. "Yeah, but it's different now. I don't dream of that anymore."

"At all?"

The corners of his lips stretched into a brilliant grin. "Not for a while now," he said, his thumb rubbing along the length of her finger. "Do you want to give it a try?" he asked, cocking his head toward the oars.

"I assume you can swim."

"Can you?"

"Thanks for your strong faith in me. But yeah, I can swim."

Tyler laughed. "Don't worry, you'll do fine."

She took the oars and did exactly what Tyler had been doing. "This isn't as easy as you made it look," she said, leaning back and pulling the oars with all her strength.

"Don't dip the oars too deep."

"Won't we be going nowhere if I just skim the top?"

"Where do you want to go?"

She smiled and continued to row for a few more minutes before Tyler took the oars from her. Though she hadn't complained, she was glad she didn't have to keep rowing them; she simply didn't have the strength.

"Why aren't you taking photos?"

"I didn't bring my phone out. I was afraid I'd drop it into the lake."

"Do you want my phone?" Even before she replied, he shipped one of the oars and reached into his pocket.

"No." She shook her head. "What if I drop it?"

"Then we'll get a new one."

"But your contacts, calendar, and all the other information inside will be lost."

"The data is backed up on my computer."

She thought about it for a moment, then shook her head again. "Forget it. I'll still feel horrible if I drop your phone."

Tyler laughed and shrugged. "If you say so." He rowed them

back toward shore, and she sat right where she was until Tyler stretched out his hand for her. "Are you afraid of the water?"

"No, I just prefer land."

"You should've told me."

"You were looking forward to it, and I didn't want to ruin your plans."

He pulled her back onto the wooden platform and ran his hand through her hair. "Next time, tell me. I want you to enjoy yourself."

"I did. It was interesting."

Chapter Twenty

Kate opened her eyes when she heard the soft knocks on the door. She glanced toward the window and groaned. It was still dark outside.

She got out of bed and groggily opened the door, squinting at the bright lights in the hallway. Tyler stepped directly in front of her and shielded her from the light.

"Get dressed. We're having a picnic."

She forced her eyes open and saw a refreshed and excited Tyler. "Oh, Ty, there's one thing you should know about me; I hate waking up early. What time is it anyway?"

"Please? I'll get it set up while you wash up. Wait for me in the house. I don't want you walking out alone in the dark."

Nodding her head grumpily, she turned back toward her bed.

"Don't go back to sleep."

Her shoulders slumped. "Five minutes."

Tyler laughed. He stepped into the room, hooked his arm around her waist, and dragged her into the bathroom. "Don't sleep in the tub. Get ready."

"Ugh. Fine."

"If I have a curse on my mood when the sun sets, you have one before the sun rises."

That brought about a sigh and a smile.

"Don't fall asleep standing."

She glowered at him, and he grinned before scooting out of her room. She patted her hands against her cheeks before splashing some cold water onto her face. She sighed again as she stretched her muscles. She would love to soak in the tub for a while, but she was certain she would fall asleep if she did.

Instead, she used the standing shower and was out in less than ten minutes.

Why couldn't they have a picnic later in the afternoon?

It was so early.

Thinking that it would be cold outside, she slipped on her jeans and wore a cardigan over her tank top.

She was fully awake by the time she plodded down the stairs, but was still peevish about having to wake up so early. Since Tyler wasn't in the living room, she flopped onto the couch and stretched out, thinking she could rest her eyes for a few minutes.

"Sleeping beauty, ready for breakfast?" Tyler asked just as she closed her eyes.

"Yes, but only because I think you'll drag me out even if I say no." She sat upright and ran her hands through her still damp hair. "You're really an early riser."

Tyler walked over to the couch and took her hand, pulling her up. "The sunrise is beautiful here, and with the colors of the trees, it'll be stunning."

His words painted a picture in her mind and she smiled. "All right." She leaned against his arm as they strolled over to the door.

"Don't fall asleep."

She widened her eyes and blinked at him. "I'm up, I promise."

Tyler pushed the door open, and she froze.

"Ty ..."

The way out to the edge of the lake was lined with tea candles. Around each candle was a transparent glass cylinder to prevent the breeze from blowing out the light. The candlelight cast a warm yellow glow in the darkness, lighting up a dazzling smile and warming up her heart.

He leaned down and kissed her hair. "Shall we?"

She inched closer toward him. "You must've woken up quite early to prepare this."

"Do you like it?"

"Yes, of course." She turned to him, kissing his shoulder.

He led her to the picnic mat he'd prepared by the lake. On the picnic mat lay a bouquet of pink tulips and a basket of food. He kept his eyes on her, grinning when she gasped.

"This is ... really sweet. I don't know what to say ..." She looked at the flowers, the candles, and the food he'd prepared.

Hooking his finger under her chin, he tipped her head up and leaned in to kiss her. His kiss was tender but intimate. Then drawing in a deep breath, Tyler broke away from their kiss, his face inches away from hers. "Let's eat."

She sat while Tyler took out the food from the basket. She picked up the flowers and took a deep breath. "Thanks, Ty, and happy birthday." She leaned across and gave him a peck on the lips.

He grinned and pushed a muffin toward her.

She ate two muffins and waited eagerly for the sun to rise.

When a tinge of pink and yellow started to emerge in the distant horizon, Tyler asked, "Do you know why I dragged you out here to watch the sunrise today?"

She continued to gaze at the emerging light while she shook her head. She had thought there was no particular reason except to let her see the beautiful sight.

"I want to start a new year, a new day with you as my fiancée."

She blinked and turned to look at Tyler, seeing him down on one knee, holding a black box in his hand.

She took in a ragged breath and her heart sped. "Ty ..."

"Kate Mitchell, will you marry me?"

She broke into a smile, and her fingers splayed across her lips. "This is crazy."

"I know we've only known each other for a couple of months, but—"

She took her fingers off her lips. "This is crazy because I know we've only known each other for a short while, but all I can think of is saying yes."

Tyler sighed, relieved, and broke into a brilliant grin himself.

"Yes, yes, and yes," she said, her eyes brimming with tears.

He took out his mother's ring from the box and slipped it onto her finger. Then he pulled her into another kiss. "I love you."

"I love you, too."

Wiping her tears away, he kissed the corner of her eye before he continued. "There's something else." He reached into his pocket and pulled out a velvet pouch. "I didn't want to give you something that cost me nothing, so I took out the original diamonds and replaced them with new ones. Since you already have a necklace, I set the original diamonds into a bracelet." He poured out the bracelet and, lifting her hand, clasped it around her wrist.

She looked at her new bracelet and ring. "I love you," she whispered and leaned onto his chest.

He held her close and kissed her hair. "You're everything I need and more."

They idled the morning away in front of the lake, lying next to each other, basking in the sun while she wriggled her finger in the sunlight, smiling as she stared at her ring.

She only sat up when she heard the cars driving up to the cabin. "They're here." She bounced up and ran toward the two cars pulling up.

The moment Evelyn got out of the car, Kate threw her arms around her.

"What got you so excited?"

"I said yes."

"You said yes?" It took Evelyn a fraction of a second to comprehend her statement. Evelyn immediately stepped out of the embrace and lifted Kate's hand. "You said yes!" Evelyn screamed and hugged her tightly.

"Said yes to what?" Marianne asked as she stepped out of the car.

Kate let go of Evelyn, but all she could do was smile.

"My proposal," Tyler stated.

Marianne's eyes widened. She half ran over and took Kate's hand in hers. "It's real! Oh, I'm so happy," Marianne said, clasping Kate's hand.

The guys all gave Tyler a pat on the back before Joseph said, "Marianne, Kate's the one who got engaged; you're behaving as if you are."

Marianne tried to scowl at Joseph, but she couldn't get the smile off her face. "I've already stopped by the grocery store in town, but I'll need more food. We'll have a feast tonight. In celebration of Ty's birthday and your engagement!"

"Good job, Ty," Ryan said.

Kate laughed and returned to Tyler's side.

"Happy birthday, Ty!" Dan exclaimed, and the rest of the guys echoed their good wishes.

"This place is gorgeous! If Lydia were here, I'd ask you to get married this weekend." Evelyn said as she pulled Kate away from Tyler. "I want her to tell me everything, so you guys go in for lunch first."

"I'm coming along," Marianne said. "You boys settle your own lunch and bring back more ingredients for me." She rattled off a list of food for them to get and caught up with Evelyn and Kate.

"All right," Dan said as the guys turned back to the cars.

"I'll stay in the house," Tyler said.

"Oh, please. Go! We'll be fine. I'm here and Marianne's here. No one can get to Kate, I promise," Evelyn said.

"Go, you should eat something."

Tyler took a step closer. "All right, but stay by the lake and don't go wandering around."

Kate nodded as Evelyn began to pull her toward the lake, waving her hand to shoo Tyler away.

Evelyn and Marianne pressed her for every single detail about the proposal, and they chatted until the guys returned from lunch.

Again, she stared at the glistening ring. She waited for some form of distress to surface in her heart.

This was by far the craziest thing she'd ever done, but everything felt so right. It felt as though everything was meant to be.

She looked up as Dan and Tyler came strolling over.

"Hungry?" Tyler asked, pulling her up to her feet.

She nodded.

"Happy birthday, Tyler. And congrats." Evelyn smiled at him. "But nothing changes. If you ever hurt her, I'll still hunt you down."

"You won't believe the grin he had on his face. He actually spoke to a sales clerk at the grocery store; he was actually polite," Dan told Evelyn and Marianne as they walked ahead of them.

"We'll go horseback riding later," Tyler said, slowing their pace further.

"All of us? Eve can't ride."

"Dan will take care of that. The rest already had basic lessons, so it looks like you're stuck with me."

"Oh, the horror! Being stuck with a polite man."

He laughed and pulled her close, draping his arm over her shoulders. "Find a place where there's joy ..." He left the sentence trailing, smiling to himself.

"And the joy will burn out the pain." She looked up at him. "Joseph Campbell."

"Pretty *and* smart." He grinned, then stopped walking. "You are my joy," he whispered in his deep voice, leaning in to kiss her.

When she got back to the cabin, she tried calling Lydia on the phone, but it kept going to her voicemail. She sighed, understanding why Evelyn was always so frustrated with her whenever she didn't pick up her call.

"You can call again later. If you're worried, we can head back tonight or tomorrow morning," Tyler said.

"No. It's your birthday, and you have wanted to come here for quite a while. We'll stay as planned."

The guys waited for Evelyn, Marianne, and Kate to finish up their lunch before heading over to the ranch.

"Ty, we know you normally go riding on your own. But since Kate's here, are you joining us in the race?" Ryan asked.

"I don't think she appreciates speed on the horse."

"You can go ahead without me. Eve and I can watch."

"There isn't any point. I'll definitely win if I join. I might as well accompany you."

Evelyn turned to Tyler. "Cocky much?"

Tyler shrugged.

"Actually, he is the best rider among us so I'd rather he doesn't join us. There are fifty bucks at stake." Ryan cracked his fingers and gave Joseph and Dan a sly grin.

The guys dove into a debate, which lasted all the way to the ranch, on who was better and had a greater chance of winning.

When they got to the ranch, a middle-aged couple came out of the house with broad smiles on their faces. "You must be Kate." The lady wearing a light blue shirt with jeans stepped forward. "Congratulations."

Kate took her hand with a smile, slightly confused at how fast the news had spread to people whom she didn't even know. "Thank you," she said uncertainly.

"This is Jenny and Matt Clark. They help me run the ranch," Tyler said.

Matt nodded when she gave him a polite smile.

"Can you prepare a horse for each of them? Kate will ride with me."

"How did they know about the proposal?" she asked as they turned away from the Clarks.

"They helped me with the flowers."

When the Clarks brought out the horses, Tyler led her over to his gray stallion. He held on to the reins and gestured for her to try getting up.

She still remembered how it was done. Bouncing off her left leg, she swung her right leg over easily.

"Good," Tyler said.

"You sound surprised."

"You were the one who said you aren't good with animals and sports."

Tyler got up behind her. Along with Joseph and Ryan, they went for a ride on a nearby trail, leaving Dan to teach Evelyn how to ride.

Halfway down the trail, Tyler told the guys to go ahead, then taught Kate how to ride on her own.

At first, he gave her instructions while he was seated right behind her. After a few rounds of that, he hopped off the horse and urged her to give it a try.

She bit down on her lips and hesitated.

Following his instructions was easy when he was right behind her. She knew that if anything went wrong, he would take over immediately.

But it was a different matter when she was alone on the horse. She didn't quite dare to move or even shift her weight. She was afraid she would do something wrong.

"You'll be fine. Ash won't hurt you."

She licked her lips nervously and let out a slow breath.

Tyler didn't rush her; he merely stood by the horse, smiling warmly and waiting patiently.

"All right, here goes." She pulled the reins back, a little too far, causing the horse to start moving backward. She panicked, tightening her hands on the reins.

"It's all right. Relax your arms," Tyler guided.

Hearing his voice, she relaxed her arms a little. Then she made the same click-click noise that Tyler had taught her and squeezed her heels gently. The horse moved forward obediently and she yelped, "I did it!"

He laughed at her excitement. "Now try to go a little faster."

Her delight faded, and she gave him a nervous smile. "I think this is good enough."

"Try it. You'll do fine."

She sighed but did as she was told. Ash trotted forward smoothly, and her anxiety quickly disappeared.

She turned back to Tyler and beamed at him.

"Let's head back to the stables," Tyler said, getting up behind her.

"But you told Ryan and Joseph that we'd catch up with them."

"We will. We're just going back to the stables first."

"Why?"

"You'll see."

She shook her head. Some things never changed. "Okay. I guess I can check on how Eve's doing, too."

271

When they got back to the ranch, Tyler helped her off the horse. "Wait here," he said before heading toward the stables.

She didn't know what Tyler was up to, so she stood where she was and glanced around the ranch.

Evelyn and Dan weren't too far away from her. A wide grin was plastered on Dan's face while merriment and distress interchanged on Evelyn's.

Kate chuckled. She understood exactly what Evelyn was going through.

A series of slow clip-clops caught her attention, and she turned back to the stables to find Tyler walking alongside a white horse. "She's so pretty."

"And she's all yours."

"You got me a horse?"

He nodded. "I told Matt to start scouting for a horse when we got home from North Dakota. After running the errand for Marianne, I came here to take a look and picked her."

"When we got back from North Dakota? That was before we —"

"I know. But you looked like you were enjoying yourself, and I wanted to teach you how to ride anyway. So I figured you should have your own horse."

"Do the guys have their own horses?"

"They are free to ride any of them, except these two."

She smiled and shook her head. According to the guys, they used to come up here whenever Ryan and Joseph could get a weekend off, but they didn't have horses. Yet before she even stepped onto the ranch, Tyler had already gotten her one.

"Why?"

His brows furrowed. "What why?"

"Why did you get me a horse when I was only going to stay with you for a year? And I would probably not come back here more than once."

He shrugged and said, "I don't know. I wanted to get you a horse, and I just knew that you'd be back here more than once. I was right." Releasing the reins, he stepped forward and pulled her into his arms. He kissed her hair and stepped behind her.

Running his fingers through the ends of her hair, he asked, "So what do you want to name her?"

"Um ..." She cocked her head to the side and racked her mind for a name. "She's white like snow; I know it severely lacks creativity."

"She's yours. You can name her whatever you want. So, Snow it is." He wrapped his arm around her waist and nudged her forward. "Give her a try."

She nodded, but her lack of confidence was making the horse jittery.

Tyler placed his hand over hers. "They can feel it when you're nervous. It makes them nervous as well. I chose her for you because she's really gentle and tame. She won't move unless you guide her." He helped her off the horse and gestured for her to try again.

She nodded, confident in the fact that Tyler did know plenty about horses. She shook off the fear and tried again.

Snow was gentle with her. She waited patiently while Kate adjusted her weight and took the reins, and she moved only when guided.

"She's perfect."

"Good. You want to ride over and ask Evelyn and Dan to join us?"

"Really?"

"Go slow."

Evelyn wasn't quite as ready to ride on her own, so she rode with Dan.

Kate was getting better and more confident with each passing second, but Tyler made sure he kept the pace slow and was always beside her.

"Am I slowing you guys down?" Kate asked.

"Please do slow us down. I have no wish for the horse to go any faster," Evelyn answered.

Kate and Dan laughed while Tyler grinned.

"You'll be fine. I'm sure Dan won't let you fall."

Neither Evelyn nor Dan gave any reaction. Dan fell silent while Evelyn stared ahead.

Though Evelyn maintained her smile, Kate knew something was wrong.

Not long after that, they saw Ryan and Joseph sitting beside their resting horses.

"Finally. You guys took long enough. We're going to race back."

"You guys go ahead," Dan said.

Kate knew Dan was rather excited about the race, but he didn't want to leave Evelyn alone. "Actually, why don't all of you race back? I'll walk back with Evelyn and Snow. I need a break from riding."

"I walk back with you," Tyler said to her.

"No, it's fine. They're betting, right? I'm putting my money on you, so make sure you win." She stood on tiptoe and gave Tyler a peck on the lips.

Tyler scanned the surroundings and looked back at her. "It's quite a distance back, and I don't want to leave the two of you alone. I'll ride slightly ahead. Shout for me if you need anything." He lifted her chin and kissed her.

She shook her head at his protectiveness. "All right."

As Tyler rode forward, she pulled Snow beside her and turned to Evelyn. "So, what's wrong with you and Dan?"

"Nothing, we're just friends. Friends having fun."

"Eve, you have great instincts. Dan isn't just one who has fun and then moves on."

"I told him. I told him right from the start that it wasn't going to lead to anything else. We hang out, have fun, and that's it," Evelyn said, the exasperation clear in her voice.

"He said he wanted more?"

"No, I just feel that he does."

"And you? Still feel the same about relationships?"

Evelyn pursed her lips into a thin line.

"That's hesitation. Whenever I asked you this question, you never hesitated. You'd tell me 'yes,' then go on about divorce rates, about how love stories belonged to Disney and that as adults we should know better."

Evelyn cleared her throat. "Seeing you and Tyler, seeing how happy you are, seeing how protective he is of you," she said. "I mean look at him. We're not too far behind him, but he has to keep turning back to check on you."

They broke into a smile as Tyler glanced over his shoulder to check on them again.

"It makes me wonder if I'm wrong."

"And I assume you're still wondering."

Evelyn sighed. Her eyes swam with a pain that Kate would never fully understand.

"At least you're beginning to wonder. May I know your definition of fun between you and Dan?"

"We talk, watch movies, and have dinners."

"You're going to start running, aren't you?"

"Not literally. But I think it's better to put some distance between us."

Kate sighed softly. "And there I was thinking that you were having a great time with him."

Evelyn didn't answer.

Kate understood Evelyn's skepticism. Having grown up in the foster system, Evelyn had seen so many broken and screwed-up families. It was difficult for Evelyn to imagine being in something she thought was bound to fail.

"So do you think Ty and I will come to one of those inevitable ends?" Kate asked.

"Of course not. You're different; you're a good person."

"As opposed to you?"

"Let's not talk about this anymore. It's Tyler's birthday, and you just got engaged. I don't want to be talking about my issues this weekend, okay? Ty, join us!"

Tyler pulled back on the reins the moment he heard Evelyn shouting his name. He turned the horse back toward them. "Yes?"

"Walk with us," Evelyn suggested. "Are you guys going to continue staying at the mansion after the year is up?"

Tyler got off the horse and took Snow's reins from Kate so that he could walk beside her. "Do you want to stay there? We have quite a few properties. I can take you to all of them and you can choose whichever you like. Then you can rent out your house as well."

"And you? Where would you prefer?" Kate asked.

"Anywhere you are."

Evelyn shook her head and laughed.

As they strolled back, they chatted about the wedding. Tyler was fine with everything except the suggestion to return the following year to have their wedding at the cabin. He was adamant that there were other scenic areas, and he didn't mind flying everyone to the ends of the earth for Evelyn to enjoy scenic views.

Evelyn laughed at his speech and declared that it was the first time he'd said so much to her at one go. When she stopped laughing, she took a good look at both of them. "You two will work." Then she gave Kate's arm a squeeze before stepping into the cabin.

Instead of trailing in after Evelyn, Tyler took Kate's hand and strolled toward the lake. "I know you don't like the mansion, but we can still redesign it, then find somewhere else to stay. We can buy a new place if you want."

She leaned against his arm. "Actually, I don't mind staying there. It doesn't seem that scary now. Besides, you love the place."

"I want a place that we both love."

"We still have to stay there for a while anyway. I'll let you know again?"

Tyler nodded and sat on the wooden bridge with his legs hanging just above the surface of the lake. She sat beside him and folded her legs in.

"What is it about the lake that you're afraid of?"

"I'm not afraid. It's just that you don't know what's underneath, and it feels as if something may grab me anytime." She laughed at her own silliness.

He laughed softly and pushed her hair behind her ears. "I won't let anything get you. And if you do get pulled down, I'll go after you."

"I'd rather just avoid the getting-pulled-down part."

He shook his head. "You have an overactive imagination."

She'd realized that after watching *The Ring*. She remembered how every creak would conjure up a crazy image of a ghost crawling out of her computer screen. "Which is why I stay away from horror movies. But I can't help that I still remember those I've already seen."

Giving her a grin, he hooked his arm around her shoulders and pulled her closer. "Is everything all right with Dan and Evelyn?"

"Not really. She'll probably start giving him the cold shoulder soon."

Tyler didn't reply, and she felt the need to clarify for her friend.

"It isn't that she's cold-hearted; she went through a lot. I want to explain it to you, but it isn't my story to tell."

"I understand."

They sat in silence for a while, watching the sky turn orange before the darkness took over. "This is a beautiful place," she said as she gazed up at the starry sky. Without the city lights, the stars were so much more prominent. Thousands of dazzling stars lit up against the dark backdrop, accompanying the lone moon hanging in the sky.

"Please don't tell me you're thinking of getting married here, too."

She laughed at his dismay. "Why are you so against it?"

"Because I don't want to wait one year for you to become my wife."

"We can discuss that later. We should go in for dinner."

That night at dinner, everyone threw around ideas on where Tyler and Kate could have their wedding. When they heard from Evelyn that Tyler was willing to fly everyone anywhere, ideas like Fiji and Bahamas started popping up from the guys.

They joked around, but each time one of them tried to push Kate into choosing a particular location, Tyler would step in and tell them to stop it.

He gave them a stern warning that no one was to sway her decision, or the guys would be barred from wherever they would be staying.

Since where they stayed equated to where Marianne would be, everyone was quick to shut up.

While everyone was still trying to finish up all the food that Marianne had whipped up, Dan cleared his plate and headed out of the kitchen.

Evelyn had chosen to sit between Kate and Ryan, ignoring Dan throughout the conversations they had around the table.

Kate knew Evelyn would do that. It was classic Evelyn; she always ran whenever an issue about relationships was at stake.

Giving Tyler's hand a squeeze, Kate stood and followed Dan.

"She told me right from the start about what you said and how she's the kind of person who doesn't want more," Dan said as he switched on the television.

"She's dodgy when it comes to relationships and all."

"If Tyler can change so drastically for you, so can Eve, right?"

She sank onto the couch, pulling a cushion up against her, and considered her answer. "I guess anything is possible, but you have to be patient with her. If you push her, she'll either run or push back. Either way, you won't make any progress."

"She talks to me about everything. I thought I was different. I thought we were like you and Ty."

She sympathized with what Dan was going through. But when it came to Evelyn, there was only one thing anyone could do—be patient. "She's a great person. She has been through hell but still turned out great. I don't know if you'll end up like Ty and me. But if you believe that you will, then don't give up. She'll run, but as long as you ease up, she'll come back. She just doesn't like pressure."

"What happened to her?"

"You'll never get that answer from me."

Dan sighed and scanned through the channels.

"I'm sorry."

"Not your fault. This is your version of her telling Tyler that she would hunt him down if he ever hurts you."

"Sort of, I guess."

* * *

The next morning, the guys had another series of competitions from horseback riding to swimming in the lake.

Once lunch was over, Tyler brought Kate to the ranch and taught her how to brush the horse and how to ride faster.

Though he was patient, he was extremely strict.

They stayed at the ranch for hours before heading back to pack up.

She wished they could stay another day, but Ryan and Joseph had to work the next day. So that night, they packed up and left after having dinner in town.

On the way home, she tried calling Lydia. But again, it kept going to her voicemail. She hung up the call and dropped the phone into her bag.

Lydia was old enough to take care of herself.

So instead of brooding over Lydia's disappearance, she turned to Tyler and discussed how they could redesign the mansion.

Chapter Twenty-One

When they were driving up to the mansion, Kate's phone buzzed. She pulled it out from her bag, thinking it was Lydia returning her calls. Instead, it was a text from Evelyn.

She read it and shook her head.

"Is that Lydia?"

"Nope. Eve says to stay away from the office today," she said, grimacing at the thought of Joanne finding out about their engagement.

The same grimace appeared on Tyler. He must've been thinking of the same situation. "Tell her I owe her one."

"Maybe we should build a gate in front of the house. That way, Joanne won't be able to get in. It's safer than having her loiter outside the house," Marianne said from the back seat.

"She's Dan's sister. I don't want to make things so ugly, and it doesn't make much of a difference with her standing outside the gate."

Mr. Sawyer turned to Marianne and asked softly, "Is this the same Joanne who splashed juice into Kate's eyes?"

Marianne nodded grimly. "Which reminds me, have you gone for the checkup that Dan paid for?"

"Nope. I doubt I can head down until the team's probation is over," she replied and looked in the rear-view mirror to observe Marianne's reaction.

Immediately, Marianne leaned over and updated Mr. Sawyer. "One of her design teams made some major mistakes, so Kate and Evelyn split them up into separate teams. Now they're missing a team and have to take over the projects themselves."

Mr. Sawyer nodded in understanding, and Kate broke into a smile.

Since taking a break from work, Mr. Sawyer had been around the house a lot, especially around Marianne. And Marianne didn't seem to mind at all.

"Don't worry about the girl; we'll be around the house," Mr. Sawyer said.

"Thanks, but I'm hoping she won't make a big deal of it."

After all, what Joanne had with Tyler was simply a childish infatuation. When Joanne had found out about them, she didn't create any drama. She kept quiet and left. Her only outburst was when Kate went after her, hoping to talk to her.

The moment that memory surfaced in her mind, she felt a twinge of guilt for how her talk ended. "Anyway, since I'm not going to work, I think I'll work on the shed later today."

"I'll go with you," Tyler said.

As they stepped out of the car, she glanced at her watch. It was nearly two in the morning. She stretched her neck and back while Tyler and Mr. Sawyer took their bags from the trunk.

After muttering the usual goodnights, Mr. Sawyer and Marianne walked toward their end of the wing.

Tyler took Kate's bag up to her room and placed both their bags by the door. He stepped aside for her to move in while he stood by the door, smiling at her.

"Did you have fun?" he asked and ran his fingers through the ends of her hair.

"I did."

His smile grew into a wide grin. "Good." Leaning in, he kissed her softly and slowly. "Goodnight. I love you."

She looked dazedly at him. Their kisses never seemed to last long enough for her. "Goodnight. I love you, too."

She plodded over to her bed. Though she hadn't driven, she was exhausted. She hadn't slept a wink on the drive back, staying awake to keep Tyler company.

Now that she was on her bed, the exhaustion left her, and she couldn't stop staring at her ring.

She still remembered the night that Mr. Sawyer had read the will. She remembered how angry Tyler was and how she'd thought the late Mr. Hayes had gone out of his mind.

She wondered if this was the ending that the late Mr. Hayes had hoped for, or if he had ever imagined that she would get together with Tyler.

So much had changed in the few short months.

I'm so happy, Lord. I really am.

She wasn't sure when she fell asleep, but the sun was already high up in the sky by the time she woke. Glancing at her cell phone, she realized it was after ten. She washed up and trotted down the stairs to see muffins, a pot of coffee, and a jug of orange juice on the table. "Marianne, you're a godsend."

Marianne laughed. "Thank you, dear, but I didn't make those. Mr. Sawyer bought them. I did make the coffee and pour out the juice into the jar."

"Still, thank you. Is Ty still sleeping?"

"No, he isn't. He's already back from a jog and was wondering when his fiancée was going to wake up," Tyler said from behind her.

She turned around as Tyler entered the kitchen. "You went for a jog? All I want to do is lie in bed the whole day."

He grinned and bent down to kiss her hair. "I can do that with you, too."

She slapped him on the chest, pushing him away.

"There are others in the kitchen," she whispered.

He shrugged. "I'm going to shower, then eat. We'll go down to the shed after that."

She nodded. Instead of walking away, Tyler leaned down until his lips were beside her ear. "Or we can follow your plan. I'm fine with both."

"Go shower!" She pushed him away. "You're irritating."

He held his position and gave her a quick peck on the cheek before heading upstairs.

She turned to Marianne.

"If you're thinking of apologizing for him, don't. I spent twenty years with a moping and morbid Tyler. It's refreshing to see another side of him."

"He does seem happy, doesn't he?" Mr. Sawyer added. "So different from when we first met him."

"Of course he is," Marianne answered.

Kate and Tyler spent the rest of the day at the shed, eating the sandwiches that they had brought for lunch. But despite having been at the shed all day, Kate hadn't done much.

For the first few minutes, Tyler sat and watched her touch up his mother's paintings. Then, he took out his phone and started snapping pictures of her. When he got bored with that, he began teasing her, and they ended up painting on each other instead of working on the wall.

"You're a major distraction," she said as she started packing up.

Tyler grinned. "You seem to have enjoyed yourself as much as I did."

She glowered at him. "I'm never going to finish it with you around."

"Take your time," he said and helped her pack. "You've already done a lot and ..." He pulled her against him and leaned so close that their lips were almost touching. "I don't see the harm of having some fun while you work." Then he kissed her.

She wrapped her arms behind him, moving herself closer.

When they finally made their way back to the mansion, both their phones started ringing with continuous text messages. They looked at each other, confused by the phone spam.

"Whoa, Eve called me like fifty times. Marianne too."

"They called me, too. And Dan."

Kate glanced up from her phone.

"Joanne," they said in unison.

At that moment, Tyler's phone rang. "Marianne." He picked it up but didn't manage to get a word in. After a few minutes, he hung up. "I think Marianne's going crazy."

She stared at him, waiting for him to explain.

"She said Joanne became you. Then I couldn't catch the rest, something about hair and clothes."

"Marianne isn't crazy," she said with her eyes staring in the direction of the mansion.

Tyler followed her gaze and saw another Kate. That woman had the same hair color and hairstyle as Kate, and she was wearing a dress that Kate had worn before.

"Please don't tell me that's Joanne."

"It's all right," Tyler said as he pulled her closer against him, draping his arm protectively over her. "Stay by my side."

She had no intention of going anywhere else.

Joanne turned around when she heard them approaching. Her usual heavily made-up face was gone. The thick mascara, eyeliner, and eye shadow that she used to wear were replaced with barely-there make-up, like what Kate always wore.

Her wavy hair had been straightened, and her blond hair dyed brown.

Even her bag was similar to the one Kate often used.

"Hi, Ty."

Kate had stopped moving, bringing Tyler to a stop beside her. She couldn't make herself take another step. She didn't know how to react. Part of her wanted to laugh at the ludicrous situation she was in while part of her wanted to run.

She wasn't the only one who was dumbfounded. Tyler stood and stared in disbelief.

After a prolonged awkward moment, the front door flew open and Marianne stood there beside Mr. Sawyer.

Kate wanted to move toward the house, but her legs refused to function. Tyler tightened his arm around her shoulders and half dragged her toward the mansion.

Joanne behaved as though Kate wasn't there. She looked at Tyler and asked, "Do you like how I look?"

Tyler cleared his throat. "I love how Kate looks when it's on her. What are you doing, Joanne? This is …" Tyler shook his head, seemingly searching for the right word. "This is insane. I need you to leave now."

Just as he finished his sentence, a flash went off behind him. Their heads snapped around to see Mr. Sawyer taking a photo.

Kate didn't know what Mr. Sawyer was doing, but that was the last thing she was concerned about.

"Wait, Ty! I did this for you. Isn't this what you want?"

Tyler's head continued to sway slowly from side to side. "I already have what I want."

They returned to the mansion, and Tyler shut the door behind them.

"What were you doing?" Tyler asked Mr. Sawyer while locking the door.

"This is proof. Now all we need is a photo of her before this. The two photos will be enough for a restraining order."

The doorbell rang incessantly as Mr. Sawyer spoke.

Irate, Tyler went over, jerked the speaker off, and removed the batteries.

"That's a great idea, Joel," Marianne said. "Kate, you need to get the restraining order and get Evelyn to fire her. This is just wrong."

Kate swallowed hard and cleared her throat, but she didn't know what to say.

Tyler went over and knelt in front of her. "Are you all right?" He took her hand and ran his finger down the side of her cheek.

His warm touch brought her back to earth. "Did that actually happen or did I imagine it?"

Tyler got up and sat beside her, pulling her into his arms and wrapping her head close against his chest. Gently, he rubbed his hand down her back. "We'll get the restraining order, and I'm sure Evelyn will fire her without you asking. Maybe you can work from home this week."

"I can't stay here tonight."

"Then we'll stay at your house. She doesn't know where you live."

"We'll go, too," Marianne said.

Kate's mind kicked into host mode. "I haven't cleaned the house in a while, and there aren't enough rooms. Not that I don't want all of you there, but the house isn't presentable, especially if Lydia has been over there recently."

As she was speaking, she could feel the vibration from Tyler's chest. She looked up to see him trying to contain his laughter. "What?"

"Really? Even now you're thinking if the house is clean?"

She scowled at him, then laughed at herself. But they weren't going to get any reprieve. Joanne must've figured out that the doorbell was no longer working; she started pounding on the door, screaming for Tyler.

The laughter was strangled in Kate's throat. "Her hair is exactly like mine. Her dress, her bag …"

"We'll go pack," Marianne said.

"But—"

"We'll make do," Tyler told her.

"Yes, I can take the couch," Mr. Sawyer offered.

Tyler nodded and smiled gratefully at Mr. Sawyer before he continued. "We'll pack whatever you need, then we'll leave after Dan gets here and collects his crazy sister," he said, pulling Kate to her feet and walking up the stairs with her.

Instead of packing her stuff, she sat on her bed and shook her head. "What was she thinking?"

"Trying to get attention? Don't worry, she doesn't look anywhere near as good as you."

She knew he was merely trying to cheer her up. "It's all right. I can pack on my own," she said when Tyler took her bag and grabbed what he assumed were essentials.

"Are you sure?"

"Most of my stuff is already there. I don't need to bring much."

Tyler placed the bag on the floor and sat beside her. "How are you doing?"

"I can't figure out how I'm supposed to feel."

He took her hand, giving it a gentle squeeze. "What can I do?"

"I don't know." She broke into a smile at her silliness. "Are you all right?"

Tyler frowned, confused by her question. "Why wouldn't I be?"

"She did all this for you. You don't think she had a breakdown, do you?"

"Please don't tell me that since you can't decide how you feel about this whole thing, you're going to settle on worrying about her. Trust me, Joanne isn't weak. Her parents coddled her, but she isn't the sort who'll break down."

"You sound rather confident about that."

"She grew up with us, with Ryan. Even though all of us simply ignored her whenever she threw a tantrum, Ryan never allowed her to get away with it. He was always taunting her. Some of the things he said to her face were cruel even for me."

She nodded. "So this is another of tantrums?"

Tyler shrugged. "I guess so. Forget about her. Pack your things, and we'll head over to your house. Marianne can take the guest room, Mr. Sawyer gets the couch, and I'll sleep on the floor in your room. That way, you'll know I'm nearby." Without waiting for her reply, he stood, gave her a peck on the head, and headed to his room to pack his things.

She sighed and went into the bathroom, packing all her essentials into a pouch before placing it in her bag. Her phone rang at the same moment.

It was Evelyn telling her to open the door.

She headed down the stairs and, for the first time in her life, went over to the window to steal a peek outside before opening the door.

"Where's Joanne?" she asked, peering over Evelyn's shoulder.

"Do you think I'd ask you to open the door if she was still around?"

Kate pulled the door wide open for Evelyn to enter.

"Dan came and got her. He'll pick up his car later tonight or tomorrow."

"We won't be here. We're heading over to my house. I can't stay here tonight."

"Okay. She's gone too far. I've already fired her, so don't worry about that. Do you want me to stay over with you?"

She was grateful for Evelyn's offer, but there was no room to put her in. "It's all right. Marianne, Mr. Sawyer, and Tyler are all going."

"Are you sharing a room with Tyler?" Evelyn asked with an arched brow.

"He says he'll sleep on the floor."

Evelyn nodded and headed up the stairs with her, accompanying her until they left for her house.

"Nice place," Marianne said as they entered her house.

She glanced around, picking up the cushions on the couch and stacking them up on the dining table. "Are you sure you'll be fine on the couch?"

"Yes, don't worry," Mr. Sawyer assured.

She smiled and turned to Marianne. "I'll show you the guest room."

"I'll show her the guest room. Why don't you go put your stuff in your room?" Tyler said and led them up the stairs.

Tyler showed Marianne the room and closed the door after nudging her in.

"Why are you rushing Marianne into the room?" Kate asked.

"So you don't start getting worried about changing the sheets and all."

She laughed softly and headed into her own room.

When she got out of the bathroom, Tyler was sitting on the sleeping bag he'd placed on the floor.

"You brought a sleeping bag?"

"I can sleep on the bare floor if that's what you want."

"I actually intended to share. You can choose one side of the bed, and I'll take the other."

Tyler cocked his head to the side. "Are you sure?"

"Yeah, the bed is big enough for both of us."

He nodded and got up on the bed. "Look what I found on your bookshelf." He waved Shakespeare's *Romeo and Juliet* in his hand. "Looks like someone has read it quite a few times," he said as he flipped through the worn-out pages.

"What are you doing with that book?"

"I figured you probably won't be able to sleep after what happened, so I thought I could read to you."

No one had read to her since her parents passed away.

"Why not?" she said, settling down beside him.

Tyler opened his arm and waited for her to lean in before he wrapped his arm around her and began reading.

She laid her head against his chest, feeling it move as he breathed in and out. She listened to the steady rhythm of his heartbeat and to him giving voice to Shakespeare's words.

"No one has taken care of me the way you do," she said.

Tyler stopped reading and placed the book down. "And I promise I'll continue to do so." He gave her a peck on the hair, then lifted her chin and kissed her.

She broke from the kiss, leaning back on his chest.

Tyler kissed her hair again and continued reading until she fell asleep.

Her eyes flew open just as Tyler suddenly tightened his arm around her.

She thought she heard glass shattering, but she wasn't sure if she was dreaming.

The earsplitting alarm answered her question.

"Are you awake?"

She sat up, running her hand through her hair.

"Stay here," Tyler said and got out of bed.

"I want to go with you." She hopped off her bed and made her way over toward him. She didn't want to be alone.

With her hand in his, Tyler opened the door. Instead of taking her down the stairs, he brought her over to the guest room. Marianne had opened the door and was standing by the doorway.

"Is it Joanne?" Marianne asked as they neared.

Kate hadn't thought about that. She rubbed her hands against her arms as thoughts of Joanne stalking them to her house took over.

Tyler cupped his hand against Kate's cheek and said, "I'll check it out. Stay here with Marianne."

Tyler strode away, checking the bathroom on that level before moving downstairs. "Mr. Sawyer?" he shouted when he was halfway down the stairs.

Instead of an answer, he heard a cry of pain before Mr. Sawyer started cursing.

Tyler hurried down the stairs just as Mr. Sawyer flipped the switch, turning on the lights.

Tyler glanced at the glass pieces scattered across the floor and the patches of blood on some of the glass shards. "Are you hurt?" he asked when he saw the blood stains leading to where Mr. Sawyer was standing.

"Just my feet. I stepped on the glass when I tried to switch on the lights. I think someone threw something through the window."

"Did you see anyone?"

"No, I only heard the glass breaking," Mr. Sawyer said and jumped when the phone started ringing.

"Leave it. It's security." He cautiously stepped across the glass pieces and looked out of the broken window. The porch lights weren't triggered, so Mr. Sawyer was probably right.

He turned back to the floor, and sure enough, not far from the window lay a rock. He picked it up, but didn't bother examining it. Placing the rock on the table nearby, he said, "I'll do a quick check around the house. Stay here."

He moved around the house, making sure that every door and window was still locked. When he was done, the phone rang again. He ignored it and jogged up the stairs. "Where's your first aid kit?"

"Are you hurt?" Kate asked, giving him a look over and searching for his wounds.

"Not me, Mr. Sawyer. He stepped on the glass."

Kate nodded and ran into the bathroom to get the first aid kit while Marianne hurried down the stairs.

"Be careful of the glass!" he shouted after Marianne.

Shortly after, Tyler and Kate joined them downstairs with the first aid kit. While Marianne attended to Mr. Sawyer, Kate went over to cut off the alarm and asked, "Should we call the cops?"

"They should be on the way. I didn't answer the security call," he said as his eyes fell on the rock sitting on the table.

He was briefly distracted when the motion sensor lights turned on, flooding bright white lights onto the front porch. He looked out of the window and saw a few people, clad in pajamas, moving cautiously toward Kate's house.

"My neighbors," Kate said as she peered over his shoulder to see what he was staring at. Then she moved toward the door.

"No." Tyler grabbed her hand.

He bent over and looked out of the window. "We're fine. The police are on the way."

Kate popped her head out.

"Are you all right?" one of the neighbors asked.

"Yes, we're fine. Sorry about the alarm." Kate turned back to him. "I should go out and talk to them."

"No. I don't want you going outside, not until the police are here."

She peered out of the window again. "Just a prank; someone threw something through the window." She smiled and waved.

That reminded him of the rock.

When he'd first picked it up, he noticed something was wrapped around it. But he was more concerned with making sure no one had actually broken into the house.

He walked over and picked the rock up for a closer look. A folded piece of brown paper was secured to the rock by rough nylon strings.

He tugged on the string and unfolded the paper.

BACK OFF OR YOU WILL PAY

The words that formed the sentence were made up of cut-out letters from magazines. Besides that line of words, there wasn't anything else on the note.

His jaws tightened as he clenched the paper in his hand.

"What is it?" Kate asked as she moved over to him.

"We're filing a report."

Kate peered over and gasped at the threat in his hand. "Is that Joanne? If we tell the police, she'll get into trouble. Maybe we should call Dan."

"If she did this, she's gone too far."

Kate stood, vacillating between obeying a seething Tyler and protecting his friendship with Dan. "Ty, she can't hurt me, not with you here. Let me call Dan. I don't want to get the police involved in a family matter."

"Joanne isn't family."

"But Dan is. Please let me call him."

He sighed and conceded. He moved over to the phone and made a call, canceling the dispatched police car.

Dan was at her house in less than thirty minutes. He shook his head when he saw the note. "I called my parents. They swore she was home all night, but I won't count on it."

"Do you think she did it?" Kate asked.

"This isn't her style. She's more likely to write across the door or window with her red lipstick."

Tyler rolled his eyes.

"But you should call the cops anyway. If she did this, she's definitely losing her mind," Dan continued.

"You mean this evening at the mansion wasn't proof that she's completely lost it?" Marianne asked.

Dan sighed. "Call the police," he said to Tyler. "I'm really sorry about everything."

"Thank you," Tyler stated as he picked up the phone. He didn't intend to let it go in the first place. He wasn't going to allow someone to threaten Kate and get off scot-free.

"Ty." Kate tried taking the phone away from him, but he was faster.

He sidestepped and moved around her while dialing 911.

"Dan, are you sure? If this is Joanne, she'll get into serious trouble."

"It's high time she learned there are consequences to her actions," he said and looked at the pieces of glass on the floor. "Do you want me to clean it up?"

"No, Ty says we should leave it for the cops to see."

The police arrived shortly after Tyler made the call. They took a look around the house and asked why he'd canceled the first report. Tyler said they thought it was a prank, then realized it wasn't when he saw the note.

The police asked a series of questions about who they thought the culprit was and if anyone would want to hurt any of them.

Tyler, Marianne, and Mr. Sawyer all brought up Joanne. Even Dan admitted that his sister was behaving erratically.

Tyler stood beside Kate while the police interviewed her. Kate agreed that Joanne had been causing problems for her, but added that it might all be an unfortunate coincidence.

As Kate defended Joanne, the policeman cast a glance at Tyler. His only response was a tight-lipped smile.

The officer nodded and, before leaving, promised he would send more patrols.

"I need to call Evelyn and tell her about this. Otherwise, she's going to get real pissed when she hears about it from you," Kate said to Dan as she picked up the phone. While she spoke to Evelyn, Dan helped Tyler clear up the mess.

"Ty, I don't think it's Joanne. *But*, for what's worth, if it's her, I'm really sorry about it," Dan said.

Tyler nodded. Even if it was Joanne, it wasn't Dan's fault. If anyone were to be blamed, it would be him. He was the one who allowed Joanne to address him as her boyfriend for that long. "You're not her keeper."

"Thanks."

"Yeah, I'm fine. Yes. Yeah, he's here. They were here, too. They took our statements and left. No, there's no need. I'll see you in the morning. Yeah, yeah, okay. Bye." Kate hung up the call and turned back to Tyler as Dan's phone began ringing.

"It's Eve," he said. "Well, I'll leave you all to sleep."

Kate waved goodbye while Dan trotted out, picking up Evelyn's call.

Tyler ran his fingers through Kate's hair and rested his hand on her back. "Go back to bed. I'll tape up the window and be right up."

"I'll do it," Mr. Sawyer said.

"Are you sure you want to stay here tonight? Without the window—"

Mr. Sawyer waved her off. "I'll be fine. Leave this to me."

"Thanks." Tyler smiled and took Kate's hand, returning to her room.

Chapter Twenty-Two

Kate shifted closer to Tyler as she felt his hand running through her hair. "Mm …" she moaned and took in a deep breath. "Are you up?" she asked with her eyes closed.

"Sorry to wake you."

"It's all right. I was half awake anyway."

She couldn't sleep. Her brain kept processing everything that had happened, and she couldn't think about anything but her new doppelganger.

She scooted closer to Tyler, listening to his steady heartbeat, allowing it to wind down her overactive mind. Then, realization hit her.

There was another possibility.

Kate hadn't been able to reach Lydia since they had gone up to the cabin. It was only over a weekend. But no matter how busy Lydia was, unless they were in one of their cold wars, she would at least reply to Kate with a text.

Maybe it had something to do with Detective Cooper.

Then again, their visit had happened so long ago, and they had nothing to go on. Why would anyone tell them to back off now?

As her mind churned through the possibilities, her concern for Lydia grew. And as that concern grew, she couldn't stay in bed.

She got up and picked up the phone.

"What's wrong?" Tyler asked.

"I need to check something with Lydia."

It was still way too early to call someone, but she dialed

Lydia's phone repeatedly, determined to speak to her even if she had to spend the entire day doing nothing but hit the redial button.

When Lydia's drowsy voice answered the call, Kate shouted into the phone, "Don't you know you're supposed to call a person back when there's a missed call? What's wrong with you? Where have you disappeared to?"

"Sorry, I was busy," Lydia said after a moment.

"Busy? So busy that you can't take one minute of your life to send me a text?"

"Sorry."

Kate sighed, crawling back into bed. After venting the pent-up anxiety, she relaxed and told her sister everything that had happened the night before.

Then she questioned Lydia, asking her if she'd received any threats and if she'd been back to Detective Cooper's house.

Lydia assured Kate that neither had happened.

"I guess she didn't get any threats," Tyler said when she put the phone down.

"Nope."

He narrowed his eyes and continued. "Why do you look like you don't believe her?"

Kate gave him a wry smile as her head bobbed up and down. "Lydia's stubborn. You don't know how many times she got into a row with my grandparents in hope of digging out more information regarding my parents' deaths. She's never stopped asking. And now with the detective being the only lead, I'm afraid she wouldn't let it go so easily."

"Then why didn't she just tell you?"

"Because she knows I'll try to stop her, and she doesn't like to entertain people who don't hold the same view as she does."

"But the visit was some time back."

"I know. It doesn't make sense. Besides, he's an old man in a wheelchair. I don't think he'd get himself here just to throw a rock through my window."

"But?"

"The last time I spoke to Lydia, she told me she was

concentrating on a cold case project and that was all. Now, she suddenly has so many reports to complete. I haven't seen her in weeks, so she could've gone back to the house a few more times or found something else. I don't know. It doesn't seem like her to let it go so simply. Like how Joanne doesn't seem the kind to throw rocks into someone's house in the middle of the night."

"Dan said the police went over to his parents' house, and Joanne was at home. His parents also vouched that she was there the whole night."

"You know what? This could be a stupid prank by some neighbor's kid. We're reading too much into it. I'm going to change and get to work."

Since Kate hadn't been staying at her own house, there wasn't anything for Marianne to cook. But even as she headed down the stairs, she could smell food. "Where did you get that?" she asked.

"Mr. Sawyer went out to get it this morning."

She pulled out a chair and slumped onto it before leaning forward on the table.

It was a four-seater table, nothing like the long oval dining table back at the mansion. It felt weird to be seated so snugly when there were so few people.

"I think you should apply for a restraining order, just in case," Mr. Sawyer said as she began eating. "I can't guarantee that we can get it. But she did hurt you once, and with her behavior last night, it should convince a judge to give you one."

"Yes, you should," Marianne said. "For your own protection."

She turned to Tyler, thinking he'd jump on the bandwagon while he had his supporters. Instead, he shrugged and waited for her reaction.

"Aren't you going to ask me to get a restraining order?"

"It's just a piece of paper; it doesn't provide much protection."

"And it seems too extreme, doesn't it? She's Dan's sister. She didn't threaten or try to hurt me. She was only focused on you."

"Then forget about that," Tyler said.

Kate saw Marianne's eyes widening even as her own eyes narrowed.

"But let me drive you to and from work. You tell either Evelyn or me where you're going and always take someone with you wherever you go, preferably Evelyn or me."

Kate laughed and shook her head. "That was why you agreed with me on the restraining order issue, so you can make me compromise on this."

"You have a choice; you can say no."

"Really?" she asked, scrutinizing his face. Tyler had been patient with her. The least she could do was to agree with him and ease his mind. "Yeah, I can do that."

Evelyn arrived just as their conversation about Joanne came to an end. After stealing a donut and catching up on what had happened, Evelyn and Kate went to work.

The moment they stepped into the office, they knew something was wrong. There was an extremely tense atmosphere, and everyone seemed afraid to make any movement.

Kate scanned the room, and her fingers reached for her necklace as she saw Joanne sitting at her temporary desk, still dressed like a replica of herself.

"Joanne, I fired you last night. What are you doing here? Get out."

Kate sighed. She'd thought that since Joanne was Dan's sister, Evelyn would at least be civil.

"You said I'll win if I can stick it out until the team's out of probation, so I'm sticking it out."

"No, you're not. This brainless stunt of yours struck you out. Get out of the office or I'll call security."

"What are you trying to do, Joanne?" Kate said, stepping forward. "You think that by dressing up like me, by sticking with this deal between you and Evelyn, you would make a difference in things between you and Ty? Even if he does accept you, it's only because you're my substitute—which makes no sense because he already has me. And do you want to live the rest of your life pretending to be someone else? So what if you aren't a spoiled brat? It appears to me that you don't need to prove that to anyone but yourself."

"No. When Ty sees that I'm not a spoiled brat, he'll see me

differently."

Kate shook her head slowly as she licked her lips. Being polite and sensitive to Joanne wasn't getting them anywhere. "Joanne, he won't care. The only thing he cares about is making sure you don't hurt me. That's the only situation when he'll even think about you."

She saw Joanne opening her mouth to speak, so she quickly continued. "When someone threw a rock through my window, he thought it was you and was hell-bent on calling the cops. He didn't care what would happen to you."

"You're lying!"

"Ask Dan, ask Marianne. They know what happened. All he cares about is me. No matter what you do, no matter how you look, you can't replace me. We're getting married, Joanne. You need to move on. Doing this just makes you look crazy."

A tear rolled down Joanne's cheek. "No! No! No! Ty's mine! You already called the cops on me last night. You can do it again. I don't care!"

Exasperated, Kate turned away from Joanne and took a deep breath.

Trying to talk sense into Joanne was impossible. Why did she even bother to try?

Looking at Evelyn, Kate gave the go ahead.

Nothing was going to enter Joanne's ears, not now. Maybe not ever.

"Insane lass." Evelyn grabbed Joanne's arm and started their tug-of-war toward the office door. "Call security!" Evelyn hollered to no one in particular, but the staff all did as they were told until one of them shouted that she had security on the line.

Kate couldn't stand watching the debacle.

She went into her office and plumped herself onto her chair. She buried her face in her hands, frustrated that things ended up in such a mess.

She'd believed that if she spoke to Joanne calmly, she could make Joanne understand that her actions weren't going to yield any of her desired results.

"Are you all right?" Evelyn asked as she came into the office.

"Please tell me you didn't kill her."

"I didn't. I dumped her outside and locked our doors. I think we should get Tyler to install a security system in the office." Evelyn waited for Kate to reply. But she didn't, so Evelyn took Kate's silence as consent. "I'll call him."

"The two of you are like a wrestling tag team."

"You should be glad that your two favorite people in the world get along well."

Kate laughed dryly, waving Evelyn away to do whatever she wanted.

She was determined to forget about everything and focus on work. She went through all the designs, discussed the changes to be made with the teams, and went through the new projects that were in line. When she was done, she began working on a few designs for the mansion's attic.

"Am I disturbing you?"

Kate looked up and broke into a smile. Without thinking, she went toward Tyler and buried her face in his chest. "She was here and it went horribly."

"I know. Let me take you out for lunch. Then we'll come back to check on the security system."

She glanced up at him, then out to the main office, seeing a group of people working on various areas of the office. "You're fast."

"Only for you."

She smiled at that. "Yeah, that sounds good."

"If we have time after lunch, we'll go over to your house and see if the window has been fixed. Dan will be there, but we should still check on it."

"I completely forgot about my window. You got Dan to fix it?"

Tyler grinned. "I didn't ask, he offered. He says he knows someone who can fix it today, and he volunteered to be there so I can be free to watch over my precious."

She laughed at that. "You don't have to watch over me."

"So, where do you want to go?"

"We'll go over with Evelyn to meet Dan, then we'll all go for lunch together."

By the time they got to the house, the window was fixed, and Dan returned the keys that Tyler had handed him that morning. "All done!"

"Thanks, Dan. You didn't have to do this," she said.

"Oh well, like Ryan says, you're like the new, likable sister in the group. That's what family does."

She chuckled. "Thanks anyway."

At lunch, she showed them the designs she'd worked on and asked which design Tyler preferred.

Dan groaned at the idea of turning the attic into a study. "How about a games room? Get a pool table."

Tyler grinned but told Kate that he loved her library idea.

"So you're staying at the mansion after you guys get married?" Evelyn asked.

She turned to Tyler. "The house is great when everyone's around. It's big enough to accommodate everyone, and it doesn't seem creepy when it's filled with all of us."

"So it's a yes?" Tyler asked with a growing grin.

"And that means we, including Joseph and Ryan, will be free to go to the mansion whenever we want, right?" Dan checked.

"Yes, to both questions," she answered. "But only if Ty agrees as well."

"I never agreed to them showing up at my apartment, but they still do. So I doubt they'll care. You'll have to fire Marianne to solve the problem."

"Over my dead body," she said.

Tyler glanced over at his phone and sighed when he saw the name on the screen.

Joanne had been bombarding his cell phone so many times that he'd decided a change of phone number would be necessary.

After all this time, even Kate had realized that nothing was going to get through to Joanne. Joanne only listened to whatever she wanted to hear and had the uncanny ability to shut everything else out.

Telling her to stop calling or stop her nonsense was a useless battle that he'd rather not engage in.

Other than the phone calls and Joanne's mother trying to barge into his office, everything had been peaceful over the past few days. He had no idea why Mrs. Riley would think she could trick or persuade her way into a security firm.

If he couldn't stop people he didn't want to see from entering his own office, his company would've folded a long time ago.

He cast a glance at Kate. She was bent over slightly as she made changes to the drawings of the attic while he drove them back to her house.

They were only going to her house so she could check her mail and bring more of her things over to the mansion.

He couldn't be more pleased with her decision.

The mansion was no longer a place she was bound to. It was going to be their home, and Kate shifting her things over seemed to finalize that.

They had also set a wedding date; another reason for the smile he was wearing. The wedding was set to be in spring. Though it was still quite a few months away, they would only have what was left of autumn and the whole winter to turn the mansion into their home.

Between having to plan for the wedding and redesign the house, Kate and Evelyn decided it was better for them to give those on probation an early reprieve.

"We're here," Tyler said as he pulled up in front of Kate's house.

He got out of the car and went to get the mail while she headed over to open the door.

He opened the mailbox and frowned when he found it completely filled. "Kate!" he shouted, stopping her immediately. He hadn't seen what was on the stack of paper, but he couldn't shake the ominous feeling.

Taking out the stack of paper, he quickly flipped through it while moving over to Kate.

"What is it?" Kate asked while she stood rooted in front of the house.

He handed her the stack of paper as he pulled her away from

the house and scanned the area.

"Oh my God," she said, flipping through the dozens of notes. Each of the notes held the same warning.

BACK OFF OR DIE

He saw Kate's shock and disbelief as she went through the notes piece by piece. He wrapped his arm around her and rubbed his palm against her arm that had suddenly gone cold.

"It's all right," he assured her and took the stack of paper from her.

Scanning the surroundings to make sure no one was around, Tyler ran his hand through her hair. "Let's get back inside the car. I'll call the cops from there."

Once she nodded in his chest, he straightened and led her back to the car.

Kate took out her phone and called Evelyn while he called the police. The police arrived soon after and were getting more details from them when Detective Allen's car pulled up.

Tyler had known Detective Allen for years, and the detective had always done whatever he could to help him. Most in the police department did. After all, quite a few of his staff were ex-police officers.

Tyler did most of the talking.

Kate simply stood beside him, answering only when a question was directed at her.

Halfway through the police questioning, Kate excused herself and called Lydia. "Call me when you get this."

"She's not answering your calls?" he said.

"I don't know what she's doing."

"I told them about Detective Cooper so they could check him out as well."

Kate nodded and leaned her head on his shoulder.

"Kate, are you all right?" Evelyn got out of Dan's car, headed over, and gave Kate a tight hug. Dan was right behind her, wearing a perturbed look.

"I'm fine."

"We should head back to the mansion. Ryan and Joseph are already there," Dan said.

"Did Joanne do this? We fired her yesterday and today—"

Kate sighed and stopped Evelyn from continuing. "I don't know. There were so many of them. It's so creepy to see the whole stack of paper with the same warning."

"Were the letters cut out from magazines?"

Kate nodded.

"Joanne loves reading magazines," Evelyn said.

"Many people read magazines. I have magazines," Kate said, shaking her head.

Tyler thought Evelyn had a valid point.

The only thing he'd ever seen Joanne read was magazines, all sorts of fashion and female magazines. But it was clear that Kate was still adamant about not jumping to conclusions.

"Let's go home." He drove back to the mansion with Dan's car behind them.

Marianne opened the mansion's door even before they stepped out of their cars. "You didn't bring anything from your house? I don't think you should go back for the time being," Marianne said as she ushered them in.

"We'll buy whatever you need." He didn't want Kate to be in her house, not even with him around.

The notes might be nothing but pranks. Still, he didn't want Kate near her house, not until they found out what was going on.

"I can live with the stuff I have here. I just thought I could bring more clothes over and all."

"Hey," Ryan and Joseph echoed as they entered the kitchen. Both of them came over and gave Kate a hug.

"You'll be safe with us," Joseph said.

"Yeah. We'll take shifts to accompany you when we're not working. You won't be alone."

Kate smiled at everyone. "I'm fine. I don't want to trouble you guys. You work horrible hours and—"

"And nothing," Joseph interjected. "You're one of us now, so we're helping no matter what you say."

"Unless Ty is intending to whisk you away to an exotic island that few know about, we'll take turns to stay with you," Ryan added.

Tyler thought that was a brilliant idea, a complete stroke of genius. It wouldn't be difficult to arrange, but it would probably be impossible to convince Kate to go along. She wouldn't want to run from the problem, not when Lydia could be involved.

"Didn't you install security cameras at Kate's house?" Ryan asked, returning to his seat.

"It only captured a partial head of the hooded culprit who threw the rock, and we don't have any camera facing the mailbox." Protecting the mails was never a priority.

"Fingerprints?" Joseph added. "You guys got a note last night, right?"

"Only my fingerprints were found," Tyler replied.

Kate arched a brow. "They checked for fingerprints?"

"I pulled in a favor to get Detective Allen on the case."

She nodded while the guys began arranging who was to accompany Kate and when.

The guys filled Tyler in on their schedules and told him when they could come over to the mansion or go to her office.

"Look," Kate suddenly said. "I've got less work on my hands now. Whatever I need to do, I can do from here. That's if it's all right with you." She turned to Evelyn and smiled apologetically.

"Of course. I'd rather you stay here than travel around."

"Then there's no need for you guys to worry about where I'll be."

"Fine, then we'll come over here to accompany you," Joseph said.

"It'll be much easier without the stupid clause in the will. We can bring some clothes and stay over. We're here all the time anyway," Ryan complained.

"Actually, there is a clause stating that if there are emergencies, and I consider this one, anyone who is helping can stay. I suppose protecting Kate puts all of you in that category," Mr. Sawyer stated.

Evelyn and the guys turned to Tyler, waiting for his approval.

He had always enjoyed his space, but he couldn't say no to this. He knew Kate enjoyed having everyone around anyway, so he nodded. "You can have the guest room near ours if you don't mind the guys crashing there during the day. Otherwise, you can stay over with Marianne in the other wing," Tyler said to Evelyn.

"I don't mind. I'll head home to pack and be back in a while."

Kate nodded, and Dan followed Evelyn out after saying he would do the same. Since Ryan and Joseph already had their change of clothes with them, they stayed and had dinner before going to bed.

"Isn't it slightly dramatic to have everyone move in to accompany me over some threats? It may just be a sick joke," Kate said as Ryan and Joseph went to their rooms.

"We don't know who is behind this or what his or her intention may be. We have to be careful. I want you to promise me that you'll take every care. Same thing we agreed on; I drive you around, and if you need to go somewhere, take someone with you—one of the guys or Evelyn."

"I promise," she said as her fingers twirled around her necklace.

He pulled her hand from the necklace, holding it tight. "Everything will be fine. Don't worry."

Kate squeezed his hand and nodded. "Okay."

Chapter Twenty-Three

Kate sat at the desk; the drawings of the attic, living room, and master bedroom lay in front of her. She flipped through the drawings, checking the designs again.

As promised, she had stayed in the house as much as she could. Everyone who needed to see her regarding work or wedding preparations came to the mansion. She felt as though she was under house arrest, but she couldn't complain.

She wasn't the only one stuck in the house.

Since she had received the stack of threats, everyone had practically moved into the mansion. Tyler was there with her every day, solving whatever problem he had at work over the phone.

The rest of the guys and Evelyn were at the mansion once they were off work. At night, Evelyn would check on her, making sure that all her windows were locked before going to bed.

Her car had been rendered useless, sitting and wasting away in the front driveway. The few occasions when she had to leave the house to look at wedding venues, and her sole trip to the office were chauffeured by Tyler.

Even with Evelyn in the office, Tyler still insisted on hanging around, citing the excuse that he had nothing else to do anyway.

He spent most of the time lounging on her couch, reading on his iPad. Sometimes, he would get up and go over to the pantry to get himself a cup of coffee.

His presence was not only distracting Kate but everyone else in the office.

He walked around the office like it was his own, not realizing that all the staff were staring at him whenever he passed by their desks.

Oblivious would be a better word for it.

At first, she had thought that everyone was staring out of curiosity, that even though he had accompanied Kate to the office more than a couple of times, it was the first time he stayed.

It wasn't until she overheard the gossip in the pantry that she realized they were ogling rather than staring.

She hadn't noticed the reaction Tyler caused the people around him. His attention had always been solely on her. Whenever she was around him, she always had his attention, and he had hers.

She returned to the office and told Tyler what she'd heard.

He shrugged and pulled her onto his lap, asking her if she was done with work, ignoring what she had just told him.

Lydia had also returned Kate's call. She swore that she hadn't been back to Detective Cooper's house and hadn't found anything else about their parents' case. Lydia did ask Kate in detail about the notes and what she was going to do about them.

Kate told her about the arrangement with the new bodyguards she now had, but before she could update Lydia on her wedding plans, Lydia told her that she was busy and had to go.

That was when Kate realized that she hadn't even told Lydia about her engagement.

"Still working on the attic?" Ryan, her bodyguard for the day, asked, bringing her attention back to the drawings in front of her.

"No, I'm thinking about what to do with the current study."

"Get rid of everything, then put in a pool table."

She chuckled as she shook her head slowly. Joseph and Dan had each *suggested* that she could change the study into a games room as well, but she couldn't quite bear destroying anything inside.

She had spent so much time with the late Mr. Hayes in there.

Sometimes, she would pass by the room and still expect to see him sitting on the black leather chair, flipping through a photo album.

"She's going to keep the room as it is," Tyler suddenly said.

"Why would you need two studies?"

"Because she isn't ready to change the room. Leave her alone."

She understood that rationally, there wasn't a need for two studies. But she couldn't make herself change anything.

Tyler was right. He had said it before she could admit it.

"We'll talk when he isn't around." Ryan winked. "Goodnight for now."

Ryan went back to the guest room while Tyler continued. "Ignore them. Keep whatever room you want. It's your house."

"Actually, it's yours. What do you think?"

"I think I want my fiancée to stop thinking of herself as a guest."

"I don't. I just want to make sure that you like what I'm changing."

"I do. I'll tell you if I don't, I promise."

"And you don't mind leaving the study alone?"

"I don't think the guys need another excuse to come over."

She laughed and kissed him. "I love you."

Tyler opened Kate's letterbox, relieved that there weren't any threatening letters. He checked to make sure that the pinhole camera he'd installed on the mailbox was still intact.

Maybe Kate was right. Maybe it was just a stupid prank, and they were overreacting.

He closed the mailbox and turned back to his car. That was when the corner of his eye caught sight of the parcel. He stared at the parcel sitting in front of Kate's house, and his brows drew closer.

Kate didn't tell him that she was expecting a package.

He strode forward, picked it up, and gave the box a light shake to gauge what was within.

Whatever was inside was light, but it seemed large.

He studied the box that was wrapped in light brown paper and addressed to the Mitchells.

There wasn't any reason for Lydia to be sending her things

here; she knew Kate wouldn't be home.

He didn't want to open up Kate's parcel, but he had a gut feeling that whatever it was, it had something to do with the threats she'd been receiving.

Sighing, he tore off the wrapping to reveal a white box. Taking off the lid, his face paled.

Two charred dolls lay side by side in the box.

Clenching his jaws, he told himself to throw the dolls into the trash can and return to the mansion.

But he couldn't move his legs. He couldn't even loosen his rigid fingers that had clenched onto the edge of the box.

He exhaled a slow, long breath and sat on the steps.

The nightmare that had eluded him for months came rushing back to his mind, and the fear was worse than he had ever felt.

The mere thought of losing Kate in a fire constricted his lungs, causing him to struggle for air. Putting the box down, he closed his eyes and made himself focus.

He called Detective Allen before calling Ryan to bring Kate over. Then he called Kate, informing her that there was another threat and that he'd told Ryan to drive her over. He tried to keep his tone as placid as he could, but he probably wasn't doing too well with that.

"What is it? Are you hurt?" Kate asked.

"No, I'm okay."

"Something's wrong. Tell me or I'm going to be worried sick all the way there."

"It isn't just notes this time. The person sent something else."

"What?"

He took a deep breath and slowly exhaled through his nose. "A pair of charred dolls. I think you're right about your sister not telling you everything. It isn't just meant for you; it's meant for both of you."

"I should call her."

"Do it on the way here."

"Okay." She paused for a moment before continuing. "Ty, I'm safe. I'll be there soon."

He continued sitting where he was until Detective Allen

arrived.

When Detective Allen's Ford Focus came to a stop, Tyler couldn't continue sitting on the porch. Despite the waves of fear crashing against him, despite the image of the charred dolls imprinted so firmly in his mind, there were things he had to do.

He wasn't a helpless kid anymore. He didn't have to hide under the table while his loved ones got snatched from him.

He could change things now. He could protect her.

He got up, connected the pinhole camera to his computer, and reviewed the footage captured.

"Did it capture anything?" Ryan asked as he peered over their shoulders.

Tyler stretched out his arm and pulled Kate tight against his side as she stepped in.

He kissed her hair and said, "Nothing, it's just the postman. I figured that when I saw the postage on the box, but I thought we could give it a try anyway."

"Send me the footage. I'll have someone look over it thoroughly to check if anyone has been watching the house," Detective Allen said.

"Do you think the person is serious about the threats?" Kate asked.

"First, it was the rock, then hand-delivering those notes. Now, whoever is behind this is taking steps to avoid getting caught," Detective Allen replied. "Makes me think that maybe he has a plan and doesn't want to risk getting caught before it can be executed."

"A plan," Kate muttered before reaching for her locket.

Tyler remained silent. He could sense Kate's eyes on him, but he didn't turn to her. He didn't want her to see the fear in his eyes. Clenching his jaws, he looked away and tried to shift his thoughts from images of his parents' being trapped in the fire; images that were quickly morphing to include Kate.

"Don't worry, Ty. We'll keep doing what we do. There's no way anyone can get close to her. She's been safe so far."

"Kate!" Evelyn shouted once she got out of the car. "Have you called Lydia?"

Kate rolled her eyes at the mention of her sister's name. "She's sticking to her story, and she's refusing to come home; says she can't leave school over some silly threats that probably meant nothing."

"Take a photo of the dolls and send it to her."

Dan was right behind Evelyn. He gave Kate a hug, then turned to Tyler. "What are we going to do?"

"We're leaving," Tyler said.

"We'll follow your car."

"No, I mean we're leaving the country. Anywhere you want to go, but we're not staying here." Before, the notes were just words. But the person had upped the game. The dolls, the fire—Tyler couldn't take the risk.

"What? We can't leave. We're planning a wedding, and we're redesigning the house. What about our work?"

"We can plan the wedding from somewhere else. We've already reserved the place. The rest can be arranged through emails or calls. You can redesign the house anywhere. All we need are the blueprints. And I don't care about work. I want you safe."

"I *am* safe. Everyone's watching me as if I'm the president of the United States. And if we run, how long do we have to run? If we never catch this guy, do we keep running forever?"

He hadn't thought that far; he only wanted Kate out of the way of danger. He could plan the rest later when she was somewhere else and when his mind wasn't drenched with fear. "We just need to leave now." He stepped forward and took Kate's hand, dragging her toward the car. "We'll go home and pack. Everyone can come with us if they want."

Kate wrenched her hand from him and stepped away. "You're going to ignore what I've said and force me to follow your ridiculous plan? It's my life, too."

"You can be angry with me; I don't mind. But we're leaving." He took a step toward Kate, but she staggered back at his advance.

Evelyn immediately stepped in front of Kate. "Tyler, enough," she said softly, but without a hint of a smile.

311

"You want her to stay? Even with the danger she's in? Move aside," he commanded.

"I'm a human, Ty. I'm not the book that your mom left behind. You can't just snatch me away and shout at whoever is trying to come near me to leave."

He knew Kate was referring to the incident of Joanne touching his *The Little Prince* book; the last book that his mother had read to him before the accident. He ran his hand through his hair and drew a long, deep breath. "Kate …"

Irate, Kate turned away from him and stalked toward Dan's car.

He watched Kate storm away. He wanted to go after her. He knew she was right; he was being nonsensical, but his legs failed him again.

When Dan's car disappeared from his sight, he got into his car and drove back to the mansion.

Once he was back at the mansion, he headed straight toward his room and slammed the door closed. He had marched past a confused Marianne, but he didn't bother to say anything to her. He was certain Ryan would bring her up-to-date with what was going on.

In his room, he sat on the floor with his back against the wall.

He knew he'd screwed up big time, but there wasn't anything he could do now. "Get out," Tyler said the moment he heard the door opening.

Undeterred, Ryan stepped in and sat beside him. "Look, I know you want your space, but I'm afraid you might take a little too long to realize what you need to do."

He closed his eyes, trying to ignore Ryan.

"I once asked Kate when was the first time she felt there could be more than friendship between the two of you. You want to know the answer?"

His eyes remained shut.

Ryan shrugged. "She said it was in North Dakota. When she told you that there would be times when she'd disagree with the decisions you made. And you told her that if she did, you'd do whatever necessary to rectify the situation. Something about buying a plane. I can't really remember. Point is, Ty, that was something you could easily solve with money, and I know you have a lot of that. But now you're in a situation where money can't solve the problem. Are you still willing to do anything to rectify the situation? Can you put your fear aside, put your parents' accident behind you, and do what is needed to appease her anger? Man up to your words." Ryan gave him a pat on the shoulder and walked out of the room, leaving him to his thoughts.

He sighed audibly and tipped his head back as the door closed. He hated to admit it, but Ryan was right.

He had told her that, and he'd meant it.

Kate wasn't a thing for him to control, and she had compromised time and again for him. This time, it was his turn to step up.

He got up and left the mansion without saying a word to anyone. He didn't have much experience with apologizing, but he was sure that flowers were a must.

He returned home once he'd bought a bouquet of pink tulips, and sat on the couch, waiting for Kate to come back.

He wanted to go look for Kate. He was fairly certain that she would be at Evelyn's house, but he was equally certain that Evelyn wouldn't give him the address to her house.

"Dinner is ready," Marianne said.

Tyler nodded, but he didn't move. Kate should be back anytime now, and he didn't have the appetite for anything until he made things right with her.

"She'll come back."

"I'll wait."

He continued sitting where he was even as the clock crawled toward twelve. As he sat and watched the clock tick away, he felt as if he were eight again, sitting in the house and waiting for his grandfather.

Every day, he'd hoped that it would be the day his grandfather would turn up.

Every day, he'd gone to sleep disappointed.

This was why he never allowed himself to care. Everything he cared about was ripped away from him. And now the unshakable fear that Kate would disappear from his life percolated through his soul.

Marianne must have noticed him staring at the clock. She picked up the phone, probably to call Kate.

"Don't." He didn't want Kate to return because Marianne called her; he wanted it to be her choice.

Just as Marianne put the phone down, the door flew open. Kate entered the house, all flustered. She glanced at her watch and sighed. "Thank God we made it in time."

Evelyn and Dan were right behind her. "Sorry. She was busy cleaning while we watched TV and lost track of time."

"Cleaning?" Ryan asked.

"She does that when she needs to blow off steam. And according to her, there's always plenty of things to clean in my house," Evelyn answered.

Tyler sighed and stood, pulling Kate into a tight embrace. "I'm so sorry. It was a stupid idea. I won't force you to do anything you don't want to."

Kate wrapped her arms around him and snuggled closer. "I'm sorry too. I know those charred dolls reminded you of your parents' accident. I should've been more understanding. I'm sorry."

He closed his eyes and held her close, refusing to budge even when he felt Kate trying to take a step away from him. He didn't want to let go. He was so afraid that if he did, she might disappear.

"What's wrong?" she asked and laid her head against his chest.

Again, he said nothing.

Kate tipped her head back and looked up at him. "I'll always come back. No matter how angry I am, no matter where I go, I'll always come back."

For the first time since Kate stormed away from him, his lips parted into a smile.

He didn't know what he'd been thinking and how he'd allowed the senseless fear to take over his thoughts. He turned to the coffee table and picked up the flowers he had bought for her. "For you."

"Thank you." Kate took the flowers and glanced around the empty room.

Everyone had escaped into the kitchen to give her and Tyler some space.

Taking his hand, Kate pulled him to the couch and sat. "I don't want to leave. I've already been leaving Eve to take care of all the work. I can't just skip town. I want to stay here. I want to sit in the rooms and redesign them. I want to be here when we turn the mansion into our home."

"Then we'll stay. But you won't go anywhere alone. Don't just take Evelyn; bring one of the guys as well. And I'm going to apologize to you in advance for how I'm probably going to behave until this thing is over. I'll probably be calling you all the time, and you may find me around your office during working hours. But I promise I won't affect your work."

Kate laughed softly. "You won't affect my work, but you'll probably affect some of the female staff."

He didn't care what her staff thought of him; he only wanted her safe. "If you want, I can stay hidden in your office."

"Thank you. I know it's difficult for you, and it means a lot to me that you're listening to what I think. And remember, above all else, God and His angels are watching over me." She leaned in and kissed him. "Is there any food left? I'm starving."

Now that she was back, he was too. "We have Marianne; there's always food."

Chapter Twenty-Four

Kate twisted to the side to have a better look at the dress she was wearing.

"I think this is the best," Evelyn said.

Of the three dresses she'd shortlisted, she loved the current one she had on. "I think so, too." She ran her hand down the smooth satin with silver and gold embroidery threads that weaved classy flowers down one side of the gown.

"It's so you." Evelyn walked around her, looking at the dress at every angle. "Perfect. This is perfect."

"The dress does look great on you. With veil or without?" Helen asked as she tugged at the excess material around Kate's waist and took note of the adjustments that had to be made.

"With," Evelyn said.

Kate nodded, agreeing with Evelyn. "Have you decided on your bridesmaid dress?"

Evelyn picked up a dark violet off-shoulder dress. "You know, most brides choose the bridesmaid's dress. They choose the ugly ones."

"Why would I do that? You're the maid of honor, so you get to decide what you want to wear."

Evelyn laughed and shook her head. "Everything is perfect. You'll have a perfect wedding, a perfect marriage, and you'll live happily ever after."

"I thought you didn't believe in happily-ever-afters."

"I believe it for you."

Kate smiled warmly at Evelyn and gave her a hug. "Thanks."

"It's settled, then. We should pack up and leave. We shouldn't be here in the first place, and where is Dan?" Evelyn checked the time on her phone.

"I'm sorry, it's just that …" Helen pursed her lips. "It's a little difficult to work on the dress at Evelyn's place."

It wasn't just difficult for Helen to work on the dress; it was impossible to walk across Evelyn's living room without dragging something under the train of the dress.

An hour before the appointment, Helen had suddenly called and asked for a change in location.

Evelyn was adamant about not letting Tyler see the wedding dress. With that, the only location left was Kate's own house.

Though Tyler was totally against the idea, it was too late to make other arrangements, so he eventually gave in after asking Dan to accompany them since he was around the area.

But they had been in the house for over an hour, and Dan was still nowhere to be seen.

"He's probably caught in a jam," Kate said.

"Tyler won't be too happy with us staying here longer than necessary."

Helen led Kate away and helped her remove the dress, making sure that the pins stayed in place.

"All right, I'm done. Do you want me to stay with the two of you?" Helen said as she packed up her bag.

Kate smiled and shook her head. Helen was already going out of her way to travel out of the studio with all the heavy gowns. Kate had told Helen the gist of what had been happening, and she had been kind enough to accommodate. "We'll be fine. Thanks for coming."

"Thanks for flying me in first-class and for the five-star hotel suite," Helen said mischievously. "I'll see you at the next fitting."

"Thanks."

Helen left while Kate and Evelyn continued waiting for Dan.

"We should head back to the mansion on our own," Evelyn said when Dan didn't pick up his phone.

"He's probably on the way here. Let's wait for a while. I can clean up a little while waiting," Kate said with her arms akimbo and her eyes scanning the room.

Even with her back toward Evelyn, she could feel Evelyn rolling her eyes.

"Fine. Fifteen minutes, then we're leaving."

Kate agreed and proceeded with her chores, trying to clean as much of her house as she could. Evelyn switched on the television and lazed on her bed, waiting for the fifteen minutes to pass.

As she was wiping the dust off her table, a sudden brightness from outside her window attracted her attention.

It was the light from the motion-sensors.

Dan. But she couldn't help wondering why Dan would walk toward the back of the house instead of ringing the bell. Curious, she peeked out the window to see what he was doing.

She couldn't see the man's face, but it definitely wasn't Dan.

Dan wouldn't be wearing black leather gloves and a ski mask.

Kate reeled back from the window. "There's someone outside." Just as she finished her sentence, the shattering of glass confirmed her statement.

Evelyn hopped off the bed at the same moment the security alarm rang. "Call Tyler now," she instructed and went over to lock the door. Taking Kate's chair, Evelyn jammed it against the doorknob. Then she reached into her bag and pulled out a handgun.

"When did you get that?"

Evelyn frowned at her. "You knew I always had a gun at home. I've kept it in my bag since you received the threats." Evelyn took a few steps back and took aim at the door. She cocked her head to the side, gesturing for Kate to move behind her. "How many are there?" Evelyn shouted over the alarm.

"I don't know. I only saw one."

Evelyn thought about that for a moment. "You should get in the bathroom. I'm the only one with a gun."

"I'm not leaving you alone out here."

Evelyn sighed and dragged her into the bathroom, locking the door.

"How does this help?" Kate asked.

"It puts more space between us and whoever is in the house." Again, Evelyn aimed her gun at the door, and the two of them fell silent as they waited.

Kate's heart pounded against her chest, and she found herself staring at the doorknob, waiting for the inevitable. She swallowed, remembering the anxiety she'd felt when watching the zombie film.

The person in her house wasn't a zombie, but this ending would affect her directly. She exhaled deeply through her nose, trying to calm her palpitating heart.

"Kate, call Tyler."

She'd clean forgotten about the phone in her hand. Her fingers moved quickly across the screen, calling Tyler.

"Done with your dress?"

"There's someone in the house. I saw him breaking in."

Tyler didn't say anything.

"Evelyn has a gun."

More silence. Kate kept her eyes on the door knob until Tyler spoke.

"Stay where you are. I'm on my way. Where's Dan?"

Before Kate could answer, a loud bang against her bedroom door and the sound of wood splintering made her scream. Her phone slipped out of her hand, crashing onto the floor. She picked it up to see cracked lines across a black screen. "No, not now."

She pressed the home button, but no light came on. Frantically, she tried the power button.

Nothing.

Nothing but a blank screen stared back at her. "Ugh!"

Evelyn held her ground and kept her eyes on the door. "Leave it. Just stay behind me."

Kate moved behind Evelyn, leaning against the sink for support. She watched as Evelyn took long deep breaths, her eyes focused on the door. Despite Evelyn's placid exterior, she was sure Evelyn was terrified.

She knew every detail of Evelyn's terrible childhood. Having to hide away in the bathroom was probably bringing up memories from the past that Evelyn couldn't forget or wait to shake.

Then, the doorknob to the bathroom started shaking violently as someone on the other side tried to open the locked door.

Without shouting any warnings or threats, Evelyn pulled the trigger and fired a warning shot through the door.

Kate cringed and bit down on her lips to stop herself from screaming while her fingers tightened around her locket.

The doorknob stilled, and there wasn't any sound. Her fingers gripped the edge of the sink, and she realized she'd stopped breathing.

Drawing a shaky breath, she flexed her fingers and shook her hand.

Jesus, please end this. Please let this be over.

Evelyn got back in position, poised for another shot.

After a few minutes, it felt as though her prayer was answered. She stepped from behind Evelyn and moved toward the door, thinking she could look through the bullet hole to see what was going on outside.

"Kate, stay behind me," Evelyn whispered harshly.

"Maybe he left."

"Maybe. Or maybe he's waiting for you to open the door. We're not leaving the room until Tyler or Dan arrives."

Resuming her position, Kate tugged on her necklace and twirled it around her fingers. The anticipation of someone knocking down the door was worse than getting killed.

She sighed, and as the thought entered her head, she had to ask, "Eve, what if your shot killed him?"

"Then we continue to wait. The security will dispatch somebody, right? We'll just wait until someone comes for us. I'm not putting down the gun, and we're staying put until someone arrives."

Moving to sit on the edge of the bathtub, Kate took a deep breath and tried to calm herself down. She wrinkled her nose and took a sniff. "Is that smoke?"

Evelyn lowered her arm and took a deep breath. "Damn!" She reached for the doorknob and screamed when her fingers wrapped around it. Jerking her hand back, Evelyn turned around to put her hand under running water.

Kate stood and saw an orange light flickering off the windowpanes in her bathroom. "There's fire downstairs, too." She pulled the towel off the rack then dumped it into her tub and turned on the water. Opening one of the cabinets, she pulled out another towel and threw it under the running water.

Evelyn took the first towel and wrapped it around her hand while Kate took the second towel from the tub and pulled it over Evelyn and herself.

"Stay behind the door!" Evelyn yanked the door open and wrapped the towel over herself.

After the initial burst of fire through the door, they kept their heads low and ran out. Instantly, the heat and smoke overwhelmed them.

Kate bent over, coughing and choking from the thick smoke. Every breath she took only made her cough more severely, and her throat quickly became sore as the smoke stung through the membranes.

Evelyn dropped to her knees and pulled her toward the door.

Kate crawled along, squinting as the smoke continued its assault. She bent low and saw the raging flames through the slit at the bottom of the door.

Reaching out, she grabbed Evelyn's arm.

She shook her head. "The window!" she shouted amid a cough, then pulled the wet towel over her mouth. She breathed through it and started crawling toward her bedroom's window.

She was no longer sure if the towel was wet from the water she had soaked it with or from her perspiration. The heat was making it difficult to take in the already pathetic amount of oxygen left in the room, and she struggled to keep her limbs moving.

Evelyn's cough caught her attention.

She paused and turned around. It was clear that Evelyn was struggling as well. "Come on!" Kate shouted through the cloth.

Evelyn coughed again, her entire frame shaking as she did. She stopped moving completely, and her arm flew to her chest.

Evelyn collapsed onto the floor, pushing Kate's arm away. "Go," the word came out in a gasp.

Even through the smoke, Kate could see Evelyn's eyes losing focus. She cast a frantic glance around.

The fire was inching closer, devouring everything in its way. She turned back to Evelyn and clamped her fingers over Evelyn's arm, refusing Evelyn's weak attempts to push her hand away.

Her lungs were throbbing with pain, and she couldn't speak. She had to get both of them out before it was too late.

Thankfully, when Evelyn realized that Kate wasn't going to leave her behind and that she was wasting precious time and strength trying to do otherwise, she cooperated.

With what little strength she had left, Kate dragged Evelyn toward the window. She pulled herself up using the window ledge and tried lifting the window pane.

She used all the strength she could gather, but it refused to budge. Desperate, she grabbed the lamp beside the window and swung her arm, smashing the window pane. The glass shattered, pieces flying everywhere. But compared to the stabbing pain in her chest, the pain from the cuts was negligible.

Fresh air hit her and she gasped, sucking in a much-needed deep breath, relieving some of the pain.

Taking another deep breath, she spun around and helped Evelyn to her feet.

Then, she heard it.

The crackling of wood. The same crackling of wood she'd heard in the hallway as the fire licked up the hardwood flooring.

The unmistakable sound of wood caving to fire.

Without thinking, she shoved Evelyn out of the window.

Ryan jumped out of the fire truck and started shouting out instructions. He couldn't believe how strong the fire had gotten within such a short period of time.

As the team got to work, Ryan noticed Tyler's car.

He'd hoped that Kate would appear beside Tyler. But when he saw the dazed look on Tyler's face, he knew Kate was inside the house.

He was about to run up to Tyler when a burst of flames shot through a window on the second floor. "Stay here! We'll find her," Ryan shouted to Tyler and sprinted up to his teammate who was carrying Evelyn in his arms. "Where did you find her?"

"She jumped out of the window. She was screaming for someone before she blacked out."

"Evelyn," Ryan said, shaking her lightly. But Evelyn was out cold.

He glanced back at the flames shooting out of the second floor.

He couldn't give up now. Maybe Evelyn and Kate got separated during the fire. "There's still someone inside. We need to find her." Ryan prayed he wouldn't fail Tyler on this.

He knew Tyler lost his parents in a fire. Tyler never spoke of it, so he didn't know the specifics. But he knew one thing for sure —if Kate were to die in the fire, Tyler wouldn't survive it either.

"The fire is too strong. The floors could give way anytime," his teammate said as Ryan moved toward the house.

"My friend's in there."

His teammate nodded, and without another word, they got to work. While the team doused water on the burning house, Ryan, along with two of his teammates, got ready to enter the house.

The raging roar of the fire took over the moment he stepped in. His gut was screaming at him to get out.

The fire was too strong.

It was too late.

"It's too dangerous! The structure isn't safe! We need to get out!"

"No!" He couldn't leave, not without Kate. But despite his best intentions, a slab of ceiling dropped heavily in front of them, blocking off their entry.

"Ugh!" Ryan shouted in exasperation and exited the house. When he stepped out, he pulled off his mask. But instead of going back to the fire truck, he turned to the side and looked for another way in.

He wasn't going to give up; his friend's life depended on Kate's survival.

He'd seen plenty of miracles in his line of work. He'd seen

impossible situations turned around by what could be nothing but God's hand at work.

Keep her safe, Lord. I know you can do it; I've seen you do it.

Chapter Twenty-Five

Kate stepped away from the window as the bookshelf came crashing down right before her, blocking out the window and the fresh air she needed.

She coughed as she drew a breath.

There wasn't anywhere else to go.

She watched the bookshelf burn as her legs crumpled. But instead of sinking onto the floor, she felt a warm arm supporting her around her waist.

"We have to go."

She turned and blinked. *It couldn't be.* She blinked again, wondering if the lack of oxygen to her brain was causing her to hallucinate. She forced herself to focus, staring at the familiar faces in front of her.

The same couple she'd seen dancing outside the mansion. The same couple she'd seen in the picture. "Mr. and Mrs. Hayes?" Kate asked as she tried to grasp what was going on.

"You can call me Diana and my darling husband, Kenneth."

"Am I dead?"

"No, but we have to hurry or that may become true. Come, quickly."

Kate coughed again. She didn't have any strength left.

Somehow, she was still standing, but that was all she could do. She couldn't move her feet. It was getting painful to breathe. Her chest was burning like her house, and she was so tired.

"Kate, Ty needs you. You have to move. Come on, just put one leg in front of the other."

A tear slipped down her cheek. Diana was right; she had to move.

With great effort, she managed to do as she was told.

"The gun, Kate. Shoot at the glass."

Kate blinked and felt her lids scratching the contact lenses that seemed to have fused to her eyes.

She was back in the bathroom. The tiles inside must have held the fire back.

She turned to look at the floor, her head spinning as she did so. She tried shaking the drowsiness from her brain, but it only made her dizzier.

Her ears rang as the gun fired, but she couldn't even move her hands over her ears. She closed her eyes and felt herself falling.

She couldn't resist the relief she felt.

"Breathe, Kate."

The voice sounded so far away. She felt the urge to hang on to the voice, but she couldn't.

The burning pain was fading.

The heat against her skin was easing.

Thank you, for keeping your promise.

Tyler's face was buried in his hands when he heard someone calling his name. He ignored it and remained in his position.

"Ty."

He drew a deep breath when he heard the voice he thought he'd long forgotten.

"Ty, Kate is safe."

His head snapped up at the news, but when he saw the familiar face in front of him, he froze.

"Kate's safe. Come with me."

He closed his eyes, thinking he was losing his mind.

"I'm sorry I was such a lousy grandfather to you."

He forced his eyes open, but his grandfather was gone. He *was* losing it.

"Ty!"

He turned as Ryan came running back toward him with Kate in his arms.

He ran his hand through his hair and got up. The strength returned to his legs, and he followed them to the ambulance. "How is she? Is she hurt?" Tyler took her hand. "Kate?"

Ryan laid her down on the stretcher, and the paramedics immediately put an oxygen mask on her.

Tyler stood aside, but refused to let go of Kate's hand even as the paramedics attended to her.

"Heart rate and blood pressure normal. She'll be fine." The paramedics pushed the stretcher into the ambulance. "Who's coming along?"

Tyler hopped up into the ambulance.

"See you at the hospital," Ryan said, then went back to put out the flames.

Tyler continued holding Kate's hand as the ambulance drove off. He brushed her hair aside and skimmed his finger down her cheek.

Kate's eyes fluttered open for a mere second.

"Kate?"

Slowly, her eyes opened. "Ty?" she mumbled, her voice deep and hoarse. She tried clearing her throat, but ended up coughing.

"Shh … It's okay, just rest."

Gently, he kneaded along her neck and noticed she was wearing another necklace with her usual locket. He recognized the necklace immediately, but he lifted the pendant for a closer look anyway.

He grunted with disbelief as he held the angel pendant in his hand.

Kate was wearing the necklace he'd given his mother. The necklace that had cost him a year's savings. The necklace that his mother never took off.

He set the pendant down and gave Kate a peck on the forehead. Maybe Kate wasn't dreaming when she saw the couple dancing. Maybe she really did hear someone playing the piano.

Maybe she was right about everything; there really were angels watching over her every move.

Once they got to the hospital, Kate was whisked off for a

thorough checkup before being pushed into a hospital ward.

By the time she got to the ward, Marianne and the rest of the gang arrived.

Tyler sat beside her on the hospital bed, keeping Kate in his arms and the rest of them away from her. He knew they were all happy to see her, but he didn't want them crowding around her; she needed her rest.

"Where's Eve?"

"Here," Dan said as he wheeled Evelyn in.

Kate stared at the cast around Evelyn's right arm and shoulder and the cuts on her other hand.

"Don't worry, the cast will come off in time for your wedding," Evelyn said.

Kate rolled her eyes. "I wasn't worried about you ruining the aesthetics of the wedding. I was just wondering if it was my push that caused your injuries."

It was Evelyn's turn to roll her eyes. "You saved my life, Kate. If you hadn't pushed me out, both of us could be dead."

"I'm sorry I was late. My car broke down and my phone was dead. I couldn't get to your house in time. Otherwise—"

"Dan, it isn't your fault. You weren't the one who set the fire. Besides, we're both fine," Kate said.

"Speaking of which, how did you get out?" Evelyn asked.

Kate chewed on her lower lip and turned to Tyler. "I'm not sure. Everything is such a blur. I thought …" She paused for a moment, then smiled wryly at Tyler. "I thought I saw your parents. They helped me get back to the bathroom and shot the window. I can't remember anything else."

Everyone stared at Kate with blank faces.

Joseph was the first to speak. "You were probably hallucinating. Your brain was lacking in oxygen and—"

"Marianne, look at her necklace," Tyler interjected.

Marianne frowned, but moved closer for a look. Even Kate looked down at the long chain holding her locket.

Tyler reached behind Kate's neck and unclasped the necklace he'd once given his mother. Holding one end of the chain, he lifted the necklace and let the rest of the chain hang freely.

Marianne gasped and took the necklace from him. "Where did you get this? Your grandfather searched everywhere for it."

"What's that?" Kate asked.

"I gave this necklace to my mother when I was young."

"And she never took it off," Marianne added.

Everyone leaned in closer to look at the necklace.

"Where did you get that?" Evelyn asked.

"I don't know."

Marianne placed the necklace into Kate's hand. "I know you're safe. That's all that matters."

Kate nodded. "And Lydia?"

"I left her a message, and she called back a while ago. She says she's fine. She wanted to come over now, but I told her you were fine and to come tomorrow instead," Evelyn said.

"Thanks." Kate yawned softly.

"We should go. She needs her rest," Joseph said.

Everyone gave Kate a hug before leaving the room.

When Ryan came over, he leaned in, and instead of the usual brotherly hug that squashed her, his hand draped lightly across her shoulders. "I believe you saw what you saw." He grinned and added, "Goodnight."

Only Tyler stayed behind. He lay in bed beside Kate while she curled up against him. He ran his hand down her face while his cheek leaned against her hair.

For twenty years, he'd thought his parents were ripped from him and he was all alone.

But he wasn't.

They were always watching over him; he just hadn't realized it until now.

Evelyn was chatting with Dan when she spotted Joanne walking past her ward and heading toward Kate's. She got out of bed and rushed out. After what they had gone through that night, Evelyn didn't want anyone disturbing Kate.

"Where are you going?" Dan asked.

But Evelyn was already out the door. She was ready to drag Joanne out when she saw her standing by the door, looking into

Kate's ward.

"Anne, not tonight. Whatever you've planned, not tonight. Ty thought he'd lost Kate," Dan said from behind Evelyn.

"He's smiling, even in his sleep," Joanne said softly, her words saturated with pain.

Evelyn gave Dan's arm a squeeze and cocked her head toward her ward. "Give us a minute."

Dan arched a brow.

She nodded, then waited until Dan was back in her ward before saying, "He does seem happy, doesn't he?"

Joanne spun around at Evelyn's voice, and she swallowed hard. "I'm not here to make a fuss."

"And you're here looking like yourself," Evelyn stated as she gave Joanne a look over, noticing that she'd returned to her former blond hair and thick mascara.

"No matter how much I change, no matter how I prove myself, he'll never look at me the way he looks at Kate."

Evelyn thought she was probably supposed to feel sorry for Joanne, but she didn't.

Joanne never had anything with Tyler; it was a childish infatuation that blew out of proportion.

"That's right."

"I'll leave now."

Evelyn reached out and gently grabbed her arm. "You should be happy. Forget about him. He never cared about you anyway."

"Is that supposed to make me feel better?"

"Yes. You don't have to be like this."

"What? A spoiled brat?"

"You don't have to be like your mother. Move out from your parents' house and find your own place. Tyler isn't your life, he never was. You can be so much more. Find your own dreams, find yourself. Whatever you want to pursue, I'm sure Dan will support you."

Joanne wiped away the tear that escaped her eye. "I don't know what I can do or what I want to do."

"It's not too late to start thinking. When you've made your

decision, we'll help you. We all will."

"They have never considered me to be one of them. I'm always chasing after them. No one tells me anything. I know they think I'm just Dan's irritating sister. Even when this happened, no one called me. I only found out because I saw it on the news."

"That's because you have never bothered about anyone but yourself."

"I care about Tyler."

"No, you don't."

"I do," Joanne said, clearly indignant.

"Why did you come here?"

"I was concerned."

"No, you weren't. You came here thinking it was a chance to show Tyler how concerned you are about him. If you were truly worried about him, you'd be smiling now. Everyone's safe and he's happy."

"You never sugarcoat your words, do you?"

Evelyn grinned and looked at her. "You're like this because you've received nothing but sugar-coated words. You should start listening to some truths."

Joanne sighed and turned to leave. "Tell Kate to take care. Goodnight."

Evelyn watched Joanne leave, then she turned back to glance at Tyler and Kate in the ward before returning to her own ward.

Dan was seated on the couch, and he smiled as she stepped in.

"Settled?"

"Yeah. I don't think we have to worry about her bothering Kate or Tyler again."

"I hope you're right."

"You sound skeptical."

"My mom brought her up with one concept. Stay pretty, marry well, and live happily ever after. For whatever reason, she was determined to have that with Ty."

"I think she's figured out that it isn't going to happen."

"Again, I hope you're right."

Evelyn glanced at the clock on the wall and said, "You should go; I'm fine. It's time for me to rest anyway."

"It's all right. I can stay with you."

"I can't sleep when someone else is around."

"I'll just sit on the couch. I won't disturb you."

Evelyn sighed and sat on the bed. "I don't like having people in my room when I'm sleeping. I know you're being nice, and I'm trying to say this as nicely as possible, but please leave."

"Are you still angry that I was late?" Dan asked.

"I just don't like having someone else in the room with me when I sleep," she repeated and drew an impatient breath.

There was more to why she didn't like people being in the room while she slept, but she wasn't going to explain. She hated being reminded of it.

"All right, I'm out of here. If you need anything—"

"If I need anything, Kate's next door."

Dan shrugged, took his coat, and left Evelyn's ward.

Evelyn wanted what Kate and Tyler had. She'd known Kate since they were in college and had never seen her happier, but frivolous things like love weren't meant for someone like her.

Chapter Twenty-Six

Kate placed the new photo frame down on the late Mr. Hayes's desk, setting it right beside the photo of young Tyler and his grandfather.

When she got home from the hospital, she'd immediately dug out the photo of the late Mr. and Mrs. Hayes. The official report stated that Kate had picked up the gun and shot the window before leaping out. But she was certain she wouldn't be alive if it weren't for God who sent Tyler's parents.

She'd just set the frame down when the doorbell to the mansion rang. It must be Lydia.

Kate trotted down the stairs and opened the door. She turned without saying a word to Lydia and sat beside Evelyn on the couch.

She'd never been angrier at Lydia than she was now.

She didn't mind helping Lydia with the investigation. She wouldn't have been pleased if Lydia had chosen to continue with it despite the lack of leads. But she hated being lied to.

And Lydia hadn't just lied to her once.

"Are you all right?" Lydia asked, breaking the silence.

Evelyn set the newspaper down and stared pointedly at Lydia.

"As you can see, we're alive and well," Kate said.

"I'm sorry."

"About the fact that we were almost burned to death or that you blatantly lied to me?"

"I thought they were empty threats. I went back to Cooper's place a few times. I might've hinted that I knew more than I was letting on and was going to uncover the truth about our parents' case."

Evelyn grunted while Kate sighed.

"But I had nothing. I was just trying to get something, anything, out of him. When you told me about the threats, I didn't think it would result in anything serious. You had so many people keeping you safe anyway. I thought my pushing was starting to scare him. The threats proved I was right; it proved he was hiding something. So I kept going back," Lydia continued.

She couldn't believe what Lydia was saying. Despite knowing about the threats, Lydia didn't think of anything else but the case.

"Well? I hope you got something major that would blow the case wide open, because your sister almost paid for your so-called justice with her life," Evelyn said. Lydia opened her mouth, but Evelyn raised her hand to stop Lydia before continuing. "And, by the way, if she'd died because of your pig-headedness and I killed you, is that justifiable in your book?"

Lydia pursed her lips and took a slow, deep breath. "I'm sorry."

"Maybe it's time for you to be more concerned about the living than the dead," Evelyn chided.

"I know you guys are angry, but I swear I didn't know he'd follow through with the threats. I thought Kate was safe."

"Thought?" Evelyn gave a dry laugh. "Yeah. It's the thought that counts, right?"

Though Kate was frustrated, she didn't want things to get out of hand. And most importantly, she didn't want Tyler to see Lydia.

"Look—"

"Lydia, I can't begin to explain or describe how angry I am with you. And seriously, I don't care what you thought. What you caused Evelyn, me, and everyone else to go through was inexcusable."

"Kate," Lydia said.

"I'm not done." Kate paused and drew a deep breath. "I know you want to know the truth about our parents' case, but I'm done with it. I'm not going to help you anymore. If you want to live your life obsessing about something that happened so many years ago, then you can go ahead and do that."

Kate strode over to her handbag and fished out her mother's locket. Taking Lydia's hand, she dropped the locket into her palm. "It's your ghost to chase."

"I didn't know you would get hurt. I didn't know things would turn out like this."

"Yeah, you've made that pretty clear," Evelyn said and rolled her eyes.

"I think you should go."

"Kate——"

"One more thing, I'm engaged. That was why I called you from the cabin." Kate opened the door and stood by it. "Bye."

"And try not to do anything that will get us killed," Evelyn shouted as Lydia plodded out.

Kate closed the door once Lydia was out.

"Don't feel bad. She deserves it," Evelyn said as Kate walked back toward the couch.

"Dan told me that you kicked him out of the ward last night."

"That's a smooth change in topic."

She shrugged. "So what happened?"

"Nothing." Picking up her phone, Evelyn focused on the screen and refused to look up at Kate.

Evelyn always did that when she wanted to avoid talking about something.

"Eve, I know how hiding in the bathroom must've brought up some forgotten nightmares."

"They were never forgotten."

Kate pursed her lips. She knew she could never understand the fear that Evelyn grew up in. "I'm sorry for what you went through, but Dan isn't like——"

"I just can't have people around when I'm sleeping, you know that," Evelyn interjected.

"You've fallen asleep with me around, so it's a matter of trust. I seriously doubt he'll mind waking up if you have a nightmare."

Evelyn ignored Kate and continued staring at her phone.

Seeing that Evelyn wasn't ready to talk about it, Kate let it drop. "You deserve to have someone who will love and protect you, someone who will cherish you and give you a family."

"I already have you for that. Or are you telling me that since you have Tyler, I'm being booted?"

Shaking her head with a grin, Kate continued. "Dan's fine, by the way. A little confused, but I assured him that he did nothing wrong."

Evelyn finally glanced up from her phone. She gave Kate a small smile, then returned to scanning through her phone.

"You're welcome," Kate said.

The next few months flew by quickly. Winter came, turning the evergreen woods that surrounded the mansion white. Snow covered the green leaves, and with the cold, a stillness took over the woods.

Things in the mansion were the complete opposite.

On top of her work, Kate was planning her wedding and redesigning the mansion. There never seemed to be enough time, making it easy for her to put the fire incident behind her.

She was worried Tyler would get all worked up and decide to ship her away from it all, but he never brought that up again.

Even when Detective Allen told them that there weren't any leads on the fire, Tyler merely requested that she be careful.

His protection was no longer overbearing. He didn't insist that someone had to be around her all the time and didn't go crazy when she went to meet a client on her own.

Maybe it was because of what Kate had seen, letting him know that his parents were watching over them. Maybe the angel necklace she now wore became a reminder that they were never alone.

Evelyn, on the other hand, was very much affected.

Kate had thought that after having gone through a near-death experience, Evelyn would realize how vulnerable life was and would finally open up her heart. Instead, she appeared to have withdrawn even further. She shut Dan out of her life and avoided him at all costs.

Kate wanted to help. But when it came to relationships, nothing she said or did would get Evelyn to change her mind.

"So, have you asked him?" Ryan asked, pushing aside the drawings that Kate had in front of her.

She sighed and shook her head. Of all the things she had to deal with, this was the worst.

Whenever the guys had the chance, they would pester Kate on who the best man would be.

Each time they had asked her, she had told them to ask Tyler. But somehow, they kept coming back to her.

"All right, all right. I'm going to ask him now." She stood and marched up the stairs, ready to transfer her vexation onto her fiancé. "Have you decided on who will be your best man? They won't stop bugging me."

"I'll tell them to stop."

She elbowed him lightly in his chest. "That isn't the point. Why haven't you made your decision?"

"They're all hoping to participate in the wedding. Since you have one maid of honor and one bridesmaid, I can only have one best man and one groomsman. That means one of them will be left out."

"That was what you were worried about?" Shaking her head, she continued. "You should've told me. I don't have anyone to walk me down the aisle, so they'll all be involved. One best man, one groomsman, and one to walk me down the aisle."

Tyler blinked while she laughed.

"All right. Now that I've solved your problem, please, please, please tell them what they're doing before I strangle someone," she said and gave him a peck on the lips. "Oh, and Joanne came over the other day."

"Here?"

"No, at the office."

Tyler's eyes narrowed.

"Don't worry, it was nothing. She was actually looking for Eve. She wants to study interior design, so she came over to ask for our opinions."

"Huh."

"She apologized."

Tyler's eyes widened. "Did she actually mouth the words 'I am sorry' or did you assume she was sorry?"

Kate rolled her eyes. "She said she was sorry."

"Why interior design?"

"I know what you're thinking. She swore she isn't trying to become me. Apparently, the only real work she'd ever done was at our office, and she loved it."

"Okay."

Kate grinned. Tyler wasn't the only one who had changed. She didn't know how to explain it, but something was different with Joanne as well.

Epilogue

With the fading of the cold and snow and the arrival of a new season, the mansion morphed from a time capsule that captured what had been lost to a home where great friends gathered. Instead of the painful memories of loved ones gone, the mansion now echoed with laughter, joy, and love.

Even Evelyn's house had been transformed.

Since Kate couldn't stay at her scorched house, she had to stay at Evelyn's to get ready for the wedding. They spent a week cleaning up the house and clearing all of Evelyn's clutter.

It was spick and span now, but Kate was certain it wouldn't last.

Kate and Evelyn lay in bed, with Evelyn scanning through the channels on TV. Kate looked at the wedding dress hanging in front of the wardrobe and smiled. "I hope he'll like the wedding dress."

"He loves everything about you. He'll love the dress," Evelyn replied monotonously.

Turning to her side, she studied Evelyn's face. "Is something wrong?"

"Nothing."

"Oh, come on," she said.

Evelyn sighed softly and stared at the television's screen. "I'm worried for you. I know it's silly, but I can't shake the notion that things will change after marriage, and he'll end up hurting you. Then I'll have to commit murder."

She laughed and looped her arm around Evelyn's. "He won't

339

hurt me. I'm sure there will be times when we'll quarrel, and I'm sure there will be times when I'll feel like killing him. But I know he'll always love me. We'll be happy. I hope that someday, you'll find someone you believe will love you no matter what. And don't say you've got me. You know what I'm talking about."

"What's that?" Evelyn snapped upright at a small thud on the window.

"What?" Kate sat up. She frowned when she heard another thud on Evelyn's window. She got off the bed and moved toward the window, gingerly pushing the curtains aside. Evelyn was right beside her when she slid the window up and peered out.

The ground outside the window was completely covered with pink and purple tulips. In the middle of it stood Tyler, dressed in an impeccable suit. Kate gasped and broke into the widest grin.

Evelyn scrambled for her phone, recording the scene below as a video.

Just as Evelyn got back to the window, Joseph, Ryan, and Dan appeared at a corner, holding a large piece of white paper with the words 'ASK: By whose direction found'st thou out this place?'

Kate chuckled at the absurdity of three grown men waving the mega piece of paper over their heads, but she complied anyway. "By whose direction found'st thou out this place?"

"By love, that first did prompt me to inquire. He lent me counsel and I lent him eyes. I am no pilot. Yet, wert thou as far as that vast shore washed with the farthest sea, I would adventure for such merchandise. Lady, by yonder blessed moon I swear, that tips with silver all these fruit tree tops ..."

Kate laughed and shook her head.

She couldn't believe that Tyler would memorize the words from *Romeo and Juliet* and display such silliness in front of their friends.

Movements from where the guys were standing caught her attention, and she turned, seeing the words that Juliet spoke next written on the paper.

She didn't need help; she already knew the words by heart. Taking a deep breath, she quelled her laughter and continued.

"O, swear not by the moon, the inconstant moon that monthly changes in her circled orb, lest that thy love prove likewise variable."

"Then I swear with my life that I love you with all my heart and soul, that I truly will go to the ends of the world for you, with you."

She laughed and sniffed, wiping the tear hanging by the corner of her eye.

Another round of movements made her turn to the guys. This time, they held another line from further down the scene.

"A thousand times goodnight."

"A thousand times the worse to want thy light. Love goes toward love as schoolboys from their books. But love from love, toward school with heavy looks."

"Good night, good night. Parting is such sweet sorrow that I shall say good night, till it be morrow," Kate said before the guys could bring up the lines.

Tyler grinned. "Sleep dwell upon thine eyes, peace in thy breast. Would I were sleep and peace, so sweet to rest."

She sighed softly, then blew him a kiss.

"Goodnight, my love," Tyler said and gave a dramatic bow.

The guys in the corner followed, bowing like true gentlemen.

Kate laughed and gave a curtsy.

A round of cheers erupted as Tyler left with the rest of the guys. When they were out of sight, Evelyn stopped the recording and laughed as she gave Kate a hug.

"He must be crazy in love to do that. But it's so sweet. He didn't take out any paper, so he memorized it. And he actually did it in front of all of us."

"I love him."

And with Tyler's voice speaking Romeo's lines, Kate fell asleep with a smile on her face, looking forward to a new chapter in her life with Tyler.

Readers' Exclusive

Did you enjoy *Moving On?* I've gotten so many emails from readers asking for more on Kate, so here's a novella I've written just for my readers. *Ghost of The Past Prequel - Letting Go.*

Where it all began
GHOSTS OF THE PAST PREQUEL

Letting Go

TRISHA GRACE

You'll get to go on a mini adventure with Kate and Tyler's grandfather, Mr. Hayes, find out how Kate and Marianne met, and see what happened between Kate and her ex-boyfriend, Benjamin.

To get this book, simply head over to my website at http://www.TrishaGraceNovels.com and sign up for my newsletter. It's a reader's exclusive, so it won't be available for sale anywhere. It's a thank-you gift I've written for all my supportive readers.

Note to Readers

Dear Reader,

I hope you enjoyed reading this book. This book was originally released as a romance/thriller book, but I've reworked it into a Christian-based book.

My friends and fiancé had advised me to move on and work on other books, but I couldn't let it go.

When I first got into writing, I had (and still have) it in my heart to incorporate God's words into my story so that I could do my little part in spreading God's love.

Right from the start, I've wanted to write this book as a Christian book. But as it was a series, I wasn't sure how I could incorporate God's words into the second book.

Once I knew how, the desire to change the book burnt in my heart.

As with the testimony of Kate's near-accident with the car that swerved past her (which really did happen to me in real life), the message in this book is that God loves you, and He is always there protecting you.

What you thought was an evil day filled with horrible events, may be God's way of keeping you from harm.

Now, in the world we live in, there are many dangers out there. But God has promised His children that no weapons formed against us shall prosper and that He is our place of safety.

I pray that the promises in Psalms 91 will keep you from all harm.

That's all for now. I would love to hear what you think about the book. Feel free to drop me an email at trishagracenovels@gmail.com.

Thanks for reading my book.

God bless!
Trisha Grace

* * *

P.S. Honest reviews on Goodreads and Amazon are always appreciated.

P.P.S. My facebook page is up at https://www.facebook.com/TrishaGraceNovels, do show it some love!

Connect With Author

Facebook:
My new facebook page is up at https://www.facebook.com/TrishaGraceNovels. Do give it some love.

Website:
http://www.trishagracenovels.com

Mailing List:
If you enjoyed this book and would like to get updated on future releases by Trisha, you can sign up for the newsletter at my website.

Twitter:
You can find Trisha on Twitter: https://twitter.com/TrishaGraceBks
Handle: @TrishaGraceBks

About Author

Trisha Grace graduated from Bradford University with an Accounting and Finance degree. She has always been an avid reader and has a passion for writing. After being a tutor for over six years, she finally sat down and penned her own novels.

More Books

Ghost of The Past Book 2 - Closing Books

© 2012 Trisha Grace

The traditional roles of man and woman become twisted with Dan and Evelyn.

Dan isn't a playboy. He doesn't have any commitment issues. In fact, he wants it all—relationship and family. Only problem? He wants it with someone who doesn't want anything to do with him.

Evelyn doesn't fool around with relationships because she's never been in one. She's certain that things like love and happily-ever-afters aren't meant for people like her. There's simply too much darkness in her past.

A past she thinks she's buried.

But she's wrong.

After more than a decade, her nightmare returns to haunt her, forcing her to face up to memories she can't seem to shake.

Can she ever close the books on her past and let go of the horrors she went through? Can she ever learn to trust again?

Enjoy the following excerpt for Closing Books:

Prologue

Evelyn and Dan strolled through the park. The light pink cherry blossoms hanging low above them. She took off her coat, folding it over her arm.

Spring was warmer than usual this year.

Children were already out in full force, running around in T-shirts and jeans.

She glanced toward the playground and smiled ruefully as she saw the huge grins plastered on the children's faces.

She loved watching children at playgrounds. She loved listening to the high-pitch, carefree laughter and shrieks of joy as they ran spiritedly, flailing their hands about.

"I used to love playing at the playground until my parents forced me to take my sister along," Dan suddenly said.

She shook her head with a grin, but didn't say anything. She felt Dan's eyes on her, waiting, she supposed, for her to share an anecdote of her own.

But she didn't like to think about the past—no, she didn't *allow* herself to think of the past.

"Do you want to head over to the mansion for dinner tonight? Or would you rather we go somewhere else?" Dan asked after a moment.

She turned her head back to him and pursed her lips. It felt weird going over to Kate's house when she wasn't around. "Somewhere else."

"Are you going to stay away from the mansion until they come back from their honeymoon?"

One of her shoulders inched up as she gave him a nonchalant shrug.

"You can still head over even though she isn't around, you know?"

"I know." She smiled, then continued. "Where do you want to go for dinner?"

She was glad that Kate's wedding had resulted in the need for her and Dan to work together. She was reluctant at first, thinking it was better that she stayed away from him.

Things between them were complicated.

They were good together, but they weren't meant to be.

She wasn't meant to be someone's girlfriend; she wasn't meant to be in a relationship.

She wished things between them could remain like this forever—simple, just two friends hanging out together.

"How about—" Dan looked down toward the floor.

A young girl wearing a bright-pink dress printed with large blue flowers ran right into Dan's legs, fell back, and landed heavily on her bum.

Dan immediately knelt down and lifted the young girl to her feet.

The young girl stared at him with wide, frightened eyes, seemingly ready to burst into tears.

Even being down on one knee, Dan towered over the girl. And his broad shoulders must have made him seem like a giant to her.

"Are you all right?" Dan asked with a small smile and a light pat on her head.

The girl nodded slowly, her lips curling to reflect Dan's.

"Are you hurt?"

"No," the young girl replied.

"Abi!" A woman wearing a light purple top came running over. "I'm so sorry; she never looks where she's going," the woman said as she scooped the young girl into her arms.

"It's okay," Dan said, grinning at the girl. "Don't worry about it."

"Bye." The young girl grinned and waved as her mother carried her back toward the playground.

Evelyn watched Dan return the girl's wave.

Dan would make a great father. The kind of father who would be there for their children; the kind of father a kid would be proud to have.

He was responsible and extremely patient.

She'd worked with him and seen how he was with his staff. When things went wrong, he never lost his temper. Instead, he always focused on solving the problem. Then he would give a stern warning that such mistakes should be avoided.

What she admired most was how he would never bring up the subject again.

Even with her, even after all that she'd put him through, he would always turn up whenever she needed him.

"Cute girl," Dan commented.

"You think every child is cute."

He grinned and shrugged.

"You'll be a great father."

"I sure hope so. I've been babysitting Joanne forever," he said. "And I'm sure you would be a great mother."

She hitched her handbag higher up against her shoulder.

"Don't you want to have a family?"

Her fingers tightened around the strap of her handbag.

This was why they weren't meant to be; they were so different. "I know you do."

"Yeah, and you don't?"

Again, she adjusted the strap on her shoulder. "I already have a family. I have Kate."

Though Kate wasn't related to her, they were closer than

most sisters were. Kate would probably be the only family that Evelyn would ever have.

His head bobbed up and down as he stared ahead.

They continued strolling through the park, walking side by side, neither saying anything.

Evelyn gazed at a mother walking past them. The young mother held a baby in her arms, rocking gently as she cooed the baby back to sleep.

She turned her head from the mother and child.

She wouldn't know how to be a mother anyway. She didn't know a single lullaby. She didn't know how to bake cookies. She didn't even know what a normal childhood was.

It was better that someone like her didn't have children.

"So what do you want to have for dinner?" Dan asked.

Dan deserved better. He shouldn't be wasting time on someone who could never give him what he wanted.

Pressing her lips into a thin line, she turned to him. "Actually …" She paused as she felt the vibrations in her bag. "One minute."

She pulled out her phone and frowned at the unfamiliar number. "Hello?"

"Hi, Mandy."

Evelyn's face blanked. "Wrong number," she said and ended the call.

"Is everything all right?"

She forced a smile as she looked up at Dan. "Yeah, but I have to go."

"Now?"

"Yeah." She turned and walked away from Dan without another word.

"And dinner?"

She drew a deep breath and turned back to him. "I don't think that's a good idea."

"Eve—"

"I really have to go."

She spun around and strode toward the parking lot, still clenching the phone in her hand.

Chapter 1

Evelyn stared at the phone number displayed on the screen of her vibrating cell phone. The originally unfamiliar number had become a source of fear and was probably the cause of the migraine she'd been suffering from.

She buried her face in her hands and let the phone vibrate a few more times before sighing and picking it up.

"I thought you were going to ignore my call," the monotonous voice said.

Tightening her grip on the phone, Evelyn clenched her jaws. She took a deep breath and quietly cleared her throat of the frustration that had lodged itself there before replying. "What do you want?"

"Money, of course. I've run out."

"I'm not your bank."

"You can always say no. But I can't say you'll like what follows."

Evelyn shut her eyes and reminded herself to take slow, deep breaths. All she wanted to do was to smash her phone into the wall and leave, to disappear to a place where no one knew her.

If only life was that easy.

"How much do you want?"

"Three thousand. Six o'clock, same place."

Evelyn ended the call without another word. Leaning back against the chair, she shut her eyes and swallowed hard. Crying wouldn't solve the problem. She needed a solution; she needed to think.

She had contemplated on making a police report, but that meant revealing the secret she'd so adamantly refused to speak of. She had thought of changing her phone number so she could live in denial. Perhaps things would simply return to normal as long as she could no longer be reached.

But as much as she tried to convince herself, she knew things wouldn't just vanish by feigning ignorance.

Since receiving the first call less than a month ago, Evelyn's bank account had been set back by over six thousand dollars, and there didn't seem to be an end to it.

Straightening herself, she stared at the photos playing as the default screensaver on her laptop, photos taken on her best friend's wedding. She stared blankly at the pictures from Kate's wedding, seeing smile after smile until a photo of her and Dan appeared.

Evelyn tilted her head back and took a deep breath, but tears still went tumbling down her cheeks. Tears stemmed from the nostalgia of joy she'd felt in the picture; a joy that seemed so far away and unattainable at the moment.

Life had been good since she got out of the foster system. She had worked hard, and now she had a successful career and a great life.

She had thought that if she were to keep her past a secret, she could bury it deep enough that someday she'd completely forget about it.

Thus far, time had proven her theory to be entirely wrong. Ghosts of the past had a way of haunting one no matter how much one had changed.

After so many years, Evelyn thought her past was so far behind that the only remnant of it was in her mind.

Again, she was wrong.

She was beginning to doubt if she would ever be free from the past she couldn't shake.

There was a simple solution, and she knew it.

All she had to do was to spill the beans. If everyone knew what had happened, the blackmailer wouldn't have anything to threaten her with.

It should have been an easy thing to do.

All those things happened so many years ago. But even after a decade, it was difficult for her to open up and talk about what had happened to her or what she had done.

Kate was the only one who knew her secret, and Evelyn

was sure that Kate would never reveal it to anyone unless she allowed it.

Before, she had kept it a secret because she didn't want to talk about it. She didn't want to discuss it with anyone and relive her nightmare.

Now, even though she didn't want to admit it, the truth behind her silence was her hope to keep Dan from ever finding out what she'd done.

She'd battled with the decision of telling Dan in order to end everything once and for all, but the resolve to do so always disappeared before it ever took root in her heart.

Each time she made up her mind to tell Dan, fear would creep in.

Fear, with its sneaky little voice, would tell her that Dan would never accept her after what she'd done and that he would be disgusted with her.

The little voice, which seemed ridiculous in the beginning, began to grow louder until she could no longer ignore it.

Soon, the voice in her mind dropped into her heart, and she was convinced that Dan would scorn her when he found out what had happened.

Though she was no longer seeing Dan, though they were never officially dating, she couldn't bear the thought of Dan finding out her past. She couldn't bear to see his reaction.

It didn't take much for the fear to convince her that she was alone in this matter. No one, not Dan, not Kate, would want to be involved with her shady past.

Brusquely, she wiped the tears on the back of her hand and picked up her bag by the side of the table. Another trip to the bank was necessary.

Evelyn drove up the lone, single driveway that led to the mansion. Green towering trees that stood throughout all seasons flanked both sides of the road. For a moment, her eyes flickered onto the trees. She forced herself to focus on the road and kept her eyes away from the never-ending woods.

Even after a year, Evelyn couldn't get over how creepy and isolated the mansion was.

Whenever her eyes wandered to the trees, thoughts of someone or something suddenly appearing out of the forest to attack her would surface.

Even with her wild imagination aside, she hated the drive up to the mansion.

She wasn't sure if it was the scenery of the impenetrable forest or the solitary drive, but a sense of melancholy always accompanied her on the drive.

If only Kate had chosen to live somewhere else, then she wouldn't have to make this drive up every other day.

She tightened the grip on her steering wheel as she turned into the mansion and saw Dan's car.

She hadn't seen him for weeks, not since Kate went on her honeymoon, not since that day at the park. But that hadn't stopped her from thinking about him.

She sighed, pushing the thoughts from her head.

They were no longer together, and for good reason.

Stepping out of the car, she strode up to the door and turned the knob. As expected, it wasn't locked.

With so many people going in and out of the house, Marianne had made it a policy to leave the door unlocked during meal times.

Evelyn stepped through the doorway, and her entrance was immediately announced by the motion sensor alarm.

She didn't understand why Tyler had bothered with that thing. The kitchen didn't offer a direct view of the main door, so the alarm did nothing to indicate who was coming in. For all they knew, she could have been a burglar.

Strolling past the luggage in the living room, she headed straight into the kitchen.

She forced her lips into a wide grin. "Hey!"

Kate turned around with a blissful smile and gave her a hug. "Sit! I'm giving out presents. These are yours," Kate said, giving the two large paper bags on the oval dining table a slight nudge.

Without even looking, Evelyn knew it was probably two new branded bags.

Bags were her sole indulgence.

Having grown up with barely anything instilled some habits in her.

She always made sure she set aside more than half of her income in the bank. She didn't go for expensive food and had been driving the same secondhand car for years.

But bags, she was always willing to cut back on other expenses for her bags.

She sat beside Kate and watched her dole out presents to Dan and Marianne. It was strange to see so few people in the usually crowded kitchen.

Kate's husband, Tyler, sat back against his chair with his arm draped lazily across Kate's chair.

The past year had brought about many changes to all their lives.

A year ago, a will left behind by Tyler's grandfather ended up bringing Kate and Tyler together. Along with Tyler, Dan, Ryan, and Joseph all tagged along. They had all become part of the regular people in her life now.

Besides Dan, she wasn't close with any of the guys.

She wasn't a sociable person in the first place. She was the sort who fared better at being alone than having to mingle with people. Having one friend was more than enough for her.

Her on-and-off relationship with Dan didn't help her score any points with the other guys as well.

Joseph, in particular, was exceptionally cold toward her. He never spoke to her directly unless necessary.

Even Ryan, the friendliest in the group, hadn't warmed up to her.

But she did have to admit that everyone had been cordial with her for Kate's sake. Even Marianne, Tyler's housekeeper, who loved all the boys like her own children, never showed any disapproval of her despite the things she had going on with Dan.

Evelyn hadn't meant to keep Dan in her craziness. Each time she had walked away from him, she'd promised herself that it was the last time and that she wouldn't get involved with him again.

Logic and rationale told her that they weren't meant to be. But each time she needed someone, she couldn't stop herself from reaching for her phone and calling Dan.

"How was the honeymoon?" Marianne asked.

As Kate launched into a speech about how perfect everything was, Evelyn took the chance to steal a glimpse of Dan.

She hadn't spoken to him since the whole blackmail began.

It was her decision, her own doing, but that didn't stop her from missing him.

She smiled ruefully as Dan ran his hand through his blond hair, causing the sleeve of his shirt to inch up, revealing the muscles under it.

Though he wasn't the largest guy in the group, his tendency to work alongside his men in his construction firm had built quite a few sturdy muscles.

Dan hated folding up the long sleeves of his shirt. He hated having to pull the edge back down his elbow whenever he lifted his arms.

Her smile faded as the dull ache in her heart worsened.

All the details she remembered about him only reminded her of how happy she was whenever they were together.

But people like her didn't get happily-ever-afters.

The blackmail she had been receiving was a reinforcement of the different world they belonged in.

Dan grew up in a complete family. It wasn't perfect, but at least he grew up safe.

The horrors she'd gone through and the things she'd done were beyond the worst nightmares that someone like Dan could ever imagine.

Pushing the thoughts from her mind, she reached into one of the paper bags on the table and took out the leather bag within. She twirled the new handbag, pretending to examine it while her thoughts were consumed by the payment due later that night.

Money was draining out of her bank account faster than before. Just two days ago, she had paid off her blackmailer. Now, she was to prepare another three thousand dollars.

It had started out with a few hundred dollars. Within two weeks, her blackmailer had quickly upgraded the demands. Besides demanding more money, her blackmailer was increasing the frequency of the demands as well.

"You don't like them?"

Kate's voice broke her thoughts. Evelyn looked up and quickly gave her a small, pleasant smile. "You know I love them. I was just thinking about some stuff at work. Speaking of which, I brought some new projects that you might be interested in. They're in my car, I'll get them."

Before anyone else could say another word, she was up from her chair and out of the kitchen, heading toward the main door.

Evelyn knew she wasn't acting like her usual self very well. Before driving up to the mansion, she'd reminded herself to behave as normally as she could. Kate was particularly astute at picking up emotional disturbances in people, and Evelyn knew she had to be careful or Kate would be all over her.

She tried; she genuinely did. But it was difficult to keep up her smile with the apprehension of meeting a ghost that had latched onto her.

Halfway through the living room, she heard the familiar ringtone she'd grown to dread.

Crap. She spun around and sprinted back toward the kitchen.

Why did she put down her phone to play with her new bag?

The moment she got back to the kitchen, she saw her phone in Kate's hand.

Without thinking, Kate tapped on the screen and answered the call. "Hello?"

Evelyn's eyes widened, and she snatched the phone from Kate's hand. "Don't pick up my calls."

She could see the confusion on Kate's face and felt the stares directed at her. She knew her strong reaction would appear to border along temporary insanity, especially when they all knew how close she was to Kate.

"I always answer your phone when you're not around," Kate stated hesitantly while Evelyn checked who the caller was.

"Stop doing that," she hissed and headed out of the kitchen with the phone in her hand.

Hastening her steps, she exited the mansion. Once the door was closed behind her, she lifted the phone to her ear. "What do you want? I know I'm supposed to hand you three thousand dollars tonight."

"Is that your friend?"

"What do you want?" Evelyn repeated, irate at the situation she was in and at how senseless she was behaving toward the only person who actually cared about her.

"I changed my mind. I need five."

"Don't push it," she said through clenched jaws.

"No, Evelyn, don't push me. I'm sure you don't want the-one-who-always-answers-your-phone-when-you-are-not-around to know what's going on, right?"

Evelyn ended the call and clenched her phone. Boiling, but with nowhere to vent, she got into her car and began to beat up her steering wheel.

She slammed her arms against the steering wheel, sending jolts of pain through them. Though her hands became the eventual victims, her anger was slightly appeased.

Pinching the bridge of her nose, she forced herself to take a few deep breaths while her arms burnt with a dull pain.

After a minute, she rearranged her features into a carefully placed smile and got out of the car.

As she entered the kitchen, everyone kept their eyes on the food that was on the table, and no one said a word to her. Although they had all been polite to her, they had never been overly concerned about her.

Evelyn didn't blame them. She was the one who kept everything to herself, and that had the tendency to keep everyone out.

In fact, she rather enjoyed people staying out of her business. It saved a lot of time and effort from having to explain things she'd rather not talk about.

Kate looked up from the table and smiled at her; a smile that didn't reach her eyes.

Behave normally. Evelyn sat and slotted her phone into her back pocket.

From the corner of her eye, she noticed Kate staring at her arms, which were red and slightly purple at certain areas where bruises were beginning to form. She quickly pulled her hands back and placed them on her legs. She was certain that if she refused to speak about it, Kate wouldn't pry it out of her, not right now anyway.

And she was right.

After a moment, Kate turned away from her and casually asked, "Where's the work you mentioned?"

"Oh, right." She got up, shaking her head at her absentmindedness. "I'll get it."

She turned and left the kitchen again. This time, she cast a brief glance over her shoulder; a glance long enough to see Dan staring at her. Their gaze held for a moment before she tore her eyes from him.

It pained her to see the questions, or maybe accusations, in his eyes.

She had only turned from Dan when he tried pushing her into a serious, committed relationship.

This time, she had simply shut him out of her life for what would appear to him as no apparent reason.

It was difficult to be so near to him and yet be so clearly separated that they might as well be a thousand miles apart. She wanted so badly to let him understand why she pulled away from him, but she could never find the words and didn't know where to begin.

Taking the files from her car, she ran her finger down one side of the files while she kicked the door close.

This was exactly what she needed—work.

With Kate being on honeymoon for the past few weeks, as her business partner, Evelyn should have been free as a bird. Instead, she scoured through the projects handled by the different teams they had and insisted on custom making pieces of furniture that were readily available in stores.

She had even begun trying her hands at keeping a good set of accounts, something she'd always avoided at all cost.

Her work was the one escape that kept her from thinking how screwed up the other aspects of her life were.

"Here are the few projects I thought you might be interested in. If you don't want them, we can assign them to the teams. Let me know," she said the moment she got back to the kitchen. "I have to go."

"Where are you going?" Kate asked as she took the files, staring intently at Evelyn.

Pausing by the chair, Evelyn hesitated a moment. A moment that turned the curiosity on Kate's face into suspicion.

"Nowhere," Evelyn quickly said. "I just need to run some errands."

Be casual, Evelyn reminded herself. She smiled and gave Kate a pat on her shoulder. "See you tomorrow."

Not giving Kate a chance to ask another question, Evelyn grabbed her bag and presents, made sure she kept a smile on her face, then left without saying goodbye.

Chapter 2

Dan forced himself to keep his eyes on his plate instead of looking up at Evelyn's disappearing figure.

"What's wrong with her?" Kate asked. "You haven't gone out with her since we went on our honeymoon?"

He pushed the food around on his plate as he looked up at Kate. "Something like that." He tried to speak as nonchalantly as possible, but when he saw Kate's lips thinning, he realized he wasn't doing a terrific job of concealing his feelings.

Months before the wedding, someone had set fire to Kate's house; a fire that almost killed both Kate and Evelyn. Immediately after, Evelyn retreated into her shell, barely speaking to him.

He'd thought that experiencing a life and death situation would bring about the epiphany of living life to the fullest and treasuring people she loved. Either that was a whole load of nonsense or Evelyn just wasn't like normal people.

Evelyn's cold-shoulder treatment toward him continued until the preparations for Kate and Tyler's wedding kicked into high gear. The planning for the wedding and the renovation of the mansion forced them to work together.

And it was clear that whenever they were together, they couldn't get enough of each other.

It was undeniable that they had terrific chemistry.

Whenever they were working together or going out on a date, they would spend half the night laughing away, and time always flew by way too quickly.

But despite all the laughter they shared, there was always an invisible barrier between them—the past she refused to speak of.

He didn't mind. He believed that with time she would trust him enough to tell him what had happened, and he was willing to wait.

When Evelyn wasn't busy pulling away from him or being all mysterious, she had a genuinely open and candid personality. He had never met anyone like her before.

He hadn't been with many women in his life. The two most prominent ones were already too much for him to handle. Throughout his life, his dramatic mother never spoke her mind and loved resorting to theatrics to instill guilt in him. Guilt was his mother's sole weapon of manipulating him into doing things her way.

Unfortunately, that unbearable characteristic had passed down to his sister as well.

Evelyn's frankness was a refreshing change. She had no problem telling the truth about anything, and they could chat about everything under the sun; everything except relationships and her past.

Each time he spoke of something that had happened when he was young, she'd laugh at his anecdote but never reveal any of hers. On occasions when Dan asked about her childhood, she would clam up and simply state that there wasn't much to talk about.

Though they weren't officially in a relationship, they spent all their time together and didn't date anyone else.

But Dan wasn't satisfied with their ambiguous status.

He knew what he wanted in life. He wasn't one of those who had flings and left a trail of broken hearts behind. He took each relationship he had seriously.

With Evelyn, he didn't even know if what they had qualified to be considered a relationship.

They always had a great time, and he couldn't think of any reason why they shouldn't be together.

But whenever he tried to push Evelyn into a relationship, she'd push as well; she would push him away. All communications would cease to exist between them, and she would treat him as if he never existed.

Initially, everyone assumed they had a fight and were in a cold war. Dan never explained to them either. How was he supposed to explain when he had no idea what was going on?

A week later, sometimes longer, sometimes shorter, she would call in the middle of the night and ask to meet up for supper. They would then begin to talk and go out again until Dan took another shot at pushing her into a relationship.

After so many cycles of this ridiculous routine, he thought he would have gotten used to it.

He tapped his fork against the plate, then pushed it away.

Everyone, especially Marianne, had been asking him about the situation between Evelyn and him. To get himself out of the need to answer the questions, he had adopted Tyler's classic style of shrugging then keeping his lips locked.

Eventually, the guys learned to stop asking questions. Marianne, on the other hand, wouldn't stop bugging him about it.

Perhaps that was how real mothers behaved. He couldn't be sure. His own mother was always more concerned about herself and his younger sister. To him, Marianne was more of a mother than his parents ever were. Despite that, it didn't change the fact that her questions were getting on his nerves.

Sometimes, he wished he had an answer for Marianne.

Despite Evelyn's straightforward personality, there was plenty that he didn't understand about her.

For one, he didn't understand why Evelyn always isolated herself and pretended she didn't care about anyone else. He was sure Evelyn wasn't such a person, and the kitchen he was sitting in proved it.

He looked up from his food and turned to the newly renovated kitchen.

The cherry wood cabinets that had been in the house for nearly three decades had been removed and was now furnished with dark brown cabinets. The wooden countertop had also been replaced with a light gray slab of granite. Those were the basic designs that Kate had chosen, but the degree that Evelyn went to customize it for Marianne showed how much she cared.

Every cabinet was designed specifically to suit Marianne's needs.

Instead of the standard shelf height, Evelyn had noted down all the things that Marianne had placed in the different cabinets and adjusted the height of the new shelves to fit those needs. She even solved Marianne's problem of having too many spices and not enough places to store them by completely revamping one of the cabinets into a multi-layered turning tray that allowed Marianne to store and reach her spices easily.

Evelyn had noted every complaint that Marianne ever had about the kitchen and designed the new cabinets to suit her needs. And she did all of that without even having to ask Marianne or Kate.

"Ryan and Joseph working?" Kate asked, bringing his thoughts back to reality.

Though Dan was glad that Kate wasn't harping on the

problem between him and Evelyn, he was hoping that he didn't have to be the one to break the bad news.

He looked over at Marianne, then back to Kate. "Joseph's working while Ryan's in the hospital."

Kate's eyes widened, and Tyler's gaze finally shifted from his beloved wife.

"He got injured at work; part of a wall fell on him," Marianne clarified. "He's recovering now, so there's nothing to worry about."

"How is he? When did that happen? Why didn't you guys tell us earlier?"

"He's fine, around a week ago, and we didn't want to disturb your honeymoon. We knew you'd want to return immediately if we had told you," Dan answered and flashed a bright smile at Kate.

Kate narrowed her eyes at his condescending answer. "I called Eve so many times, and not once did she think to tell me what happened."

"She didn't know."

"Huh," Kate said, studying his expression before she continued. "We should visit him, *now*."

Tyler hesitated. "Are you sure? I thought you were tired?"

"I'm fine. We should go see him. How bad is it?" She turned back to Dan and glared at him, warning him from lying to her.

"Got some slight burns, dislocated his right arm from his shoulder, and tore a ligament in his leg."

Kate cringed.

"There's good news, though; for him at least," Dan said and continued when he saw Kate frowning. "He gets to stay home for three whole months. And since Marianne didn't want him staying in his apartment alone, he'd accepted the invitation to crash here until he recovers." As Dan finished his sentence, he turned to look at Tyler, grinning when he saw Tyler shaking his head.

Before Kate came into his life, the guys always made sure

they gave Tyler his space. They only appeared to devour Marianne's cooking before disappearing. Now, all of them had become semi-permanent residents of the mansion.

Before, Tyler had no qualms about chasing them out of his house, but Kate loved their presence in the mansion and he loved seeing her smile.

"I can't believe you're joking about his injuries. It sounds serious; we should visit him right away."

Tyler smiled and stood, stretching out his hand for Kate.

"I'll drive," Dan volunteered. He didn't want to be left behind in the house, where he was certain Marianne would ask him over and over again if he was serious about Evelyn and why hadn't he taken a stand on the relationship he wanted them to have.

He trailed out of the mansion along with Kate and Tyler, watching Tyler run his fingers down Kate's hair.

When Tyler met Kate, his personality changed so drastically that it made Dan believed it was possible for things to turn around with Evelyn, too.

Kate had once told him that Evelyn treated him differently, and it was something she hadn't seen before, just like how Tyler treated Kate completely different from everyone else. Dan had come to believe that he would be different enough for Evelyn to break free from the mysterious shadow of her past.

The secretive past that Kate refused to talk about, even to her dear husband.

The two women were like sisters, and Kate guarded Evelyn's secret fiercely.

Dan understood Kate's reason; it wasn't her story to tell. Still, it didn't change the fact that the whole secrecy around it was frustrating.

Tempted as he was to ask Evelyn, Dan hadn't dared to step over that particular boundary. Each time he'd pushed Evelyn into taking a step closer, he'd only succeeded in pushing her further away. He had an inkling that if he did push Evelyn on this particular subject, she would close her door to him completely.

Looking up at the genuine smile on Tyler's face, a smile that was non-existent until Kate appeared in his life, Dan felt a sense of jealousy surging through him. In spite of the many things Tyler had, Dan never coveted any of them except for what he now had. Someone whom he could love; someone who would reflect the joy that he had; someone who only had eyes for him.

"Are you all right?" Kate asked when they got into his car.

Dan's face blanked, and he stared back at her. He had missed her question.

"What happened this time?"

She didn't have to elaborate; Dan knew exactly what she meant. Though she was the newest member of his group of friends, Kate was the only one Dan had spoken to about Evelyn. Perhaps he was hoping that Kate's understanding of Evelyn would help shed some light on what he was doing wrong.

"I don't know. I swear I didn't push her this time." He thought back on the last time they met. "She had this strange look after picking up a call, then she hurried away. After that, she just cut me off," he said. "Maybe she's seeing someone else."

Kate nodded. "She's acting weird over the phone, but I'm sure she isn't dating someone. She would've told me."

He didn't make any comment. He didn't believe Evelyn would hide such information from Kate, but based on her behavior, he couldn't help thinking otherwise.

Evelyn was clearly secretive when it came to those calls, even Kate wasn't allowed to answer her phone.

"I'm sorry. I wish I could help. It's just that she's *really* touchy when it comes to relationships. I love her, but I hate to see you like this. Maybe you should stop running around in circles with her."

Dan sighed heavily. Of course he'd thought about that. Basic logic told him that they weren't going anywhere and that he should put a stop to the crazy cycles. Yet whenever she called, his logic and reasoning would leave him.

Whenever they were in the cold stages, he couldn't stop checking his phone to make sure that he hadn't missed her call.

And when she did call, he couldn't help but feel relieved. "I tried." *I really did.*

He heard Kate sighing softly before she changed the subject. "When is Ryan getting discharged from the hospital? He'll need someone to help him up and down the stairs. And his clothes? Anyone helping him to bring them over?"

He grinned and looked at Kate through the rear-view mirror.

Since Kate entered their lives, she had become the linchpin that held all of them closely together. With Kate, they'd all become a family, all except Evelyn.

He wasn't sure if it was the way she refused to reveal information about herself or the formality with which she treated everyone, but there always seemed to be a wall between her and everyone else.

Refusing to dwell on thoughts of Evelyn, Dan shook his head and returned his focus to the conversation. "Marianne has already brought his stuff over. He'll be staying with her in the other wing."

"Why? That's quite a long walk from the kitchen, and we all know how much he loves the kitchen." Kate looked up and grinned at Tyler.

Tyler beamed back in return and said, "There are three guest rooms near our room. He can stay there."

"Marianne says it's easier for her to take care of him. Plus, there's a room right on the first floor, so he won't have to climb the stairs." He kept his eyes on the road and smiled to himself. That was the exact reason Marianne had told them though they all knew Marianne just didn't want anyone disturbing the newlyweds.

When they got to the hospital, Dan and Tyler gave a nonchalant "hi" to Ryan before settling on the couch while Kate went to fuss over him.

Among all the guys, Ryan was the muscular one. His shirts always fitted him so snugly that the contours of the muscles were easily seen through the stretched T-shirts.

Dan knew Kate would be shocked to see their own giant

lying in bed with a heavy cast on his arm and a huge brace on his leg.

"Gosh, I'm so sorry we didn't visit you earlier," she said, sitting on the edge of the bed.

"Don't be. I was in on the decision of not telling you guys. Where's my present?" Ryan asked with his boyish grin and usual upbeat tone.

"Back at the mansion. Don't worry, she knows you love her. She won't forget your present," Tyler answered from the couch.

Dan laughed when he heard how disgruntled Tyler was.

Besides being the strongest among all of them, Ryan was also the friendliest. His initial friendliness toward Kate had bothered Tyler, especially when Ryan openly professed how he loved her. Tyler knew Ryan had spoken jokingly, but he simply refused to let it go.

"How are you doing?" Kate asked after shaking her head at Tyler's childish behavior.

"Great, especially since I get to stay at the mansion for three whole months. I'll get to eat Marianne's food for three whole months!"

Kate laughed softly at Ryan's equally childish answer. "You guys deserve each other."

Dan joined in the laughter. "I think he won't mind being paralyzed if you tell him that he'll get to enjoy Marianne's food for the rest of his life."

Tyler grinned at Dan's words.

"When will you be discharged? We'll come and get you," Tyler said.

"You can take him back now if you want."

Everyone turned toward the door as Joseph entered. Kate got up from Ryan's bed and gave him a hug. "Are you coming with us? We can wait for your shift to end."

"That's still hours away. You guys must be tired from your flight. Go back and rest. How are your eyes?"

After much pushing, Kate finally found time to get her Lasik surgery done before the wedding. In the beginning, she had complained that her eyes felt dry rather easily, so Tyler had bugged Joseph on checking her eyes whenever he was at the mansion.

"Fine. I still can't believe I have perfect eyesight. Sometimes I go to bed thinking I should remove my contacts."

Tyler walked up to his wife and ran his fingers through her hair. In reaction, Kate gazed up at him and leaned against the length of his arm.

Again, the simple intimacy they displayed reminded Dan of the ache in his heart. "I'll get the papers settled while Kate fills him in on Marianne's menu for the night." He stood and walked out without a second look at the rest of them.

"Hey," Joseph said as he followed him. "Evelyn again?"

"I'm fine." There wasn't much he could say. How was he supposed to explain to his friends that Kate's best friend was driving him crazy, but he couldn't get himself to stay away from her?

"Ryan may be quitting his job," Joseph said after a moment of silence.

"Really? I thought he loved being a firefighter."

"Actually, after the fire at Kate's house, he started having second thoughts. Then this accident."

"So what is he going to do?"

Joseph shrugged. "I don't think he's put much thought into it."

Chapter 3

"Good morning," Evelyn said as she entered the kitchen. The kitchen was crowded with the entire gang, all of them sitting in their respective seats around the dining table. Only plates and utensils were on the table, but the aroma from the food was already making her stomach growl.

Evelyn's brows flitted up when she saw Joanne sitting

next to Dan.

Since the fire, Evelyn had been working with Joanne on her application for an interior design course. They had looked at dozens of schools, narrowed them, prepared her portfolio, and submitted applications.

Helping Joanne was another secret that Evelyn had been keeping from Dan.

Initially, she was surprised that Joanne came to her for advice. She wasn't the kind of person whom people looked to for help, but she couldn't turn Joanne down. She knew Dan had hoped that Joanne would grow up and stop behaving like his mother. He wanted Joanne to have a life of her own, to have her own ambitions and desires beyond having Tyler as her boyfriend.

Evelyn smiled as she thought about the series of debacles that Joanne had resorted to when Kate first moved in.

Things were different now. Joanne was no longer creating problems for Kate and was serious about finding a future for herself.

Evelyn was glad to help. She was certain Dan would be elated to know that his sister was finally ready to start living her own life.

She pulled out the chair between Kate and Dan, joining the rest of the group around the crowded table.

The mansion was now the focal point of their lives. Even with the crazy work schedules that Ryan and Joseph had, they always came over whenever they had the time. If they couldn't make it for dinner, they'd turn up for breakfast or lunch or to chat with Kate and Marianne for a while before heading to crash in the guest rooms.

Evelyn didn't stay over as the guys did, except during the brief period of time when Kate had received threatening notes.

She didn't like staying anywhere except her own apartment. Her apartment was a place where she was used to, a place where the noises at night wouldn't startle her, and a place where she could lock her bedroom door without having to explain why.

"Hey! The food will be ready soon," Ryan said.

"How are you feeling? Kate told me what happened."

"Good. Still in one piece."

Evelyn smiled and stole a glimpse of Dan as she pulled her chair closer to the table, slightly disappointed that he wasn't looking at her.

She had no right to be, but she was.

She knew what Dan wanted: relationship, marriage, family. Everything that she couldn't give him. Everything that he wouldn't want from her if he found out about her past.

But when she wasn't with him, all she could think about was him. When she tried seeing other guys, all she could see was how they failed to compare to him. When she told herself that she wasn't going to keep Dan in her craziness and that it was time to bring things to a complete end, she'd have an overwhelming urge to see him.

Her hands would then betray her, picking up the phone and calling Dan before she could stop herself.

Dan would turn up; he always did. And they would have as much fun as they always had. They'd laugh and flirt. Dan would lean in close, push her hair back, then skim his finger down her cheek.

His soft touch, along with his warm and clear emerald eyes gazing into hers, never failed to capture her heart. His gentleness with her spoke of more affection than any words ever did. Selfishly, she didn't want to let that feeling go, so she persuaded herself into believing that they could always remain the way they were.

But what she wanted wasn't good enough for Dan. He'd always push her into formalizing their relationship, and she would take a thousand steps back away from him.

She didn't do that to punish him or to prove her point. She needed to stay away from him to remind herself that she wasn't girlfriend or wife material. She was damaged beyond repair; it was impossible to fix her.

Things that are impossible to men are possible with God.

Evelyn shook Kate's voice out of her head.

She had to remind herself that she and Dan were only

meant to be friends, and she had to stay away to make sure she got her perspective right.

When she was with him, she sometimes fell into the daydream on the possibility of a future together with Dan. She'd allow herself to play with the thought for a few minutes, just a few minutes.

She wasn't the naive sort of person.

No one would ever want someone like her as his girlfriend or wife.

As if the universe were reminding her of why she could never be in a relationship, her phone buzzed, and she jumped from the shock of the vibration. She checked her phone, then dropped it back onto the table when she saw that it was just an advertisement.

The reminder of the blackmail took her mind into a dark turn.

What had she done to God to make Him abandon her and be so cruel to her?

She didn't doubt that a God existed.

He existed for Kate. He protected Kate when she was in trouble, but He had never bothered with her. If He did, He shouldn't have allowed her to go through what she did.

Unconsciously, her hand moved toward her left shoulder and her fingers grazed across her shirt, over where the scar was located.

Who would be interested in a woman with such a dark history?

"Ryan, Joe said you're thinking of quitting your job," Dan said.

Dan's voice easily cut through her thoughts, capturing her attention. Realizing where her hand was, she immediately dropped her arm back onto her legs.

Ryan nodded. "Maybe, but I don't know what else I can do."

"Open your own gym and produce more incredible hulks," Joanne teased.

"That's actually a brilliant idea," Kate said. "That way,

you don't have to work those horrible shifts, and it's much, much, *much* safer than being a firefighter."

All of them echoed their support of the idea.

"Are you guys serious?" Ryan asked, half laughing.

"Why not?" Kate said. "You can get Joseph to come up with healthy meals that would help in weight loss or muscle gain. He can even give check-ups to track their progress."

Ryan turned to Joseph with a raised brow.

Joseph brows drew closer together, seemingly considering the possibility of doing so.

While Marianne began placing food on the table, more ideas were thrown around.

Evelyn tuned out the conversation and turned to Dan again.

She was tempted to talk to him, to ask him about his day. She missed hearing his voice, seeing the smile he always had for her, and feeling the warmth of his finger skimming down her cheek.

She closed her eyes, hoping that removing him from her sight would get rid of the thoughts in her mind.

This is better for everyone, she reminded herself.

Just then, her phone vibrated again, and another jolt of shock reverberated down her spine. Hastily, she grabbed the phone from the table. Relieved that it was just about work, she sighed softly and returned the phone to its position on the table. When she glanced up from her phone, she found Kate staring at her, probably waiting for an explanation on her neurotic behavior over her phone.

"Lack of sleep." A pang of guilt besieged her as she looked away from Kate. Though it was true that she wasn't sleeping well and her nightmares were back, compared to the other problem she was facing, the nightmares were insignificant.

She hated having to lie to Kate, and Kate's response only doubled her guilt.

"Do you want me to stay over at your house tonight? If you want, I can accompany you. Maybe tomorrow we can buy some chamomile tea and essential oils. I heard they work miracles for some who can't sleep."

"Don't worry, I'm fine." Evelyn kept her eyes from Kate, letting her know she had no intention of continuing that particular line of conversation.

It was better for Kate to know nothing about what was going on. There wasn't any need to pull another person into her mess.

The next morning, Evelyn pulled up in front of the mansion, surprised to see Lydia's car parked by Joanne's pink mini.

Everyone, including herself, had treated Kate's sister like an outcast since the fire. Though only her and Kate confronted Lydia, everyone else blamed Lydia for what happened as well.

Since finding out that their parents didn't die from an accident like their grandparents had told them, Lydia had been obsessed with finding out what caused their brutal murder.

Even though Lydia wasn't the one who set the fire, she was undeniably the cause of it.

To Evelyn, the actual fire didn't scare her; it was the events leading right up to it that did. The whole incident brought back the unwanted memories that she'd been trying to bury.

Even seeing Lydia's car brought back those memories.

She remembered how her heart pounded while she hid in the bathroom with Kate. She remembered how she kept her gun aimed at the door while fear ran rampant in her mind.

The suspense of knowing someone was heading for them reminded her of how she had felt while hiding in the bathroom as a child, of the futile prayers she had made, and of the eventual punishment she had to endure.

She was no longer a child, and she had practiced hard at using her gun. Still, no amount of logic helped as the same fear that used to surge through her veins every night raked her once again.

Evelyn rubbed her palms against her arms, getting some warmth back to her suddenly cold hands.

"Hey, you're late," Ryan said as she entered the kitchen.

Everyone else echoed some form of greeting and went

back to the food on the table.

Without command, her eyes moved in search of Dan's, then immediately darted away the moment they met his.

She took her usual spot, sitting between Kate and Dan. Since his eyes were obviously avoiding her, Evelyn took the chance to observe him.

He kept his eyes on his plate, taking a bite of food then looking up at the selection on the table. He looked well to her. The brilliant smile he used to wear was missing. But besides that, he appeared to be doing fine without her.

She couldn't help wondering if he was already seeing someone new and if she could handle sitting at the same table with whoever it was.

"Now that you're here, we're ready to make the major announcement," Ryan said, swallowing a mouthful of food. He nudged Joseph and gestured for him to continue.

Seeing Ryan's excitement made her smile.

She wished she had his personality; he was always smiling and chirpy. She wondered how he did that. The things he must have seen in his line of work: the carnage, the deaths … Yet he seemed untouched by them.

"We've decided to leave our jobs and start a gym like you guys suggested."

Joanne laughed. "Are you guys serious? I was only joking."

"We are. The only gym in this area isn't very good. Many of Ryan's fellow firefighters and friends he worked out with had complained about it. It's definitely viable," Joseph answered.

"That will be great," Kate said, her eyes bright. "That way, you guys won't have to deal with all the shifts anymore."

Dan nodded. "That's true. I can help with the finding of a location; I have contacts."

"And of course, Evelyn and I will design the place for you guys," Kate added.

"Before any of that, we'll have to come up with an actual proposal and get a bank loan," Joseph interjected before anyone else could continue.

Dan's brows drew closer in confusion. "You do know there are a few multi-millionaires sitting around this particular table, right? If the richest guy …" He cocked his head in Tyler's direction and continued. "Isn't willing, his wife definitely is."

Kate's smile widened. "Of course I'd support you guys. I've lots of money, and I can't find anywhere to use it."

Evelyn cleared her throat to conceal her laugh and hid her smile behind her hand.

Kate had inherited a sizable amount of money from Tyler's grandfather; money that was doing nothing but lying around in the bank. Since they got married, Tyler had refused to let her pay for anything.

"I have money," Tyler stated. "You guys get it from me."

Kate rolled her eyes. "Seriously? I can't even support them? What's the point of having all that money in the bank if I can't spend it?"

"You bought Evelyn's handbags with your money."

That began a banter that lasted for a few minutes, ending with Tyler hooking his arm over Kate and holding her against his chest.

Dan shook his head as Tyler grinned despite Kate's struggle to get out of his arms. "I don't think there ever was any couple who vies for the chance to pay for stuff."

Ryan nudged Joseph in his elbow. "Told you they'd help." Then he turned back to Tyler. "But no charity, we'll repay it. I'm sure Mr. Sawyer can draw something up for us."

"Of course," Mr. Sawyer said.

Evelyn looked at the now-retired lawyer sitting next to Marianne, another addition to the group due to the will left behind by Tyler's grandfather. Mr. Sawyer had moved in last year to ensure that every condition of the late Mr. Hayes's will was met.

Now that Kate and Tyler were married, Mr. Sawyer had moved back into his own house, but that hadn't stopped him from dropping by during meal times.

The difference between him and everyone else who was

there to sponge off Marianne was that he wasn't there for the food.

"So, what are you guys intending to do?" Tyler asked.

Kate elbowed Tyler softly in his ribs and finally managed to break free from his arms. "Yeah, what's the plan?"

Evelyn leaned on her arm and looked at the blissful couple beside her.

A corner of her lips curled as she thought about the shopping trip she had with Kate. They were at the counter, getting ready to pay for their stuff, when Kate took out her wallet and noticed the cards. Kate pulled out all the credit cards in her wallet with a gaping mouth, surprised that Tyler had substituted all her cards without telling her about it.

The bewilderment caused by the sight of the new cards was quick to pass while annoyance took over.

Once they were out of the shop, Kate called Tyler and gave him an earful. Despite her rant, Evelyn knew Kate hadn't been happier.

Whenever Evelyn looked at how Tyler and Kate interacted, a part of her longed for a relationship like theirs; a relationship where she would be loved and accepted despite all she'd done and all she might do.

She blinked, feeling a hint of moisture at the corner of her eyes, and turned away from the blissful couple.

Such fairytale love was for people like Kate, the kind of woman everyone loved. She was always sweet and amiable, and she never turned anyone down whenever they needed help. In less than a year, Kate was able to turn the aloof Tyler into someone who could never stop smiling whenever she was around. In less than a year, everyone in the room loved her like a princess.

Evelyn, on the other hand, wasn't that kind of lady.

She was one who could never trust enough to be nice to everyone.

While Ryan and Joseph rattled off their plans for the place, Evelyn suddenly felt a gentle squeeze of her hand.

She looked down at Dan's hand, and her head snapped over to him.

She pulled her hand back as she looked away. She couldn't allow herself to become needy now. Now, more than ever, she had to be strong. She promised herself that she wouldn't let a demon from her past destroy what she'd built for herself, and she couldn't be the tough Evelyn when she had Dan to rely on.

She had grown so used to Dan being her comfort that each time she woke from her nightmare, her thumb would hover over the phone while her heart and mind went into battle; a battle between satisfying what her heart wanted and complying with what her mind knew was right.

She wanted to kick herself when Dan withdrew his hand and pretended as though nothing happened.

She shouldn't have pulled her hand back that way. He was merely concerned about her, and all she did was hurt him in return.

Dan could see that Evelyn was already deep in her own thoughts, dismissing him from whatever or whoever was occupying her thoughts.

He looked away and caught Marianne staring at him.

Throughout the whole hot and cold cycle that Evelyn and Dan were going through, Marianne had been nagging him to step up and show Evelyn that he was serious about being together.

Each time, he had trusted Marianne and did what she said.

Each time, the result that followed was a period when he became the invisible man to Evelyn.

When that happened, Marianne would tell him that he wasn't serious enough, and he didn't show her that he'd meant what he said.

Sometimes, he was tempted to snap back at Marianne and tell her to stop meddling in his business. It was easy to blame Marianne for things going downhill, but he had to admit that she was only giving him the push he needed.

He did know what he wanted, and he wanted everything

with her.

He'd heard people talk about how they knew the person they were with was *the one*, and he knew.

It didn't matter that they were running in a circle. It didn't matter that they might be with someone else in between. There was a knowing in his heart that they would end up together.

She would be the one he would grow old with; the one he would create great memories with; the one he would have a family with.

Dan had lost count of the number of times he'd looked at Evelyn and heard the small voice in his heart telling him that they belonged together.

But Evelyn didn't seem to agree. She knew what she wanted as well.

She had told him right from the start that she wasn't interested in relationships, never had and never will. Still, he dove in head first, thinking things would change.

There was nothing for him to complain about. Evelyn did tell him straight to his face; it was purely his stupidity in thinking that he could change things.

Maybe he was wrong. Maybe it was just the spillover effect of Tyler finding love that made him think otherwise. Maybe this time, things were really through between them.

Pushing the food away from him, he tuned in to the conversation around the table.

"Eve always said she wanted to learn self-defense. We just never got to it. If you start one, I bet she'll be your first customer," Kate said.

He had tuned in just in time to disapprove of Kate's idea.

"Yeah, of course," Evelyn replied after a moment's lapse as if she, too, was daydreaming. "It shouldn't be too difficult for you guys to come up with the lessons. You guys learned judo, right?"

Ryan raised his brows. "True."

"Will you ladies be our guinea pigs?" Joseph asked Kate.

"Why not?" "No."

Two people spoke at the same time, but all heads turned toward Tyler. Even if they hadn't recognized his voice, it was obvious he was the one rejecting the idea.

"They're clumsy; you might get hurt," Tyler said to Kate.

"Thanks for thinking about me, too," Evelyn stated sarcastically.

"*Both* of you may get hurt," Tyler corrected.

For once, Dan was grateful for Tyler's protective nature.

Dan grew up with the guys and had lost count of the injuries he'd sustained while playing basketball with them. He didn't think it would be dangerous; he knew it would be. But unlike Tyler, he'd no right to speak up about it.

A silent frustration over the ambiguity of their relationship bubbled within him; a frustration over his lack of rights to be frustrated.

Though he never fooled around in relationships, he'd never felt so possessive over someone, especially someone whom he wasn't even officially dating.

The worst of it was knowing how ridiculous it all seemed. He wasn't in high school anymore; such trivial and petty relationship problems should no longer be an issue. Why couldn't he just close the chapter he had with Evelyn and move on?

"I don't think Ryan's in a position to hurt anyone," Kate said, pointing to the cast on his hand. "And Joseph is a doctor, I'm sure he'll be careful. *And* I'm going to ignore you now."

"Don't worry, Ty. We won't risk your *precious* in any way. I promise," Joseph assured.

There wasn't any point in trying to fight it, Tyler seemed to know it was a lost cause. He shrugged and smiled at Kate. "You do know they'll be dead if you end up getting hurt."

"Ignore him," Kate said.

Dan turned to Evelyn and saw, for just a moment, the hint of sadness in her eyes.

Perhaps her words meant more than she let on.

His fingers twitched as he fought to keep his behavior in

check. She didn't want him touching her, not even to comfort her, so he pulled his hand back a few inches and tightened his grip on his fork.

A moment of silence took over as everyone continued to devour the food Marianne had prepared. There was nothing more to discuss until Ryan and Joseph put more work into the gym.

"Are you interested in being part of the self-defense guinea pigs?" Mr. Sawyer said to Lydia. "After all, lawyers work horrible hours. It's good to learn something to keep yourself safe."

Lydia's head shot up. She blinked and looked around the table, clearly surprised that a question was directed at her.

Although Dan wasn't magnanimous enough to forgive Lydia, he did admire her courage to show up each time Kate invited her over. Everyone was angry with Lydia for various reasons. For Dan, it was because Evelyn could have died in the fire.

The thought of losing Evelyn in the fire was too much to think about, and each time he saw Lydia, he was reminded of the fact that the arsonist was still at large and Evelyn's life might still be in danger.

"Sorry, maybe another time," Lydia finally said.

Without much subtlety, Ryan rolled his eyes.

Lydia didn't have to explain her lack of time. Everyone knew she was still obsessed with the cold case.

Then, Ryan suddenly asked, "What about you, Joanne? Everyone's offering some form of help. What are *you* going to do?"

"Marianne and Mr. Sawyer didn't offer their help," Joanne retorted.

Laughing, Marianne said, "If Joe is planning healthy meals, who do you think will make it edible? And of course, Mr. Sawyer will be taking care of all the legal matters."

Having no other defense, Joanne turned and shared a look with Evelyn.

"Stop disturbing her," Evelyn interjected.

Dan narrowed his eyes at Joanne. He saw the look between Joanne and Evelyn; something was wrong.

Joanne had been disappearing a lot lately, and she would get all flustered each time he asked her what she was up to. Now, there seemed to be some shared camaraderie between Evelyn and Joanne.

"Yeah. What are you so busy with that you can't help? You've been rather secretive lately, Anne." Dan stared at his sister, worried that she was getting into some sort of trouble.

"Everyone has secrets. Let her be," Evelyn stated.

You definitely have yours. He pried his eyes from Evelyn and turned back to Joanne, waiting for her explanation.

Dan saw Joanne swallowing hard and ducking her head as her eyes moved to her plate.

He held his stare; he wasn't going to back down. If Joanne was up to something, he was going to find out right now.

"I'm leaving for Paris next week, and I won't be back for at least a year," Joanne rushed through her words while her eyes remained fixated on the plate.

"What?" Dan exclaimed. "Why?"

"To study. I'm going to study interior design. Everything is settled. Evelyn found an apartment for me and went shopping with me for all the necessities I need."

Evelyn knew all along? "And how long ago was this decision made? Do Mom and Dad know about this? You've never been away on your own for so long. How are you going to survive?"

"Oh, Dan, you should be glad. It's a fantastic opportunity; it'll be good for her," Marianne said. "Good luck with your studies, Joanne."

"Glad? She's never done her own laundry. She doesn't know how to cook—"

"This is why I didn't want to tell you. I'm always just your baby sister. I don't want to be just your sister anymore."

Clueless about what Joanne was talking about, Dan turned to Evelyn with a slight frown.

"Let her go. She'll be fine," Evelyn stated simply.

Dan sighed softly.

"Look, Evelyn taught me how to do my laundry, how to cook can food and ramen noodles," Joanne said.

Evelyn taught her?

Joanne continued to rattle on, "Always lock my doors and windows when leaving the house and when going to bed. Do not walk in dark alleys. Always be aware of my surroundings, and a whole load of other stuff that Evelyn has already been nagging me about."

"Nagging?" Evelyn arched a brow.

"Kidding … kidding." Joanne gave Evelyn a nervous smile.

"How long have you been preparing for this?" he asked.

"A while."

And Evelyn had been helping her.

Evelyn wasn't fond of Joanne at all, not after all that Joanne had done to Kate. So why was she doing this?

His gaze fell on Evelyn. If only he could read minds.

"I'll be fine," Joanne continued when he said nothing.

Evelyn had been living on her own since she was sixteen. There couldn't be a better person helping Joanne. And for the first time since the conversation took a turn, he finally breathed easier.

He leaned back and nodded. "When were you intending to tell me?"

"Soon, in a less public scene."

His head bobbed up and down as he thought things through. "Everything is settled? School admissions … money?"

"Yes, and probably yes. Evelyn settled all the admission stuff for me. I *think* Mom and Dad will help me with the money. Otherwise, Kate has agreed to help me with whatever I need while I find a part-time job."

He turned to Kate and smiled gratefully. Though he was somewhat offended that Joanne hadn't come to him for help, he was glad that she'd chosen the next best alternative.

"I'm sorry. She made me promise not to tell," Kate said with a wry smile.

He already knew how good Kate was at keeping secrets,

but he couldn't believe that Evelyn hadn't told him anything when they were going out. Then, a sudden realization hit him. "Kate knew, so that means you knew," he said while glaring at Tyler.

Applying his signature style to avoid talking, Tyler merely shrugged.

"I made him promise not to tell," Kate interjected. "Joanne wanted to make sure that everything was settled before announcing it."

There was no way he was going to win the war. Putting aside his bruised ego for being blindsided, he had to admit that it was a positive step forward for Joanne. "Looks like you've got everything covered. If you need anything else, I hope you'll remember that you have a brother."

Joanne laughed. "I will. Now that I know you're not going to stop me, I will."

With that, all the guys wished her well while Dan dove into his own interrogation, prying all the details from Joanne.

When everyone was done with breakfast, Joseph helped Ryan back to his room, and Lydia left for her own house. Dan lingered in the kitchen; he wasn't through with Joanne.

"Going to the office today?" Evelyn asked Kate.

"Yup."

"All right. Tyler can drop you off, right? I'm going to head off first," Evelyn said and strode out of the kitchen.

Kate made no objection, but Dan saw how her eyes bore into Evelyn's back. Kate wasn't the sort who'd pry information out of people, but she'd definitely be keeping a closer watch on Evelyn.

Since he wasn't able to do so, he was glad someone would be watching Evelyn's back.

To continue reading Closing Books (Ghost of The Past book 2), you can get it on Amazon.

Made in the USA
Columbia, SC
11 March 2019